Critical acclaim for Madeline Baker's previous bestsellers:

APACHE RUNAWAY

"Madeline Baker has done it again! This romance is poignant, adventurous, and action packed."

—*Romantic Times*

CHEYENNE SURRENDER

"This is a funny, witty, poignant, and delightful love story! Ms. Baker's fans will be more than satisfied!"

—*Romantic Times*

THE SPIRIT PATH

"Poignant, sensual, and wonderful....Madeline Baker fans will be enchanted!"

—*Romantic Times*

MIDNIGHT FIRE

"Once again, Madeline Baker proves that she has the Midas touch....A definite treasure!"

—*Romantic Times*

COMANCHE FLAME

"Another Baker triumph! Powerful, passionate, and action packed, it will keep readers on the edge of their seats!"

—*Romantic Times*

PRAIRIE HEAT

"A smoldering tale of revenge and passion as only Madeline Baker can write....without a doubt one of her best!"

—*Romantic Times*

MADELINE BAKER

Winner Of The *Romantic Times* Reviewers' Choice Award For Best Indian Series!

"Lovers of Indian Romance have a special place on their bookshelves for Madeline Baker!"
—*Romantic Times*

LAKOTA RENEGADE

Creed looked at Jassy as if seeing her for the first time and slowly shook his head. "It won't work, Jassy."

"What do you mean?"

He let out a long sigh. "You and me—it just won't work."

"Why?"

"You're too young, for one thing."

"I am not!"

"Then I'm too old."

She shook her head vigorously.

"Jassy, it's not just the difference in our ages; it's my whole life. I can't outrun my past." Suddenly restless, he stood up. "I can't outrun who and what I am, not even for you."

Other *Leisure* and *Love Spell* Books
by Madeline Baker:

APACHE RUNAWAY
BENEATH A MIDNIGHT MOON
CHEYENNE SURRENDER
WARRIOR'S LADY
THE SPIRIT PATH
MIDNIGHT FIRE
COMANCHE FLAME
PRAIRIE HEAT
A WHISPER IN THE WIND
FORBIDDEN FIRES
LACEY'S WAY
FIRST LOVE, WILD LOVE
RENEGADE HEART
RECKLESS DESIRE
LOVE FOREVERMORE
RECKLESS LOVE
LOVE IN THE WIND
RECKLESS HEART

Writing As Amanda Ashley:

EMBRACE THE NIGHT

LAKOTA RENEGADE

MADELINE BAKER

LEISURE BOOKS  NEW YORK CITY

A LEISURE BOOK®

September 1995

Published by

Dorchester Publishing Co., Inc.
276 Fifth Avenue
New York, NY 10001

Printed in the United States of America.

To Julie, Marian, and Marciela
for bringing happiness to my three sons,
Bill, John, and David—
and for bringing love and laughter
into my life, as well.
May you all live happily ever after!

LAKOTA RENEGADE

Chapter One

Harrison, Colorado, 1872

Creed Maddigan stood on the porch of Gratton's Mercantile, his right shoulder propped against the whitewashed upright that supported the sloped overhang of the general store. His left hand rested negligently on the ivory handle of the Colt holstered on his left hip.

He swore under his breath, his eyes narrowing as he watched the confrontation taking place in the narrow alley that ran between the rear entrance of the general store and the row of two-room shacks where most of the town's prostitutes lived.

Shacks was a flattering description, he mused. Most were made of inferior lumber and tar paper. He'd only been back in Harrison a couple of weeks, but he'd heard there was a big push by some of the local ladies to have the shacks torn down and their occupants run out of town.

Maddigan grunted softly. He didn't spend enough time in Harrison to care what happened to the town or its lightskirts. Truth be told, he didn't spend much time in any one place, although he had a permanent room in the hotel. It gave him a place to hole up when he wanted to be alone and a mailing address so people interested in hiring his services could get in touch with him without too much trouble. The room at the Harrison House was the closest thing he'd had to a home in the last ten years.

The argument in the alley was getting louder now as three boys, who appeared to be seventeen or eighteen years old, continued to harass a red-headed girl who looked to be several years younger.

Creed frowned as they teased her about the color of her hair, about the fact that her mother and her older sister worked the cribs in the Lazy Ace Saloon across the street.

Tears formed in the girl's eyes as the tallest boy shoved her up against the wall, his body pressing suggestively against hers.

"One kiss," he cajoled. "That's all." He nodded toward his two companions. "One kiss for each of us."

The other two boys grinned and punched

each other on the shoulder.

"No, Harry!" The girl jerked her head aside when he tried to cover her mouth with his.

"Come on, gal, give me a little kiss," Harry demanded. "My dad told me you'll be working in the saloon in a couple of months anyway."

"No!" Struggling to free herself, the girl drove her knee into the boy's groin. It was a direct hit and had the desired effect.

Yelping with pain, Harry doubled over, his hands cradling his injured manhood. The girl tried to dart past him, but Harry's hand snaked out and grabbed her by the arm. He hung on to her in spite of her wriggling—waiting, Creed knew, for the worst of the pain to pass.

And then the boy slapped her. Hard. Twice.

The two other boys exchanged uneasy glances.

"Harry, you don't have to hit her."

"Shut up, Billy!"

Billy tugged on the third boy's shirt sleeve. "Come on, Trent, let's go."

Trent glanced at Harry and the girl and then, apparently deciding that what had started out as a lark wasn't fun anymore, he followed Billy down the alley.

From the porch, Creed shook his head. If only the kid hadn't hit her. Disgusted with himself for what he was about to do, he pushed away from the upright and vaulted over the porch railing.

Jassy McCloud gasped as the tall, black-clad

man jumped the railing and dropped lightly to his feet. She had seen him before. You didn't forget a face like that. He had been a frequent patron at the Lazy Ace Saloon during the last few weeks. She had heard all kinds of stories about him from her mother and from her sister, Rose. Maddigan, his name was. Creed Maddigan. He was a loner, a fast gun with a formidable reputation. A man without pity or mercy. It was rumored that he was half Sioux Indian. Some said he'd even taken a scalp or two.

Now, seeing the determined expression on his face, Jassy believed every lurid story she had ever heard.

Afraid the gunman had come to help Harry Coulter, Jassy tried to wrest her arm out of Harry's grip.

Unaware of the man coming up behind him, Harry swore at Jassy, cussing her with all the finesse of a hard-rock miner, only to fall silent as Creed Maddigan's fingers closed over his shoulder like the hand of doom.

"That's enough, kid."

Jassy stared up at the half-breed, surprised that he had come to her rescue. She tried to pull away from Harry again, but he kept a firm grip on her arm.

The gunman's hold tightened on Harry's shoulder. "Let her go."

Sullen-faced, Harry released Jassy's arm.

Creed yanked Harry around so they stood face to face. "That's better. What's your name?"

"Coulter. Harry Coulter."

"You think it's fun, hitting girls?"

Harry's expression was defiant; then, to Jassy's delight, the man slapped Harry. Hard. Twice.

"Go on, get out of here," Creed said, giving the boy a shove. "If I ever see you picking on her again, I'll break your arm. Do we understand each other?"

"You'll be sorry for this," Harry said, his hand massaging his cheek.

"Yeah? Why?"

"I'll tell my old man, and he'll . . ."

"He'll what?" Creed took a step forward, his stance filled with menace.

"Nothing," Harry muttered. He shot a fulminating glance at Jassy, then turned and ran down the alley.

"You all right, girl?"

Jassy nodded.

Creed's gaze moved over her in a long, assessing glance. She was a little bit of a thing, with huge brown eyes. She wore a baggy blue dress that looked to be several sizes too large and a pair of ugly black shoes badly run down at the heels. Her hair, as red as autumn leaves, was pulled back from her face and tied at her nape with a narrow black ribbon.

"You sure you're all right?" Creed muttered, thinking she looked awfully scrawny in that hideous dress.

Jassy nodded again, unable to draw her gaze

from his. His eyes were as black as the finely woven shirt stretched taut over his broad shoulders. He was tall and lean, with skin the color of her mother's old copper kettle.

"What's your name, girl?"

Jassy blinked up at him, mesmerized by the sound of his voice. It was deep and soft, almost gentle. "Jasmine Alexandria McCloud. And I'm not a girl. I'm a woman."

Creed grinned. The name was bigger than she was.

"Most people call me Jassy."

It suited her, he thought, right down to the ground. "You'd best go on home, Jassy girl. And stay out of alleys from now on, hear?"

"I will. Thank you."

To his amazement, she dropped a proper curtsy, then ran across the street and up the outside stairway of the Lazy Ace.

With a rueful shake of his head, Creed resumed his place on the porch, a wry grin twisting his lips as he thought of that little bit of a girl curtseying to him like he was somebody.

Creed swung his legs over the side of the bed, grimacing as his hand rubbed his left thigh. The wound, inflicted by the last man he had hunted down, was only half healed and still tender.

Reaching for the Colt hanging on the bedpost, he crossed the room, wondering who would be knocking at his door at this hour of the morning. He didn't have any friends in town, at least none who'd be out and about this early in the day.

With his thumb poised over the hammer of the Colt, he unlocked the door to find Jassy McCloud standing in the hallway. He wouldn't have been more surprised if he'd come face to face with Saint Peter.

"What the hell are you doing here?" he asked.

"I . . ." A wave of color swept into the girl's cheeks. "I just came by to . . . to thank you for what you did yesterday." She thrust a napkin-covered plate at him. "I made these for you."

Frowning, Creed shoved his Colt into the waistband of his pants. Taking the dish from her hand, he lifted the cloth.

"Cookies?"

"Ginger snaps," she said shyly. "I hope you like them."

It was all he could do not to laugh out loud. Cookies! He was a hired gun on the down side of thirty, and she brought him cookies. "Thanks."

Jassy stared up at Maddigan. It was obvious she'd gotten him out of bed. His hair, as black as his reputation, was sleep-tousled. The beginnings of a beard shadowed the firm, square line of his jaw. He wasn't wearing a shirt or shoes, and she experienced a funny fluttering sensation in the pit of her stomach as her gaze moved over him, imprinting images in her mind. Finely chiseled lips. Prominent cheekbones. A broad slash of a nose. Well-muscled shoulders and arms. A deep chest sprinkled with curly black hair. A flat stomach ridged with muscle. Slim hips. His skin was the same copper color all over, not just where the sun had touched him.

He was, without doubt, the most handsome man she had ever seen. And he'd been kind to her. Suddenly, impulsively, she wanted to know him better.

Creed endured the girl's scrutiny in amused silence. A lot of women were fascinated by his reputation and the color of his skin. He'd seen that same appraising look countless times before. Only Jasmine Alexandria McCloud wasn't a woman, just a kid who probably didn't realize what that look inevitably led to.

Jassy dragged her gaze from Maddigan's rugged physique and glanced up and down the hall, hoping no one would see her standing outside a man's room so early in the morning, knowing what conclusions were sure to be drawn.

"Can I come in?"

"What?"

Jassy swallowed hard. "Can I come in?"

Creed's eyes narrowed thoughtfully. That young pup, Harry, had said the girl's mother and sister both worked at the Lazy Ace. Maybe the girl was older than she looked. Maybe she was hoping to get in a little practice before she took her place in one of the cribs, but it wouldn't be with him. He'd never cared much for robbing cradles.

"I don't think that's a good idea."

Jassy glanced past him, catching a glimpse of an unmade bed. The rumpled sheets reminded her of what her mother did for a living; suddenly, going into a man's room didn't seem like such a good idea after all.

"I . . . thanks again," she stammered, and almost ran down the hall.

Creed watched her round the corner, then stared at the plate in his hand.

"Cookies," he muttered with a wry grin.

He was still grinning when he closed the door.

Chapter Two

Creed sat across the table from Jassy, rolling a cigarette while she wolfed down a huge slice of chocolate cake. He didn't see how she could possibly have room for dessert, considering the enormous meal she'd just put away, but she was lighting into that cake as if she might never eat again.

It was funny, he thought. He'd been in town for almost a month and he'd never laid eyes on Jassy McCloud until that day two weeks ago when he'd gone to her rescue in the alley. Since then, he seemed to run into her everywhere he went.

If he walked over to Gratton's to buy a sack of Bull Durham, she was there, likely at the counter, browsing through a mail-order catalog.

If he went down to the livery to check on his horse, he invariably met her somewhere along the way.

If he stopped in at Jackson's Restaurant for a cup of coffee, she was sure to show up with a bright smile on her face.

Inevitably, he invited her to sit with him. And because he thought she was too thin, he usually ended up buying her something to eat.

Creed took one last drag on his cigarette before snuffing it out. They were in Jackson's now. It was Creed's favorite restaurant, mainly because most of Harrison's high-class citizens ignored it in favor of the Morton House, which was a fancy eatery located uptown.

Creed sat back in his chair, rolling a fresh smoke as he watched Jassy nibble her way through a second slice of chocolate cake.

She was wearing a brown print dress today, similar in cut to the baggy blue one.

He struck a match on the sole of his boot, lit the cigarette, and took a deep drag. Why was he wasting his time in Jackson's when he could be at the saloon? Why was he spending so much time with Jassy when he'd sworn never to get involved with another white woman as long as he lived?

But then, he thought wryly, Jassy McCloud hardly qualified as a woman.

"So," he drawled, blowing out a thin column of smoke, "tell me about yourself."

Jassy shrugged, suddenly embarrassed. How

could she tell him about her life, about having a mother who worked in a saloon and liked it? How could she tell him that Rose didn't know where her father was and didn't seem to care?

"There's nothing to tell."

"You live with your folks?"

"My mama and my sister."

"They pick out your clothes for you?"

Jassy looked away, embarrassed. "Mama does."

"Where's your father?"

"I don't know. He left when I was six."

Creed nodded, wondering if he'd misjudged the reason Jassy was following him around. Maybe she wasn't infatuated with him at all. Maybe she was just looking for someone to take up where her old man had left off. It rankled that he was probably old enough for the job.

Jassy put her fork down and stared at the crumbs on her plate. She could still remember the day her father had walked out. She'd come home from school to find him throwing his clothes into an old cardboard valise. Her mother had been standing beside the bed, crying, begging him to stay, promising that it wouldn't happen again.

At the time, Jassy hadn't understood exactly what was going on. But later, bit by bit, she had learned the whole story from Rose, who had told her how Gregor McCloud had met their mother, Daisy Shaunessy, in a saloon down in West Texas, how he had fallen in love with

Daisy and asked her to marry him.

But it wasn't in Daisy's nature to stay true to one man. And finally Jassy's father couldn't put up with it anymore. So he had left, just like that, and Jassy had never seen him again.

Creed took a last draw on his cigarette, wishing he hadn't asked Jassy about her folks. It was obvious she'd had a rotten childhood; judging from what he'd seen so far, her life hadn't gotten much better since.

"Come on." He tossed a couple of greenbacks on the table. "Let's get out of here."

"Where are we going?"

"To Gratton's."

Jassy grinned, pleased that he wanted her to go with him. She loved to browse through the store, to look at the bolts of calico and gingham, to wander down the aisles. She didn't go there too often because old man Gratton always followed her around, as if he expected her to steal something. But she loved the store. Mr. Gratton stocked a little bit of everything—pots and pans, straw hats, coffee, wheels of tangy cheese, barrels filled with crackers and pickles and sauerkraut.

"You're limping," Jassy remarked, wondering why she hadn't noticed it before.

"Yeah."

"What happened?" She hurried to catch up with him as they crossed the street.

"I got shot."

"Shot! How? When?"

"Couple weeks back." It was the reason he'd come to Harrison, to lick his wounds while he decided on his next move.

"Does it hurt very much?"

"Not anymore."

"How did it happen?"

Creed let out a weary sigh, wondering if all girls were as curious as this one. "I was trying to take a man to jail. He had other ideas."

"It's true, then? You're a bounty hunter?"

"Sometimes."

"And other times?"

"I do whatever I'm hired to do. You gonna ask me questions all day?"

"Just one more," Jassy said as they climbed the steps to Gratton's. "What are you going to buy?"

"A dress."

"A dress!"

She stared up at him, a cold knot forming in her stomach. She should have known. He had a girlfriend. Or a wife. Maybe both.

Creed shook his head, amused by the jealousy he saw lurking in the depths of her eyes.

"It's for you, girl. I'm sick of looking at those baggy things you wear."

"A dress," Jassy murmured. "For me?"

The mere idea rendered her speechless, and she trailed along beside him, wondering if he really meant it. A dress. One that fit. Oh, but her mother would never let her wear it. Daisy insisted that Jassy wear clothes that hid her burgeoning figure, telling her she wasn't to "flaunt" herself until she was old enough to get paid for it.

Jassy followed Creed into the store, trying to think of a polite way to tell him she couldn't possibly accept such a gift, but the words died in her throat the moment he picked a frock off the ready-to-wear rack inside the door. It was just a simple day dress, made of dark green gingham. Modest in cut, it had a round neck with a prim white lace collar, puffy sleeves edged in the same delicate lace, and a full, ankle-length skirt. A wide, light-green sash tied in a big bow in the back.

It was the prettiest thing she had ever seen.

Creed held it up to Jassy, his eyes narrowed. He didn't know the first thing about buying female duds, but anything had to look better on the kid than what she was wearing, and the green looked pretty with her hair.

"You like it?" he asked, though he could see she did.

"Oh, yes."

He grunted. "Go pick out a pair of boots to go with it. I'll meet you at the counter."

"Mr. Maddigan, I . . ."

"Creed," he said. "Just call me Creed. Go on now, before I change my mind."

Hugging the dress to her, Jassy hurried down the aisle to the back of the store where Mr. Gratton kept the shoes. A new frock and new shoes! It was better than Christmas.

* * *

Daisy McCloud glared at her youngest daughter. "And just what did you give him in return for those things, Jasmine Alexandria?"

"Nothing, Mama."

"Nothing! No man spends that kind of money on a girl unless he expects to get something in return."

"I didn't give him anything, Mama, I swear it."

"We'll just see. I think I'll have the doc take a look at you to make sure."

Jassy took a step back, the dress crushed against her breasts. "What do you mean?"

"I mean there are ways to tell if a girl's been foolin' around."

"I haven't! Please believe me, Mama. I haven't done anything wrong."

Daisy stared at Jassy for a long moment, then let out a sigh. Jassy had always been young for her age. She was going on seventeen, and she was still as innocent as the day she was born, though how she'd managed to stay that way in a town like this was a miracle. Of course, dressing the girl in drab, shapeless clothes helped some. So did the fact that Jassy wasn't as blatantly pretty or buxom as Rosie. Nor did Jassy seem to crave the kind of male attention that had cost Daisy a husband.

"You didn't tell me his name," Daisy said.

Jassy licked her lips nervously, wishing she was a better liar. "It was Billy, Mama."

"Billy Padden? The preacher's kid? You can do better than that, Jasmine."

Jassy let out a sigh of resignation. There was no point in lying. All Daisy had to do was ask Mr. Gratton who had bought her the dress. She should have just told the truth in the first place.

Daisy tapped her foot impatiently. "I'm waiting, Jasmine."

"It was Maddigan."

Daisy stared at her daughter. "Creed Maddigan? The gunfighter?"

Jassy nodded.

"Saints preserve us," Daisy murmured. And then she slapped Jassy across the face. "That's for lyin', and this is for—"

Jassy took a hasty step back as her mother raised her hand again. In an effort to avoid being slapped, she tripped over the wood box and fell backward, hitting her head against the edge of the hearth.

"Creed Maddigan," Daisy exclaimed, her voice filled with disgust. "Girl, you haven't got the sense God gave a goose. You stay away from that half-breed, you hear? Men like that are nothing but trouble."

Creed frowned at Jassy. "What happened to your face?"

"Nothing. I fell down."

Jassy looked away, ashamed to meet his eyes. Usually, she tagged after him, hoping he would notice her, but today, of all days, he had come looking for her.

"Why aren't you wearing your new dress?"

"I didn't want to get it dirty."

Creed cupped Jassy's chin in his hand and forced her to meet his gaze.

"Tell me the truth, Jassy."

"Mama took it back. The boots, too." She tried without success to keep the disappointment out of her voice. "She told me to stay away from you, that . . . that men like you are nothing but trouble."

Creed grimaced. He couldn't argue with that, much as he'd like to.

"Did she hit you?"

"No. She slapped me for lyin', and I fell and hit my head."

A muscle twitched in his jaw. "Does she hit you very often?"

"No."

"What'd you lie about?"

Jassy's gaze skittered away from his. "Nothing."

"Did it have to do with me?"

Jassy nodded, though she refused to look at him. "I told her Billy Padden bought me the dress."

Swearing under his breath, Creed carefully probed the ugly black-and-blue bruise near the corner of Jassy's left eye. She didn't have to tell him why she had lied to her mother. He knew why. Even a whore would consider herself a step above a half-breed who earned his living as a hired gun. It was no wonder Jassy had been reluctant to tell her mother where the dress came from.

He stroked her cheek lightly, marveling at the silkiness of her skin beneath his calloused hand. "Does it hurt much?"

Jassy shook her head. It didn't hurt at all, not when he touched her like that, his big hand achingly gentle. His dark eyes caressed her face and she wished suddenly that she were pretty, like Rosie, or high-spirited and vivacious, like her mother.

"Go on home, Jassy," Creed said. "Put a cold cloth on that bruise."

"Where are you going?"

"I've got some business to take care of," he replied, his voice harsh.

She watched him walk down the street, glad that his business didn't concern her.

Daisy McCloud frowned as she saw the tall gunfighter enter the saloon. He was a frequent customer, but she had always avoided him. She liked men who knew how to have a good time, men who laughed and joked and made her feel like she was still young and pretty. She had never seen Creed Maddigan so much as crack a smile. And his eyes . . . There was something about those fathomless black eyes that frightened her on some primal, instinctive level.

She felt a shiver of apprehension as he

crossed the room toward her.

"You Jassy McCloud's mother?"

Daisy's first thought was to deny it. But she knew, somewhere deep inside, that lying to this man would be a big mistake. She lifted her chin defiantly, not wanting him to know she was afraid of him.

"What's it to you?"

"Don't hit her again."

"I beg your pardon?"

"Jassy. Don't hit her again."

"Who the devil do you think you are?" Daisy exclaimed, her anger making her reckless. "She's my daughter and no concern of yours."

"I'm making her my concern. You lay a hand on her again, and you'll live to regret it."

"Are you threatening me?"

"No ma'am," he replied quietly. "You can take my word to the bank."

The retort that sprang to Daisy's lips shriveled and died, unsaid. She took an involuntary step backward, repelled by the menace in his soft-spoken words, and by the warning she read in his eyes. This was what death looked like, she thought.

He took a step forward, his size intimidating her. "Do we understand each other?"

"Y-yes."

"Good. I want Jassy to have that green dress. And those boots."

Daisy nodded. She'd already spent the money she'd gotten for the dress and the boots on a bottle of Paris perfume, but he didn't have to know that.

She'd make sure he didn't know that.

Chapter Three

Creed stretched the kinks out of his legs as he studied his cards. Four queens and a trey. Lady Luck had been sitting on his shoulder all night, he mused as he tossed five silver dollars into the pot, and she didn't seem to be in any itching hurry to leave.

He was raking in his winnings when there was a sudden commotion at a nearby table. Instinctively, his hand dropped to his Colt as he glanced over his shoulder, but it was just a brawl between a couple of soiled doves. All he could see was a swirl of red satin skirts and thrashing arms and legs as the two women tumbled to the floor.

With a shake of his head, he turned his attention back to the game, only to spring to his feet when a single gunshot echoed and reechoed off the walls.

A sudden hush fell over the saloon as the crowd stared at the still female form on the floor. Then it seemed as if everybody was talking at once, taking sides over who was to blame for the altercation.

"It was Mae who started it," one of the house dealers said, nodding with an air of absolute certainty. "I saw the whole thing."

"I didn't start it!" the woman called Mae shrieked. "She did. I warned her not to try to cut in on my customers."

Without warning, Mae began to cry. "It was an accident, Coulter, honest. I didn't mean to hurt her." She dabbed at her eyes with the hem of her skirt. "You've got to believe me, Ray. It wouldn't have happened if she hadn't pulled that gun."

Creed slid a glance at the dealer, wondering if he was related to the kid who'd been giving Jassy a hard time. Ray Coulter wore the look of a man who was accustomed to trouble. A narrow scar marred what some might have called a handsome face. He wore his dark brown hair cut short; his eyes were a pale green, as cold as gunmetal.

A couple of the doves started crying when the body of the dead woman was carried outside.

A few minutes later, the sheriff arrived and began asking questions. At that point, Creed scooped up his winnings and left the saloon. He didn't much care who'd been shot, and the less he had to do with the law, or lawmen, the better.

News of the shooting in the Lazy Ace was all over town the following day. The good ladies of Harrison gathered together, telling anyone who would listen that the latest episode at the Lazy Ace only proved what they'd been saying all along—it was time to burn down those awful shacks and send the soiled doves packing. Let them go to Dodge or Kansas City or some other hell-town.

Sitting in his favorite rocker on the porch of the general store later that afternoon, Creed heard bits and pieces of what had happened from people passing by. He hadn't stayed around long enough to find out the name of the dead woman, but the general consensus was that the shooting had been an accident.

The incident at the Lazy Ace was the farthest thing from his mind as he re-read the letter in his hand. It was an offer of a job over in Black Hawk. A miner by the name of Reid Burton was having trouble with his claim and wanted Creed to "come over and put things straight." An easy job, Burton wrote, but he was willing to pay three grand for Creed's services.

Creed grimaced as he shoved the letter into his shirt pocket. If the job was easy, Burton would do it himself.

Still, three grand was nothing to sneeze at.

Between bounty hunting and hiring out his gun, he managed to earn a fair living that allowed him to keep his own council and work his own hours.

Creed had sent the miner a reply that morning, saying he'd be there as soon as his leg healed up. He had meant to leave town weeks ago, but then Jassy had come into his life and he had found himself making excuses to stay another day, and then another. But he couldn't put it off any longer. He'd leave tomorrow for sure.

The sun was setting and he was thinking about heading down to Jackson's for dinner when he heard a muffled sob from the direction of the shacks along the alley, followed by some noisy sniffling. And then, as if a dam had burst, he heard the sound of crying. Not the kind associated with minor discomfort, but gut-deep, heartrending sobs.

And for the second time in two weeks, Creed Maddigan did something completely out of character. He went to see if he could help.

Maybe, unconsciously, he had known it was her. She was wearing one of her baggy dresses, and he made a mental note to have another little talk with her mother about getting that green dress back.

"You need help, girl?"

Jassy's head came up at the sound of his voice. She could hardly see him through her tears, but she would have recognized that soft drawl anywhere.

Sniffling, she dabbed at her eyes with a corner of her skirt. "N-no. I'm . . . I'm fine."

"You sure?"

She nodded solemnly, but began to sob again.

Feeling completely out of his element, Creed closed the distance between them and drew the girl into his arms. For a moment, he thought she was going to pull away. Her whole body tensed at his touch, and then she crumpled against him, her face buried against his chest, her shoulders shaking with the force of her tears.

He held her for several minutes, aware of people passing by only a few feet away. A couple of cowboys whistled and made crude remarks as they ambled down the alley toward Front Street.

Muttering an oath, Creed swung Jassy up into his arms and carried her across the street to the hotel, deciding she didn't need the whole town to see her crying in his arms.

Ignoring her protests, Creed carried Jassy up the stairs to his room, closed the door behind him, then sat down in the big, overstuffed chair beside the bed.

"Go on," he said gruffly. "Cry it all out, whatever it is."

His shirt front was soaked with her tears when, with a shudder, she finally fell silent.

"Want to tell me about it?" he asked, figuring

that she'd probably had a fight with her boyfriend.

"My . . . my mother's dead."

Creed swore softly. "I'm sorry. Was it sudden?"

"Yesterday. At the saloon."

So the dead woman had been her mother. Rotten luck, he thought, then frowned into the gathering darkness, wondering what he could possibly say that would make Jassy feel better.

"The funeral's tomorrow," she remarked tonelessly. "Would you . . . would you come?"

He hated funerals, all that weeping and carrying on, people saying things they didn't mean. "I don't know . . ."

"Please. You're . . ." She sniffed. "You're the only friend I have."

He let out a deep sigh of resignation. "All right. What time?"

"Nine. I know it's early," she added quickly, remembering that he liked to sleep late, "but . . ."

"I'll be there."

She looked at him solemnly, her brown eyes shining with tears, her nose red, her lips slightly parted.

"How old are you?" he asked, wondering why he cared.

"Seventeen."

Seventeen! Creed swore under his breath. He'd known she was young, but hearing just how young made him feel as if he'd just been sucker-punched.

"Almost seventeen," Jassy said quickly.

"Come on," he said, sliding her off his lap. "I'll walk you home."

"You don't have to."

He nodded, feeling as though he'd aged ten years in the last ten seconds. "I know. Come on."

She lived in one of the shoddy tin-roofed shacks that backed up to the alley. The paint was peeling. One of the front windows was covered with oilcloth; the other was boarded up.

Jassy paused at the door, her face a pale oval in the gathering twilight.

"I seem to be thanking you a lot lately," she said quietly.

Creed shrugged. "Don't worry about it. And don't think you have to make me any more cookies."

"Didn't you like them?"

He had, but he didn't know if it was wise to admit it. Still, she was looking up at him expectantly, her expression as vulnerable as a newborn babe's, and he couldn't bring himself to hurt her feelings.

"I liked them fine," he admitted gruffly. "See you in the morning."

There were only seven people at the grave site, including the preacher.

Creed stood a little way off by himself, hat in

hand, while the parson talked about hell and damnation and the sure hope of forgiveness in the next life. He rambled on and on, warming to his subject as he talked of Mary Magdalene and how her accusers had quietly dispersed when the Saviour suggested that the one without sin cast the first stone.

All in all, Creed thought the whole sermon was in pretty poor taste, but he didn't think anyone else was listening. Jassy, wearing a long black dress that obviously belonged to someone else, was staring down at the plain wooden coffin. Her face was pale, and her eyes were red-rimmed and swollen with tears.

Beside her stood a tall, slender woman, also dressed in black. Creed recognized her as one of the soiled doves from the Lazy Ace. He couldn't remember her name. She was a pretty woman, with dark brown hair and brown eyes. A nice shape, too. And not bad in bed.

Milt Cambridge, owner of the Lazy Ace, stood on the far side of the grave, flanked by two of the doves from the saloon.

Creed watched Jassy's face as the preacher said the final amen and the coffin was lowered into the ground. The tall, slender woman tossed a handful of dirt into the grave, and it occurred to him, with sickening certainty, that she was probably Jassy's sister.

The parson took his leave, and shortly thereafter the grave site was deserted save for Creed and Jassy. She was crying now, making no effort to wipe away the tears running down her cheeks.

Shaking his head, Creed pushed away from the tree he'd been leaning against and started down the hill. He'd done what she'd asked; he'd attended the funeral.

Settling his hat on his head, he took a few more steps and then, cussing himself for being seven kinds of a fool, he went back to the grave and drew Jassy into his arms, wondering what it was about her that made him feel so uncharacteristically protective.

A sigh slipped past Jassy's lips as Creed's arms wrapped around her. There was comfort in his arms, in his mere presence. She didn't stop to wonder why he made her feel so safe; she knew only that she wasn't afraid of anything when he was near—not the past, not the future.

She closed her eyes, wishing he would hold her like that forever. He smelled of whiskey and cigarette smoke, things she had always hated until now. He didn't say anything. No empty words of solace, no promises of a glorious reunion on the other side. He just held her close, one big brown hand gently stroking her hair.

Gradually, she became aware of other things: —the silky texture of his shirt beneath her cheek, the strong, steady beat of his heart, the fact that she barely reached his shoulder.

Creed blew out a deep breath, a little bewildered by the emotions this girl aroused in him and even more puzzled by her effect on his anatomy. She wasn't much to look at, and he'd never been partial to red-headed women, yet she had taken up a good part of his thoughts since the first time he had seen her in that alley. He couldn't help noticing how right she felt in his arms, and that scared the hell out of him, because she was far and away too young for him—and not just in years.

"Feelin' better now?" he asked after a while.

Jassy nodded. Just being in his arms made everything seem all right.

"You ready to go home?"

Jassy thought of the dreary little shack in the alley, and the room she shared with Rose, and shook her head.

"Well, we can't stand here all day. Come on, I'll buy you some lunch."

She smiled up at him as if he'd just offered to buy her a coach and four.

It crossed his mind that it probably wouldn't do Jassy's reputation any good, being seen in the company of a half-breed gunfighter, and then he grinned. Hell, her mother had been killed in a saloon brawl, so being seen with him probably wouldn't tarnish her reputation much more than it already was.

He took her to Jackson's, where he ordered steak and potatoes for both of them, a glass of milk for Jassy, and a cup of coffee for himself. And then, as the silence stretched between them, he wondered what he was doing, sitting there with a girl almost half his age.

"What are you gonna do, now that your ma's gone?"

"I don't know," Jassy answered dully. "Rosie says I'll be able to work at the saloon pretty soon."

"Rosie?"

"My sister."

Creed's grip tightened around the cup in his hand. "She the dark-haired one standing beside you at the funeral?" he asked, praying that the answer was no.

Jassy nodded. "She says it isn't so bad, most of the time."

It caught him unaware, the sudden killing rage that washed through him when he thought of Jassy going to work at the Lazy Ace, serving drinks to a bunch of no-good cowboys, letting strangers take her upstairs. . . .

Get hold of yourself, Maddigan, he chided himself. *She's nothing to you.*

"Is that what you want to do with your life?" he asked gruffly.

"No. I want to get married and raise a family. I don't want to have to—to, you know."

He did know. He'd done it with her sister. The thought slashed through him like a Lakota skinning knife.

"Tell me about you," Jassy said. "Rosie says that you hire out your gun for a living, that you've killed hundreds of men."

Creed chuckled. Hundreds of men, indeed. "You believe her?"

A guilty flush stained Jassy's cheeks. "I . . . I don't know."

"Her count's a little high, but I've killed men, I won't deny it. And I've been known to hire out my gun, if the price was right."

He thought briefly about Burton. If he didn't get to Black Hawk pretty soon, the man would likely find somebody else for the job.

Jassy stared at Creed, trying to reconcile the man who had come to her rescue, the man who had comforted her such a short time ago, with the kind of man he said he was.

"Have you ever thought about . . . about getting married?"

"No."

"Oh."

Creed frowned. Surely she wasn't thinking about him as a possible husband? Hell, they'd just met a couple of weeks ago. Besides, she needed a young man, one who wasn't always looking over his shoulder, waiting for that one gunfighter who was just a fraction of a second faster on the draw, that one man who wouldn't flinch from shooting him in the back.

The waitress brought their dinner then, and they ate in silence.

Jassy finished her steak in record time and Creed insisted that she finish his as well. He ordered apple pie for dessert and urged her to have another glass of milk. She didn't argue, and he wondered if she was getting enough to eat at home. Surely her mother and sister made enough money to put food on the table, even if they couldn't afford to buy the kid a decent dress.

Jassy picked at her pie, not wanting the meal to end. Ever since the night her father had walked out, no one had paid much attention to her. Daisy had slept days and worked nights, so she had never had much time to spend with her youngest daughter, leaving most of Jassy's upbringing to Rosie, who was three years older than Jassy. And then, when Jassy turned fifteen, Rosie had gone to work in the saloon, too, leaving Jassy pretty much on her own.

Not that she had minded. She liked to be alone, with only her books for company. Her father had been a scholar, and though she hardly remembered him, he had left a large box of books behind when he left. Her mother would have thrown them out, but Jassy had begged to keep them because they had belonged to her father. Grudgingly, Daisy had taught her to read. She had given Jassy the gold pocket watch Gregor had left behind too. It was Jassy's most valuable possession.

She glanced at Maddigan. She knew he was a frequent visitor to the Lazy Ace, and she wondered if he had paid to take Rosie—or, heaven forbid, her mother—upstairs.

"You about finished there?" Creed asked, wondering why she was staring at him that way.

"Yes."

Creed tossed a couple of dollars on the table,

plucked his hat from the rack, and held the door open for her.

"Could we . . ." She looked up at him shyly. "Could we go for a walk?"

He hesitated a moment. "Sure, kid."

"I'm not a kid!"

"No?" He bit back a grin as he glanced down at her. She looked like a kid, he thought. Her black mourning dress was too large, the style far too mature, for a little bit of a girl like her, making her look like a youngster playing dress-up in her mama's old clothes. "Where do you want to go?"

Jassy shrugged. "I don't know. Anywhere."

Creed dragged a hand over his jaw, then grunted softly. "Come on."

Happy just to be with him, Jassy followed Creed down the street, aware of the glances that fell their way—some curious, some disapproving, but she didn't care.

Soon, they had left the town behind and they were walking alongside the narrow stream that cut across the prairie south of Harrison.

Jassy had never dared wander too far from town. Her mother had warned her time and again of dire consequences if she strayed too far from home and Jassy had known, without being told, that men would consider her fair game, since her mother and sister both worked in the saloon.

Her mother had been right, too, Jassy thought bitterly. Harry Coulter certainly felt that way. He didn't dare frequent any of the saloons because his daddy was too well known, but he wanted the same thing from Jassy that men had wanted from her mother, only Jassy wouldn't give it to him. Ever. She wasn't going to live the kind of life her mother and sister lived. She wanted to get married and have children, dozens of children whom she would love and cherish, children who would never grow up feeling unwanted or unloved. Children who would know who their father was.

"What?" Jassy looked up, aware that she hadn't been paying any attention to where they were going.

"I asked if you wanted to sit down for a while?"

She nodded, her eyes widening as she looked around. They were in a secluded valley. Tall trees, their branches covered with bright shades of green, grew all around. A small blue lake sparkled in the sunlight. Multicolored flowers bloomed on the hillsides and along the water's edge. It looked like a fairy place, Jassy thought. She wouldn't have been surprised to see a knight on a white charger riding out of the trees.

Charmed by the quiet beauty of the place, she sat down beside Maddigan.

"Pretty, huh?" he remarked.

"Oh, yes," she breathed. "It looks like something out of a storybook."

"Does it?"

Jassy nodded, a smile curving her lips as she watched a small gray squirrel scoot along a tree limb. "Do you come here often?"

"Once in a while."

"Wouldn't it be wonderful to build a house here?" She glanced around, imagining it in her mind. "I'd put the parlor here, with a big window looking out over the lake. And the kitchen over there, and the bedroom there, and maybe a nursery . . ." She smiled inwardly, watching the house take shape in her mind. "It's a perfect place for a house. Just perfect! Don't you think so?"

She was looking up at him expectantly, her eyes bright, as she waited for a reply. Young, he thought ruefully. She was so damn young.

"It's as good a place as any, I reckon."

She was disappointed in his answer. Her smile faded and the exuberance went out of her voice. "You think I'm silly, don't you, because I want a home and a family?"

"No. I hope you get what you want out of life, Jassy."

She leaned toward him, her head canted to one side, her dark eyes intent on his face. "What do you want?"

Creed shrugged. "I don't know."

"Don't you want a home someday? A wife, children?"

"Men in my line of work don't stay in one place long enough to settle down and raise a family."

She felt as if the sun had suddenly lost its warmth. "You aren't leaving town, are you?"

It was in his mind to tell her that he was planning on leaving in the morning. But he knew suddenly that he couldn't go. Not now. Not when she was looking at him like that.

"No, Jassy, I'm not leaving. Not for a few days anyway."

"Do you have to go?"

"There's a job waiting for me in Black Hawk. I should have left two weeks ago." And he would have been long gone, if it hadn't been for her.

"A job?" Her gaze strayed to the gun holstered low on his left hip.

Creed's gaze followed hers. "It's what I do, girl."

"And you're good at it, aren't you?"

Creed nodded, frowning a little at the dismay he heard in her voice. He wasn't just good. He was one of the best.

"You could stop."

"Could I?"

Jassy nodded.

"Maybe I don't want to."

"Why? Do you like killing people?"

He glared at her. If she'd been a man, he'd have known how to handle her, but she was just a kid.

"Well," she insisted. "Do you?"

She had guts, he'd give her that. Most men knew better than to push him.

"Listen, Jassy, I do what I have to do to get

the job done. It's not always pretty."

"Take me with you when you go."

She looked up at him, her dark brown eyes filled with despair. For the first time, he noticed the light sprinkling of freckles across the bridge of her nose. Her lips were a beguiling shade of pink, the color of the summer roses that grew along the banks of the Little Big Horn. Her cheeks were flushed. Sometime during their walk, she'd taken the ribbon from her hair and now it fell down her back and over her shoulders in a riot of soft red waves.

Her lips were far too tempting, he thought bleakly. Her hair invited the touch of his hand, and her eyes . . . He swore under his breath and then, without realizing what he meant to do until it was done, he lowered his head and kissed her, his fingers tunneling into the silky mass of her hair.

He knew immediately that she had never been kissed by anyone who knew how. And so he kissed her gently at first, his lips playing softly over hers, encouraging her to tilt her head to one side, to open her mouth so he could sample the honey sweetness within.

She was a quick study. In a matter of minutes, she was kissing him back, and what had started as an innocent expression of affection quickly escalated to something much more dangerous.

Desire streaked through him like chain lightning, startling in its intensity. He was breathing hard when he took his lips from hers.

"Will you, Creed?" she asked breathlessly. "Will you take me with you when you go?"

"No."

"Please."

He shook his head. There was no place in his life for a woman, especially a white woman. Especially one as young and innocent as Jassy McCloud. He'd learned long ago that getting mixed up with white women was a big mistake. He was a half-breed, a man caught between two worlds who was never at home in either, and so he had made his own world, taking what he liked from each and to hell with the rest.

With an oath, Creed released her and stood up. "Come on, kid, it's time to go back."

"I'm not a kid!" Jassy exclaimed, confused and hurt by his curt tone of voice.

"I'll say." His gaze lingered on her lips for a moment, and then he started walking.

He'd always been able to spot trouble a mile away, and this girl was trouble of the worst kind. Soft, warm, innocent trouble that caught a man unaware and snared him in his own trap.

Jassy scrambled to her feet and hurried after him. She had always said she would save herself for marriage, that she would never part with her virginity until she had a ring on her finger, but suddenly that didn't seem important anymore. What mattered was that Creed was going away and she would never see him again.

Her mouth was suddenly dry, and she licked

her lips nervously. And then, not knowing how to say it any other way, she just said it straight out.

"Would you make love to me?"

"What?"

He halted in mid-stride. Jassy, coming up behind him, slammed into his back, then stumbled backward.

Whirling around, he grabbed her by the arm to steady her. Then, remembering what she had asked, he let go of her and took a step backward. Stunned by her request, he could only stare down at her, wondering if he had heard her right.

"Make love to me. Please, Creed."

"Jassy . . ." He took a deep breath. "Why, Jassy? Why would you want me to make love to you? We're strangers."

"I love you."

Taken aback, he could only stare at her.

Suddenly bold, she burrowed into his arms. "Don't you want to?"

"Jassy, you don't even know what love is."

"Then show me."

She wrapped her arms around his waist, pressing herself against him, her eyes filled with silent entreaty.

Creed swore under his breath. Maybe he'd been wrong about her from the first. Maybe she was more like her mother than he had realized. And maybe she was just feeling lost and confused.

"Jassy . . ."

"Rosie says no one but Milt or one of the other saloon owners will hire me. If that's so, if I'm gonna have to work in that awful saloon and—and do what Rosie does, then I want to do it with you first."

She went up on her tiptoes, her hand slipping around his neck, pulling his head down to meet hers, and then she was kissing him.

It was hard to remember she was young and innocent when she kissed him like that, her lips warm and sweet and softly yielding, her tongue a welcome invasion.

Creed cussed himself then, because he knew he was the one who had taught her to kiss like that, and now it was coming back to taunt him. Her body was soft and supple where it pressed against his, her warmth beckoning to him, teasing him.

His hands slid up and down her back, then settled on her hips, pulling her hard up against him, letting her feel the heat of his desire, hoping it would scare her off.

But that backfired, too. She moaned low in her throat and strained against him, wanting to be closer, and he knew if he didn't back off soon, it would be too late.

Letting her go was the most difficult thing he'd ever done, and he managed it only by reminding himself that she was just a kid. Just a kid who was vulnerable and unhappy and looking for love wherever she could find it.

"Creed?" She blinked up at him, her eyes heavy-lidded, her voice uneven. "What's wrong?"

"It's time to go, Jassy." He stepped away from her and took a deep breath. "This isn't the time or the place."

"When?" she asked. "Where?"

"In about four years," he muttered, and resettling his hat on his head, he started walking before lush pink lips and luminous brown eyes changed his mind.

Chapter Four

She was still following him. Creed let out a long sigh, bemused by his feelings for Jassy McCloud. On the one hand, it was kind of flattering having her trail after him like a love-starved puppy. There was a sweetness about her, a vulnerability, that made him feel protective of her, especially now that her mother was dead.

On the other hand, he spent far too much time thinking about her. He didn't need a distraction like Jassy McCloud in his life, and one night, when he'd had a little too much to drink, he had told her so.

Follow me all you want, he had said, his voice harsh and unrelenting, *but it won't do you any good. I'm not taking you with me. Now get lost.*

She had nodded that she understood, but she

had kept following him, hiding in doorways, watching when he left the hotel, waiting outside Jackson's while he ate breakfast, trailing after him when he went to the saloon. Whenever he caught her at it, she just smiled, her eyes glowing with hope.

It was time to leave town, he mused, before he started giving some serious thought to taking her with him. He had done a lot of fool things in his life, but getting mixed up with a little bit of a girl who wanted a home and a dozen kids would make all his other mistakes look like accomplishments. So he'd head out of town and that would put an end to it.

Tomorrow, he thought. He would leave for Black Hawk tomorrow.

But tomorrow came and went, and Creed didn't leave town.

Jassy stared at her sister. "You're leaving town? Where are you going?"

Rose smiled a secret smile as she folded her best dress and added it to the small pile of clothing on the bed. "Ray wants me to meet him in Denver."

"Denver! But . . ."

Rose's eyes narrowed ominously. "But what?"

"He's . . . he's married."

"No, he's not."

"But . . ."

"He's not married to Tess."

"Oh."

"He's only stayed with her this long because of Harry. But Harry's a big boy now."

Jassy clasped her hands together. "Are you coming back?"

"I hope not." Rose made a slow pirouette, a dreamy expression on her face. "Wouldn't it be great if he asked me to—"

"To what?" Jassy stared at her sister. Surely Rose didn't think Coulter would marry her.

"Never mind." Rose shoved a couple of crumpled greenbacks into Jassy's hand. "We'll be gone a week or so. You stay in the house until I get back, hear?"

"What if you don't come back?"

Rose made a broad gesture with her hand. "Then I guess all this will be yours."

A lump of fear congealed in Jassy's stomach. She wasn't all that crazy about her sister's company, but she had never lived alone, had no way to support herself, except . . . She swallowed the fear rising in her throat. No matter what happened, she wasn't going to end up working at the Lazy Ace.

"Oh, for crying out loud, don't fret about it," Rose said irritably. "If we decide to stay in Denver, I'll send for you."

"You promise?"

"Sure."

"When are you leaving?"

"On the evening stage."

Creed paused on his way out of Roscoe's Tobacco Shop. Across the way, he saw Jassy's sister being helped aboard the stage bound for Denver. His gaze swept the boardwalk for some sign of Jassy, but she was nowhere to be seen.

Creed frowned, wondering what Jassy would do if Rose was leaving town for good, and then he swore under his breath. It was none of his business. Jassy was none of his business.

His business or not, he found himself walking down the boardwalk toward Gratton's. Inside, he quickly wrote a list—sugar, coffee, flour, potatoes, onions, a dozen eggs, a slab of bacon—and handed it to Gratton.

The shopkeeper looked a little surprised as he rang up Creed's purchases. Creed supposed he couldn't blame the man. Until today, he'd rarely stepped foot in the place.

After paying for his purchases, Creed made a stop at Mulsteins's Meat Market, then headed for Jassy's. With each step, he told himself he was making a big mistake, but he didn't turn back.

Minutes later, he was knocking at her door.

Jassy stared up at Creed in astonishment, the beat of her heart increasing with each passing second.

"Creed." She murmured his name, unable to believe he was really there. "What are you doing here?"

"I saw Rose over at the stage depot."

"She's on her way to Denver to meet a—a friend."

"Is she coming back?"

"Oh, yes," Jassy said, injecting a note of conviction into her voice. "Next week."

Creed grunted softly. "Where do you want this stuff?"

She noticed the box in his arms for the first time. "What is it?"

"Just some stuff I picked up. Coffee, flour, things like that."

"Why?"

Creed shrugged. He wasn't prepared to explain what he didn't understand himself. "Where do you want it?"

"In here," Jassy said and led the way down the narrow, paint-peeling hallway toward the dingy kitchen.

Creed dropped the box on the rickety table, his gaze sweeping the room. He guessed the walls had once been green, though now they were a dingy shade of gray. The floor was warped and discolored. The homemade table and chairs had obviously seen better days. The cupboard doors hung askew, and the oilcloth that covered the window over the dry sink was ripped down one side.

Damn, he thought, he wouldn't stable his horse in a dump like this.

Jassy felt the heat rise in her cheeks as she followed Creed's gaze. The house had always been ugly but now, seeing it through his eyes, it seemed even worse.

She lowered her head so he couldn't see her

embarrassment, wishing she'd never let him inside the house.

"Jassy?"

"What?" She mumbled the word, refusing to meet his gaze.

Creed placed a finger beneath her chin and forced her head up so he could look into her eyes.

"You don't have anything to be ashamed of, Jassy," he said quietly. "It isn't your fault."

She felt a small glow begin inside her, a flickering flame of gratitude because he understood what she was feeling.

"Think you could fix me something to eat?" He cocked an eyebrow at her. "You can make something besides cookies, can't you?"

Jassy nodded, warmth flooding through her.

"There's a couple of steaks in there," Creed said, gesturing at the box. "I like mine rare."

"Me too."

He stared down at her, wondering what the hell he was doing. The silence stretched between them, thick, palpable. He was aware of the faint scent of soap and sunshine that clung to Jassy's hair and skin. Her eyes were a warm luminous brown, completely without guile as she returned his gaze.

Creed dragged a hand through his hair. What was he doing here?

"I'm going outside for a smoke," he muttered, leaving the kitchen before her nearness made him forget she was just a kid.

Minutes later, he was sitting on the top step, the cigarette in his hand forgotten as he stared into the distance. He wasn't doing Jassy any favor by being here, he mused bleakly. People being what they were, they would no doubt jump to the conclusion that Jassy had decided to ply her sister's trade and that Creed was her first steady customer.

Personally, he had never cared what people thought about him, but he hated to be responsible for blackening Jassy's reputation. She was a good girl. She deserved a better life than the one that seemed to be waiting for her—certainly a better life than he could give her.

He swore under his breath. Where had *that* thought come from? He didn't need a woman in his life, especially a white woman, not after what had happened the last time.

Tomorrow he would buy her enough groceries to last the rest of the week, and then he'd hightail it out of town before he got in any deeper than he already was.

Creed ignored Gratton's inquisitive gaze as he entered the mercantile the next morning. He heard several curious whispers as he stood at the counter, waiting for Gratton to fill his order, and he knew that the news of his visit to Jassy's house the night before was already being reported by the good women of the town.

Damn! Well, he'd give them something else to talk about, he thought as he walked back to the ladies ready-to-wear department and picked out a pale pink blouse and a flounced skirt made of a dark pink print. He looked around for the green dress, but it was gone.

He told Gratton to add the clothing to his other stuff, dropped a handful of greenbacks on the counter, and left the store, conscious of the speculative stares that followed him out the door.

Jassy looked up at Creed, genuinely surprised to see him. He hadn't said anything about coming back after last night. She had never spent an evening alone with a man before, and dinner the previous evening had been awkward at best. Alone with Creed, all rational thought had fled her mind. Time and again, she had found herself staring at him, unable to believe that he was there, that he had chosen to spend the evening with her.

"Mornin'," Creed said.

"Good morning."

He shifted the box in his arms. "I probably ate up most of the grub I bought yesterday," he said with a wry grin, "so I thought I'd better restock your shelves for you. Here."

He shoved a paper-wrapped parcel into her hands. "This is for you. To replace the one your mother took back."

"You don't have to do that."

"I know. I want to."

Jassy clutched the package to her chest and a smile bubbled up inside her as she stepped aside to let him in. "Have you had breakfast?"

He shook his head. "Not yet."

"Are you hungry?"

"Yeah."

"Eggs and bacon all right with you?"

Creed nodded. Last night, she had proved herself to be a good cook.

He followed her into the kitchen, placed the box on the table, then sat down in one of the dilapidated ladder-back chairs and watched her fry the bacon and eggs. She could probably get a job cooking at one of the restaurants, he thought, admiring the sway of her hips as she crossed the floor to take a couple of plates out of the cupboard. The pay wouldn't add up to much, but it would beat working in one of the cribs.

Jassy smiled shyly as she offered Creed a plate piled high with fluffy scrambled eggs, bacon, and fried potatoes. She filled his coffee cup, then sat down across from him. Unable to help herself, she pretended that Creed was her husband, that they ate breakfast together every day, that soon he would go off to work and she'd spend the day cleaning and sewing, all the while waiting for his return.

Creed ate in silence, aware of Jassy's covert glances, of the flush in her cheeks and the sparkle in her eyes. He wondered what she was thinking that kept the color high in her cheeks, but decided it wouldn't be prudent to ask.

With a sigh, he pushed his plate away and sat back in his chair, one hand wrapped around his coffee cup.

"What are you gonna do today?" he asked.

"I don't know. Rosie told me to stay in the

house and keep out of trouble."

Staying out of trouble sounded like good advice, Creed thought. Too bad he wasn't smart enough to take it.

"How'd you like to go for a ride?"

"Really? Where? When?"

"Any place you like. Now."

She jumped to her feet, ran around the table, and hugged him. "Oh, Creed, could we go back to the valley where we went before?"

Warning bells went off in his mind as he remembered the kiss they'd shared that day, remembered the way Jassy had molded her body to his, begging him to make love to her.

She read the uncertainty in his expression. The excitement faded from her eyes and she stepped away from him, her hands clenched.

"I'm sorry. You don't have to take me anywhere, Creed."

"Jassy . . ."

"It's all right. I understand."

She squared her shoulders and lifted her chin in a defiant gesture that went straight to his heart.

"You don't have to feel sorry for me, Mr. Maddigan. I can take care of myself."

"Do you want to go riding or not, Jassy?"

His quiet voice punctured her anger. "Yes, very much."

"How soon can you be ready?"

Jassy glanced around the kitchen. She'd have to put the rest of the groceries away, wash the dishes, change her clothes. "Half an hour?"

Creed nodded. "Don't be late," he said with a wink, and settling his hat on his head, he left the house, whistling softly.

Chapter Five

Creed headed out of town the back way, hoping no one would notice the two of them riding out together. He had stopped at the livery stable and rented an even-tempered bay gelding for Jassy to ride. She had smiled her thanks as he helped her mount. She looked pretty as a picture in her new clothes.

Jassy was quiet the first mile or so, and Creed wondered again why he was spending so much time with her, why he didn't head for Black Hawk and get on with his life. But then he slid a glance in her direction, and he knew why he hadn't left town. The sun seemed to dance in her hair, making it glow like living fire. Her gaze darted from side to side, her eyes bright with the wonder of discovery, and it occurred to him that she probably didn't get out of town very often. Seeing the world through her eyes would be like seeing it for the first time.

She looked over at him and smiled, her expression radiant, her eyes shining with such happiness that it made him ache inside. Time and again, she leaned forward to stroke her horse's neck, and each time Creed's body hardened as he imagined those untutored fingers running over his chest and down his thigh, imagined her beautiful dark eyes staring up at him, hazy with passion. . . .

Muttering an oath, he slammed the door on his rampant thoughts.

As they rode alongside the stream, Jassy marveled anew at the beauty of the prairie that stretched ahead of them for miles. But it was Creed's face that drew her attention over and over again. She never tired of looking at him, of watching the easy way he sat in the saddle, the way his gaze moved over the countryside, ever wary, missing nothing. She loved to watch the play of muscles in his back and shoulders when he moved.

Occasionally she met his glance and felt the heat that smoldered in the depths of his eyes. He was a man grown, she mused, not a boy like Harry Coulter. The thought should have frightened her; instead, it filled her with a sense of exhilaration, as if she were on the verge of some wondrous discovery.

Her heartbeat quickened when they reached

the valley. Creed had kissed her here. Unconsciously, she licked her lower lip, remembering, wondering if he would kiss her again.

Creed drew his horse to a halt beneath a lacy willow tree. Dismounting, he lifted Jassy from the bay and slowly lowered her feet to the ground.

She gazed up into his eyes, her every thought, her every desire, shining in her dark gaze.

And in spite of every warning he'd given himself, Creed Maddigan lowered his head and kissed her, his lips drinking deeply from hers, as if she were life itself and he was a man on the brink of destruction.

Her lips were soft and smooth and warm. At the touch of his tongue, she swayed against him, her breasts pressing against his chest as her lips parted in silent invitation.

Creed wrapped his arms around her, and together they slowly sank to the ground. He kissed her for a long time, his mouth playing softly over her lips, her eyelids, the curve of her cheek, the tip of her nose, the lobe of her ear. His hands burned to explore the gentle contours of her body, but he knew that if he touched her, he'd be lost. And so he kissed her instead, his tongue laving the sweet length of her neck, the pulse that vibrated in the hollow of her throat. It was the most exquisitely painful pleasure he had ever known, touching without taking, exploring without possessing.

Jassy moaned softly as the tender torment

went on and on. She pressed herself against Creed, her hands roaming over his broad back and shoulders, delighting in the play of powerful muscles beneath her questing fingertips. His body was hard and firm and infinitely fascinating. His kisses made her yearn for something she didn't fully understand, made her blood race and her heart pound with such ferocity that she feared it might burst within her breast. Heat flowed in her and through her, until she was on fire for him. And when she thought she might die of the ecstacy wrought by his lips and his tongue, he let her go and stood up.

For a moment, she could only stare at him, too dazed to speak. He stood with his back to her, his hands clenched at his sides, as he drew in several long, shuddering breaths. Then he turned around.

"Come on," Creed said, offering her his hand, "we'd better go for a walk."

"A walk?" She blinked up at him through eyes cloudy with desire.

"A walk," Creed said.

Confused, she placed her hand in his and let him pull her to her feet. "But . . ."

"But what?"

"I . . ." She glanced away, embarrassed. "I want you to kiss me some more."

"And I want to kiss you," Creed said, his voice raspy and uneven. "And that's why we're going for a walk."

"Is walking a good idea? I mean, what about

your leg? Does it still hurt?"

"Not as much as some other places," Creed muttered. "Come on, let's walk."

She didn't argue. She was too happy to be with him, too caught up in his nearness, in the taste of his kisses, to let anything dull her happiness.

Hand in hand, they walked across the valley floor, their footsteps muffled by a carpet of thick grass. She listened to the birds singing in the trees, remembering how she had thought the valley looked like a fairy place the last time they had been here.

Now, with her lips still tingling from Creed's kisses, she knew that it was, indeed, a fairy place, a magical place where old dreams came true, and new ones were born. She slid a glance at Creed. She had read a story once of a frog who had been turned into a prince.

Perhaps, if she believed strongly enough, the same magic could be worked on her gunfighter.

It was near dusk by the time they returned to town. It had been one of the best days of Jassy's life. They had taken a long walk, not saying much, but Jassy's insides had been aflutter with happiness. She had loved the feel of Creed's hand holding hers. His fingers were long and strong, his palm callused and warm. Time and again her gaze had strayed to his face, admiring his profile, feeling her heart swell with happiness when his gaze met hers.

They had stopped to rest beneath a tree. Jassy had made a daisy chain, but lacked the nerve to put it around his neck, afraid he would think it foolish. And then, unexpectedly, he had picked a wild rose and handed it to her.

Now she held the fragrant flower in her hand as he tethered the horses to the porch rail.

Creed removed his hat and ran a hand through his hair before settling his Stetson on his head again.

"I had a nice time, Creed," Jassy said shyly. "Thank you."

"You're welcome."

"Would you like to stay for supper?"

He meant to say no, but it came out yes, and when he saw the smile that lit up her face, he knew he'd made the right decision.

"You go on inside," he said. "I'd best get this horse back to the livery before old man Crowley accuses me of stealing one of his broomtails."

"I'll start dinner," Jassy said. Whirling around, she hurried inside. He was staying!

She had a couple of steaks frying when he got back. The rose he had given her was in a chipped glass in the middle of the kitchen table.

For a moment, Creed stood in the doorway, a frown on his face as he watched Jassy. She had tied an apron over her dress, and he could hear her humming softly as she turned the steaks. What would it be like, he wondered, to have a woman to look after him, to fret over him and fuss at him?

He swore softly. Now, where had *that* thought come from?

Jassy turned away from the stove, and her face lit up the way it always did when she saw him. He tried not to admit how much he liked that smile, which seemed to be for him alone.

"Sit down," she said. "Supper's almost ready."

He tossed his hat on the counter, dragged a chair out from the table, and sat down.

"You must be getting tired of cooking for me," he muttered.

"No, I like it," Jassy said quickly, then flushed. "I mean, well, I like to cook, but Rosie eats out most of the time, and it's no fun to cook for myself."

She bit down on her lower lip, one hand fisted around a large wooden spoon. "I do like cooking for you, Creed. I like having you here with me."

He swore under his breath, then admitted, reluctantly, "And I like being here."

"You do?"

"Honey, I wouldn't be here if I didn't."

Honey. He'd called her honey! The word flowed through her, warm and sweet, and curled around her heart.

When supper was ready, she sat across from him, almost too happy to eat. They didn't say much, but the silence between them wasn't the least bit awkward.

When the meal was over, Creed went outside to smoke a cigarette while Jassy washed and dried the dishes. Then they sat on the porch together, his arm around her shoulder, while they watched the stars come alive in the sky.

"I'd better be going," Creed said after a long while, and when she didn't reply, he realized she'd fallen asleep.

Lifting her in his arms, he carried her to bed, removed her shoes, and covered her with a blanket. He was about to leave when she caught him by the hand.

"Stay," she whispered.

He looked down at her and slowly shook his head. "I don't think that's a good idea."

"Please. I'm afraid to be here alone."

"Afraid? Of what?"

"Of being alone in the dark." Her hand held his tighter. "I . . . I had a nightmare last night, and I'm afraid to go to sleep."

"What kind of nightmare?"

"I don't remember. Only that it terrified me. I woke up crying, and there was no one here."

He placed his hand over hers and gave it a squeeze. "Sure, honey, I'll stay."

"You can sleep in Rose's room, if you want."

Creed shook his head. "I'll bed down on the sofa in the front room." He kissed her fingertips, then let go of her hand.

"Thank you, Creed."

"No thanks needed, honey. You get some sleep now."

"Would you kiss me good night?"

He took a deep, steadying breath, then bent

down and kissed her cheek.

"Good night, Jassy," he said hoarsely, and got himself out of there before he succumbed to the sweet temptation of pale pink lips and beguiling earth-brown eyes.

Chapter Six

Creed woke early the next morning, irritable after having spent a long, sleepless night on the broken-down sofa in the parlor.

Sitting on the edge of the sofa with his head cradled in his hands, he quietly cursed his desire for the girl sleeping in the next room. What was there about Jassy McCloud that sent his blood racing and made him feel as randy as a fifteen-year-old boy who'd just discovered that girls were different?

Hell and damnation. He should have left town weeks ago, yet here he was, playing nursemaid to a kid with big brown eyes and soft pink lips . . . Except Jassy was no kid. She was young, there was no arguing with that, but she kissed like a woman who knew her own mind.

And that was his undoing, because no other woman had ever kissed him with such guileless passion, such innocent longing.

It was as seductive as hell.

He stomped his feet into his boots, grabbed his hat, and left the house, knowing he had to put some distance between the two of them. He'd check in on her later to make sure she was okay, and he'd spend the night again if she needed him, but right now he needed some time alone.

Outside, he threw a saddle on his horse and rode to the nearest saloon. Early as it was, there were a couple of old-timers hanging over the bar.

Creed ordered a bottle of whiskey and carried it to one of the tables in the back of the room. Sitting back, his feet propped on a chair, he poured himself a drink, then let out a sigh. No doubt Burton had found someone else to handle his problem in Black Hawk, Creed thought, and shrugged. He was tired of hiring out his gun, tired of putting his life on the line to settle someone else's problems.

Hell, he was just tired.

Taking the bottle, he left the saloon. He'd grab a quick breakfast over at the hotel, get some sleep, and then lose himself in a poker game for a couple of hours.

"Three queens." Creed spread his cards on the table, then raked in his fifth pot of the night.

There was some good-natured grumbling from the four other players, but Creed quickly dispelled it by ordering a round of drinks.

He glanced around the saloon while the man on his left dealt them a new hand. Usually there was nothing he liked better than a good card game in a smoke-filled saloon, but tonight . . . He shook his head as he picked up his cards. Tonight he'd rather be with Jassy, which was why he was staying right where he was.

The evening might have passed quietly if the man sitting across from Creed had just kept his mouth shut. But he didn't.

"So," Ray Braddock remarked, grinning. "How is she?"

Creed's face remained expressionless. "She?"

"Daisy's daughter. She as good in the sack as her old lady was?"

"I wouldn't know," Creed replied, his voice deathly quiet.

"Come on," Braddock urged, "you can tell us. It's all over town that you two have been shacking up since Rosie took off."

Creed swore under his breath. "Is it?"

Braddock nodded. "So, how is she?"

There was a moment of silence and then, in the blink of an eye, Creed was on his feet, reaching across the table. Grabbing Braddock by the shirt front, Creed slammed his fist into the man's face, hard, twice, relishing the pain that splintered up his arm, the warm rush of blood that spread over his hands.

When Creed spoke, his voice was lethal. "If you ever lay a hand on Jassy McCloud, I'll kill you."

Ray Braddock glared up at Creed, his eyes bright with pain and humiliation, and though he didn't say a word, gut instinct told Creed he'd better watch his back whenever Braddock was around.

Creed held the other man's gaze for a long moment, then shoved him back in his chair. "Remember what I said."

Creed's gaze swept over every man in the room, a silent warning blazing in the depths of his eyes.

Collecting his winnings, he left the saloon.

Outside, he drew in a deep breath and then, unable to fight it any longer, he headed for the ugly little shack in the alley.

She'd been crying. He knew it the moment he opened the door. And knew, with equal certainty, that he had been the cause of her tears.

It was time to cut and run, he thought, before he got in any deeper, before it was too late for both of them.

And then she was in his arms, and he knew it was already too late.

"Jassy . . ."

She buried her face in the hollow of his shoulder. His shirt smelled of lye soap and cigar smoke and man.

"I got up and you were gone," she said, her

words muffled. "I thought . . ."

"I know," he said, stroking her hair. "I know." He swore under his breath. When had his concern turned to caring, his affection to something deeper, something he refused to put a name to? And what the devil was he going to do about it? About her?

"Don't cry, honey. I'm here now. Please don't cry."

They rode to the valley again the next day. It had become their place, Jassy thought as they walked hand in hand toward the pool. If she could have one wish, it would be to build a house here and share it with Creed.

"Want to go for a swim?" he asked when they reached the pool.

Jassy glanced at the pool, then back at Creed. "Is it cold?"

"Not very. Are you game?"

She nodded. Turning her back, she removed her shoes, stockings and dress; then, clad only in her camisole and drawers, she slid into the water. Creed watched her swim for a moment, then removed his boots, socks, shirt and gunbelt and joined her in the water.

They swam and splashed until Jassy was breathless; then Creed helped Jassy out of the pool and they sat on the grass, letting the sun dry their hair and clothes.

"I love it here," Jassy remarked. "I wish we

never had to leave. It's such a pretty place. So peaceful."

Creed nodded, but it wasn't the beauty of the land he was admiring. It was Jassy.

With a sigh of resignation, he pulled her into his arms and kissed her. She melted into his embrace, a soft moan whispering past her lips as their mouths fused together.

Creed drew in a sharp breath as Jassy ran her hands over his bare back. He heard her gasp with shock when her questing fingertips encountered the first scar. Her hands stilled for a moment, and then, very slowly, moved across his flesh, tracing each one.

"What happened to you?" she asked.

"I was on the wrong end of a whipping."

She looked up at him, distress evident in her expression. "Someone beat you?"

He nodded curtly.

"Who?"

He let her go then, the pain of that whipping and the reason for it as vivid in his mind as if it had happened yesterday instead of almost thirteen years ago.

"Can't you tell me?" Jassy asked softly.

"I'd rather not talk about it."

She nodded, but he could see the hurt in her eyes.

"It was a long time ago, Jassy," he said.

"I understand."

"No, you don't."

"Then tell me."

"Jassy . . ." He cussed under his breath and then, with a sigh of exasperation, he pulled her back into his arms and rested his chin on her head. "When I was eighteen, I fell in love with a girl. A white girl. Her father didn't approve of me, and neither did anybody else in town, so we ran away."

He paused, remembering the joy he'd felt when Deborah had agreed to go away with him, to marry him. Sweet, beautiful Deborah Carey with hair as pale as sunlight, eyes as blue as a Colorado sky, and skin the color of fresh cream. Never in his life had he known anyone as beautiful; never had he dreamed that she'd learn to care for someone like him. They had made it as far as New Mexico before Gareth Carey and his men caught up with them. Carey had slapped Deborah several times, calling her an Indian lover and a whore, and then Carey's men had tied Creed to a tree and whipped him until he lost consciousness. When he'd come to, he was lying facedown in the dirt, naked as the day he was born. Carey had taken his clothes, his boots, and his horse.

"Creed?"

"We ran away," he said again, then shrugged, as if it no longer mattered. "We ran away, and we got caught."

"And her father whipped you?"

Creed nodded.

"Did you ever see her again?"

"No." By the time he had healed up

enough to go after her, it was too late. Carey had sent her away. Creed had tried for two weeks to find out where she was, but it was as if she had disappeared off the face of the earth.

"I'm sorry," Jassy murmured. Gently, she touched her fingertips to each scar as if it were a badge of honor.

"Don't."

"Why not?"

He caught her hands in his. He hated being reminded of those scars. Nothing in his whole life had hurt as much, or been as humiliating, as that whipping.

"Creed?"

He looked at her as if seeing her for the first time and slowly shook his head. "It won't work, Jassy."

"What do you mean?"

He let out a long sigh. "You and me. It just won't work."

"Why?"

"You're too young, for one thing."

"I am not!"

"Then I'm too old."

She shook her head vigorously.

"Jassy, it's not just the difference in our ages; it's my whole life. I can't outrun my past." Suddenly restless, he stood up. "I can't outrun who and what I am, not even for you."

A sigh of regret rose up from deep within him.

He'd been running his whole life, Creed thought bleakly. He had run away from the reservation when life got too hard, he had tried to run away with Deborah, and he was running now, running away from responsibility, running away from his feelings for Jassy.

"Forget it, girl," he said curtly. "I've got no future to offer you."

"I don't believe that!"

"Dammit, Jassy, what can I say to convince you?"

"Nothing, Creed. I know you think I'm too young, that I don't know my own mind, but I do." She met his ominous stare directly. "I know you care about me, whether you want to admit it or not. You need me, Creed Maddigan, and if you turn your back on me now, you'll regret it as long as you live."

A slow smile spread over his face as he stared down at her. "Is that what you think?"

"It's what I know. You'll never find anyone else who'll love you as much as I do, who—who needs you as much as I do."

She smiled up at him, a tenuous smile that wrapped around Creed Maddigan's heart and held on for dear life.

"Jassy, honey . . ."

Jassy took a deep breath. "I love you, Creed," she said fervently, and then her smile turned impish. "And I don't have a father for you to worry about."

He couldn't help it. He threw back his head and laughed. Then he took her in his arms and kissed her.

"I'm not making any promises," he said, hugging her tight. "But we'll give it a try, Jassy girl, if that's what you want."

Chapter Seven

The next five days were wonderful. For Jassy, it was like playing house. She cooked Creed's meals, washed his clothes, and mended his shirt. They usually slept late, then went out riding or walking in the afternoon. About nine o'clock, Creed went to the saloon for a few hours, because, as he said, he had to do something to earn a living since it seemed he was through hiring out his gun for a while.

For Jassy, the hours without him seemed to last forever. She always met him at the door, her heart swelling with gladness as she welcomed him home. He continued to spend his nights at her house because he knew she didn't like to be alone, but he always slept on the sofa. A part of her appreciated his gentlemanly conduct while another, less honorable part wished he'd try to take advantage of her.

She spent the hours waiting for Creed to come home from the saloon by reading her father's books, losing herself in faraway places, imagining herself as a beautiful lady in distress and Creed as her brave knight in shining armor.

Now, sitting on the lumpy sofa waiting for Creed to come home, Jassy pondered their relationship. She hadn't known him very long, but after the last few days, it seemed as if they had always been together.

Hearing footsteps on the porch, she closed the book she had been reading and ran to open the front door, smiling because he was early tonight.

"Rosie!" Jassy exclaimed, the smile fading from her lips. "What are you doing here?"

"I live here, remember?" Rose retorted. She pushed past Jassy to drop her suitcase on the floor, then whirled around, her brows drawn together in a frown. "Just who were you expecting?"

"Me? Expecting?" Jassy shook her head. "No one."

"So that big smile was for me?"

Jassy nodded vigorously. "Of course. I'm—I'm glad to see you."

Rose muttered a crude oath under her breath as she glanced around the room. The parlor had been swept clean, and the rickety furniture had been dusted and waxed.

Still frowning, she went into the kitchen. There was a new cloth on the table, together with a tin can filled with wild daisies. She opened the cupboards, surprised to see them stocked with food.

"You've been busy," Rose remarked, returning to the parlor. "Where'd you get the money to stock the shelves?"

"I . . ."

"You've had a man here, haven't you?" Rose demanded.

"No, of course not!"

"You're lying. Who was it? How much did he pay you?"

"Nothing, Rose, I . . ."

Rose took a threatening step forward. "Don't tell me you gave it away?"

"No!"

"You'd better not be lying to me," Rose warned. "You can only sell your virginity once, and I already know six men who are willing to pay a high price for it."

Jassy stared at her sister, momentarily stunned. And then she shook her head. "How can you talk like that? How can you even think it?"

"Don't be an idiot, Jassy. Your innocence is the only thing of value we've got, and we're gonna take advantage of it."

"No. Never."

"Now, Jassy," Rose said, wrapping her arm

around her sister's shoulder, "it won't be so bad. We can use the money to fix this place up a little, maybe buy some new clothes. You'd like a new dress, wouldn't you? Something pretty?"

"I don't need a new dress."

"Well, I do! And I'm tired of living in this hovel."

"How was Denver?" Jassy asked, hoping to change the subject.

"Fine, just fine. Ray said he'd take me with him the next time he goes out of town. Maybe to San Francisco next time."

"Why would he go to San Francisco?"

"I don't know, I didn't ask. I think he's going to leave Tess, Jassy. I really do." A smile softened the harsh expression on Rose's face. "Maybe he will ask me to marry him."

"Maybe," Jassy agreed doubtfully.

Rose blew out a long sigh. "And maybe not. In the meantime, he gave me enough money to pay the rent on this dump for another two months. And he bought me a beautiful new coat, and a hat to match."

Rose sat down on the sofa and took off her shoes. Leaning back, she closed her eyes. "Get me a cup of coffee."

Jassy hurried to do as she was bidden, hoping that Rose wouldn't bring up the subject of working for Milt again. Maybe it would be a good thing if Coulter married Rose. Maybe he'd take them out of this dump. Maybe they could move to Denver and start a new life.

Jassy made a sound of disgust low in her throat. She was getting as bad as Rose, day-dreaming about things that were never going to happen. There was no reason for Coulter to marry Rosie, not when she gave him everything he wanted.

Standing at the window while she waited for the coffee to heat, she stared at the jagged rip in the oilcloth, wondering what she would do when Creed arrived.

She was pouring Rose's coffee when she heard the front door open, followed by the sound of Rose's voice.

"What are you doing here?" Rose demanded, her voice high-pitched and shrill.

Jassy held her breath, but Creed's voice was low and indistinct.

She heard Rose say, "We need to talk," and then there was only silence.

Jassy peered around the door frame. She could see Rose and Creed standing on the porch, talking. She saw Creed jerk Rose up hard against him; his face was dark with anger. She saw the fear in Rosie's eyes when he pushed her away. If only she could hear what they were saying!

She ducked back into the kitchen when she heard the front door slam open. A moment later, Rose was standing in the kitchen doorway. "You want to tell me what the hell has been going on here?"

"What do you mean?"

"You know what I mean. How long has that half-breed been stopping by to look in on you?"

Jassy squared her shoulders. There was no point in lying. Too many people had seen Creed coming and going. "Just since you've been gone. I mentioned that I didn't like being home alone at night, so he stopped by to make sure I was all right before going to the hotel."

"And just when did you tell him you were afraid to be home alone?"

"I don't remember."

"You're not to see him again, do you understand?"

"Why not?"

"Because he's a dirty Injun, and because I said so. I'm responsible for you now, and I won't have you shaming me by associating with scum like that."

"Shame you!" Jassy exclaimed, her anger making her reckless. "You work in a saloon. How could my talking to Creed shame you any worse than that?"

Rose's face turned suddenly ugly, and Jassy knew she had gone too far. For a moment, she thought Rose was going to hit her, and she wondered if maybe she deserved it.

And then Rose smiled, and it was more frightening than her anger. "I'll be talking to Milt about you in the next day or so, little sister," she said nastily, "and then you'll find out what shame really is."

And with those spiteful words, Rose left the house.

Jassy gave Rose enough time to get to the saloon before she hurried outside, anxious to find Creed, to learn what Rose had said that had made him so angry. She went to the hotel first, but he wasn't in his room, so she headed for the Lazy Ace.

Slipping through the back door, she glanced around the crowded saloon, finally spying him playing poker at a corner table.

Taking a place under the staircase that led to the second floor, she stood in the shadows, watching him. Jealousy stabbed at her heart when she saw one of the saloon girls hovering over Creed's shoulder, flirting with him. Of course, he flirted back, and she wondered how many of the girls he had taken upstairs. It was obvious that he was a special favorite with the doves, and it was easy to see why. He had a roguish smile, a voice like black velvet, and a laugh that made her stomach quiver. After a while, he slipped the girl a couple of dollars. She whispered something in his ear, kissed his cheek, and left the table.

Creed's presence had a definite effect on the men, too. The women might find him fascinating, but Jassy could tell the men were afraid of him.

In the last few weeks, she had often stood there, watching Creed. She had seen the wariness in the eyes of the other men whenever

Creed took a seat at one of the tables. His mere presence made them nervous. Once, when he had accused a man of cheating, she had understood why. His eyes, those deep black eyes, carried the promise of death. The man had quickly apologized, then practically ran out of the saloon, not caring what anyone thought of his actions. Jassy realized that it would take a mighty brave man, or one who was a complete fool, to challenge Creed Maddigan.

When she saw Creed grab his hat and leave the table, she slipped outside, keeping to the shadows so no one would see her waiting for him.

She was about to cross the street to meet him when a voice cut across the stillness of the night.

"Make your move, Maddigan."

The voice, filled with menace, hissed out of the murky darkness.

Jassy came to an abrupt halt, her gaze focused on Creed, her hand pressed to her heart as he whirled around, his left hand streaking toward his gun with the speed of a striking snake.

She had never seen anything so fast. He drew the Colt with practiced ease, his thumb cocking the hammer as he drew the gun. The barrel cleared the holster in a smooth, flowing motion as it searched for the source of the threat.

There were two blinding flashes, and the

sharp staccato reports of two guns fired almost simultaneously.

Jassy held her breath, but Creed remained on his feet, apparently unhurt.

A moment later, Harry Coulter staggered into the center of the street.

Images imprinted themselves in Jassy's mind: Creed's eyes, hard and cold, as black as ebony. The bright red slash of blood spreading across the front of Harry's shirt. The gray smoke curling from the barrel of Creed's gun.

Harry stood there for stretched seconds, his hands pressed to the bleeding wound in his chest. He stared at Creed in mute appeal, and then his eyes glazed over and he toppled forward.

He was dead. Jassy felt sick to her stomach. Even before that day in the alley, she hadn't liked Harry Coulter very much. He had always been something of a bully, always bragging about how tough he was, how he was gonna make a name for himself. He'd boasted on several occasions that he was fast with a gun, but she'd never dreamed he'd actually try to outgun anyone, least of all someone like Creed.

Saloon doors were flung open on both sides of the street as people converged on the scene, all talking at once. And then the sheriff was there, demanding that Creed surrender his gun.

From the shadows, Jassy saw the hesitation in Creed's eyes; then, with a sigh of resignation, he handed the sheriff his Colt.

"Let's go," Sheriff Harrington said curtly.

"It was self-defense," Creed said.

"That's what they all say," Harrington muttered. "Anybody see anything?" the sheriff asked, his gaze sweeping the crowd. "That's what I thought. Let's go, Maddigan."

"Dammit, the kid called me out, then fired at me from between those two buildings. What was I supposed to do?"

Harrington snorted in disgust. "Why would a kid like Harry come gunning for you?"

"We had some words a while back. He must have still been upset."

"Words? About what?"

"I caught him trying to force himself on a girl, and I set him straight."

"And that's why he tried to kill you?" Harrington shook his head. "Who was the girl?"

"It doesn't matter."

"I'm afraid you'll have to do better than that. Harry Coulter was a good kid and well-liked in this town. Come on, let's go."

Jassy started to run forward, but a hand on her arm restrained her, and when she looked over her shoulder, she saw Rosie standing behind her.

"Let me go," Jassy said.

"You're not getting involved."

"But I saw the whole thing."

"I don't care. That man can take care of himself. You stay out of it."

"But Creed's telling the truth. Harry tried to

kiss me in the alley behind Gratton's. He hit me when I wouldn't let him. Creed made him let me go."

Rose shook her head. "All the more reason to keep your mouth shut. Ray thinks—thought the world of his kid, and I'm not gonna have you saying anything to change his mind. Come on, we're going home."

Still holding Jassy's arm, Rose started down the street, dragging Jassy behind her.

Jassy glanced over her shoulder, but Creed was already out of sight. "Rosie, please . . ."

The slap was hard and completely unexpected. "I said stay out of it! I told you I don't want you to have anything to do with that man."

Jassy pressed a hand to her throbbing cheek, surprised by the anger glinting in her sister's eyes.

"I mean what I say, Jasmine. You stay away from him, understand? A man like that can talk a girl out of anything, including her bloomers. You're gonna hang on to your innocence if I have to tie you to the bedpost, hear? That's something we can only sell once, and it's gonna be worth a small fortune."

Jassy nodded, hardly able to believe what her sister was saying. Harry Coulter had just got himself killed, and all Rosie was worried about was money.

"I shouldn't have hit you," Rose mumbled as they reached the front door of their house, and Jassy knew those few words were all the apology she was likely to get.

Going to her room, Jassy closed the door, then fell across the bed, her eyes filling with tears. And even as she cried, she wasn't certain if she was crying for herself or for Creed.

In spite of the time they had spent together, she really didn't know very much about him, but she knew on some deep, instinctive level that he wouldn't like being locked up.

He didn't. Creed flinched as the lawman slammed the cell door behind him. Damn!

Tossing his hat on the foot of the cot, Creed went to the narrow, iron-barred window and stared out into the darkness.

On the way to the jail, Harrington had remarked that the circuit judge wouldn't be riding through town again for at least a week.

A week! Creed ran a hand through his hair, then rubbed the back of his neck. He'd go crazy if he had to stay cooped up in this place for a week.

He paced for an hour, then stretched out on the hard, narrow bunk, one arm flung over his eyes. A week! And what if they decided he was guilty? He could spend years behind bars, if they didn't hang him.

It wasn't a thought conducive to pleasant dreams. Every time he closed his eyes, he saw himself walking up the thirteen steps to the gallows, felt the hood cover his face, shutting out his last glimpse of the sun, felt the rough hemp noose closing around his neck, growing tighter, felt the trapdoor fall away, leaving him to swing in the cold empty air, his body convulsing, his feet kicking . . .

Muttering an oath, he swung out of bed and paced the floor until dawn.

"Hey, Maddigan, you got a visitor."

Creed came awake instantly, his hand automatically reaching for the gun that was no longer on his hip. A vile oath escaped his lips when he remembered where he was.

"You want to see her or not?"

Her? A wry grin settled over Creed's face. He should have known she'd show up. "Yeah."

She entered the cellblock as though she were the one being led to the gallows. Her face was scrubbed clean, her freckles all bright and shiny. She was wearing the skirt and shirtwaist he had bought her. He wished she had left her hair down, but it was pulled back from her face, secured at her nape with a bit of frayed yellow ribbon.

"Still following me, I see," Creed said, grinning at her.

Jassy nodded, her eyes wide as she took in the rumpled cot with its uncovered pillow and gray blanket, the battered chair, the slop jar under the bed, the cold iron bars that separated them. How could he make jokes at a time like this?

"What are you doing here?" he asked, wondering at her silence. "Your sister made it pretty clear that she didn't want you to have anything to do with me."

Jassy shrugged, as if what Rose wanted was of no importance. "I brought you something."

She'd been holding one hand behind her back. Now she brought it out, revealing a brown paper bag.

Creed arched one black brow. "Cookies," he guessed. Taking the bag from her hand, he placed it very carefully on the foot of the cot. "You shouldn't have come here, Jassy."

"I thought you might be lonely."

Lonely? He was madder than hell at being locked up. He was more than a little worried about the outcome of his trial, especially considering his reputation, but he hadn't realized he was lonely until the words fell from her lips. It hit him with stark clarity that he'd been lonely most of his adult life.

And for the first time in his life, he was worried about someone besides himself. He couldn't go to prison! Damn, he hated to think what would happen to Jassy when he was gone. Anger roiled within him, threatening to choke him, as he recalled how Rose had offered to sell him a few hours of Jassy's time.

Damn. "Jassy . . ."

"I saw what happened in the street last night."

Creed frowned. "You did? How?"

"I wanted to see you, to ask you what Rosie said."

"Hell of a time for a girl your age to be prowling around," Creed muttered.

"I wasn't prowling around. Oh, Creed, I was

so scared. You might have been killed."

Relief washed through him, sweeter and more potent than wine. She'd seen it. He had a witness who could testify in his behalf.

Creed swore under his breath. He hadn't wanted to involve Jassy in this mess, but now it couldn't be helped.

"Are you all right?" Jassy asked, frowning at him.

"Yeah." Lord, he hated it when she looked up at him like that, her brown eyes all soft and warm, her lips slightly parted. It made him think of warm summer nights along the Powder River, when he had been young and anything had been possible.

Unable to help himself, he reached through the bars and took the ribbon from her hair, running his hands through the silken strands until they framed her face.

"Why did you do that?" she asked.

"Damned if I know."

But he did know. He liked the way she looked with her hair down, and he wondered when red had become his favorite color.

"You never told me what Rose said."

And he never would, not when a lie would be kinder than the truth. "She told me to stay the hell away from you if I knew what was good for me."

"Oh."

"The hell of it is, I do know what's good for me."

Jassy looked up at him, her brown eyes glistening with unshed tears. "Do you?" she asked, her voice quivering.

"You're good for me, Jassy," Creed murmured. "Too good, but I can't seem to leave you alone."

His words were the sweetest she'd ever heard, and she swayed toward him, unmindful of the bars that crushed her breasts. Slowly, she rose up on her tiptoes, her gaze quietly beseeching him to kiss her.

Creed hesitated for a moment, and then he put his arms around her as best he could considering the bars that stood between them and kissed her, savoring the taste of her lips. She was sweet, so sweet. She tasted of youth and innocence, of burgeoning womanhood. He'd never known anything so exhilarating, never felt such an intense need to possess or such a powerful urge to shelter and protect, which was pretty funny, seeing as how he was the one locked up.

"Ah, Jassy," he murmured and kissed her again, his tongue delving into the dark, secret recesses of her mouth.

Jassy's legs went weak, and she leaned against the bars, her arms wrapping around Creed's waist. She had been so afraid he would refuse to see her, afraid Rose had made him change his mind, but he was kissing her as if he would never let her go. She felt as if her blood was on fire, as if every nerve ending in her body had suddenly come to life, as if she had been asleep, like the princess in a fairy tale, until this very moment.

She felt bereft when he took his lips from hers. "Don't stop," she begged.

"Jassy . . ."

"Please."

It was madness to kiss her again, but it would have been easier to break the bars than to keep his mouth from hers. He let his tongue slide over the inside of her lower lip, savoring the warm silkiness.

She moaned low in her throat, her arms tightening around his waist, and the heat of her, the scent of her, the touch of her, made him ache with bittersweet pain.

Hearing the sound of approaching footsteps outside the cellblock door, Creed put Jassy away from him and took a step away from the bars.

She blinked up at him, her eyes cloudy with passion, her lips swollen with the force of his kisses.

"Go on," he said, not wanting to give Harrington anything to gossip about, "get out of here."

Jassy stared at him, confused by his curt tone. Had she done something wrong?

Creed swore under his breath when he saw the hurt in her eyes, but there was no time to explain.

"Go home, girl," he said brusquely. "Go on, get!"

Fighting tears, she practically ran out of the building.

"A mite young, ain't she?" Harrington remarked as he ambled down the aisle.

Creed shrugged. "She's just a friend." He jerked his chin toward the sack on the bed. "She brought me some cookies."

"Right."

Creed shoved his hands into his pants pockets, wishing he could wipe the smirk off the lawman's face.

"You want something, Sheriff?"

Harrington shook his head. "No. Just came to make sure she didn't slip you a weapon of some kind."

"She didn't."

"You won't mind if I check for myself? You know the drill, Maddigan. Move away from the door and put your hands against the wall."

Grimacing, Creed did as he was told, a muscle working in his jaw as Harrington searched him. He almost made a grab for the lawman's gun, but Harrington had a reputation of his own, and Creed wasn't ready to see if Harrington could live up to it. Not yet.

Taking a step backward, Harrington picked up the brown paper bag and looked inside. Grunting softly, he helped himself to one of Jassy's sugar cookies and took a bite.

"Not bad," he muttered as he stepped out of the cell. "Not bad at all."

Creed didn't expect to see Jassy the next morning, not after his abrupt dismissal the day before. But she turned up bright and early.

"Good morning, Creed," she said, her voice hesitant.

The hurt in her voice, the wariness in her eyes, made him feel things he didn't understand, want things he couldn't put a name to.

"I . . ." Her gaze slid away, then returned to his face. "Do you want me to go?"

"No." He ran a hand through his hair, wondering how things had gotten so complicated. "I'm sorry about yesterday, Jassy. I just didn't want you to be subjected to any of Harrington's crude jokes. I . . . I didn't mean to hurt your feelings."

The look of relief on her face made him ache inside. Lord, she was so young.

Her sweet smile drove everything else from his mind, and he was reaching through the bars, needing to touch her, to feel her softness, to taste her goodness. And for a few minutes, nothing else mattered.

Jassy came to see him every day for the next five days. She always came early in the morning, and it didn't take a genius to figure out why. He knew she snuck out of the house when Rose was asleep. No doubt Rose would throw a fit if she knew Jassy was making visits to the jail.

Creed could understand that. He didn't like the idea of Jassy coming to the jail, either, but he couldn't bring himself to tell her to stay away. And he couldn't seem to keep his hands off her, either. He told himself repeatedly that she was way too young and that as soon as he got out of jail he would be moving on and would never see her again. But, right or wrong, he simply didn't have the willpower to resist the silent invitation in her eyes.

She wanted a kiss hello, she wanted a kiss good-bye, and she wanted several more in between, and he was happy to give them to her.

He discovered the curvy, little figure that had been hidden beneath the baggy dresses, and he realized that was probably the reason her mother had insisted she wear it. Jassy might be small, she might have the face of a child, but the rest of her was all woman.

And if he thought about hangmen and iron bars during the long tedious hours of the day, it was Jassy's big brown eyes and provocative lips that filled his dreams. He was sinking in quicksand, he mused ruefully, fast getting in over his head, and he didn't seem to care.

He loved holding her in his arms, and he loved the way she looked up at him as if he were some kind of white knight. He loved the way her voice turned husky after he'd kissed her a few times and the way her eyes clouded with desire.

Damn. He'd be safer with the hangman.

He had been in jail eight days when Harrington informed him that the judge had arrived. His trial would commence the day after tomorrow at ten sharp.

He couldn't sleep that night. Hour after hour, he paced the narrow floor. Eight days he'd been locked up. Eight days. Thank God for Jassy. She had come every morning, bringing him cookies and apples and newspapers, her ready smile cheering him. But for her, he would surely have lost his mind. But it was almost over now. The day after tomorrow he would be a free man.

It occurred to him that he had never asked her to come to the trial. He had been so wrapped up in his desire for her that he had never thought to talk about the trial at all. But of course she would be there. She knew how important it was, knew that she was the only witness to the shooting.

Lord, how he hated being locked up!

Chapter Eight

"Maddigan, you've got a visitor."

Creed sat up. A visitor? It couldn't be Jassy. She'd been there earlier.

"This here's your attorney," Harrington said with a lopsided grin. He unlocked the cell door to admit a thin, wiry man carrying a black leather satchel.

Brown, Creed thought. Unruly brown hair, listless brown eyes, limp brown suit, scuffed brown shoes.

"Neville Durning," the lawyer said.

With obvious distaste, the attorney stepped into the cell and sat down on the wobbly chair in the corner.

"Give me a holler when you're through," Harrington said. He locked the cell door with a flourish, then ambled out of the cellblock, whistling softly.

Creed took one look at his lawyer and knew he'd have a far better chance in court if he was on his own.

"The trial's tomorrow," Durning said, as if Creed wasn't already painfully aware of the fact. "From what the sheriff tells me, it doesn't sound like you have much of a case."

"You come here just to tell me that?"

"I need to hear your side."

"Why? You've already decided I'm guilty."

A flush crept into Durning's cheeks. "Be that as it may, you're entitled to council."

"I've already got the whole town against me," Creed muttered ruefully. "You'd think they could have found me a lawyer who'd side with me."

"It doesn't matter what I think," Durning said. He adjusted the narrow, wire-rimmed glasses perched on the edge of his nose. "It's what we can prove."

"The kid called me out and I shot him. It was self-defense."

"I see. Harrington says there were no witnesses."

"There's one. Jassy McCloud. She saw the whole thing."

Durning frowned. "McCloud? The whore's kid?"

Creed stifled the urge to throttle the man. Instead, he nodded.

"You don't really expect me to put her on the stand? Who would believe her, especially when everyone in town knows she's sweet on you? Several people have seen you going into her house late at night." Durning shook his head. "No, I don't think putting that little tramp on the stand is a good idea."

Creed came off the cot, his hands knotted into fists as he stood over Durning. "Don't ever call her that again, you understand me?"

Durning glared at him. "A jury would have no doubt about your ability to gun a man down in cold blood if they could see you now," he remarked contemptuously.

Creed took a deep, calming breath. He had to admire the little weasel. Durning put up a good front, but Creed saw the fear in the man's eyes, the tremor in his hands.

"She saw what happened," Creed said, biting off each word. "Ask her. She's the only witness I've got."

With a nod, Durning stood up, hollering for Harrington to let him out.

Jassy didn't come to the jail in the morning. Creed tried not to let it bother him. After all, the trial was in less than an hour. She'd need time to eat breakfast and get dressed. They'd have plenty of time to be together later.

Sitting on the edge of the cot, he stared at the floor, his insides coiled tight as a spring. In a few hours, it would all be over.

He glanced up at the sound of footsteps.

"Thought you might like to wash up," Harrington said, sliding a basin and a towel through the narrow slit at the bottom of the cell door.

"Thanks."

"Whole town's talking about your trial. Reckon it'll be standing room only. Good for business."

"Glad I could be of help."

The sheriff chuckled. "Can't wait for the hangin'."

"I haven't been tried yet."

"True, true," Harrington agreed. "But Judge Paxton ain't known as the hangin' judge for nothin'. Harry's mama has been crying to the whole town, tellin' them what a good boy her son was, how he went to church every Sunday. The hell of it is, it's all true. She's got the whole town on her side. People hereabouts are partial to the Coulters."

Including my lawyer, Creed thought bleakly. "You finished jawin' yet?"

"Yeah, yeah. I'll be back in twenty minutes. Be ready."

As the sheriff had predicted, the whole town seemed to have turned out for the trial. Men, women, and children crowded into the courthouse, and it was indeed standing room only.

Creed's gaze swept the spectators, but there was no sign of Jassy. He sat down where Harrington indicated, telling himself not to worry, she'd be there.

A few minutes later, Neville Durning entered the courtroom. He took the seat next to Creed with great diffidence, his expression clearly indicating that he was there solely because he had been designated as counsel for the defense.

The bailiff called the court to order, Paxton took the bench, and the trial began.

The prosecution's case was short and direct. Harry Coulter had been a decent, God-fearing, law-abiding citizen, an upright young man who had attended church every Sunday and often sang in the choir. He had never been in trouble with the law.

"Never in trouble with the law." The prosecutor repeated the sentence, clearly enunciating each word, then went on to point out that Creed Maddigan was a well-known killer, a notorious gun for hire, fully capable of gunning down an innocent young man like Harry Coulter. As far as the prosecution was concerned, Creed Maddigan was guilty as charged.

Ray Braddock was called to the stand. With a smirk in Creed's direction, he testified that Creed Maddigan had threatened to shoot him down in cold blood.

Two other men, whom Creed recognized as having been at the poker table with Braddock the night he had warned Braddock to keep away from Jassy McCloud, testified that they had heard the threat, and that Maddigan had been cold sober when he made it. Neither had any doubt that Creed Maddigan was capable of murder.

The prosecution's only other witness was the sheriff. Harrington was sworn in and testified that Harry had been dead when he arrived on the scene, shot once through the heart. A single round had been fired from his weapon.

Neville Durning called Creed to the stand.

"Please tell us, Mr. Maddigan, what happened on the night in question."

"I was leaving the Lazy Ace Saloon," Creed said. "About midnight. Coulter called me out. I didn't know who it was at the time. I fired at his muzzle flash."

"And killed him?"

A strangled sob came from the front row. Creed glanced at the woman sitting there. Harry's mother, he thought bleakly. Ray Coulter, dressed in a tweed suit and vest, sat beside the woman, his arm around her.

Durning cleared his throat. "Would you please answer the question, Mr. Maddigan? Did you kill Harry Coulter?"

A muscle ticked in Creed's jaw. "Yes."

"Thank you. Your witness, Mr. Von Meter."

"Did you know Harry Coulter?" Von Meter asked.

"Not really."

"Would you care to elaborate on that?"

"I met him once."

"Under what circumstances?"

"I caught him bothering a girl, trying to kiss her. He hit her when she tried to fight him, and I broke it up."

"And you think that gave him cause to want to kill you?"

"I don't know what his reasons were."

"You expect the court to believe that a young man of Harry's sterling reputation would challenge a well-known gunman to a duel simply because you'd hurt his pride?"

"I don't know what his reasons were," Creed repeated. "I'm telling you what happened."

"We have only your word for that."

Creed's gaze settled on Durning's face. "There was a witness."

"No one came forward," Von Meter remarked, his voice thick with skepticism.

"Call Jassy McCloud," Creed said. "She saw the whole thing."

"Why wasn't she subpoenaed to court?" the judge asked.

Neville Durning stood up. "She's been very ill, your honor." Durning handed a sheet of paper to the judge. "This is her statement, duly signed, which states that she was at home in bed at the time of the shooting."

Creed swore under his breath. Jassy had failed him, and his own lawyer had just driven another nail in his coffin.

"Duly noted and accepted as evidence," the judge said. "Any other witnesses, Mr. Durning?"

"No, your honor."

"Excuse me, your honor," Von Meter said. "I've just been handed a note. It seems the prosecution has another witness, after all."

"This is highly irregular, Mr. Von Meter," the judge replied.

"I'm aware of that, your honor, but we beg the court's indulgence."

"Very well, call your witness. Mr. Maddigan, you may step down."

"The prosecution calls Rose McCloud to the stand."

Creed swore under his breath as Jassy's sister took the stand, then proceeded, very calmly, to testify that she had seen the whole thing on her way home from work. According to Rose, Creed Maddigan had bullied young Harry Coulter into drawing his gun and had then shot him down.

"Thank you for coming forward, Miss McCloud," Von Meter said. "Your witness, Mr. Durning."

"The defense has no questions for this witness, your honor," Durning stated.

Creed swore under his breath. He could almost feel the rope around his neck because he knew there was no way in hell the jury would believe him now. Rose might be nothing but a saloon girl, but she was a white girl, and he knew from past experience that no white man would take the word of a half-breed over that of a white woman, even if she was a whore.

Both sides gave their closing arguments, the

jury went to deliberate, and Creed was taken back to his cell.

Jassy's head jerked up when she heard the key turn in the lock. "What happened?"

Rose shook her head. "I don't know. The jury was still out when I left."

Jassy tugged against the rope that bound her wrists to the bedpost.

"Rosie, please, you've got to let me go to him."

"No."

"But why? He's innocent, Rose. It was self-defense."

"I don't care. He's a half-breed, Jassy, lower than poor white trash. He deserves whatever he gets."

"How can you say that?"

"Because it's true!" Fists clenched at her sides, Rose took a deep breath. "Anyway, Ray wants him to pay for killing Harry, and he told me . . . Never mind what he told me."

"He threatened you, didn't he?"

"Of course not!"

"What then? Did he promise to marry you if Creed went to jail?"

"I don't want to discuss it."

That was it, Jassy thought. Rose was convinced that Ray Coulter would marry her, and Jassy knew she'd do anything to make that happen, even send an innocent man to jail.

"Creed didn't do it, Rose. You can't let them send him to prison."

"I'll be back when it's over."

Rose knew a moment of guilt as she left the room. Everything she had told Jassy was true, but the real reason she wanted Creed Maddigan dead had nothing to do with Ray Coulter.

Rose had heard the affection in Maddigan's voice when he had come to see Jassy the night Rose returned from Denver. She had known right then that Creed Maddigan wanted Jassy. Why he hadn't already taken the little chit was beyond Rose's comprehension, but she knew lust when she saw it. Maddigan wanted Jassy, and Rose had figured he just might be willing to pay for what he hadn't taken.

With that in mind, she had taken Maddigan outside and offered Jassy to him, for a price. She hadn't been prepared for the sudden cold rage that had flared in the depths of the half-breed's eyes. His hand had closed over her arm and he had jerked her up close, warning her in a whisper-soft voice that if he ever found Jassy working in the Lazy Ace, he would cut Rose up so bad no man would ever look at her again.

The expression in Maddigan's eyes, as hard and cold as stone, had frightened her as nothing else ever had. Now all she wanted was to be rid of him once and for all, to know that she would never have to look into those cold black eyes again.

The jury wasn't out long. No more than thirty minutes had passed when court was reconvened.

Creed sat on the edge of his chair, his gaze moving over the faces of the twelve jurors. He didn't like what he saw there. In his gut, he knew they'd found him guilty even before the judge read the verdict. Hell, they'd decided he was guilty before the trial ever started.

A cold hand, like the hand of doom, settled on Creed's shoulder when the judge read the verdict, then sentenced him to twenty years.

Twenty years.

The words echoed and reechoed in his mind as he left the courthouse.

Twenty years.

Twenty years. He wished they'd decided to hang him instead.

So did Harrington. "Can't understand it," the lawman muttered as he locked the cell door. "He ain't never disappointed me before."

But Creed was too immersed in his own misery to care what the sheriff thought.

Twenty years.

He sat down on the edge of the cot, his head cradled in his hands, and stared at the stone floor.

Twenty years. He saw his future stretch ahead of him, his freedom gone, his days and nights spent imprisoned behind iron bars and high stone walls, and knew he'd rather be dead.

Chapter Nine

"Is it over?" Jassy stared at her sister through eyes swollen with tears.

"Yes. They gave him twenty years."

"Twenty years," Jassy repeated. She tugged against the rope that bound her wrists to the bed. "Let me go! I've got to go to him, to help him."

"You're not going anywhere."

"Yes, I am. You're not going to get away with this, Rose. I'll tell the judge what I saw. I'll tell the sheriff." Jassy tugged on the rope again, oblivious to the pain as the rough hemp dug into her wrists. "I'll tell the whole damn town!"

"Go ahead. No one will believe you." The candlelight flashed on the knife in Rose's hand as she cut the ropes from Jassy's wrists. "Milt says you can start working in the saloon as soon as you turn seventeen."

Jassy fought the despair that welled up within her. She'd be seventeen next week. "I don't want to."

"I don't see that you have much choice," Rose replied coldly. "I'm not making enough to support both of us."

"I'll get a job somewhere else."

Rose laughed mirthlessly. "Yeah? Where? Who's gonna hire you?"

"I don't know. Do we have to talk about this now?" Jassy stood up and smoothed the wrinkles from her dress.

"Where do you think you're going?" Rose asked suspiciously.

"To see Creed."

"I don't think so."

Rose gave Jassy a push that sent her sprawling backward on the bed. Hurrying from the room, she locked the door.

"Rosie, let me out of here! Rosie!"

"You're not running over to the jail to see that 'breed."

"Rosie, you've got to let me go see the judge. It isn't fair. Creed didn't do anything. Please, Rosie. I'll do anything you say."

"Damn right you will. Now shut up. I need to get some sleep before I go to work."

Jassy's shoulders slumped dispiritedly when she heard the door across the hall slam shut. Since their mother's death, Rose had moved into their mother's bedroom, giving Jassy a room of her own for the first time in her life.

For a time, she sat on the edge of the bed, staring at the raw plank floor. She didn't want to work in the saloon. Even if she could avoid working upstairs, she didn't want to have to wear one of the skimpy costumes Rose wore; she didn't want to have to serve drinks and smile at a bunch of men she didn't know and didn't want to know.

But where else could she work? Rose was right. No one in town would hire her for anything respectable. Everyone in town assumed she would follow in her mother's footsteps. *Like mother, like daughter*, everyone said, assuming that because her mother and sister did what they did, Jassy would do the same. But she wanted so much more out of life. She wanted to be respectable. She wanted a home of her own, a husband, children. She wanted to be able to hold her head up when she went to church on Sunday. She wanted to be able to look people in the eye without shame.

She wanted Creed Maddigan.

Rising, she began to pace the small room. Her stomach growled loudly, reminding her that she hadn't eaten all day. Going to the door, she rattled the knob. Even if she could get out of her room, there probably wasn't anything in the house to eat. A tiny smile curved one corner of her mouth. She'd had plenty to eat in the last few weeks, thanks to Creed.

Creed. He'd given her so much. She stared at the oilcloth that covered the room's small window, wondering what her mother had done with the money she made. She knew the rent on their ugly little house was high. Her mother had complained about it to the landlord often enough, but he'd just laughed and told Daisy that if she didn't like it, she could get out, knowing that no one else would give them a place to live.

She knew what her sister did with her money. After paying her share of the rent, Rose spent the rest of her money on lavender toilet water and pots of rouge, black net stockings, and scandalous undergarments. Apparently food had never been a high priority for either her mother or her sister, Jassy mused.

But none of that was important now. She pressed her ear to the door. The house was quiet. Rose must be asleep.

She wiped her face and brushed her hair, leaving it loose about her shoulders because she knew Creed liked it that way.

Looking at herself in the cracked mirror over the bureau, she wished she had a new dress to wear for him, but her mother had never returned that green dress. She'd never get it now.

Taking a hairpin from her dresser drawer, she went to work on the lock.

A half hour later, she was tiptoeing out of the house.

Jassy almost ran to the jail, so eager was she to see Creed again.

The sheriff gave her a knowing look as he unlocked the cellblock door. He thought she was Creed's lover. The thought made Jassy's cheeks burn with shame that he would think of her in that way, and with humiliation because she wished it were true.

Moments later, she was standing before Creed's cell and everything else faded from her mind.

He stared at her for a long moment, his dark eyes filled with quiet rage, his hands fisted at his sides.

"It wasn't my fault," she said quickly, wishing he wouldn't look at her as if she'd betrayed him. "I wanted to come."

He didn't say anything, only continued to stare at her as if he hated her.

"Rose forged my name to that paper. She tried to make me do it. She even threatened to sell me to one of her customers if I refused, but I still wouldn't do it, so she signed my name. You've got to believe me, Creed. It's the truth."

"Why didn't you come to the trial?"

"I couldn't. Rose kept me tied up in my room until it was over."

"She tied you up so you couldn't testify?" he asked, his tone incredulous.

Jassy nodded, embarrassed to admit that her sister would do such a despicable thing.

"She tell you why?"

"She said something about doing it for Coulter, about Coulter wanting revenge. I'm sorry, Creed."

Jassy slipped her arms through the bars, wanting to touch him, but he was just out of reach.

Creed swore under his breath. He knew damn well why Rose wanted him out of the way, and it had nothing to do with his being a half-breed, or with Ray Coulter, either. But he couldn't tell Jassy the truth. Not now. She would have to live with Rose long after he was gone.

"I would have been there, Creed. You've got to believe me."

"I believe you," he said, feeling his anger toward Jassy wash out of him as he closed the distance between them.

Reaching through the bars, he wrapped his arms around her, drawing her as close as possible. Lord, she was sweet.

His touch redeemed her, banishing her fears and the awful sense of emptiness caused by his anger.

"I'll go see the judge, Creed. I'll tell him everything."

"It's too late, Jassy. He left town after the trial."

"Then I'll tell the sheriff."

Creed nodded, though he doubted it would do any good. Still, if Jassy could plant a seed of doubt in Harrington's mind, the sheriff might keep him in jail until the circuit judge rode through again. Maybe they'd re-try him. And maybe hell would freeze over.

He knew, deep in his gut, that Harrington would just laugh in Jassy's face, especially after Rose's damning testimony. No matter what Jassy said, Harrington would think it was just a last, desperate effort to keep her lover out of prison. But it was worth a chance. Hell, it was the only chance he had.

"Creed?"

He gazed into her eyes and felt his heart quicken at what he saw there.

Slowly, he bent his head and kissed her, damning the bars that separated them. He wanted to bury himself within her, surround himself with her goodness, her sweetness. Maybe, if Jassy had come into his life sooner, he wouldn't be in such a mess now. And maybe he belonged in prison for wanting her the way he did, he mused with a wry grin. Heaven help him, he knew it had to be a crime for a man of his age and experience to desire a girl as young and innocent as Jassy. At least if they locked him up, she'd be safe—from him anyway.

He kissed her harder, his lips bruising hers, as he thought of other men touching her.

He remembered the night on the porch when Rose had callously offered to sell him Jassy's virginity, if the price was right, remarking that it would be his only chance to bed her while she was still untouched, because pretty soon she would be available to anyone who could buy her time. The thought twisted through his gut like a hot brand.

"Jassy." He dragged his mouth from hers and cupped her face in his hands. "Listen to me. Go to my room in the hotel. I've got better than four thousand dollars in my saddlebags. I want you to have it."

Jassy blinked up at him. Four thousand dollars! That was all the money in the world.

"Won't they have rented your room to someone else by now?"

Creed shook his head. "I did George Walker a favor a while back with the understanding that he'd have a room for me as long as I wanted it."

Reaching into his pocket, he withdrew a key and pressed it into Jassy's hand, folding her fingers over it one by one.

"You take that money and get the hell out of this town before it's too late. Go someplace where no one knows you, start a new life for yourself."

"No, I won't leave you."

"You won't be leaving me. If the sheriff won't listen to your story, I'll be on my way to Canon City at the end of the week. You take that money and get out of here before your sister has you hustling drinks at the Lazy Ace. Promise me, Jassy. I don't want to think of you ending up like Rose."

"He'll believe me, Creed. He has to."

"I hope so, honey. But if he doesn't, you do like I said."

Jassy nodded, unable to speak past the lump rising in her throat. Tears burned her eyes and she clung to him, feeling that everything would be all right so long as she didn't let him go.

She closed her eyes as she felt his hand moving in her hair, his fingers gently caressing her nape. He bent to press a kiss to the top of her head, and the warmth of his lips went clear to her toes. She loved him. She didn't care that he was a bounty hunter and a hired gun. It didn't matter that he was older than she was, or that she knew almost nothing about him. She loved him.

She drew back a little, wanting to tell him so, but before she had a chance, the door to the cellblock swung open.

"Time's up," Harrington called.

"I'll tell him right now," Jassy promised. She slid the key into her skirt pocket; then, standing on tiptoe, she kissed him, hoping he could hear the words in her heart.

Creed watched her walk down the narrow aisle, and then Harrington closed the door between the cellblock and the sheriff's office, leaving him alone in the gloomy cell.

"It was self-defense," Jassy said. She placed her hands on the desktop and leaned toward Harrington, who sat in the chair behind the desk, his expression skeptical. "It was! I saw the whole thing. Harry called Creed out, and Creed shot him."

"That's not what your statement said."

"I never signed any statement. My sister forged my name."

Harrington sighed wearily. "Go home, girl."

"It's the truth! Get my sister in here and make her tell you what really happened."

"I'll tell you what I think happened. I think you've been whoring for that gunfighter, and you just now realized you're about to lose your meal ticket."

"That's not true!"

"Isn't it? I'm not blind. I've seen how he looks at you." Harrington snickered. "And how you look at him. Well, you'll have to find yourself a new sugar man come Friday."

Jassy bit back the angry words that rose in her throat. "Please, Sheriff Harrington, you must believe me. It was self-defense. I'll swear to it here. I'll swear to it in court."

"You had a chance to do that this morning."

"I . . . I couldn't."

"Couldn't? Something more important come up?"

"Rose wouldn't let me."

"Wouldn't *let* you?" Harrington looked skeptical. "What'd she do, tie you up?"

Jassy nodded, sickened by the memory of how Rose had wrestled her to the bed, then straddled her to hold her down while she tied her hands to the bedpost. It had been frightening, humiliating.

Harrington looked temporarily taken aback; then he snorted. Tied her up, indeed! No doubt the little chit would say anything if she thought it would get Maddigan out of jail.

He rustled the papers stacked on the corner of his desk. "You're wasting my time, Jassy. Go on home. I've got work to do."

Tears of frustration filled Jassy's eyes. Creed had been right. Harrington didn't believe her. "Can I see him again before I go?"

"Twenty minutes a day. You know the rules."

"Please."

"Dammit, girl, go home!"

She stared at him a moment more and then, afraid to make him angry for fear he wouldn't let her see Creed the next day, she headed for the door, her steps heavy with despair.

In three days, he'd be gone, and she'd never see him again.

Chapter Ten

"Tumbleweed wagon's here."

Creed grimaced as Harrington entered the cellblock, followed by his deputy, Jace Rutledge.

"Stand away from the door, Maddigan," Harrington ordered as he slipped the key into the lock.

Creed's gaze washed over Rutledge in a long, assessing glance. The kid was young and eager. Judging from the look in Rutledge's wide-set brown eyes, Creed knew the deputy was hoping he'd make a break for it or jump Harrington, anything to give Rutledge an excuse to pull the trigger.

Heaven save him from young men with guns. He stepped away from the cell door.

"Turn around," Harrington said brusquely. "Put your hands behind your back. And don't try anything stupid."

Creed did as he was told, the place between his shoulder blades itching furiously. He could feel Rutledge's gun trained on his back and knew the deputy's finger was caressing the trigger, hoping, waiting for Creed to make one wrong move. Jace Rutledge wanted a reputation of his own, and taking down a known gunman would give him a start.

Creed flinched as the cuffs were locked in place, knowing he had just given up any chance he'd had of escaping.

"Let's go."

Harrington led the way out of the cellblock, his hand hovering over the butt of his gun. Rutledge brought up the rear.

Outside, Creed blinked against the sunlight. As his eyes adjusted to the glare, he saw Jassy standing across the street, her cheeks wet with silent tears. She was wearing a green dress, although it wasn't the same one he had bought her, and the boots he had picked out for her. Creed smiled a little, knowing she had picked that particular dress because of the color.

Jassy. She had come to the jail every day. Like a single bright ray of hope, she had come to him, smiling bravely. Each kiss had been sweeter than the last, and he had wished that his life had been different, that he had met her in another time and place.

She had cried when she told him that Harrington had refused to believe her, but Creed hadn't expected anything else. No one was going to take the word of a seventeen-year-old girl—or of a gunfighter with a bad reputation.

"Move it, Maddigan," the sheriff said, prodding him in the back with the barrel of his Colt. "Wagon's ready to roll."

"Give me a minute. I want to tell Jassy goodbye."

Harrington snorted. "Why? You ain't never gonna see her again."

"That's why," Creed snapped.

"All right, but make it quick."

"I don't suppose you'd take these cuffs off for a couple of minutes?"

"Not a chance."

"Dammit, Harrington—"

"You're wasting time, Maddigan."

Muttering an oath, Creed started to cross the street but Jassy was already running toward him. She threw her arms around him, hugging him close.

"Oh, Creed, it's so unfair!"

"Nobody ever said life was fair, honey."

She pressed herself against him, not caring that Harrington and Rutledge and half the town seemed to be staring at them. What did that matter now? She wished Creed's hands were free so he could hold her one last time. She felt a fresh wave of tears well in her eyes as his lips moved in her hair.

"You look real pretty," he murmured, wishing he could run his fingers through her hair just once more, feel the warmth of her skin beneath his fingertips, taste the innocent sweetness of her kisses.

"Thank you." She didn't tell him she had bought the dress with money she had taken from under Rose's mattress. "I'll write you every day," she promised.

"And send me cookies?" He tried to keep his voice light, but the thought of never seeing her again, of spending the next twenty years caged up, made anything resembling humor impossible.

She looked up at him, her gaze moving over his face, memorizing every detail. His hair was long and thick and black, his skin the color of smooth copper, his jaw strong and square. His eyes were as deep and black as a pool of liquid ebony, framed by thick black lashes and straight black brows. And his mouth . . . She had learned to love his mouth, the shape of it, the texture of his lips, the slick velvety warmth of his tongue that tasted faintly of tobacco and whiskey.

Creed was doing the same, imprinting her image on his mind to hold as a talisman against the empty years ahead. The sunlight danced in her hair, threading the red with gold. Her eyes were as brown and warm as a handful of sun-warmed earth. He loved the way her nose tilted up just a little at the end, the soft curve of her cheek, the pouty fullness of her lips . . . ah, those lips that made him ache with desire even now.

"You take that money, Jassy," he said, his voice suddenly husky. "Take it and get away from here."

"No. I'll wait for you, no matter how long it takes."

Creed shook his head. "No, Jassy. I don't want anybody waiting for me. You've got your whole life ahead of you. You take that money and get out of this town. You forget what happened here. Forget about me. Make a new life for yourself. Promise me."

"I can't. This is all my fault. If only I'd been there—"

"You'd have been there if you could, honey. I know that. Don't waste your life like I wasted mine. You find yourself a decent man and have that family you want." He gazed deep into her eyes. "Promise me, Jassy. Please."

She nodded, unable to speak the words, her heart breaking because he was facing a long prison sentence and he was still worried about her. How could she help loving him? He was the only one who had ever cared whether she lived or died.

Creed closed his eyes, his chin resting lightly on the top of Jassy's head. Her arms were tight around his waist, her breasts crushed against his chest. Twenty years. He'd be an old man when he got out. And she'd be all grown up, married, with a passel of kids. As much as it hurt to think of her with another man, he knew it was the life she wanted, the kind of life she deserved. The kind of life he could never give her.

"You about done there?" Harrington asked impatiently.

"Keep your shirt on, lawman," Creed muttered.

"I'll miss you," Jassy whispered. Standing on tiptoe, she pressed her lips to his, and he tasted the salt of her tears. "I'll pray for you every day."

"Jassy, I . . ." The words backed up in his throat. What was the point of telling her he loved her? It didn't matter now. "Take care of yourself."

She nodded, her throat clogged with tears. One more kiss, one more touch, and then Harrington stepped between them, shoving Creed into the back of the prison wagon and locking the door.

The image of his face staring at her through thick iron bars imprinted itself on her mind, and with it the knowledge that she would never see him again.

She ran after the wagon until she couldn't keep up anymore, her tears blurring his face. Then she sank down in the dirt and cried until she had no more tears left.

Her steps were heavy as she made her way

toward the Harrison House. The hotel clerk stared at her, a salacious gleam in his eye, as she crossed the lobby, but he didn't try to stop her.

The room was small, not much bigger than her bedroom at home. She wandered around the room, running her hand over the bed he had slept in, picking up his razor, his hairbrush. She went through the chest of drawers. He didn't have much. Several changes of clothing. Another pair of boots.

She found his saddlebags under the bed. Inside, she found an extra pistol and a couple of boxes of cartridges. A doeskin shirt that was almost white in color. A pair of well-worn moccasins. A choker made of blue and yellow beads. And four thousand dollars stuffed into a small buckskin pouch.

She counted the money three times, unable to believe it was hers, knowing she would gladly give it all away to have Creed with her again. Four thousand dollars.

A sudden rush of pleasure warmed her heart. She had money now. She could leave Harrison. She could go to Canon City to be near Creed.

Humming softly, she counted out enough money to replace what she had taken from Rose and dropped the rest back in the pouch.

She stuffed Creed's belongings back into his saddlebags. Rising, she considered packing his clothing and taking it with her, but in the end she decided against it because she didn't know how she'd explain it to Rose.

She was about to leave the room when she turned and went back to the bed. Picking up the pillow, she shoved it into the saddlebag, too. She had never stolen anything in her life, but Creed had slept on that pillow. Now she would sleep on it, too, and dream of him.

She crept into the house, peeking into Rose's room to make sure she was still asleep before going into her own bedroom. For once, she didn't notice how dark and dismal her room was.

Shutting the door, she removed the money pouch from the saddlebags, then slid the heavy leather bags under her bed. Crossing the floor, she lifted from the wall a wrinkled picture of an angel holding a little girl. There was a small hole behind the picture where Jassy kept her father's watch. She held the money pouch for a few moments, then tucked it into the hole with her father's watch and replaced the picture.

She smiled as she looked around the room. She wouldn't have to stay here much longer. There would be a stage leaving for Canon City in a couple of days, and she'd be on it.

Finding a sheet of paper, she began to write a letter to the judge, telling him everything that had happened, swearing it was the truth, vowing she would take an oath on the Bible, if only he would believe her.

When that was done, she wrote a long letter to Creed, pouring out her heart and soul, telling him that she would never forget him and didn't want to forget him. With tears staining the page, she wrote that she loved him, that she would wait for him no matter how long it took.

She was sealing the envelope when the door swung open and Rose entered the room. "What are you doing?"

"Nothing."

"What've you got there?"

"A letter."

Rose shut the door behind her, then leaned against it. "A letter? To who?"

"To Creed."

"Give me that!"

"No. I can write him if I want to."

"You little tramp. If you can put out for that 'breed, then you can start working tonight."

"He never touched me!"

Rose snorted, her disbelief evident in her tone.

"It's true."

Rose held out her hand. "I'll take that letter."

"No!"

"Very well."

With a shrug, Rose opened the door. She had a friend who worked at the general store. All she had to do was ask, and Tug would destroy any letters Jassy tried to send.

Rose paused, her hand on the doorknob as she glanced over her shoulder.

"Don't you go anywhere until you've made the beds and washed up the dishes, hear?"

Jassy nodded. She frowned as she watched

her sister leave the room, surprised that Rosie had given up so easily. She had never understood why her own sister disliked her so much. In the past, Jassy had tried to win Rosie's affection, but all her attempts at amity had been rejected. Now, after what Rosie had done to Creed, Jassy no longer felt any fondness for her sister, only a deep and abiding anger.

Tucking the two letters inside her bodice, Jassy went into the kitchen. She had expected to find Rosie there, but apparently her sister had left the house. Perhaps she had gone to work early, Jassy mused. She did that sometimes, when she knew Coulter was going to work the early shift at the saloon.

With a sigh, Jassy poured some water into a kettle and put it on the lopsided cast-iron stove to heat.

She thought of Creed as she washed and dried the dishes, wondering how far the wagon had gone in the last few hours, praying that he would be well treated, that he'd be pardoned in a short time, that he would answer her letter. She smiled as she thought how surprised he'd be when she came to visit him.

Putting the last chipped plate into the cupboard, she went into Rose's room. She made Rosie's bed quickly, slipping the money she had borrowed under the mattress, then went into her own room and straightened the bedspread, making sure Creed's saddlebags were out of sight.

When that was done, she left the house and made her way across the street toward Gratton's Mercantile.

The post office was located in the back of the store. Tug Harper smiled at her as she slid the letters toward him.

"Hi, Jassy. Don't think I've ever known you to send a letter before, and now you've got two."

Jassy smiled as she pulled a twenty-dollar gold piece out of her pocket and handed it to Tug. "Would you send them out as soon as possible?"

Tug whistled under his breath as he took the coin. "Twenty dollars. Where'd you get this?"

Jassy licked her lips nervously. "I earned it."

Tug looked skeptical.

"How long will it take for my letter to reach Canon City?"

"I don't know. Probably two weeks, maybe longer, depending on the weather."

"And the other one?"

Tug made a vague gesture. "About the same, I reckon." He counted out her change and handed it to her. "Say hi to Rose for me."

"Yes, I will. Bye, Tug."

"So long, Jassy."

Tug watched her out of sight, wondering where she'd gotten hold of a twenty-dollar gold piece. Earned it, she'd said. If that was true, he'd like to be her next customer.

He stared at the two letters in his hand, frowning when he read the address on the first one. Why would Jassy McCloud be writing to Judge Parker? He swore softly when he saw the address on the second envelope. Creed Maddigan!

Tug Harper grinned. That explained everything. Jassy had been hanging around with the gunman. Apparently that hadn't been all she'd been doing.

Humming softly, he pulled the shade over the window. Rose had come in earlier, promising to make it worth his while if he intercepted any letters from Jassy. The way Tug figured it, two letters ought to be worth twice as much.

"Four thousand dollars!" Ray Coulter whistled softly. "Are you sure?"

"That's what the letter says." Rose pressed a hand over her heart. Creed Maddigan had left Jassy a fortune in cash, and the ungrateful little chit hadn't said a word about it.

"We could go places with that kind of money," Coulter said, his voice soft and silky. "Get married, even."

"Married!" Rose squealed. "Do you mean it?"

"Why not? I got no reason to stay in this jerkwater town now that my boy's dead. We'd be good together, Rosie. Married, with that much money, we could be respectable. We could go west, to California maybe, or east, to New York. What do you say?"

Rose stared at him, her mind reeling. It was everything she had ever dreamed of.

"We could even take your sister, if you've a mind to," Coulter offered generously. Jassy McCloud was a pretty little thing. He'd always wondered what was hiding under those shapeless rags Daisy had dressed her in.

Rose shook her head. She'd never felt any affection or warmth for her sister, nothing but jealousy. Daisy had always protected Jassy, coddled her. Jassy had always been Daisy's favorite, and everybody knew it. Jassy could have gone to work at the Lazy Ace any time, but Daisy had kept her home, saying she wanted to keep Jassy out of the saloon until she was eighteen, even though she'd let Rose go to work at sixteen. In spite of all her talk that Jassy was too immature, Rose knew that Daisy had secretly hoped some decent man would come along and offer to marry Jassy and thereby spare her a life of degradation.

"Rose?"

She blinked at Coulter. "What?"

"You haven't answered me."

"Jassy's a big girl now. Milt will hire her." Rose chuckled, thinking there was justice in the world, after all. "She can take my place."

"Does that mean it's you and me?" Coulter grinned at her. "Come on, girl, let's blow this town and head for the big city."

"You got any money of your own, Ray Coulter?"

"I've got a few hundred stashed away." Taking her hand in his, Coulter gave her his most se-

Chapter Eleven

Creed stared, unseeing, at the passing countryside as the wagon lurched over the badly rutted road that led out of town. The handcuffs chafed his wrists and ate at his pride. As the miles passed by, he cussed Harrington for shackling his hands behind his back, making it impossible to swat the fly that was buzzing around his head.

He was vaguely aware of the desultory remarks of the other two men in the iron-barred wooden cart. One had been convicted of murder, the other of bank robbery. Both claimed to be innocent, but then Creed had yet to meet a felon who admitted to being guilty. But, dammit, he *was* innocent, at least of the crime they'd convicted him of.

Of course, he was guilty of a number of other things, not the least of which was falling in love with a girl who made him feel as if he had hung the moon and the stars just for her.

Jassy. Sweet, sweet Jassy with a mane of dark red hair and luminous brown eyes. Jassy, with lips as warm as sunshine, as soft as dandelion down, as intoxicating as hundred-proof whiskey.

Jassy. He wished now that he had made love to her that day in the valley, that he had buried himself in her sweetness, immersed himself in her youth and goodness. Right or wrong, he wanted to be the one to show her how good love could be between a man and a woman. He wanted to watch her eyes as he sheathed himself within her, hear the harsh rasp of her breath as she discovered what passion felt like.

And yet, perversely, he was glad he hadn't touched her. It would have been a crime to steal her innocence, to rob her of her virtue and leave her with nothing. She deserved more than that. So damn much more. He'd done what he could. He had given her a stake. Now all he could do was hope she would use it to make a new life for herself.

Sunk in despair, he withdrew into himself as Black Otter had taught him to do so many years ago. Staring at the raw planks beneath his feet, he blocked out the voices around him, the iron bars, the dismal future that awaited him. Traveling down the corridors of the past, he thought of places he hadn't seen since childhood, of people he had loved who were long dead.

He didn't realize the wagon had come to a halt until one of the guards jabbed him in the back with the barrel of his rifle.

"You there, Maddigan, haul your butt out here."

Choking back the angry retort that rose in his throat, Creed stood up and made his way toward the door and down the narrow steps.

There were three men guarding the wagon. Jack Watkins was the eldest, an easygoing Texan who knew all the tricks. Joe West was only a couple of years younger. He was tall and lean, with a pockmarked face and deep-set brown eyes. Mort Sayeski had only been on the payroll a short time. He had a shock of red hair and a temper to match.

"Rest stop," Sayeski explained curtly. "Sit down over there and don't try nothing funny."

Creed glared at the guard. Sayeski reminded Creed of a banty rooster, all bluff and bluster. He had scared eyes and a finger that constantly stroked the trigger of his rifle.

"I need to take a leak," Creed said.

Sayeski raised the barrel of the rifle until it was leveled at Creed's chest. "So do it."

"Can't." Creed felt his jaw clench. Damn, but it was humiliating to have to ask a snot-nosed kid's permission to relieve himself.

Mort stared at the prisoner for a moment before understanding dawned. "Turn around," he ordered. "Jack, keep him covered."

A muscle worked in Creed's jaw as the young guard unlocked the cuffs. He knew they wouldn't take the cuffs off him again until they reached Canon City and he knew a sudden, irrational urge to make a run for it before it was too late, before his freedom was taken from him forever. But the sure knowledge that he couldn't outrun a .44 slug squelched the urge.

Obligingly, he turned around and held his hands out in front of him so the guard could slip the cuffs back on.

Mort Sayeski swallowed hard as he saw the black rage smoldering in the half-breed's eyes. Unable to help himself, he took a step backward, then brought his rifle up, his finger curling around the trigger.

"Stay where I can see you," he warned. "And don't try nothing."

"Kid, if we were alone, I'd wrap that Winchester around your neck," Creed retorted. Turning his back on the bug-eyed guard, he walked into the bushes.

He'd bide his time, he thought. Sooner or later, he would find a chance to escape and he'd take it. He had to take it, because there was no way in hell he was going to do twenty years behind bars.

Jassy pulled the covers up to her chin, blinking against the bright morning sun that filtered into her room. Her first thought was of Creed.

The second was of the letters she had sent. She knew, she just knew, that the judge would believe her story and that Creed would be acquitted. Only two more days, she thought, two more days until the stage bound for Canon City arrived; when it left again, she'd be on it.

Smiling, she turned over and buried her face in his pillow. She took a deep breath, inhaling the faint scent of talc and tobacco smoke that lingered in the pillow covering. Closing her eyes, she relived those moments in Creed's arms, remembering the taste of his kisses, the feel of his arms around her, the husky sound of his voice when he whispered her name.

"Creed." Just saying his name made him seem closer somehow.

She remembered how he had come to her rescue in the alley, jumping into the fray like a hero in a storybook. He had been there to comfort her when her mother died. He had bought her the first nice dress she'd ever had. He was, she thought, the first real friend she had ever had. And even though he was gone, he was still taking care of her.

Scooting over to the edge of the lumpy mattress, she lifted the bedspread and reached under the bed for Creed's saddlebag.

Sitting up, she dumped the contents on the bed, her hands moving lovingly over the soft doeskin shirt. Picking up the choker, she fastened it around her neck, her fingertips sliding over the smooth blue and yellow beads.

She picked up the moccasins and turned them over in her hand. It made her feel good, wearing something he had worn, touching something he had touched.

Slipping out of bed, she went to her hidey hole. Removing the wrinkled picture from the wall, she reached into the narrow opening. Her fingers closed on empty air. Standing on tiptoe, she peered into the opening. Her father's gold watch was gone. And so was the buckskin pouch.

Feeling sick to her stomach, she hurried out of her room and went into Rosie's bedroom. It was empty. The bureau drawers were open and empty, as was the small wardrobe that had held Rose's clothes.

Shaking her head in disbelief, Jassy went into the small parlor and then into the kitchen. Both were empty.

Rosie was gone, and she had taken Creed's money with her.

Feeling lost and completely alone, Jassy sat at the table, put her face in her hands, and began to cry.

When she had no tears left, she washed her face and brushed her hair, then put on her green dress and new boots. Taking a deep breath, she left the house, determined not to return until she had a job.

It took nearly three weeks to reach Canon City. During that time, Creed's nerves grew ever tighter as rage and anger built within him. The slow-moving cart seemed to close in around him, growing smaller and smaller each day. The cuffs that shackled his hands were a constant reminder of the freedom he had lost. He resented being told what to do, when to eat, when to sleep, and he knew it would only get worse.

The young guard, eager to prove he wasn't afraid of a half-breed gunfighter, rode him hard after the first day. As if to prove his bravery, Sayeski began ordering Creed around, demanding that he gather wood for the fire, that he unharness the horses at night and put them in the traces in the morning. He was constantly making snide remarks about Creed's ancestry or derogatory comments about hired guns, declaring they were the lowest scum on the face of the earth.

Creed took it as long as he could and then, unable to control his temper any longer, he did what he'd been longing to do since he was first arrested. He gave in to the urge to hit something.

Mort never saw what hit him. One minute he was relaxing against the wagon wheel, jabbering about the superiority of the white race, and the next he was flat out on the ground with blood pouring out of his nose.

Creed was breathing hard as he stepped back. It had been a stupid move, hitting the boy, and he knew he'd pay for it, but damn, it had felt good.

Retribution was swift. Watkins and Joe West came running to the boy's rescue. Creed grunted with pain as the Texan struck him across the back with the butt of his rifle.

"You okay, Mort?" West asked.

"He broke my nose," Mort complained, using a dirty kerchief to mop up the blood.

"Want me to break his?" Joe West grinned at Creed as if he'd be only too happy to oblige.

"No, I'll do it."

Creed braced himself as Sayeski lurched to his feet. He glanced briefly at the other two guards, who were standing on either side of him now, and then at the other two prisoners, who were sitting in the shade of the prison cart.

Creed swore under his breath as Sayeski came to stand in front of him.

"Why'd you hit me?" the kid demanded.

"Because you're a little shit with a big mouth."

A flush crept into the kid's cheeks as his two companions started to laugh, obviously agreeing with the gunfighter.

Creed saw the indecision in the kid's eyes, and knew the exact moment when Mort decided that hitting back was the only way to save face. Avoiding the kid's fist was no trouble at all.

The flush in Mort's cheeks went from bright pink to dull red as his fist closed on empty air.

Watkins and Joe West were laughing out loud now, clearly enjoying the boy's embarrassment.

"Hold him!" Mort shouted.

"What?" Watkins stared at Mort, then shook his head. "Forget it."

"I said hold him!"

Joe West shrugged. "What'll it hurt to let the kid take a few swings?"

"I don't know." Watkins shook his head. "It don't seem right."

"Just hold him, Watkins, or I'll tell Joe about that little escapade in Amarillo."

Watkins glared at the younger man. "The 'breed's right, Mort," he muttered as he grabbed hold of Creed's right arm. "You do have a big mouth."

Joe West was grinning as he grabbed hold of Creed's left arm, then drew his sidearm and jabbed it in the half-breed's side. "Just so you don't try anything stupid."

Creed stared at Mort, his gut clenching as he waited for the kid to get down to it. The boy was short and stocky, his arms and legs well-muscled from years of hard living.

With slow deliberation, Mort propped his rifle against a rock, rolled up his shirtsleeves, and flexed his arms and hands. Standing in front of the half-breed, he took a boxer's stance, hands up, legs slightly spread. And then he lashed out, landing two short hard jabs to the prisoner's midsection.

Creed grunted as the breath was driven from his body. Pain spiraled through him, and he would have doubled over if not for the two men holding him up. The kid had a hell of a right hand, he mused, he'd give him that.

For the next ten minutes, Mort vented his humiliation on the half-breed, not content to stop until there was blood running from the prisoner's nose and mouth. Stepping back, he rubbed his bruised knuckles. Then he glanced at his companions, seeking their approval.

Watkins shook his head. "I hope Maddigan never catches you alone in an alley," he remarked, releasing his hold on Creed's arm.

Sayeski snorted disdainfully. "I ain't afraid of him."

"You would be, if you had the sense God gave a goat," Watkins retorted.

"Is that what you think, too, West?"

Joe grinned. "A smart man knows when to back off."

Sayeski swelled up like a balloon about to burst. "You sayin' I ain't smart?"

"I'm not saying anything, kid." Holstering his sidearm, West released Creed's arm. "But Jack's right. You've got one coming."

Ignoring Mort and the others, Creed bent at the waist, taking deep breaths as he sought to control the pain knifing through him. Blood oozed from a cut in his lower lip, and he wiped his mouth on his shirt sleeve, then lifted a tentative hand to his nose. Sayeski hadn't managed to break it after all.

They reached the prison at midday. Creed knew all about the penitentiary. It had once been his misfortune to share a jail cell with an ex-con who had done some time at Canon City. Built by convict labor, it was made of cut stone. The prison itself fit inside the main building and contained thirty-nine cells arranged in three tiers. The roof was made of tin to reduce the risk of fire. The floors were of brick. Adjoining the prison was a bakery, kitchen, and quarters for the staff. A massive stone wall surrounded the prison site. All work done within the prison was done by convict labor. Prisoners were also put to work quarrying stone and making brick, which had been used in the building of the town.

An hour after the wagon arrived, Creed found himself locked in one of the dismal little cells. He'd been informed of the rules, and just in case he forgot what they were, a copy was posted on the wall, right next to a copy of the Bible. There was to be no talking except outside the cellblock and then only about the task at hand. He would be required to clean his cell each morning at reveille. The blankets were to be folded and placed at the head of the narrow iron bedstead, the litter swept into the passageway outside his cell, the slop jar emptied. He would be allowed to write one letter a month and to receive letters on Sundays.

Letters, he thought bleakly. He had no one to write, no one who would write to him . . . except maybe Jassy, and even that was a slim hope. He had made her promise to start a new life for herself, to forget about him. He shook her image from his mind. He hoped she had done just that.

He spent the rest of the afternoon pacing his cell, silently cursing the prison garb he was forced to wear. He'd worn custom-made shirts and boots most of his adult life, and he didn't like the feel of the rough cotton against his skin or the fit of the heavy black shoes.

He spent the next week locked in the cell, endlessly pacing. His only relief came at mealtimes, and then only for a few moments when he was allowed to leave his cell to fill his plate from the large table that stood in the passageway. He hated the regimentation of meal times, hated the guard who unlocked his cell, hated being treated like a trained animal. At a ring of the bell, he was expected to step out of his cell with the other prisoners, fold his arms and face left. At the sound of a second bell, he was to march in single file around the table, take his plate, and return to his cell, all in complete silence.

The meals were filling, but unimaginative—bread, meat, and coffee for breakfast; soup made of cabbage, potatoes, beans, and peas, rice and hominy, meat and bread for dinner; mush and molasses and coffee for supper.

He longed for a thick steak, fresh vegetables, and fruit. And sweets. He admitted to a craving for apple pie and chocolate cake, fried chicken and dumplings. For sweet pink lips and luminous brown eyes.

Lord, he thought in dismay, twenty years of this slop.

Twenty years without a woman.

Twenty years behind bars.

Chapter Twelve

Jassy let out a sigh, one hand massaging the small of her back. She had been working at Mrs. Wellington's boardinghouse for over a month. Every day she made the beds, swept the floors, emptied the slop jars, and dusted the furniture. Once a week, she washed and ironed the sheets, turned the mattresses, and mopped the hard wood floors. She washed the windows, set the table at mealtimes, and did the dishes afterward. She had never worked so hard in her life.

A week after Rose had left town, the landlord came to collect the rent. When Jassy couldn't pay, he had tossed her out. To her relief, Mrs. Wellington had reluctantly agreed to allow Jassy to occupy the small room under the stairwell, deducting the rent and her meals from her meager salary. But she wasn't complaining. She was grateful to have a place to work and a bed to sleep in.

Taking a deep breath, Jassy finished making the bed in Mr. Cuthbert's room. Only four more beds to go. Then it would be time to go down and help Mrs. Wellington prepare the noon meal.

Jassy made the rest of the beds automatically, her thoughts centered on Creed. She wondered how he was doing, if he had received her letter, and if he had, why he hadn't written her back. Every day, she stopped at the post office, hoping for a letter from Creed, for some word from Judge Parker. And every day she left the building empty-handed and heavy-hearted.

Last night, she had written another letter to the magistrate, begging him to reconsider Creed's case, to see that justice was done. She had mailed the letter first thing this morning.

After considerable deliberation, she had written to Creed, too, but then she had crumpled the paper and tossed it into the fireplace. She couldn't write and tell him she loved him, not when he hadn't cared enough to answer her first letter, not when he had made her promise she wouldn't wait for him, that she would leave town and make a new life for herself. She couldn't bring herself to tell him that Rose had stolen the money he had left her and run off with Ray Coulter.

To her shame, she had overheard two of the town ladies gossiping just yesterday, talking about Rose and Coulter and how they'd run off together.

Headed for San Francisco, Mrs. Norton had said, shaking her head with such vigorous disapproval that her hat had almost fallen off. *I always thought Ray Coulter to be a decent sort, even if he did work in a saloon. Who'd have ever guessed he'd run off with a harlot?*

Mrs. Watson had nodded in agreement. *Poor Tess. I don't know how she'll hold her head up after this.*

Jassy had felt her cheeks burn when the two women turned around and saw her.

The twig doesn't fall very far from the tree, Mrs. Norton had remarked, and the two women had left the mercantile, their noses in the air.

Creed sat on the edge of his cot, staring at the floor. It was Sunday, the longest day of the week. He'd gladly have worked if they'd let him, because anything beat sitting in his cell, waiting for a letter that never came. Of course, he had no one to blame for that but himself. He'd told Jassy to forget about him, to make a new life for herself, and apparently she'd done just that. He wondered if she had taken his advice and left town, if she was happy, if she ever thought of him. He thought of writing her, just to see how she was, but he never did. They had made a clean break, and it was best to leave it at that.

But damn, it would be nice to hear from her just once.

Stretching out on his bunk, his hands locked behind his head, he closed his eyes. His mind wandered back in time, back to the carefree days of his childhood.

He had spent the first twelve years of his life living with the Lakota. His father, Rides the Wind, had been a *wichasha wakan*, a holy man. His mother had been a white woman. She had been badly wounded in a raid. Black Otter, the warrior who had captured her, had taken her to Rides the Wind, who had treated her wounds and cared for her during her long convalescence. By the time she was well again, Rides the Wind had fallen in love with the white woman, and so he had bought her from Black Otter and married her according to the customs of the People.

But Heather Thomas hadn't returned his father's love. She had hated the Indians, and she had hated her husband. She had tried to turn her son against Rides the Wind, but Creed had loved and admired his father, and nothing his mother had said could change that.

It had been during the summer of his thirteenth year that the Army attacked the village. Rides the Wind had been killed defending a handful of children, and Heather had been rescued from the savages at last. Creed had begged his mother to let him go, to let him see if he could find Black Otter and his family, who had managed to escape the slaughter, but his mother had refused. Turning a deaf ear to his pleas, she had dragged Creed back East, where she spent the next two years trying to civilize him.

Determined to turn her son into a gentleman, she had burned his clothes, cut his hair, and refused to let him out of the house until he agreed not to speak the Lakota language. To her everlasting regret, Creed had refused to become a gentleman. To spite her, he got involved with a bunch of young toughs. He smoked cigars and drank cheap whiskey; he got into street fights and saloon brawls. And because she abhorred guns and violence, he bought a .44 Colt and practiced with it every day.

By the time he was seventeen, his mother had given up on him. He had been nearly full-grown by then, ornery as sin, and when he was arrested with three other boys for busting up a saloon, she had refused to bail him out. Instead, she had let him sit in that damn jail for two months. When he got out, he sold everything he owned and headed West. He had intended to return to his father's people, but by the time he made his way back to the Lakota, it was too late. Most of Black Otter's band had been killed in a skirmish with the cavalry the winter before; the survivors had been sent to the reservation in chains. As much as he had wanted to stay with his father's people, he couldn't. He had stayed a year, and then he had run away. The reservation had been too much like jail, and he had vowed never to go to jail again.

Creed stared at the iron-barred door and swore softly. So much for never going to jail again, he thought bleakly.

After leaving the reservation, he had gone to Denver looking for a job, but the only thing he was any good at was fast-drawing a Colt, so he had hired out his gun, riding shotgun for the stage line. He had prevented six robberies in the first nine weeks, killing four men and capturing seven others.

That quick, he had a reputation as a fast gun. Men who had once looked at him with scorn because he was a half-breed now treated him with respect. Miners and bankers sought his services, hiring his gun, paying him sizeable amounts of money to guard a mining claim, a bank payroll, a gold shipment.

And what did he have to show for it? Not one damn thing.

With an oath, he slammed his fist into the wall, relishing the pain that splintered through his hand because it gave him something else to think about besides luminous brown eyes and his own wasted life.

Jassy's steps were slow and heavy as she walked back to Mrs. Wellington's boarding-house. She hadn't really expected to find a letter from Creed, but she couldn't help being disappointed just the same. She had been so sure he had cared for her, and even though she'd promised to forget him and make a new life for herself, she had hoped that they could still be friends, that he would at least answer her letter.

"Hey, Jassy."

She glanced up at the sound of Billy Padden's voice.

"Where've you been keeping yourself?" Billy asked, falling into step beside her.

"I've been working."

"Working? You? Where?"

"At Mrs. Wellington's boardinghouse."

Billy frowned in disbelief. "Mrs. Wellington hired you? To do what?"

"Everything she doesn't want to do, that's what."

"How about meeting me tonight?"

"I don't think so."

"C'mon, Jassy. I'll take you to dinner at the Morton House." His hand slid up her arm. "And then maybe we can take a walk down by the river."

"No, Billy." Firmly, she removed his hand from her arm.

"Why not?"

"You know why not."

"Aw, don't be like that. I won't do anything you don't want me to do."

"Hah!"

"I promise."

"No, Billy."

"Tomorrow night?"

"We'll see," she said, hoping he'd go away.

That night, overcome with loneliness, Jassy sat in her room staring out the window. Maybe she should go out with Billy Padden. He wasn't a bad sort. But he wasn't Creed.

With a sigh, she found a sheet of paper, then sat down and wrote a long letter to Creed, telling him that she had lied when she promised to forget him, that she loved him and would always love him. She told him all about Rose and how her sister had stolen the money he had left her and run off to San Francisco with Coulter. She told him about her job at the boarding-house, making light of the hard work, assuring him that she was doing fine, that she was saving her money for a trip to Canon City so she could visit him.

She touched the choker at her throat, and then, feeling shy, she poured out her heart, telling him how she treasured the things she had found in his saddlebags, that she wore his beaded choker every day, that she slept on the pillow she had stolen from his hotel room.

In closing, she told him she had written to Judge Parker again, and then she begged him not to give up hope, telling him she was sure that he would be acquitted.

She signed her name and sealed the letter before she had a chance to change her mind.

* * *

Creed stared at the guard, unable to believe his ears.

"For me?" he asked. "You're sure?"

"It's addressed to Creed Maddigan," the guard replied, fanning himself with the envelope. "But if you don't want it, just say so."

Creed held out his hand, his gaze fixed on the envelope. "I want it."

"Hope it's good news," the guard remarked. Slipping the letter through the bars, he moved on down the cellblock.

Creed stared at the envelope for a long time, his thumb caressing Jassy's name. Bless the girl, he thought, and sitting on the edge of his cot, he opened the envelope and withdrew a single sheet of white paper.

> Dear Creed. Please don't be angry with me, I know I promised to leave town, to forget you and start a new life, but I can't. I think about you every day and wonder how you are. It must be awful, to be locked up. What do you do all day? Is the food terrible?

Creed grunted softly. The food was the least of his problems.

He frowned when he came to the part about her working at Wellington's Boardinghouse, cussed long and loud when he read that Rose had stolen his money and run off to San Francisco with Ray Coulter. Coulter. Creed couldn't explain it, but he knew, deep in his gut, that it had been Coulter's idea to take the money. He'd met men like Coulter in every town west of the Missouri. Sweet-talkin' men who could charm the birds out of the trees—and fleece a woman out of a fortune before the sheets were cold. Rose would be lucky if she ever saw San Francisco.

He read the letter three times, his thoughts chaotic.

I love you. . . .

I haven't forgotten you. . . .

Rose stole the money and left town. . . .

I'm working at Wellington's Boardinghouse . . . saving my money so I can come to Canon City . . . wear your choker every day . . . sleep on your pillow at night . . .

She loved him. He bolted off the cot and began to pace the floor. How could she love him? She didn't even know him, didn't know anything about him.

She hadn't forgotten him. Lord knew, he hadn't forgotten her. She had been in his thoughts every day, in his dreams every night, his beautiful child-woman with hair as red as fire and eyes as warm and brown as sun-kissed earth. Even now, just thinking about her made him ache in ways he didn't understand, made him yearn for things he knew he'd never have.

Jassy. She had looked at him as if he was something more than just a half-breed gunfighter with a bad reputation and no future.

He thought about her wearing the beaded choker that his Lakota grandmother had made for him. Okoka had given it to Creed shortly before she passed away, a gift of love so that he would always remember her.

As if he could ever forget her. He had known little kindness from his mother while they lived with the Lakota. She had been too wrapped up in her own misery, too bitter about her captivity, to have much thought or feeling for a child she had never wanted. But his grandmother, bless her, had had time enough and love enough to spare. And now Jassy wore the choker.

And slept on his pillow. He closed his eyes, and an image of Jassy curled up in bed, her rich red hair spread across his pillow, jumped to the forefront of his mind.

Creed groaned low in his throat as heat spiraled through him. Muttering an oath, he opened his eyes and stared at the letter in his hand. Her writing was small and neat, blurred in places, as if the ink had gotten wet before it dried. And he knew, with heartrending certainty, that it had been Jassy's tears that smudged the words.

"Jassy." Murmuring her name, he dragged a hand through his hair, his gut clenching when he thought about Rose making off with his money and leaving Jassy to fend for herself.

Damn! He knew she'd made light of working in the boardinghouse, that she'd purposefully neglected to mention the long hours, the back-breaking work, the low pay—if she was getting paid at all.

He stared down at his hands, picturing them around Rose McCloud's throat. One of these days, he thought, one of these days, he would make her pay for that lie she'd told on the stand, for stealing Jassy's money, for . . .

He swore under his breath. Who was he kidding? Rose was long gone, and he wasn't going anywhere for another nineteen years, eight months, and thirteen days.

Another month passed, and Creed grew more and more restless. His temper flared at the slightest provocation. He spent three days in solitary for fighting with one of the other prisoners. He'd never realized how much he hated small places, how much he'd prized what little freedom he had, until it was gone.

When he was returned to his cell, he vowed to keep his temper in check, but it was easier said than done. He was constantly on edge, his thoughts churning with images of Jassy being forced to work because Rose had stolen his money. He read her letter until it was almost illegible, warmed by her words of love, enraged at the thought that her own sister had gone off and left her alone.

He had to get out. He had to know for himself that Jassy was all right.

Six weeks after Creed received Jassy's letter, he overheard some of the cons talking about an escape. He sought out their leader, George Westerman, the next day.

"Do you need an extra man?" he'd asked, keeping his voice hushed.

"Maybe."

"I want in."

"Can I trust you to keep your mouth shut?"

"Damn right."

Westerman had looked him over, then nodded. "It's set for tomorrow. Gresham will fill you in tonight, in the mess hall."

Creed didn't have much more than a nodding acquaintance with the seven prisoners who had concocted the plan. He knew that the ringleader, George Westerman, had been convicted of murder and sentenced to life in prison. Westerman was about twenty-four, heavily built, with a sandy complexion, curly brown hair, and blue eyes. He had a brother on the outside who was in on the breakout.

Billy Gresham had drawn two years for robbery. The others were serving terms of eighteen months to ten years for a variety of other crimes. The last man, Ryan St. John, had only a few months left to go.

But that didn't matter. They all wanted only one thing—to be free again.

As it turned out, the escape was so simple that Creed wondered why they hadn't tried it before.

At the appointed time, Gresham called for the night guard, stating that he was sick and in need of medication. When the guard was out of sight,

Westerman and St. John, who had adjoining cells on the main floor, opened their cell doors using knives they'd stolen from the kitchen. They hid in the shadows until the guard returned, then jumped him. Westerman threw a blanket over his head and held him while St. John choked him until he was unconscious.

After stripping the guard of his revolver and taking his keys, they left him bound and gagged in Westerman's cell.

Creed's heart was pounding with excitement as Westerman unlocked his cell door. Grabbing Jassy's letter, he followed the others into the clothing room, where they changed out of their prison garb, then made their exit from the prison compound by one of the windows on the north side. To Creed's amazement, the guard they'd left in Westerman's cell appeared to be the only guard on duty.

From the prison, they went into the office, where they took six Spencer rifles, a couple of handguns, and several boxes of cartridges.

"We're headin' for Texas," Westerman told Creed as he fed shells into a rifle. "Why don't you come along?"

Creed shook his head. "Can't. I've got a little unfinished business waiting for me back in Harrison."

Westerman grunted. "Hope you find him."

"Her," Creed said, his hands clenching as he imagined his fingers locking around Rose McCloud's throat.

"Even better," Westerman said with a leer. He tossed Creed a holstered Peacemaker, then pressed a wad of crumpled greenbacks into his hand. "Good luck."

"Yeah." Creed shoved the cash in his pocket, then buckled on the gunbelt. "Same to you."

On silent feet, they made their way toward the gate.

Westerman's brother, Charlie, was waiting for them, a big grin on his face.

"Any trouble?" George asked.

Charlie jerked a thumb over his shoulder. "Just him."

"Is he dead?"

"No, but he's gonna have a hell of a headache when he wakes up."

George Westerman spared hardly a glance for the body sprawled facedown in the dirt. He was far more interested in looking over the horses his brother had brought. Taking up the reins of a rangy gray gelding, he climbed into the saddle and rode into the darkness, followed by Charlie and the others.

Swinging onto the back of a big blue roan, Creed took a deep breath, then headed West.

Damn, he thought bleakly, he was running. Again.

Chapter Thirteen

It was a little after midday when Jassy left the boardinghouse and walked down the dusty street to Gratton's Mercantile.

She had been working for more than two months now and slowly, gradually, the townspeople had started to accept her, seeing her as Jassy McCloud, a person in her own right, instead of just a whore's daughter. She had never thought it would happen, never dreamed the people of Harrison would be able to overlook her past.

For the first time, she knew what respect was, what it meant to be able to walk down the street with her head held high. She went to church on Sundays, finding comfort in the hymns and the psalms.

She smiled at Kate Bradshaw, owner of the Harrison Tea Shoppe, and exchanged greetings with Elizabeth Wills, who was standing on the boardwalk, sweeping. She was making friends. It was a good feeling.

Climbing the stairs of Gratton's Mercantile, Jassy nodded at Mr. Thomas, feeling a strange catch in her heart as she realized that the old man was sitting in the rocking chair that had been Creed's favorite.

Mr. Gratton's blue eyes were twinkling as he came around the counter. With his white hair and rosy cheeks, Jassy often thought he looked like Santa Claus.

"Good afternoon, miss," he said cheerfully.

"Hello, Mr. Gratton. I don't suppose . . ."

"It's here," he said, wiping his hands on his apron.

"It is?"

Gratton nodded. "A letter," he said, beaming at her.

At last! She hurried after him as he made his way to the post office in the back of the store, her heart hammering in her breast as the storekeeper reached into a cubbyhole and withdrew a long brown envelope.

Her smile faded a little when she saw the return address. It wasn't from Creed after all. She opened the envelope, her eyes flying over the words. It was a letter from the judge, asking her to write out what she had seen exactly as she remembered it, sign it, date it, and have it notarized.

In the meantime, he would send word to the warden at Canon City and ask that Creed write out his version of what had happened the night Harry Coulter had died. If he felt there was a possibility that Creed had been wrongly convicted, he would consider a retrial.

"Good news?" Mr. Gratton asked.

"The best!" Jassy exclaimed. Hugging the letter close to her heart, she ran out of the store.

It was well after midnight when Creed reached Harrison. He sat on the outskirts of town for a long while, contemplating his next move. On the long ride to town, he'd come to the conclusion that the best thing, the smart thing, would be to get out of Colorado as fast as his horse could carry him and to stay as far away from Jassy McCloud as possible.

Creed nodded to himself. He should just ride on. Sooner or later, Jassy had to learn to take care of herself. Sooner or later, she'd meet some decent guy who could give her the kind of life she wanted, the kind of life she deserved.

There was no reason for him to see her, no reason at all. He'd go to Frisco, find Rose if she was there, get his money back, send it to Jassy, then get on with his own life and let Jassy get on with hers.

He should just ride on, he thought again. It would be better for both of them. But he continued to sit there, watching the windows in town go dark until the Lazy Ace Saloon was the only place with lights still showing.

He'd ride on, he told himself, just as soon as he made sure Jassy was all right.

Knowing he was making a mistake, yet unable to help himself, he headed for the alley behind Martha Wellington's boardinghouse.

Dismounting, he tried the back door. It opened on well-oiled hinges, and he stepped into a large, square kitchen. He caught the lingering scent of fresh-baked bread, the sharp smell of lye soap.

He stood there for a long moment but heard nothing to indicate anyone in the house was awake.

He moved silently through the dark rooms and down the hall until he came to the room under the stairs that Jassy had written was hers.

His heart was racing like a runaway train as he put his hand on the knob and tried the door.

He was relieved to find it unlocked; relieved and angry. Relieved because he wouldn't have to break the darn thing down; angry because anyone, including a no-account gunfighter, could walk in on her in the middle of the night.

Stepping into the room, he closed the door behind him, his gaze intent on the narrow bed against the far wall. Three long strides carried him across the room. For a moment, he stood beside the bed, watching her sleep. Her hair was spread like a flame across the snowy pillow slip. One hand rested beneath her cheek; her lips were slightly parted.

Drawn by a power he was helpless to resist, he brushed a wisp of hair from her brow. Lord, she looked so young lying there, so innocent. He had no right to be in her room, no right to want her.

"Jassy." Kneeling beside the bed, he placed his hand over her mouth. "Jassy."

She woke with a start, her eyelids fluttering open. In the dim light cast by the moon, he saw the fear that flickered in her eyes, a fear that was quickly replaced by disbelief, and then joy.

The happiness in her eyes brought a smile to his face. Removing his hand from her mouth, he replaced it with his lips. She tasted clean and fresh, like sunshine on a summer morning.

"Creed." She whispered his name when he came up for air. She pulled him down on the bed beside her, hugging him fiercely, then drew back. "What are you doing here?"

"I broke out of prison."

She blinked at him as if she couldn't believe her ears. "You what?"

"You heard me."

"Oh, Creed."

"You sound disappointed."

"I heard from Judge Parker," she said, and quickly explained about the letter she'd written, about how the judge had promised to look into Creed's case.

He swore under his breath. Hell and damnation, he'd only made things worse. Still, just because the judge said he'd look into things didn't mean they'd find him innocent.

"Maybe you could turn yourself in," Jassy suggested.

Creed looked at her as if she'd lost her mind. "No. I'm not going back. Not ever."

"But—"

"No, Jassy." He ran a hand through his hair. "I never should have come here," he muttered, "but I had to make sure you were all right."

His gaze moved over her face, memorizing every sweet line and curve, the dark sweep of her lashes, the stubborn tilt of her chin, the deep brown of her eyes.

He stood abruptly. "I've got to go. Take care of yourself."

"No!" She grabbed his hand and held on to it tight. "I missed you." She tugged on his hand, pulling him down beside her once more. "Don't go. Not yet."

She sat up, her arms reaching for him, her mouth seeking his. He couldn't go, not now.

With a low groan, he wrapped his arms around her and held her close. His hands roamed restlessly over her back and shoulders as he drew her up against him and held her tight. She was hope and love, sustenance for a starving man, and he thought he might never let her go. She made little mewling sounds deep in her throat, like a satisfied kitten, as he rained kisses over her face and neck.

"Jassy." Her name was a groan on his lips, a plea, a prayer.

"I'm here." She locked her arms around him, holding him tight, the voice of budding feminine intuition telling her that he needed to be held.

"Oh, girl," he murmured, and with a sigh, he pillowed his head on her breast, content for the moment to be held and petted.

Closing his eyes, he listened to the sound of her voice as she murmured his name, telling him that she loved him, that she had missed him, that everything would be all right now.

She was so young, he thought. So innocent. And he wanted so badly to believe her. But he couldn't stay in Harrison. He was on the run now, a wanted man with a price on his head. He'd go, he promised himself, in a minute he'd go.

Her hand was small and warm against his cheek, her lips incredibly soft as they brushed his forehead.

"I can't believe you're here," she said, kissing the top of his head. "I'm afraid it's just another dream, and in a minute Mrs. Wellington will be knocking on my door, telling me it's time to get up."

"I'm here," he assured her. *I'm here, and I don't want to leave.* She felt so good in his arms. Warm and sleep-tousled, she smelled of soap and sunshine. Her skin was as soft and smooth as a baby's, tempting his touch.

Time seemed to lose all meaning as they held each other close. She kissed him over and over again, her hands moving over the taut muscles in his arms, measuring the width of his shoulders, tracing the dark shadows on his jaw, until he ached with wanting her.

Only then did he draw away. Rising, he walked to the window and stared out at the sky. The moon was high now. Time to move on.

He thought of what it meant, being on the run, avoiding large towns, sleeping with one eye open, always glancing over his shoulder. Long days and longer nights.

He sensed her presence even before he felt her arms slip around his waist.

He shouldn't have come here. Leaving now would be that much harder.

"Jassy, I've got to go."

"Where? Why?"

"To find Rose. She took something that wasn't hers, and I intend to get it back."

"The money," Jassy said.

"Right."

"I'll go with you."

"No, Jassy."

"She's *my* sister," Jassy said emphatically. "And she didn't steal that money from you. She took it from me, along with my father's watch."

"Right on all counts," Creed allowed, "but you're not going with me, and that's final. I'll see you get the money back. And the watch, too, if she hasn't hocked it."

"I don't want the money. I want you. I won't be any trouble, I promise."

He turned to face her, his finger tracing the delicate curve of her cheek. "Honey, I'm in trouble enough for both of us."

"I thought . . ." She lowered her head so he couldn't see the tears that burned her eyes. "I thought you . . . that you cared for me a little."

"I care for you a lot, Jassy. And that's why you're staying here."

Two huge tears slid down her cheeks. "Please take me with you."

Creed gazed down at her. Her brown eyes were luminous, pleading, hopeful.

He swore under his breath. She stirred him in ways no other woman ever had, and she wasn't even a woman yet, just a girl who made him yearn for things that were forever out of reach, things he had never even known he wanted until Jassy McCloud entered his life. Things like a home, a wife, kids—things he had forfeited any right to the first time he took a gun in his hand.

"Jassy, honey . . ."

He ran his finger over the beaded choker at her throat. It gave him a funny feeling in his gut, knowing she wore it to bed.

"Jassy, dammit, you're only seventeen. You don't even know what life's all about."

"Eighteen."

"What?"

"I'm eighteen. I had a birthday a couple of weeks ago."

"Eighteen," he murmured, and wished he could have been there to share it with her, to wish her a happy birthday. "All grown up now, huh? A woman of the world?"

She sensed him weakening and she tightened her arms around his waist, pressing herself against him, her hands kneading his back.

"Please, Creed," she begged fervently. "Please take me with you."

"I can't." He ran a hand through his hair. "Don't you understand? I'm a wanted man now."

"I don't care!"

"I do."

"Creed . . ."

"You don't know what it means, Jassy," he said gruffly. "I'll be riding the outlaw trail, depending on a poker table for cash, always looking over my shoulder. It's a miserable life for a man, and no life at all for a little bit of a girl like you."

She didn't care. All she knew was that he was leaving her, just like everybody else. First her pa, then Daisy, then Rose. She couldn't let Creed go. If he walked out of her life now, she knew she'd never see him again.

She gazed up at him, wondering how she could penetrate the hard shell he seemed to have drawn around himself. She knew she would never change his mind, not with words.

But there were other methods of persuasion.

Standing on tiptoe, she pressed her mouth to his and kissed him with all the passion that had been smoldering in her heart. She caressed his lower lip with her tongue, felt an exhilarating surge of power when he groaned deep in his throat, and then he was kissing her back, his arms closing around her like steel bars.

His tongue slid sensuously over hers, sending tremors of delight skittering through her.

"Oh girl . . ." His senses were reeling with her nearness. Her hair was like soft silk beneath his cheek. He could feel the curvy length of her body pressed against his, her warmth melting the coldness in his heart. Every breath he took was permeated with the warm, sleepy scent of her skin. With Jassy in his arms, in his life, he would never be cold or lonely again.

He held her close, his body aching with need. Her bed, that narrow little bed that she had been sleeping in, sent out an invitation that was darn near impossible to resist.

He had to get out, he thought desperately, now, while he still could, before he carried her to that bed and buried himself deep inside her. He was no good for her, no good at all. Even if he wasn't on the dodge, he was a half-breed. She wanted respectability. Well, she'd never have that if she married him. People might forgive her for being a saloon girl's daughter, but they would never forgive her for marrying a half-breed gunfighter.

Chapter Fourteen

Jassy watched him go, unable to believe Creed was really leaving her, unable to believe he *could* leave her. He cared. She knew he did. She had seen it in his eyes, tasted it in his kisses, heard it in the husky tremor of his voice.

Of course he cared, she thought. If he didn't, he wouldn't give two hoots in hell about what happened to her. He would have taken her with him, then dumped her somewhere along the way when he tired of her.

Jassy's heart swelled with tenderness as she realized the magnitude of the sacrifice Creed was making. He wanted her, but he was leaving without her, determined to go on alone rather than put her life in jeopardy.

But she couldn't, wouldn't, let him go. He had

been alone all his life, she knew, alone and lonely. And she knew all too well what that was like.

She was rummaging through her dresser, trying to find something suitable to wear on the trail, when the door burst open. She glanced over her shoulder to find Creed standing in the doorway.

"Jassy." He lifted one hand, then let it fall in a gesture of helplessness. "I . . . I got to the edge of town and then . . ."

He crossed the room in three long strides and jerked her up hard against him.

"I tried to do the right thing," he muttered ruefully. "I told myself all the reasons why I should leave you here, but . . ."

He let out a deep sigh of resignation and despair. "Come with me."

Laughter bubbled up in Jassy's throat. "Oh, Creed, I was coming after you."

He looked surprised. "You were?"

She nodded. "I told myself you were being noble, leaving me behind because you were afraid for me. But I don't want to be alone anymore. And I don't want you to be alone, either."

"Noble, huh?" He grinned at her. "I'm no good, honey. I told you that a long time ago, and I guess this proves it."

Her face glowed in the candlelight. "It only proves you love me."

Love. Creed swore softly. Did he love her? How could he help it?

"Come on," he said gruffly, more certain than ever that he was making a mistake. "Let's get out of here."

"Just let me get a few things together."

"Hurry it up. I'll wait outside while you change."

Hurry she did. In less than ten minutes, she had donned her baggy blue dress, stuffed her few belongings into Creed's saddlebags, and tucked the pillow she had stolen from his hotel room under her arm. With a last look around, she opened the door, then closed it firmly behind her. It was symbolic, she thought, like closing the door on her old life.

Creed grimaced when she stepped into the hallway. "If it's the last thing I ever do, I'm gonna burn that dress," he muttered as he took the saddlebags from her hand.

Jassy nodded, her heart pounding wildly. She was going with Creed, and she didn't care where, as long as they were together.

She followed him down the hall, through the kitchen, and out the back door.

Creed's horse whinnied softly as they approached, and Creed shook his head, irritated by his lack of foresight. He would have to find Jassy a horse before long, not to mention a heavy coat and a hat to shade her face from the sun.

An unexpected wave of protectiveness swept through Creed as he thought of caring for Jassy, providing for her, loving her.

He took up the reins, but made no effort to mount as second thoughts crowded his mind.

"What is it?" Jassy asked.

Creed swore under his breath. In all his adult life, he had never been responsible for anyone but himself. What if he failed her? She was so young. She had no idea what she was letting herself in for. Even if he wasn't too old for her, even if he wasn't on the run, he was still a half-breed and nothing on God's green earth could change that. People would belittle her, shun her presence, treat her worse than poor white trash when they saw her with him.

He couldn't take her with him, he thought ruefully. He had already made a mess of his life. He couldn't ruin hers, too.

"Jassy."

She looked up at him, her face dappled by moonlight, her eyes shining with eagerness and trust.

"Jassy, I . . ."

"Is something wrong?"

Creed groaned low in his throat. Everything was wrong.

"Did you forget something?" Her smile faded as she saw the bleak expression in his eyes. "You've changed your mind, haven't you?"

Her voice was flat, devoid of emotion. But the look in her eyes threatened to rip his heart to shreds.

"Jassy, listen . . ."

"It's all right. You don't have to explain."

Bravely, she lifted her chin and squared her shoulders, like a soldier facing a firing squad.

"Here." Her voice quivered as she handed him the pillow she'd taken from the hotel. "You might need this."

Damn. He couldn't leave her. Her father had run out on her. Daisy had failed her. Rose had stolen every cent she had and skipped town without a backward glance. He couldn't walk out on her, too. Right or wrong, he couldn't leave her behind.

"Hang on to it, honey," he replied ruefully. "You might want to use it before the night's over."

She gazed up at him, a glimmer of hope rising in her eyes.

Tenderly, Creed drew her close. Wrapping his arms around her, he pressed a kiss to the top of her head.

"Promise you won't hate me, Jasmine Alexandria McCloud. No matter what happens, promise you won't hate me."

"I promise," she replied, her words muffled against his chest. "I could never hate you."

"I hope not," he muttered as he boosted her into the saddle, then swung up behind her. "I hope not."

It was three hours past midnight when Creed reined his horse to a stop. Jassy had fallen asleep in his arms long since, giving him plenty of time to chastise himself for bringing her with him, but, even knowing it was a mistake, he couldn't have left her behind. She needed someone and, right or wrong, that someone seemed to be him. He would find Rose, get his money back, get Jassy settled in some nice little town, and then he would get the hell out of her life before it was too late.

"Jassy. Wake up."

She stirred in his arms, snuggling against him.

He kissed her cheek. "Come on, Jassy, wake up."

Her eyelids fluttered open and she stared up at him. "What's wrong?"

"Nothing. We're gonna bed down here for what's left of the night."

Dismounting, he lifted her from the saddle, then removed his bedroll from behind the cantle and spread it on the ground.

He glanced briefly at Jassy, then at his blankets, and swore softly, knowing they would have to share his bedroll. Knowing it wasn't a good idea.

"Come on, honey, let's turn in."

She was too tired to argue. Fully clothed, she crawled under the blanket and curled up into a ball. She was asleep by the time he crawled in beside her, careful not to touch her in any way.

Folding his arms behind his head, he stared up at the sky, trying to ignore the woman beside him. How many nights had he tossed and turned on that damned narrow cot in prison, dreaming of a woman, of Jassy, in his bed? Never in a million years had he imagined those dreams would actually come true.

He turned on his side, his back toward her, and listed all the reasons why he was no good for her, and when that failed to quell his desire, he started over again. He was too old. She was too young. He was a half-breed. She was a nice girl in spite of the way she'd been raised. She deserved the best. He was a wanted man. She was too young, too young, too damn young! . . .

He groaned deep in his throat as Jassy rolled over and molded her body to his, one arm sliding over his waist.

The heat of her breasts pressed against his back.

Her scent, warm and womanly, hovered in the air.

He swore softly as she snuggled closer, seeking the heat of his body.

It was going to be a long night.

Chapter Fifteen

Jassy pulled the blanket over her head, reluctant to let go of the beautiful dream she'd been having. Abruptly, she realized that her bed seemed awfully hard. The whinny of a horse brought her fully awake.

With a start, she sat up. It hadn't been a dream after all. Creed really had come for her.

Glancing over her shoulder, she saw him standing a few feet away, saddling the roan. For a moment, she sat there watching him, admiring the width of his shoulders, the way his muscles bunched and relaxed as he moved. The early morning sun glinted in his long black hair.

She felt a blush rise in her cheeks when Creed turned away from his horse and saw her staring at him. She had spent the night sharing his bed and had awakened just before dawn to find herself wrapped around him.

"Morning," he said, walking toward her.

"Morning."

He extended his hand and helped Jassy to her feet. "Are you ready to go?"

"Go?"

"I don't know about you, but I'm hungry. We need to find a town, lay in some supplies."

"I'm ready."

"Do you need to—ah, you know?"

The fire in her cheeks burned hotter. Head down, she hurried toward the shelter offered by a clump of bushes.

She refused to meet his eyes when she returned a few minutes later.

"Jassy?"

"What?"

"We're gonna be spending a lot of time alone on the trail. There won't be a lot of privacy, so I don't want you feelin' embarrassed about . . . about anything, okay? If you need to stop, you let me know."

Jassy nodded.

"Okay, then, let's ride."

Jassy's stomach was rumbling loudly by the time they reached the next town. To her dismay, Creed's first stop was at the livery stable, where he instructed the owner to give the roan a good rubdown and a generous helping of hay and oats.

"Always take care of your horse first," Creed remarked as he took Jassy's hand and started walking down the street. "You take care of him, and he'll take care of you."

Jassy nodded, though tips on horse care were the furthest thing from her mind. She was acutely aware of the tall man walking beside her, of his hand holding hers, his palm callused, his long fingers gripping hers with quiet strength.

As they neared a small restaurant, her stomach began to growl again.

Creed grinned down at her as he opened the door. "Think you can wait another couple of minutes?"

"If I have to."

The waitress brought them coffee, her gaze hardening when she looked at Creed. As she took their order, it was blatantly obvious that she objected to having a half-breed in the place, and just as obvious that she didn't have enough sand in her craw to refuse to serve him.

Jassy frowned at Creed. "What's wrong with her?" she asked when the waitress went into the kitchen.

"Same thing that's wrong with most people," he muttered.

"What do you mean?"

"Most people don't take kindly to half-breeds, Jassy. Some of 'em are downright nasty about it."

"Oh."

"And most of them won't think much of you for associating with one," Creed said flatly. "You'd best get used to it if you plan to travel with me."

"Creed, people have been looking down on me all my life," Jassy replied candidly. "Don't you think I'm used to it by now?"

"I don't know. Are you?"

She lifted her chin defiantly. "Yes."

"But you don't like it?"

"Of course not, but I can't do anything about it."

"Maybe, maybe not."

"What do you mean?"

Creed shook his head. "We'll talk about it later."

She wanted to pursue the matter, but their food arrived then, and eating suddenly seemed more important than answers.

Twenty minutes later, she sat back, utterly content.

"Don't tell me you're finished," Creed remarked, amazed, as always, by the amount of food she put away.

Jassy nodded. "I couldn't eat another bite."

"It's a good thing," he muttered with a wry grin. "Another bite, and I doubt if my horse could carry us both."

Jassy made a face at him. "Very funny, Mr. Maddigan."

"Sure you don't want another stack of pancakes? More bacon? Eggs? Another cup of coffee?"

Jassy made a face at him. "I'm sure."

"Let's go then."

Lifting his hat from the back of his chair, Creed stood up and dropped a couple of dollars on the table.

Their next stop was the mercantile. Creed bought Jassy a pair of levis, a long-sleeved flannel shirt, thick wool socks, a pair of sturdy boots, a wide-brimmed hat, and a bedroll of her own.

"You can change on the trail," he said as he thrust the clothing into her hands.

"But I've never worn pants!" she exclaimed, scandalized by the mere idea.

"Well, I'm sure they'll be less trouble than a dress and a dozen petticoats. And I'm sick of that blue thing."

"I just wore it to travel in. I have another one."

"Good, 'cause I'm burning that blue one tonight."

"No, Creed, I don't have that many clothes."

"Then get yourself another dress, 'cause that blue one's about to be history."

Jassy smiled. There was no arguing with the man, she thought, and that was fine with her. She hadn't had many new dresses in her life, and she was as sick of that blue dress as he was.

She picked out a pink muslin and held it up for Creed's approval.

"Just as long as it's not blue," he muttered.

She trailed after him while he bought supplies, conscious of the looks of disdain and distrust that followed him. Funny, back in Harrison it had never occurred to her that people held Creed in contempt because he was a half-breed. She had always thought their apprehension was because of his reputation as a hired gun.

Now, paying more attention, she saw the fear in the eyes of the women, the wariness in the eyes of the men.

She lifted her chin and squared her shoulders when she overheard a couple of the women whispering about her behind her back, declaring that she must be no better than white trash to keep company with a dirty half-breed.

Tears of anger and hurt stung her eyes, and she blinked them back. Narrow-minded old biddies. What did they know about anything, about being poor and hungry, about being ashamed of living in a dirty little shack in a dirty little alley? Fat, rich old crones, what right did they have to judge her?

Hands balled into tight fists, she followed Creed out of the store.

"You okay, honey?" Creed asked.

"Why wouldn't I be?"

"I heard what they said."

"Nasty old . . . old . . ." She stamped her foot because she couldn't think of a word bad enough to call them. "I'm not white trash!"

"I know."

"What right do they have to call me names? I could understand it in Harrison, where everybody knew who I was, who my mama was. But those women don't even know me."

A shadow of regret passed across Creed's eyes, and she saw a muscle twitch in his jaw before he said, "They knew you were with me."

"They don't know you, either!"

"Jassy . . ."

She was getting angrier by the minute. "Doesn't it make you mad, having people look down on you like that?"

He loosed a weary sigh. "It used to, but what the hell, you can't change the world." He slid his knuckles over her cheek. "I warned you how it would be."

"I know."

"But you didn't believe me."

Jassy shrugged. "I guess not."

"Come on, let's go get my horse and get the hell out of here."

Later that night, Jassy was still fretting over what she'd heard in town. Sitting beside the campfire, her hands wrapped around a cup of hot black coffee, she stared into the dancing flames, wondering why those women had felt the need to judge her. She'd heard the disdain in their voices, the righteous indignation, but she couldn't understand it. They didn't know anything about her except that she was with

Creed, and they had labeled her as white trash. It was so unfair!

"Jassy?"

She glanced up to find Creed standing beside her.

"You okay?"

"Yes."

"You're not still brooding about what those women said, are you?"

Her gaze slid away from his. "Sort of. I just want to be respectable, Creed. Is that asking too much?"

"No, honey. But if you're after respectability, you're keeping the wrong kind of company."

She wanted to argue with him, but deep down she knew he was right, at least in part. No one would ever call Creed Maddigan respectable. Right or wrong, she knew now that there were those who would never forgive him for being a half-breed, even though he had nothing to do with the circumstances of his birth. She knew, too, that his reputation as a hired gun would never be socially acceptable.

Nevertheless, he was the kindest, most wonderful man she had ever known. Even though she had known him only a short while, he'd always been there when she needed him, whether it was saving her from Harry Coulter's rough handling in an alley or comforting her after her mother died, Creed had been there, giving her a strong arm to lean on and a shoulder to cry on.

Creed added some wood to the fire, then glanced down at Jassy, his stomach clenching when he saw her pensive expression.

"You wouldn't be having second thoughts about running off with me, would you?" he asked.

Jassy shook her head vigorously. "No. I just don't understand why people think the way they do. Everybody in town thought Harry Coulter was such a decent, upstanding young man because he went to church with his mother on Sunday. And all the ladies thought Billy Padden was a nice boy just because his father's the preacher."

She gazed at him intently, her eyes luminous. "Neither of them was half as honorable as you are."

Creed snorted with disdain. "Honorable? Me?"

"Yes, you. I've thrown myself at you several times, and yet you've never taken advantage of me." Her cheeks were on fire, but she couldn't seem to stop the flow of words even as she wondered whatever had possessed her to broach the subject in the first place. "I even asked you to make love to me, and you refused."

"Don't ask me again."

"What?"

"You heard me. I'm not an honorable man, Jassy, and I'm not a saint. I want you more than I've ever wanted anything in my life."

"Really?" His words pleased her, filling her

with delight, and confusion. "Then why didn't you . . . ?"

"You said it yourself. You want to be respectable, and that's something I'll never be. Something I've never wanted."

Jassy stared into the depths of Creed's turbulent black eyes and all thought of being respectable fled her mind. He was so tall, so breathtakingly handsome. The firelight played over the hard planes and angles of his face, so that his profile was half in shadow. She remembered the feel of that hard muscular body pressed against her own, the taste of his kisses. Would he really make love to her if she dared ask him again? He might claim that he had no honor, he might very well ravish her, but she knew deep in her heart that, once he had made love to her, he would never abandon her.

Slowly, her heart pounding wildly, she stood up. "Creed." Rising on tiptoe, she wrapped her arms around his neck.

"Jassy, don't."

"I'm asking, Creed. Make love to me."

"Jassy . . ."

"I don't care what people will think. I don't want to be respectable if it means I can't have you."

Slowly, deliberately, he removed her arms from around his neck.

"Jassy, think about what you're doing. When we get to Frisco, no one will know who you are or where you came from. You can start a whole new life for yourself, a decent life."

"What good's a decent life if you won't share it with me?" she cried, unable to keep the hurt from her voice. "I thought you cared for me, at least a little."

"I do, and you know it."

"Why did you bring me with you if you're just going to dump me in San Francisco?"

"You ask the damnedest questions," Creed muttered.

"Why, Creed?" she whispered.

He looked deep into her eyes, beautiful brown eyes filled with love and hope.

"Creed?"

He swore softly, viciously, and then he yanked her up against his body and covered her mouth with his. It was a rough kiss, harsh and demanding, filled with passion and anger and an overriding sense of helplessness. He'd fought rustlers, he'd faced armed men, but he had no defense against the sweet innocence of Jassy McCloud.

Jassy clung to his shoulders as the world spun out of focus. He'd kissed her before, sometimes gently, sometimes passionately, but never like this. His arm was rock-hard around her waist, imprisoning her body against his, while his other hand moved restlessly up and down her back, then cupped her buttocks, drawing her up against him so that she could feel the evidence of his desire.

She returned his kiss, glorying in his touch,

in his nearness. He wanted her. And she wanted him.

His kiss deepened, his tongue teasing hers, until she felt as though her whole body was on fire. With a soft moan, she stood on tiptoe and pressed herself against him, her breasts crushed against his chest, her whole body quivering with need.

He groaned, as if he was in pain, and then, abruptly, he pushed her away.

"What is it?" she cried. "What's wrong?"

"Not here, Jassy. Not like this."

"Damn you, Creed Maddigan, if you don't finish what you started, I'll never forgive you! Not the longest day I live!"

He threw her a maddening grin. "Yes, you will."

"I won't!" She glared up at him, her whole body tingling with need and unfulfilled desire.

"Jassy, listen." He reached for her, but she backed away, her eyes mutinous, her lips bruised from his kisses.

"Leave me alone."

"Jassy, I want your first time to be special. I . . ." he broke off, feeling suddenly embarrassed.

"Go on."

"I want it to be in a nice hotel, with a feather tick. I want to . . ." He swore softly. "I want to seduce you with flowers and champagne and carry you off to bed. I don't want to take you here, in the dirt, like some stag in rut."

"Oh, Creed," Jassy murmured, her eyes shining. "I hope there's a hotel nearby."

"Not near enough," he muttered.

This time, when he reached for her, she didn't back away, but went willingly into his arms.

"I can't fight it any longer, Jassy," he murmured helplessly. "I can't fight you any longer." Resting his chin on the top of her head, he let out a sigh of resignation. "But if we're gonna do this, we're gonna do it right."

"What do you mean?" she asked, her voice muffled against his chest.

"I mean we're getting married in the next town."

"Married!"

"I haven't done many things right in my life, but this is one time we're doing it by the book, if you'll have me." He tipped her head up so he could see her face. "Will you marry me, Jasmine Alexandria McCloud?"

"Oh, yes."

"I think you're making a big mistake."

"Why, Creed Maddigan," she purred, batting her eyelashes at him, "you say the most romantic things."

"I can't help it, Jassy girl," he replied solemnly. "As your friend, I'd advise you to say no."

Jassy laughed softly. "I'm sure no girl in all the world has ever received a proposal quite like this one."

"I only want what's best for you, honey, and I'm afraid I'm not it."

"I think you are."

He grinned ruefully. "I hope you're right." Lowering his head, he kissed her brow, her cheeks, the tip of her nose. "Go to bed, Jassy, before all my good intentions go up in smoke."

Happiness bubbled inside her as she rose on her tiptoes to kiss him good night.

"I love you, Creed. I'll make you a good wife, I promise." She looked up at him, hoping he'd say he loved her, too, but not expecting it. Some men found it hard to say the words, but she was certain he cared, certain that, in time, he'd say the words she longed to hear.

He stood by the fire, watching while she climbed under the covers. There was no doubt in his mind that Jassy would make him the best wife a man ever had.

He only wondered if he was capable of being the kind of husband she deserved.

Chapter Sixteen

He knew, even before he opened his eyes, that something was wrong. Then he heard it again, the sound of wary footsteps muffled by the soft dirt.

A whiff of rawhide and bear grease seeped into his nostrils.

Indians, he thought. But how many?

For a moment, Creed lay still, all his senses alert. A prickling along his spine warned him that any sudden move could cost him his life, and Jassy's as well.

Very slowly, he opened his eyes.

Warriors stood on either side of him, just out of reach, their faces streaked with war paint, their long black hair adorned with feathers. The man to Creed's left held a reasonably new Winchester rifle, the barrel aimed at Creed's chest. The warrior to his right held a war lance decorated with a single white eagle feather. And a pair of long blond scalps.

Without moving his head, Creed glanced at Jassy. She was still asleep, her cheek pillowed on her hand, her hair spread over the ground sheet like a burnished halo.

Two warriors stood at the foot of her bedroll, both armed with repeating rifles.

Out of the corner of his eye, he could see two more warriors standing a few yards away. Both were well-armed.

In the distance, Creed spotted a novice warrior holding the Indians' horses.

Creed swallowed hard. The Indians were Crow, judging by their shields and moccasins. Had they been Lakota, he might have been able to convince them that he was one of them. Unfortunately, the Crow didn't care much for the Lakota. But then, the Lakota had no use for the Crow, either. In order to gain the support of the Federal Government in protecting their hunting lands, the Crow had served as scouts for the Army, a fact that did nothing to endear them to the Lakota.

"Creed." Jassy's voice called out to him, quivering with fear.

"Don't move," he warned, keeping his voice low, hoping he didn't sound half as worried as he felt.

The warrior with the lance prodded Creed in

the side, gesturing for him to stand up.

Slowly, Creed did as he was told, noticing as he did so that the Indians had already ransacked their camp, helping themselves to their supplies, to his weapons, and Jassy's new clothes.

He heard Jassy shriek with alarm as one of the warriors grabbed her by the arm and hauled her to her feet, then pushed her toward the small, stone-ringed pit that had housed last night's campfire.

"I think they want you to fix them something to eat," Creed said.

He looked at the Indian nearest him and made motions like he was eating. The warrior nodded.

While Jassy prepared breakfast, one of the warriors lashed Creed's hands behind his back, then forced him to his knees. Another warrior knelt beside Creed and began going through his pockets—taking his tobacco, slipping the knife from inside his boot, and tossing a handful of greenbacks into the fire.

Giving Creed a shove that clearly told him to stay put, the Indian went to join the others, who had gathered around Jassy, talking and gesturing while they watched her fry up bacon and potatoes.

Jassy's hands were trembling so hard that she could barely hold on to the frying pan. Never, never, had she been so frightened. Time and again she glanced over her shoulder at Creed, and each time he smiled reassuringly, but even that didn't allay her fears.

These were Indians, wild Indians, capable of atrocities beyond her imagination. She hadn't missed the long blond scalps fluttering on the end of the lance. She had heard enough about Indians to know war paint when she saw it, to realize that her life and—she swallowed hard—her virtue were in danger.

She had heard countless stories about women who had been taken captive, who had been tortured and raped by savages. She had listened in horror to lurid tales of women who had killed themselves rather than submit to rape and degradation.

Of course, there were almost as many stories of women who had embraced the Indian way of life, who had married their captors, learned their language and customs, and borne their children. Outrageous stories of women who had refused to be rescued, who had gone running back to their Indian men when they were forcibly taken away.

She glanced at the faces of the Indians as she opened a can of beans, looking for some sign of mercy or compassion, but it was impossible to see any kind of expression, any kind of emotion, beneath the grotesque paint.

When the food was ready, the warriors gathered around, eating with their fingers and their knives. As casually as she could, Jassy started walking toward Creed, only to have one of the warriors grab her by the ankle.

"You. Stay."

She stared at the Indian mutely, then glanced at Creed.

"Do what he says, honey."

In minutes, the Indians were through eating. The warrior nearest Jassy grabbed her by the arm and quickly tied her hands behind her back.

The other warriors surrounded Creed, their dark eyes malevolent, their voices angry.

His stomach churning with dread, Creed scrambled to his feet. Head high, he glared at his captors, wondering if they were going to kill him outright or drag it out.

He glanced quickly at Jassy. Her face was beyond pale; her eyes were wide with fear. He'd failed her, he thought bleakly, and felt a gut-wrenching ache. They would probably kill him; slow or quick, in the end it wouldn't matter, but Jassy . . . He groaned low in his throat as he thought of her being passed from one warrior to another.

And then there was no more time to worry about Jassy's fate.

The first blow was no more than a slap, meant to humiliate, not hurt. The second was a little harder, the sound of flesh striking flesh echoing loudly in the stillness of the morning.

Jassy cried out as one of the warriors struck Creed across the face with the end of his bow, raising a long red welt. She covered her eyes as the Indians circled Creed, closing in on him like wolves around a bloody carcass as they repeatedly struck him with their fists and their weapons.

With his hands bound behind his back, Creed was virtually helpless, although he managed to kick one of the warriors in the groin before the others overpowered him, driving him backward to the ground.

Creed drew his knees up to his chest and bowed his head in an effort to shield his face and groin from the blows that were coming harder and faster. Fists and feet pummeled his back, drove the breath from his lungs, until his whole body was throbbing with pain. A red mist clouded his vision; blood spurted from his nose and trickled down the side of his mouth. He heard the faint sound of weeping, and then blackness washed over him, mercifully sucking him down, down, into nothingness . . .

Jassy was crying openly now, the tears flowing down her cheeks. She flinched each time she heard a fist strike flesh. Blood dripped from multiple cuts on Creed's face and neck and arms. When would they stop? Why wouldn't they stop? They were killing him. She closed her eyes, unable to watch any longer. She wished she could block out the sound as well.

And then, abruptly, the Indians turned their backs on Creed and walked away.

Jassy stared at Creed. His clothes were torn,

splattered with blood. And he didn't seem to be breathing.

"No," she whispered. "No, please."

She started to go to him, but the Indian nearest her grabbed her around the waist and tossed her, none too gently, onto the back of a horse. With a grunt, he swung up behind her and rode away.

Twisting around, Jassy gazed over the warrior's shoulder. Creed lay as before, limp and unmoving, his face and body covered with dirt and blood.

Pain. Waves and waves of pain washed over him and receded, only to return. The pain grew in intensity as he swam through thick layers of darkness toward consciousness.

Creed groaned low in his throat as full awareness returned. There was the taste of blood and dirt in his mouth. His left eye was swollen almost shut. He lay still for a long while, learning to live with the pain, and then he began to work the rope that bound his hands. He grimaced as the narrow strip of rawhide cut deep into his wrists.

He was sweating and swearing profusely, the skin on his wrists slick with blood, before he managed to free his hands.

Feeling sick and exhausted, he closed his eyes, felt himself again spiraling down, down, into blessed oblivion.

It was dark and he was shivering with the

cold when he awoke the second time. Moving carefully, he sat up, one arm wrapped protectively around his midsection. Every breath sent new waves of pain skittering through him. He figured he had a couple of badly bruised ribs, but he didn't think anything was broken, thank God.

Cautiously, he tried to stand up, but he just didn't have the strength. Fighting the urge to vomit, he sat with his back against a tree, taking slow, shallow breaths. After a while, he lifted a hand to his face. There was a deep cut across his left cheek, his upper lip was split, and his lower lip was about twice its normal size. His nose, though caked with blood, didn't seem to be broken.

He swore softly as he began to shiver uncontrollably. He was cold, so damn cold. And thirsty. It would be so easy, he thought wearily, so easy to just lie down and surrender to the cold and the pain.

But he couldn't stay where he was. He had to go after Jassy, had to get her away from the Indians before it was too late, before they reached the safety of their village.

Teeth clenched against the pain, he struggled to his hands and knees, feeling the nausea roiling in his gut. Eyes closed, head hanging, he panted softly for a few minutes and then, swearing softly, he admitted defeat.

He wasn't going anywhere, not tonight.

Tomorrow, he thought. He'd start at first light

tomorrow. He couldn't track them in the dark, anyway. For now, he needed to sleep.

Closing his eyes, he curled up into a tight ball, his pain-wracked body shivering violently as it tried to warm itself.

"Jassy." He murmured her name over and over again, like a prayer, until sleep overtook him.

Her fear grew with each passing mile. Fear of what would happen to her when the Indians reached their destination. Fear for Creed. She prayed fervently that he was still alive, even though she knew he must be dead. No one could endure such a beating and survive.

It was near dawn when the Indians made camp. The Indian who had taken her pushed her down on the ground, then covered her with a blanket. Jassy went rigid with horror and shock when he crawled under the blanket with her.

He mumbled something she didn't understand, then turned on his side. A moment later, she heard him snoring softly.

The tears came then. Tears of fright. Tears of grief. Tears of relief because she was still alive. She thought of Creed, picturing him lying dead in the middle of the prairie, his body being mutilated by wild animals. The knowledge that she would never see him again was more horrible than the unknown fate that awaited her.

She tossed and turned for hours, unable to

sleep. Every time she closed her eyes, she saw Creed sprawled in the dirt while the Indians hit him over and over again. She could hear the sounds of their fists and their blows striking his flesh, hear Creed's muffled grunts of pain. And now he was dead and she would never see him again. Her father had left her; her mother was dead; Rose had taken her money and run off. And now Creed was dead, and she was alone in the world, at the mercy of savage Indians. . . .

Jassy's eyes were gritty with lack of sleep when her captor rolled nimbly to his feet early the following morning. He untied her hands, which had gone numb long since, then spoke to her in a harsh, guttural tongue, gesturing toward the chaparral with his hand.

Hoping he was saying what she thought he was, Jassy picked her way toward the brush. Squatting behind a tall shrub, she relieved herself, thinking that she had never in her life felt so utterly filthy. Her hair needed combing. Her mouth tasted like the inside of a spittoon. Her clothing was dirty and wrinkled. Her wrists were sore from being bound; her hands were numb.

And then she remembered that Creed was dead, and her discomfort no longer seemed important.

After adjusting her skirts, she peered around the scrub brush. The Indians were breaking camp. No one seemed to be paying any attention to her.

Quick as a wink, she lifted her skirts and began to run, away from the savages who had killed Creed and killed all her hopes for the future with him.

She ran blindly, not knowing or caring where she was going, knowing only that she had to get away.

The ground blurred beneath her feet. Her heart was hammering wildly. A sharp pain darted along her side, and still she ran—away from the horror and the memory of Creed's death, away from the terror that awaited her at the hands of her captor.

Her blood was pounding in her ears like thunder and the pain in her side was knife sharp, when the strength went out of her legs and she sprawled facedown in the dirt.

Sobbing, she scrambled to her knees, knuckling the tears from her eyes.

It was then that she saw the Indian. He was sitting on his horse a few yards behind her, his expression as empty as the sky.

"No." Jassy shook her head.

She stood up as he rode toward her. It had all been for nothing.

Left. Right. Left. With dogged determination, Creed put one foot in front of the other.

Each step sent knife-like slashes of pain lancing through him.

Each step carried him that much closer to Jassy.

He squinted up at the sun. He'd been walking for about two hours, although it seemed like two days. Every inch of his body ached. His throat was as dry as the dust beneath his feet. His stomach alternated between hunger and nausea, and still he kept going.

When he saw the stream, he thought it was an illusion conjured up by his thirst.

"It isn't real," he muttered, but he flopped down on his belly and buried his head beneath the water.

It was real. Cold and wet, it was sweeter than anything he had ever tasted. He drank slowly, only a small amount at a time, knowing he'd vomit it all back up again if he drank too much too fast. But, Lord, it was tempting, so tempting.

When he had taken the edge off his thirst, he stripped off his tattered clothing and sank down in the water, letting the current rinse away the dirt and the blood that covered him from head to foot.

He felt considerably better when he emerged from the water. Moving upriver, he took another drink, rinsed the dirt and blood from his shirt and pants as best he could, then spread his clothes over a rock to dry.

Buck naked, he stretched out on a scrawny patch of yellow grass and closed his eyes, basking in the heat of the sun.

It was late afternoon when he woke. His clothes were dry and stiff, and he groaned softly as he pulled on his pants, then shrugged into his shirt.

Damn, but he felt like the very devil, he mused as he dragged a hand across his jaw. His left eye was still swollen, the cut on his cheek throbbed with a dull ache, and his whole body felt as if it had been stomped by a loco bronc.

But he was alive.

Alive and hungry.

And there were fish in the stream.

Stretching out on his stomach on the bank, he cupped his hands in the water and waited.

Twenty minutes later, there was one less trout in the stream.

The Indians had taken his tobacco, but they hadn't found his matches. In a short time, he had the fish spitted over a small fire.

A slow grin spread over Creed's face as he stared into the flames. Now, all he needed was a horse, a gun, and a little luck.

"Hold on, Jassy," he muttered softly. "I'm coming."

She was tired and hungry and frightened out of her mind. Every minute took her farther away from civilization and deeper into the heart of Indian country.

She was keenly aware of the warrior riding behind her, of the heavily muscled arm that curved around her waist.

They rode steadily for hours, stopping only once to water the horses. Jassy needed to relieve herself, but the Indian didn't offer her the chance and she had a terrible feeling that, if she wasn't allowed a few minutes' privacy, she was going to embarrass herself.

It was near dusk when the Indians made camp for the night. Her backside was numb from spending so many hours straddling a horse, and her back and shoulders ached. Her legs felt like rubber when her captor lifted her from the back of his pony. Desperate to relieve herself, Jassy stumbled into the bushes.

Squatting in the short yellow grass, she closed her eyes, fighting back the urge to cry. What good would crying do now? There was no one to hear her, at least no one who cared.

Totally dispirited, she stared into the gathering darkness, wondering if she dared risk running away again. But where would she go? She had no idea where she was. Still, it would be infinitely better to die in the wilderness than be ravished by savages.

She was trying to decide which way to go when her captor appeared, a knowing smirk in his deep black eyes as he gestured for her to return to their campsite.

Feet dragging, she did as she was told. When they reached the others, her captor gave her a shove, then leaned down and tied her hands together. She felt a surge of gratitude because he hadn't secured her hands behind her back, and then she thrust the thought away. She wouldn't feel anything for this man except hatred. She glared at him as he thrust a hunk of jerked meat at her.

It looked dry and old and decidedly tasteless, but she was too hungry to be choosy. Scowling, she reached for the jerky, wishing she had the nerve to throw it back in his face. She accepted the bladder he offered her, shivering with revulsion as she put her mouth where his had been, but a raging thirst overcame her squeamishness and she took a long drink of the water, which was warm but still quenched her thirst.

Jassy gnawed on the jerky as she stared into the flames. Creed was dead. She couldn't seem to think of anything but that. She'd never see him again, never hear his laugh or feel the touch of his hand, so gentle in her hair. She lifted her hands, fingering the beaded choker at her throat. It was all she had left of him now, that and her memories.

She remembered the way Creed had come to her rescue in the alley, the sound of his voice, so deep and soft, when he'd asked her name. She recalled how he had looked the following morning when she had gone to his hotel room to thank him for his help, the odd expression in his eyes when she had handed him a plate of cookies. She remembered staring at him, at his naked chest, at the gun he had shoved into the waistband of his trousers. He'd bought her a dress—the first new dress she'd had in years. He had comforted her the day she buried her mother. No one else had offered her a word of solace. Not the minister, who might have at least lied and said he was sorry. Not even Rose. Only Creed. He had held her while she cried, gently stroking her hair. He had kept her company when Rose went off to Denver with Ray Coulter. Like a guardian angel, he had always been there when she needed him the most. And now he was gone.

Steeped in sorrow and despair, she curled up on the ground, her cheek pillowed on her bound hands.

Creed was dead, and she felt empty and alone. She tried to cry, wanted to cry, but the tears wouldn't come.

Dry-eyed, she stared into the darkness. Creed was dead, and nothing else mattered.

Chapter Seventeen

Creed stared into the distance, wondering why he didn't just lie down and die. He'd been walking for two days, quietly cussing himself for staying in Harrison when he should have gone to Black Hawk. He cursed the Indians, the heat, and the burning sand. He cursed Jassy for being young and irresistible, and himself for not having the good sense to admit he was licked.

He was tired and hungry, sore from head to foot, and madder than hell.

And more worried than he cared to admit.

Two days. Anything could have happened to her in that time. She could have been raped. Killed.

He shook the thought from his mind, refusing even to consider such a thing.

He focused his attention on the pony tracks that stretched northward. Except for their trail, the Indians had left little sign of their passing.

A faint line of greenery promised water, and Creed quickened his stride, one arm wrapped protectively around his mid-section.

When he reached the stream, he dropped to his knees, grunting softly as he jarred his bruised ribs.

For a moment, he just sat there, waiting for the pain to pass, and then he stretched out on his belly and took a long, slow swallow. When his thirst was quenched, he splashed water over his face and chest.

Closing his eyes, he rested his head on his forearm. From a distant corner of his mind came near-forgotten Lakota words of gratitude.

"Pilamaya, Ate."

Thank you, Father. For the tall grass. For the clear water. For the warm sun. For the buffalo. As a child, he had been taught to be thankful for so many things. What had happened to that gratitude, that sense of wonder, that had filled his mind and heart when he was young?

Thank you, Father. For life. For wisdom. For a warrior's strength and courage. For Jassy.

Jassy. She had restored his faith in people, given him a new sense of wonder. She had baked him cookies! The memory made him smile. What other woman would bring cookies to a hired gun? He had taken her to the valley outside Harrison and seen it again, new and fresh, through her eyes. How long had it been since he'd taken time to appreciate the beauty of the wildflowers that bloomed in the valley, the way the sunlight danced and shimmered on the small blue pool, the stately grace of the trees that housed the birds and provided shade in the summer's heat?

Jassy. In spite of her dismal upbringing, in spite of the fact that her mother and sister were whores, Jassy had remained untouched by ugliness, by bitterness, though she had every right to be bitter. Somehow, she had managed to hang on to her youth, her innocence, her faith that things would get better. He thought of her wearing the beaded choker his grandmother had given him.

His grandmother, bless her. Except for Jassy, Okoka was the only woman who had ever loved him wholly and completely, who had expected the best of him and refused to settle for less. Jassy, with hair like a dull flame and the spirit of a Lakota warrior. He couldn't let her down now.

Eyes closed, he murmured a fervent prayer to *Wakan Tanka*, praying for the Great Spirit's help in finding Jassy, praying for the strength to go on.

He took another drink from the river, savoring the sweetness of the cool water. Then he stood up, determined to find Jassy or die trying.

It was near dusk when Creed neared another water hole. Covered with dust, his throat as dry as the ground at his feet, he almost spooked the horse before he saw it.

Halting in mid-stride, Creed held his breath while his gaze moved over the animal. It was an Indian pony, rawhide tough, with a deep chest and wide, intelligent eyes.

Extending one hand, Creed approached the horse, surprised that the pinto didn't bolt. Then he saw the rope tangled around the horse's fore-legs.

Eyes wide, nostrils flared, the horse backed up, but the rope acted like hobbles, preventing the animal from running away.

"Easy, girl," Creed said softly. "Easy. I'm not gonna hurt you."

The mare's ears twitched at the sound of his voice, and then she lowered her head and sniffed his hand. Careful not to make any sudden moves, Creed patted her neck, a little awed by the mare's unexpected appearance. A lucky coincidence, he mused, or a gift from the Great Spirit?

"Easy, girl." Taking hold of the horse's mane, he untangled the rope from her legs and fashioned a rough hackamore.

"Pilamaya, Ate," Creed murmured, and wondered how much better and simpler his life might have been if he'd adhered to his grandmother's teachings, if he'd put his trust in *Wakan Tanka* instead of a steady hand and a fast draw.

But there was no point in rehashing the past

or wondering what might have been if he'd followed a different road. It was too late to turn back now, too late to abandon the habits of a lifetime. He was a hired gun, and no fit company for decent people. If he'd remembered that sooner, Jassy's life wouldn't be in danger now.

Gritting his teeth, he swung onto the pinto's back. "I'm coming, Jassy," he murmured. "God help me, I'm coming."

Jassy pulled the blanket over her head. Three days had passed since the Indians had abducted her. Three days. And nights.

Tears stung her eyes. It had been the worst three days of her life. Worse than the day her father left home. Worse than the day her mother was killed. Worse than having Rose run off.

She closed her eyes, and immediately Creed's image rose up in her mind, his hair as dark as the night, his eyes as deep and black as a bottomless pit—sometimes cold and unfathomable, sometimes blazing with desire.

Tears coursed down her cheeks. He was dead. She wished the Indians had killed her, too. At least then her troubles would be over and she wouldn't be afraid anymore. And she was afraid. Horribly, terribly afraid. Of the Indian who had captured her. Of the look in his eye. Of what would happen when they reached their destination. So far, he hadn't touched her. She should have been relieved, but for some reason, that only frightened her more. If he didn't intend to rape her, what was he going to do with her? Visions of being cruelly tortured crowded her mind during the day and haunted her dreams at night.

They reached the Indian village late the following morning. Jassy stared at the numerous lodges and experienced a heart-stopping sense of fear. She tried to find comfort by reminding herself that Creed had been half Indian, but it didn't help.

Black eyes filled with distrust and hatred stared up at her as they rode into the camp. A woman spat in her direction, others reviled her in a harsh, guttural tongue, and Jassy realized that some words sounded the same in any language.

Her captor reined his horse to a halt in front of a large tipi. Vaulting from the horse's back, he lifted Jassy to the ground, then shoved her into the lodge.

The inside was cool and dim. Jassy glanced around, her gaze resting on what she assumed was a pile of furs, until the pile moved and she saw two dark eyes staring at her and realized that an old woman lay under the furs.

Her captor spoke to the woman for several minutes and then, using gestures and a few words of English, informed Jassy that she was to care for the old woman.

For Jassy, the next few days were like something out of a nightmare. She was scorned and reviled by the Indian women whenever she left the lodge to fetch water or wood or to try her hand at cooking in the huge iron pot that hung on a tripod outside the tipi.

Her days were spent looking after the cranky old woman—bathing her, cooking for her, feeding her, dressing her, helping her outside to relieve herself.

The old woman, who was partially paralyzed from the waist down, spent most of the day sleeping, which left Jassy with a great deal of time on her hands with nothing to do but sit outside and try to ignore the jeers and dirty looks that came her way, or sit inside the dusky lodge and lament her fate while she listened to the old woman snore.

Nights, she slept beside the fire, wrapped in a buffalo robe, afraid to close her eyes for fear her captor would try to molest her, though he had made no move to touch her in any way.

A week passed. In that time, Jassy learned that the warrior who had captured her spoke more than a little English. She learned that his name was Chah-ee-chopes, that the old woman was his mother, and that his wife and little daughter had been killed by soldiers in the same attack that had crippled his mother.

In stilted English and sign language, Chah-ee-chopes told her that he had been on a raid of vengeance when the war party found her and Creed. He had thought it a fitting form of revenge that the white man should be killed and a white woman should be forced to look after his mother, whose name was Oo-je-en-a-he-ha, since it had been a white man who had crippled her.

Chah-ee-chopes' story touched Jassy's heart and eased some of her fears. He hadn't captured her to abuse her or torture her, but to care for his mother.

As the days passed, Jassy learned a little of the Indians' daily routine. Early every morning, the herald called for the people to get out of bed, bathe, and drink all the water they could.

"Put water on your body," he called. "Get up and drink your fill. Make your blood thin."

Jassy questioned Chah-ee-chopes and learned that the Crow believed that drinking plenty of water kept the blood thin, which would keep a person from getting sick. Thin blood wouldn't clog, but ran freely through a person's veins. A person who didn't drink a lot of water wouldn't live long.

She learned that when there was meat in camp, a man who was not concerned with joining a war party or taking part in a ceremony tended to idle away his days in his lodge. Jassy realized, of course, that among the Indians, going to war and providing meat were a man's main occupations. Occasionally, she saw men making arrowheads of stone or bone, but shafts and bows were made by experts. Only little boys used bows made of wood; a warrior's bow was made of horn or antler with a backing of sinew.

Still, Crow men appeared lazy when compared to the women, who were never idle. They spent their days sewing, mending, drying meat, tanning hides, and cooking.

Now that she was no longer quite so afraid of him, Jassy realized that Chah-ee-chopes was a handsome young man. She noticed that he was greatly admired by the Crow women and that the men held him in high esteem.

One night, there was a large gathering in the middle of the camp. Jassy sat in the shadows, watching as the men danced.

When the dancing stopped, Chah-ee-chopes stood up and began to speak. He would say something, then pause, and one of the drummers would strike the drum.

When Chah-ee-chopes sat down, another man stood up to speak. And then another.

Later, Jassy asked Chah-ee-chopes what he had said and learned that at most large gatherings, the men enumerated their deeds. There were four deeds of valor that brought special honor to a warrior. The first was counting coup on an enemy, the second was taking a bow or a gun from an enemy in hand-to-hand combat, the third was the theft of a horse picketed within a hostile camp, and the fourth was being the pipe-owner or raid-planner. A man who could claim any of these deeds was called *araxsi'wice*, or an honor-owner. To be a chief, a man must have accomplished at least one deed of valor.

"You must have done many brave things," Jassy mused, remembering how many times the drums had beat.

Chah-ee-chopes nodded. "I have counted coup. I have captured a gun and a bow. I led a war party. I have raided the enemy for horses and scalps. I have been to war many times."

Jassy nodded. He was, indeed, a warrior. And yet, for all that, he had treated her with kindness and respect.

That night, curled up in the warmth of a buffalo robe, Jassy offered a silent prayer, thanking God that she was still alive, that she wasn't being mistreated, and that the warrior who had captured her seemed to be a man of honor.

Lying there, listening to the faint sounds of the night, she prayed for Creed's soul.

The tears came then, tears of grief because she would never see him again, never hear his voice murmuring her name, never again feel the touch of his hand.

Her eyes burned and her throat ached as she wept for the life they might have shared, a life that was now forever lost.

As the last of her tears dried, Jassy vowed to stop feeling sorry for herself. Creed was gone, and all the crying in the world would not bring him back.

Tomorrow, she would try to make the best of her life. She would endeavor to learn the Crow language. She would be nicer to Oo-je-en-a-he-ha. She would wear the doeskin dress, leggings, and moccasins that Chah-ee-chopes had provided for her.

A single tear trickled down Jassy's cheek as she touched the beaded choker at her throat. It was all she had left of Creed.

Ruthlessly, she wiped the tear away. The time for tears was past.

Chapter Eighteen

Creed sat huddled near a small fire. He'd spent thirteen hours in the saddle, and his bruised ribs ached like the very devil.

He grimaced as he lifted a cautious hand to his face. The swelling in his left eye was almost gone. His fingertip traced the edges of the gash on his left cheek and he swore softly, knowing there would be a jagged scar when the cut healed. As if he didn't have enough scars, he mused ruefully, and then shrugged. Another scar was the least of his problems.

He stared into the dancing flames and thought about Jassy, always and forever Jassy. It had been almost a week since the Indians had abducted her. He wondered how she was getting along, how the Indians were treating her.

Creed swore softly, the thought of Jassy being manhandled by the warrior who had taken her tying his stomach in knots.

Iyokipi, Ate . . . Please, Father, let her be alive. Please, Father, don't let them hurt her. Please, please, please . . .

He ran a hand through his hair. With luck, he would catch up with the Crow sometime tomorrow. And then what? He had no weapons, nothing to bargain with. And yet he couldn't just leave her there. He'd got her into this mess, and by damn, he'd get her out!

He just wished he knew how.

Jassy was returning from the river when she heard the commotion. Curious, she walked toward the center of camp, wondering what was causing such a ruckus in the middle of the afternoon.

Standing on tiptoe, she peered over the shoulder of the warrior in front of her. For a moment, she could only stare, unable to believe her eyes.

"Creed." His name whispered past her lips. He was alive. Relief and joy erupted within her and as quickly disappeared. He was alive, but for how long?

She glanced at the faces of the Indians around her. The women looked at Creed with hatred, but there was curiosity and admiration in the eyes of the men.

And then Creed's gaze met hers, and for a moment she forgot everything but the fact that he was alive, that he was there. He gave her a reassuring wink, then turned his attention to the warrior who was speaking to him in sign language.

She had no idea what they were saying, but after several minutes, Creed dismounted, handing the reins of his horse to a young boy.

A moment later, Chah-ee-chopes led her into his lodge and closed the door flap. "White man says he is husband. Is true?"

Jassy nodded vigorously. "Yes."

Chah-ee-chopes grunted softly.

Oo-je-en-a-he-ha sat up, her dark eyes narrowed as she fired off a burst of rapid Crow. Chah-ee-chopes silenced the old woman with a wave of his hand, then fixed Jassy with a long, assessing glance.

"You, here, wait," he said and left the lodge.

Jassy paced back and forth for several minutes, wondering what was happening outside. Finally, unable to stand the suspense, she peered out the door flap.

It looked as if every Indian in the village had assembled in the middle of the camp. She could hear voices raised, not in anger, but in anticipation, reminding her of the noisy excitement that had preceded horse races or fisticuffs back in Harrison.

Curious, she left the lodge, ignoring Oo-je-e-en-he-ha's admonition to stay inside.

No one paid her any mind as she took a place in the back row of onlookers. She knew immediately what was happening. Chah-ee-chopes, stripped down to only a breechclout and moccasins, a knife in his hand, stood to her left. Creed, wearing only his trousers, stood across from the Crow warrior. His face and body still showed the effects of the beating he had received. Faint bruises could be seen on his chest; his left eye, though no longer swollen, was still discolored.

She saw him flinch as he accepted a knife from an aged warrior in the crowd, and she wondered how he was going to fight when he was still hurting.

Creed and Chah-ee-chopes stared at each other for an endless, silent moment, and Jassy knew with terrible certainty that they were fighting over her.

They circled each other warily, like two wolves on the scent of blood. Creed was taller, broader, and heavier. At any other time, he would have won hands down. But now he moved stiffly, one arm curved protectively around his ribcage.

The knowledge that his opponent was not up to full fighting strength made Chah-ee-chopes reckless. With a cry, he lunged forward, his knife eager for blood, but he had badly underestimated his adversary and his blade found only empty air as Creed sidestepped at the last moment, his knife making a wide slashing arc that sliced into Chah-ee-chopes' right shoulder.

With a cry of rage, Chah-ee-chopes whirled

around and lashed out, his blade missing Creed by inches.

Heart pounding with fear, Jassy watched as they circled each other, coming together again and again, with Chah-ee-chopes always on the attack. It was only a matter of time, Jassy thought hopelessly. Creed was tiring fast. All Chah-ee-chopes had to do was wear him down until his reflexes slowed, then close in for the kill. And yet, in spite of everything, Creed had managed to avoid the warrior's knife while he himself had drawn blood three times.

From the corner of his eye, Creed saw Jassy in the crowd, her eyes wide, her face drained of color. Seeing her filled him with a renewed sense of urgency. Taking a deep breath, he faced Chah-ee-chopes and waited.

The next time the warrior lunged at him, Creed let him come, and then, at the last possible second, he stepped aside and brought his fist down on the back of the warrior's neck. Chah-ee-chopes hit the ground hard.

Ignoring the throbbing ache in his side, Creed straddled the Crow. Grabbing a handful of the warrior's hair, he jerked his head back and placed his knife at the man's throat.

Jassy held her breath, waiting to see whether Chah-ee-chopes would die or yield. The seconds ticked by, each one seeming longer than the last as everyone waited for Chah-ee-chopes' decision.

Slowly, the tension drained out of the warrior's body. Reluctantly, but resolutely, he dropped his knife.

Creed loosed a long sigh as he stood up. Tossing his own weapon aside, he wrapped one arm around his middle. Then he made his way toward Jassy.

The Indians made no move to stop him.

"Creed."

"It's all right, Jassy," he murmured as he drew her into his arms. "Everything's gonna be all right."

She gazed up at him, her heart beating fast. "I thought you were dead," she whispered, and burst into tears.

The sound of someone clearing his throat drew Creed's attention. Glancing over his shoulder, he saw a tall warrior standing behind him.

"You, come this way."

Wrapping one arm around Jassy's shoulders, Creed followed the warrior toward a small lodge located near the outskirts of the village.

"You will stay here," the warrior said. "My woman will bring you food and clothing."

"My thanks," Creed said, and taking Jassy by the hand, he entered the lodge.

"What are they going to do to us?" Jassy asked.

"Nothing."

His gaze moved over her, noting the doeskin dress, the moccasins, the bit of red ribbon tied at the end of her braids. Her cheeks were tanned, her eyes luminous with tears. He felt a peculiar catch in his heart when he saw that she was still wearing his grandmother's beaded choker.

Murmuring a silent prayer of thanks that she was alive and well, he held out his arms.

"Come here, Jassy."

She flew into his arms and hugged him tight, her face pressed to his chest, her shoulders shaking as she began to sob.

"It's all right, honey," he murmured soothingly. "Don't cry. Everything's all right."

Lord, he thought, she felt good in his arms.

"Did they hurt you?" he asked.

"No."

"Did he . . . he didn't . . . are you sure you're all right?"

Jassy sniffed. "I'm fine. Oh, Creed, I didn't think I'd ever see you again." She drew back so she could see his face. "I thought they'd killed you."

"Not quite." A long, shuddering sigh rippled through him. "I think I need to sit down."

She watched him anxiously as he carefully lowered himself to the ground. Then she dropped down beside him.

"How did you find me?"

"Followed your trail, of course." He lifted one dark brow. "You didn't think I'd leave you here, did you?"

"I thought you were dead."

Creed grunted. "No, just tired. So damn tired."

"Sleep then," she urged softly.

She didn't have to tell him twice. Pillowing his head on her lap, one arm snuggled possessively around her waist, Creed Maddigan closed his eyes. And slept.

Jassy gazed down at him, unable to believe she wasn't dreaming, that he was really there, alive and whole.

An Indian woman arrived a short time later, bringing bowls of venison stew and dried meat, as well as a change of clothing and moccasins for Creed. She also brought a waterskin, two wooden cups, and two spoons made of buffalo horn.

Jassy smiled her thanks, and the woman left the lodge.

And still Creed slept. She covered him with a robe, then smoothed the hair from his brow. She frowned at the half-healed cut on his cheek. It would leave a nasty scar, she thought sadly, but a hundred scars couldn't change the way she felt about him. He was the bravest, most wonderful man she had ever known.

And she was going to be his wife.

She held on to that thought as she watched him sleep, trying to imagine what it would be like to be married to this man, to lie in his arms after they made love, to bear his children, to grow old at his side.

Missus Creed Maddigan.

"Missus Jassy Maddigan." She smiled as she whispered the name aloud.

She was still smiling when she fell asleep.

Chapter Nineteen

Creed woke slowly, aware of being warm for the first time in days. A familiar scent tickled his nostrils. A lock of silken hair lay across his chest. An arm spanned his waist; a long, slender leg was pressed close to his.

Jassy. His body's response to her nearness was immediate and unmistakable. For a moment, he kept his eyes closed, content to stay as he was, to bask in her warmth, to imagine what it would be like to wake beside her each morning of his life.

He shook the thought from his mind. He'd been a fool to think he could settle down, and an even bigger fool to think he could just walk away from his past. Trouble seemed to dog his every step. Until Jassy came along, he hadn't cared. But now . . . He shuddered to think what could have happened to her.

"Pilamaye, Ate," he whispered softly. Thank you, Father. For letting me find her, for keeping her safe.

Jassy stirred beside him, but didn't awake, and Creed opened his eyes. How beautiful she was! Her skin was soft and smooth and lightly tanned. The wealth of her hair was like molten flame, spilling over her shoulder and across his chest.

Unable to help himself, he caressed the curve of her cheek with his knuckles. Soft, so soft. Creed bit back a curse. What kind of life could she have with him? He was a half-breed. A hired gun. An escaped convict. Lord knew she deserved more out of life than he'd ever be able to give her. Even if he somehow managed to clear his name, he would still be a half-breed, a man straddling two worlds, at home in neither.

Creed stared up at the small patch of sky visible through the lodge's smoke hole. Jassy deserved the kind of life a decent man could offer, and he intended to see she got it.

He glanced down to find Jassy gazing up at him, a smile curving her lips.

"You are here," she murmured. "I was afraid I'd dreamed you, that I'd wake up and you'd be gone."

"No."

She reached for his hand and held it to her heart. "I missed you."

Creed nodded. "I missed you, too."

"Will they let us go?"

"Yeah." He smiled down at her. "I wasn't just fighting for you, you know, but for our freedom as well. We'll leave this morning."

Jassy's expression was dubious. "Do you feel up to riding?"

"Not really, but I want to get you out of here."

"We can stay another day or two if you want. I don't mind."

"I mind. I don't like the way he looks at you."

"Who? Chah-ee-chopes?"

Creed snorted. "Who else?"

"He's been very kind."

"I'll bet."

"Creed, it's not like that."

"Like hell. I saw the way he looked at you." Creed stared at Jassy, his eyes narrowing thoughtfully. "Maybe you want to stay here. With him."

"Don't be silly."

"I'm sorry." Creed ran a hand through his hair, wincing slightly as the movement put pressure on his bruised ribs.

"I think we should wait," Jassy said.

"And I think we should go. And that's the end of it."

It was just after noon when they rode out of the village. To show there were no hard feelings, Chah-ee-chopes had provided them with a couple of parfleches of food, a waterskin, and a rifle. He had offered Creed a pair of buckskin leggings, a loose-fitting shirt, and a pair of moccasins, which Creed had accepted with a terse word of thanks.

Before saying good-bye, Chah-ee-chopes had given Jassy a pretty little bay mare, apparently as a going-away present of some kind, or perhaps a token of his esteem. Creed hadn't missed the possessive way the warrior had looked at Jassy when he handed her the mare's reins, or the way his hands had lingered at Jassy's waist when he lifted her onto the bay mare's back. Nor had Creed missed the scorching glance of jealous hatred that Chah-ee-chopes had sent in his direction.

Gritting his teeth, Creed had swung up on the back of his horse. They weren't getting out of the village any too soon, he had mused ruefully.

And now it was dark. He had insisted on traveling until well after nightfall, in spite of Jassy's suggestion that they make an early camp.

He grimaced as he overheard her muttering something about "stupid, stubborn men" under her breath, but he wanted to put as many miles between themselves and the Crow as possible, and if it meant aggravating his already sore ribs, then that was just too damn bad; he had seen the way Chah-ee-chopes had looked at Jassy, and he hadn't liked it one damn bit.

Though he refused to admit it, he was exhausted by the time he agreed to make camp. The beating he had taken, the long ride to the

Crow camp, and the fight with Chah-ee-chopes had all taken their toll on his endurance. His ribs ached like the very devil, and all he wanted to do was lie down and close his eyes.

He grunted softly as he slid from the back of his horse. And suddenly Jassy was there beside him, her arm slipping around his waist, her brow furrowed with concern.

"I'll take care of everything," she offered. "Don't move."

She was as good as her word. She found a smooth stretch of ground and spread a blanket for him to lie on, unsaddled and hobbled the horses, and built a small fire.

When that was done, she knelt beside him. Removing the wide strip of cloth she used as a belt, she soaked it in water and carefully bathed his face and neck. She helped him out of his shirt, then bound his ribs with the cloth.

"Does that help?" she asked as she tucked the end in place.

"Yeah. Thanks."

"You rest now," she said with a smile. "I'll fix us something to eat."

Creed nodded, but his battered body needed rest more than food, and he was asleep within minutes.

Stretched out beside Creed, Jassy stared up at the stars. He'd been asleep for hours. She had eaten dinner, washed her hands and face and neck, and run her fingers through the tangles of her hair.

Turning on her side, she studied his face. It still amazed her that he had survived the brutal beating, that he had traveled across miles of barren ground to find her. Like a mythical hero in one of her father's books, Creed had risked his life in her behalf, rescuing her from the clutches of the black knight.

With a sigh, she combed a lock of hair from his forehead. Even bruised and battered, he was the most handsome man she had ever seen.

Handsome and brave, she thought, and because she had to say the words or die, she whispered that she loved him.

Creed felt better after a good night's sleep. He woke a couple of hours after dawn, aware of Jassy lying beside him, her head pillowed on his shoulder. Last night, she had whispered that she loved him. The memory of those three words, fervently and sincerely spoken, had kept him awake long after Jassy had fallen asleep.

She loved him. And he loved her. But was that enough? How could he ask her to share his life when he had no life? He was a bounty hunter with a price on his head. Hardly the type of man for a woman to pin her hopes on.

He swore softly as he became increasingly aware of her body pressed against his. He loved her, loved everything about her, and that was why he was going to let her go.

Carefully, he eased away from her, then made his way to the shallow stream that cut across the prairie some fifteen yards away from their camp.

It was a pretty spot, sheltered by slender cottonwoods and shrubs. The stream was wide and shallow, with a slow current and a sandy bottom.

He removed the cloth that bound his ribs, shucked off his pants and moccasins, and rolled everything together. Tossing the bundle onto a flat-topped boulder, he plunged into the deepest part of the stream, gasping as the cold water swirled around him.

He sat on his haunches, his eyes closed, while the water flowed past him. He would take Jassy to Frisco, find her sister, get his money back, get Jassy settled somewhere, and then get out of her life before it was too late, before she wrapped herself so firmly around his heart that he would never be able to let her go.

Abruptly, he stood up, shaking the water out of his hair. It wouldn't be easy to let her go, but he'd done difficult things before, and somehow he would get through this, too.

The sound of muffled footsteps interrupted his thoughts, and he swore softly when he realized that he'd left the rifle back at camp.

He whirled around, then dropped to his knees. "Dammit, girl, what are you doing creeping up on me like that?"

Jassy shrugged, her eyes wide as she took in

the broad expanse of Creed's bare chest. Water droplets clung to his copper-hued skin, twinkling like diamond dust in the early morning sunlight. His hair fell over his shoulders, as sleek and black as a raven's wing.

"I came down to wash," she said, unable to keep her gaze from straying downward. The rippling water covered him from the waist down, blurring what lay beneath.

She felt the blood rush to her face, but she couldn't seem to stop staring. She'd seen naked men before. Considering what her mother and sister did for a living, it had been inevitable. But she had never been in love with any of those men. Never wanted them to hold her, to touch her.

She had never wanted to touch any man the way she wanted to touch Creed Maddigan. Just looking at him made her want to slide her hands over his hard-muscled chest, to trace the outline of his jaw with her fingertips, to soothe the half-healed scar on his cheek, to run her fingers through the heavy thickness of his hair. She yearned to caress the thick muscles in his arms, to explore the black hair sprinkled across his chest. To feel his hard body pressed against her own.

"Jassy." Creed's voice sounded strange, as if he were in pain.

"What?"

Her hair was like a living flame in the sunlight. Her cheeks were a becoming shade of pink. Her brown eyes were wide. And curious. Like Pandora's before she lifted the lid. Like Eve's, when she first saw Adam.

Creed swore under his breath. Her every thought was mirrored in the depths of her eyes, magnifying his desire until the need within him grew painful. Immersing oneself in cold water had long been touted as the best way for a man to cool his lust, but in this case it was like trying to put out a raging forest fire with a cup of water. It just wasn't working.

"Dammit, girl, you'd best stop looking at me like that."

She met his gaze then, a saucy grin curving the corners of her mouth as she fisted her hands on her hips. For the first time since she'd known him, he looked disconcerted. It gave her a sudden sense of power.

"Like what?" she asked innocently.

"Like a hungry kitten contemplating a bowl of fresh cream."

She took a slow step forward. "And if I don't?"

"I won't be responsible for what happens," he growled. "Now go on, git!"

She shook her head as she walked closer to the water, her hips swaying provocatively. "Aren't you getting cold in there?"

Cold, he thought. Hell, he was surprised the water wasn't boiling.

She lifted a hand to the ties that fastened her dress. "Shall I join you?"

The sound that emerged from his throat was

a strangled gasp, like that of a man going down for the third time.

"Jassy, for the love of heaven," he pleaded, "go back to camp."

"Why, Creed? Why can't I stay here?"

"You know damn well why."

She grinned, and then she laughed. Why hadn't her mother ever told her how delightfully exciting it was to charm a man, to flirt, to tease? She felt a kind of power she had never known before, a sense of daring, of exhilaration.

Creed glared at her, his eyes narrowed. "I'm gonna count to five," he said, clipping off each word, "and then I'm coming out. One . . ."

She resisted the urge to stick her tongue out at him.

"Two."

He wouldn't do it, she thought confidently. He was only bluffing.

"Three."

Her confidence began to wane. "Creed . . ."

"Four."

Fire blazed in his black eyes. A muscle ticked in his cheek. Slowly, he began to rise out of the water.

For a moment, Jassy stared at him, the images of sleek black hair and smooth skin glistening like wet bronze imprinting themselves on her mind. Tiny rivers of water cascaded down his broad chest, arrowing down, down. . . .

With a startled cry, she turned on her heel

and raced back to camp.

The sound of arrogant masculine laughter rumbled behind her.

She knew, in that instant, that he had been bluffing.

For a moment, she was tempted to turn right around and go back, to prove that she wouldn't be made sport of, but then she remembered the fire blazing in the depths of his black eyes, the tension that had been evident in every taut line and muscle of his body.

Perhaps, in this instance, prudence had been the wisest course of action.

But it galled her just the same.

Creed swore under his breath as he watched Jassy's headlong flight back to camp. How was he going to keep his hands off her on the long journey to San Francisco? He wanted her as he had never wanted a woman in his entire life, wanted to bury himself deep within her sweetness. But that wasn't all. He wanted her heart and her soul. He wanted her smiles and her laughter. He wanted to comfort her when she cried, to share her heartaches and her joys. He wanted her face to be the first thing he saw in the morning, the image he carried into sleep at night.

He wanted her.

And she wanted him.

How was he going to keep his hands off her?

More importantly, how was he going to keep *her* hands off him? She wouldn't run forever.

She thought they were going to be married, and that implied a certain amount of intimacy—hugs, at the least, followed by long, slow kisses, and maybe a caress or two.

Muttering an oath, he submerged himself in the water, knowing that even a dip in Arctic waters in mid-winter wouldn't be cold enough to cool his desire.

Chapter Twenty

Snuggled in her bedroll, Jassy gazed up at the night sky. Stars by the millions twinkled like diamonds scattered across an indigo canvas.

But it wasn't the stars that she was thinking about. It was the way Creed had looked in the river that morning, his dark bronze body shining wetly in the sunlight, his long black hair framing the most handsome, masculine face she had ever seen.

Creed . . . Just thinking of him caused her pulse to race and her stomach to curl with pleasure.

She slid a furtive glance at him from the corner of her eye. He was lying on top of his bedroll, fully clothed, his arms crossed beneath his head, apparently lost in thought. Was he thinking of her? What would have happened if she had stood her ground by the river? At the time, she had been certain he was bluffing, but what if she hadn't run?

A hot flush washed into her cheeks as she imagined what might have happened, imagined Creed emerging from the water, taking her in his arms, kissing her, making love to her. . . .

He wanted her. She wanted him. Why did they have to wait?

She chewed thoughtfully on her lower lip. What if she went to him now? Would he send her away again? Or take her in his arms and make love to her?

Only a few feet of ground separated them. She was gathering her courage when Creed's voice bridged the gulf between them.

"The Lakota call the Milky Way *Wanagi Tacaka*, the Spirit Road," he remarked quietly. "They believe the *nagi*, or spirit, travels the Milky Way to *Wanagi Yatu*, the Place of Souls. It's a long journey. *Tate*, the Wind, guards the Spirit Trail, but there are some who believe the spirits of the departed must pass by an old woman before they can enter the land of many lodges. This old woman, whose name is *Hihankara*, the Owl Maker, looks for certain tattoo marks which must appear on the chin, wrist, or forehead of the deceased. If she can't find a tattoo, she pushes the spirit off the trail, and it falls back to earth to become a ghost."

Jassy smiled, charmed by the tale. Creed's description made it easy to picture an old woman with long gray braids standing at the edge of the Milky Way, her black eyes sharp as she checked for the necessary tattoo.

"Is that what you believe?" she asked, certain he wouldn't admit to believing such a fanciful thing even if he did.

"I'm not sure," Creed answered. "My grandmother believed it, though. I guess if it's true, I'm destined to become a ghost."

"Didn't your grandmother give you a tattoo?"

"No. My mother wouldn't permit it. She said it was a heathen tradition. I always meant to get one, but somehow I never did."

Jassy stared at the Milky Way, trying to imagine what it had been like for Creed, growing up with the Indians. It must have been nice, having grandparents, being part of a family. She fingered the beaded choker at her throat. She had never known her own grandparents. She knew almost nothing about her mother and father, except that her mother had been born on a farm in Pennsylvania.

"It's pretty—the Milky Way, I mean," she mused.

"Yeah."

"Do you believe in heaven?"

"I don't know. I believe in hell, though."

"I don't think you can have one without the other," Jassy remarked. She rose onto one elbow and faced Creed. "Reverend Padden always said my mama's soul was bound for hell. Do you think he's right, Creed? Do you think my mama's burning in hellfire?"

Creed shook his head. "I don't know, honey. I'm in no position to judge anyone else." He turned on his side, facing her, his jaw cradled in his palm. "I wouldn't pay much attention to what that Bible-thumper said if I was you, Jassy. Your mama did what she had to do, same as the rest of us."

"I guess so." Jassy looked up at the sky again. Overwhelmed by the beauty of it all, she felt suddenly small and vulnerable. Stars without number, she thought.

"Good night, Jassy."

"'Night, Creed." She snuggled under the covers, and then, before she could change her mind, she scrambled out of her bedroll and slid in beside Creed.

"Jassy, what the . . . ?"

"I don't want to sleep alone, Creed, please."

"This isn't a good idea, Jassy, believe me."

"I don't care. I'm . . . I'm afraid."

"Of what?"

"I don't know. Ghosts, maybe."

Creed grunted. He didn't have the heart to send her back to her own bed, not if she was really scared, but he knew there was no way he was going to get any sleep with her lying there beside him. No way at all.

Nevertheless, he turned his back to her and closed his eyes.

She stirred beside him, her body brushing

against his as she curled up against him.

Her scent rose all around him, warm and sleepy, soft and feminine. Alluring. Desirable.

He swore under his breath. If there was indeed a hell, no doubt he would burn in it for all eternity for his thoughts alone.

He woke before dawn to find Jassy's arms and legs entwined with his. Her hair was spread over his arm like a living flame. Her skin was slightly flushed; a faint smile played over her lips. He would have given a month's pay to know what she was dreaming about.

And then she murmured his name, her voice thick with unfulfilled desire, and he knew. He tried to ignore his body's instant reaction, but she was too near, too tempting.

Unable to help himself, he rolled onto his side, gathered her into his arms, and kissed her.

He had meant it to be a quick, passionless kiss, but as soon as his mouth covered hers, he was lost, drowning in sweetness.

He was holding her, kissing her, whispering her name. The words became clearer; the shadows became substance. She was aware of the gentle abrasion of whiskers against her cheek. She drew a long shuddering breath and inhaled the scent of man and sweat and dust. She heard a moan, and realized it wasn't hers . . .

Jassy's eyelids flew open as her dream merged with reality, and she realized that Creed was indeed holding her, kissing her. Her arms slid around his neck, drawing him closer. Pressing herself against him, she parted her lips and let her tongue taste his. And suddenly she was holding empty air.

Creed swore softly as he scrambled to his feet. Another minute, and she would have been his in every sense of the word. And then what? Once he had taken her innocence, he would never be able to let her go.

Jassy sat up, looking confused. "Creed, what's wrong?"

"Nothing." Nothing, he thought ruefully. How was he going to keep his hands off her when she came alive at the slightest touch, when she offered herself to him without hesitation? She was like fire and silk in his arms, hot and soft and smooth.

Turning on his heel, he headed for the river.

"Creed, where are you going?"

He paused, but didn't look at her. "I'm going to take a . . . I need some privacy, so unless you want a first-hand education in male anatomy, don't follow me."

Glancing over his shoulder, he fixed her with a warning stare, then headed for the river. He doused his head and neck in the chill water, then sat back on his heels, his gaze fixed on the opposite bank.

If his calculations were right, they weren't more than twenty or thirty miles from Rock Springs. If they rode hard, they could be there late tomorrow afternoon. With luck, he could sell their horses for enough money to buy some decent clothes for the two of them and have enough left over for a couple of second-class tickets on the Union Pacific. Three days on the train should get them into Sacramento. From there they would take the stage into San Franciso. He'd find Rose, get his money back, get Jassy settled someplace, and clear out of her life once and for all.

He'd miss her. Still, it was for her own good. He was never going to amount to anything, and she deserved a decent life, marriage to a respectable, church-going, stay-in-one-place man, a home of her own, children. What did he know about any of those things? He had never been respectable and never would be. Worse, he had no desire to be respectable. He had never been one for going to church. Never had a home of his own. Didn't want children.

But he wanted Jassy. There was no question about that. Wanted her with every breath he took, with every beat of his heart. What was worse, he needed her. He, who had never needed anyone, found himself needing this woman-child in ways he didn't fully comprehend.

Muttering an oath, he surged to his feet. He would never be good for her. He had never been good for anyone. But Jassy deserved the best, and he aimed to see that she got it. The sooner the better.

She was sitting on her bedroll when he returned to camp.

"Let's go," he said curtly. "We've got a lot of riding to do today."

"What about breakfast?"

"We'll eat on the trail."

"But . . ."

"Don't argue with me, Jasmine."

Jasmine! He had never called her that. Confused by his anger, she rolled her bedding into a compact cylinder and tied it behind the saddle. She braided her hair, pulled on her moccasins, and saddled her horse, all without speaking to him. Head high, chin jutting out, she dug a piece of jerky out of her saddlebags, then climbed into the saddle.

Moments later, they were riding north.

Jassy stared at Creed, wondering what was wrong. Ever since she had flirted with him beside the stream, he had been trying to ignore her. At first, she had thought he was angry with her, but he didn't seem angry, just withdrawn. His face was like something cast in stone—hard and unyielding. He spoke only when necessary, insisted they ride from dawn till dark, and then, as soon as they'd eaten and the horses were settled for the night, he had taken refuge in his bedroll, pretending to be asleep even though she knew he was awake. Awake and on edge, just as she was.

The attraction between them hummed like a

telegraph line, sizzling like summer lightning. He had only to look at her, and her whole being seemed to come alive. Colors were brighter, sounds more clear. Her skin tingled with longing whenever he was within reach, though he made a determined effort not to touch her in any way.

He had kissed her. Kissed her and liked it. And she wanted more. More of his kisses, more of everything.

He had told her they would reach Rock Springs sometime tomorrow and that they would take a train to San Francisco. But Jassy had lost all interest in finding Rose. The money was no longer important. Nothing mattered except Creed and the wall he was erecting between them.

She stared at his profile, mentally running her fingers through his hair, tracing the hard planes of his face, lingering on the sensual line of his mouth.

Tonight, she thought, tonight she would find out what was wrong. One way or another, she would find out.

She was up to something; he could smell it in the air, the same way he smelled the promise of rain before the night was over.

He had been aware of her covert glances all day. Even now, as she spread their bedrolls beside the fire, he could feel her furtive gaze. She was as nervous as a new bride.

He swore softly. What the hell had made him think of that? Lurching to his feet, he headed for the shallow water hole located a short distance from their campsite.

"Creed?"

Her voice stopped him in his tracks. "What?" He didn't look at her, merely waited.

"Will you be gone long?"

"I don't know."

He waited a moment to see if she had anything else to say, then stalked into the darkness. He was burning up inside. His blood was on fire. His skin felt tight. And he ached. Oh, how he ached for her.

He flopped down on his belly at the water hole and buried his face in the cool water. Jassy. She was like a song he couldn't get out of his mind. Her sweetness, her ready acceptance of him in spite of who and what he was, drew him like a lodestone. He wished suddenly that he could be the man she wanted, the man she deserved.

For the first time in his life, he regretted the choices he had made and the kind of life he had lived. The ghosts of the men he'd hunted rose up to haunt him, their skeletal faces accusing and damning. There was blood on his hands, on his soul, and he would never be free of it, any more than he would ever be free of his past, of the fact that he was an escaped convict, a man on the dodge.

He swore under his breath. Life had been so uncomplicated before he met Jassy McCloud, and yet he knew, deep down, that he wouldn't give up a minute of the time he had spent with her.

Sitting up, he shook the water from his face and hair, then prowled the darkness, edgy as a long-tailed cat in a room full of rockers. He paced for almost an hour to give her time to get to sleep, and then he padded silently back to camp.

The first thing he noticed was that there was only one bedroll, and Jassy was in it, her hair a riot of color against the dull brown blanket.

A muffled oath escaped his lips as he stared at her, his breath catching in his throat as she slowly sat up, letting the covers pool around her waist.

The firelight caressed her, glinting in her hair, shimmering on her naked shoulders and breasts. Wordlessly, she held out her arms, the silent invitation as old as time.

His feet felt like lead as he moved toward her. His voice was ragged as he whispered her name, and then he dropped to his knees beside her and wrapped her in his arms. Her skin was warm and moist. Inviting. Tempting.

He felt her arms go around his waist, heard his name on her lips, and then she was kissing him, pressing her body to his, drawing him down onto the blankets.

A distant corner of his mind told him this was wrong, urged him to resist, but the passion of her kisses made his blood flow hot and thick, like lava, drowning out everything but the taste of her, the touch of her.

He covered her body with his, his hands gliding over her silky flesh, his mouth hot and hungry as he kissed her. He was a condemned man, and she was his only hope of salvation.

His arms tightened around her as he deepened the kiss, his tongue searching for hers. A muffled groan of pain and pleasure was trapped in his throat as her tongue met his, inviting him to taste, to explore.

Her hands roamed over his back and shoulders and chest, nervous, eager. She delved under his buckskin shirt, moaning softly as her fingertips came in contact with warm skin. She heard the sharp intake of his breath as her hands skimmed across his chest.

He wanted her. Every kiss told her so. She could feel it in the tension that caused him to tremble, in the sudden hard heat pressed against her belly. She heard it in the harsh rasp of his voice as he murmured her name, the sound filled with yearning, with need.

And she was trembling, too, longing for something she didn't quite understand. She wasn't ignorant of the act itself, but no one had ever told her of the wild tumble of emotions that accompanied the act of love. She felt afraid, excited, eager. And in the very depths of her being, she felt the need to give, to soothe Creed's doubts, to give him the love she knew he had never had.

She tugged on his shirt, and he shrugged it off. The touch of his bare flesh against her own was exhilarating, and she drew him closer. His skin was dark bronze; hers was translucent ivory. He was strong and hard; she was yielding and soft.

She gazed into the smokey depths of his eyes and saw her own yearnings, her own hunger, mirrored there. But more than that, she saw doubts. His doubts.

Hoping to erase his misgivings once and for all, she murmured that she loved him.

She had hoped to make him smile. She had thought he might reply that he loved her, too.

She did not expect him to draw back as if he had been slapped.

Creed stared down at Jassy for a long moment. Her lips were swollen from his kisses, and her eyes glowed with the flame of desire. He knew in that instant that he couldn't do it; he couldn't take her innocence. She was only seventeen, with her whole life ahead of her. She deserved more out of life than a used-up, half-breed gunfighter.

"Don't, Jassy," he said curtly.

"Don't what?"

She reached for his hand, but he caught both of hers in one of his, his grip merciless.

"I won't let you waste your love on a man like me," he said. Releasing her hands, he threw the covers over her and walked away.

"Creed! Damn you, Creed Maddigan, don't you dare turn your back on me!"

"Go to sleep."

"No."

He refused to look at her, knowing how dangerous it would be, knowing he would be sorely tempted to forget his good intentions and crawl back under the covers. "Dammit, Jassy, do what I say!"

"You're not my father." Her eyes narrowed angrily. "Or my husband! You can't tell me what to do."

He started to turn, then caught himself. *Don't look at her,* he told himself. *You'll be fine if you just don't look at her.*

"I want you," she said softly. "I love you and I want you, and I know you want me."

"I want a lot of things."

"Please, Creed, don't shut me out."

"This was a mistake from the beginning, Jassy. I'm no good for you. I never have been. I thought . . ." He blew out a long, weary sigh. "Hell, it doesn't matter what I thought."

"It matters to me."

He turned to face her then, his eyes dark and haunted. "Jassy, you don't know anything about me." He held up a hand when she started to protest. "Just listen. I'm a wanted man, and nothing's going to change that. I thought if I took you far enough away, it wouldn't matter. But it won't work. I can't ask you to spend the rest of your life on the run, always looking over your shoulder because of something I did."

"Creed, you're forgetting about the letter from Judge Parker! He said he'd look into your case. We could go back. I could tell him what I saw—"

"No, Jassy. I've made up my mind."

"But . . ."

He shook his head. He should have left her in Harrison, he thought bleakly. At the time, he had convinced himself that he was doing the right thing, rationalizing that he couldn't walk out on her, that he couldn't leave her alone. He knew now it had been a mistake. She had been captured by Indians because he had been too damned selfish to leave her behind. If Chah-ee-chopes hadn't taken a liking to her, Jassy could have been killed, or worse. Somehow, he had to make her understand.

"Jassy, Harry's not the only man I ever killed. If Parker starts nosin' around in my past, there's no telling what skeletons he's liable to dig up."

"Why didn't you ever tell me that before?"

He shrugged. "I don't know. It didn't seem important at the time, and then . . . I guess I just didn't want you to know."

He drew in a deep breath and let it out in a long sigh. It had all happened so long ago, he hardly ever thought about it anymore, but it was there, a dark shadow in his past, the only killing he had ever been ashamed of.

"And now you want me to think you're all bad, is that right?"

"Think whatever you like."

"I don't understand you, Creed Maddigan," she exclaimed, her anger rising. "You keep telling me you're no good for me, that I'm too young. Well, you're wrong! I'm not too young. A lot of girls are married and have a couple of kids by the time they're my age. And as for your not being good enough for me . . ." She shook her head. "My mother was a whore, Creed. Maybe what you really mean is that I'm not good enough for you!"

"Dammit, Jassy, that's not true and you know it! And in spite of the way you grew up, you're still just a kid, and if you don't want to end up like your mother, then you'd best hang on to your virginity for as long as you can!"

There was no use arguing with him, not now, when they were both angry, when anything she said would only make him more determined to leave her behind.

"Very well, Creed," she said with feigned resignation. "If that's the way you want it."

"It is."

She gave him a long, accusing look and then, with a sniff, she turned her back to him and closed her eyes. That might be the way he wanted it, she thought, but that wasn't the way it was going to be.

She smiled into the darkness. She might have lost the battle, but she was determined to win the war.

Chapter Twenty-one

Creed's gaze darted left and right as they rode down the dusty street that was Rock Springs' main thoroughfare. Back in the 1860s, Rock Springs had been a trading post and stagecoach station on the Oregon Trail. Now it was a coal mining town for the Union Pacific Coal Company. The population, mostly male, numbered less than two hundred.

Four years had passed since peace had been made between the settlers and the Sioux. In that same year, 1868, Wyoming had been organized as a Territory. A year later, the new Territory had granted women the right to vote.

Even though Rock Springs wasn't much of a town, and they were pretty far from Harrison, there was always a possibility that a wanted poster carrying his description might turn up, although Creed thought the chances were slim. But there was no help for it—they were out of supplies and out of money. He'd sell the horses and buy two tickets to Sacramento. For Jassy's sake, the sooner he got her settled and got the hell out of her life, the better. For both of them.

There was only one store in town. Located on the south side of the tracks, it was officially known as the Beckwith Quinn Store, but everybody called it The Big Store.

Creed had never seen the place before now, but he'd heard about it. Besides being the company store for the mine, it housed the mine office and the post office. It was also the undertaking parlor, with the delivery wagon doubling as a hearse when necessary. The Big Store sold everything from blasting powder to clothing, mining tools to groceries. When the miners needed entertainment, they used the counters for a stage and danced in the aisles.

Jassy wandered through the store while Creed haggled with the owner about what their horses and saddles were worth. There were several men in the place, and they all turned to stare at her.

Feeling uncomfortable, she made her way back to Creed, who was waiting for her near the door.

"Did you get a good deal?" she asked.

"Good enough to get us a couple of train tickets and a change of clothes."

Jassy nodded, trying not to notice the way the miners were staring at her. Creed didn't look too out of place in buckskins, but she was acutely conscious of her fringed doeskin dress and moccasins.

"So," Creed said, "what do you want first? Something to eat, or something to wear?"

"Clothes, please."

The Big Store might be big, Jassy thought, but there weren't a lot of choices in ladies ready-to-wear, and even less in her size. She finally settled on a blue gingham dress, since the only other choice was an ugly brown wool. Shoes were the next item of business, and she picked out a pair of low-heeled black leather boots. Cheeks flushing, she selected a pair of cotton stockings and garters. Lastly, she bought a hair-brush and a packet of hairpins.

"That all?" Creed asked.

Jassy nodded. Her chemise and pantalets were still in reasonably good condition, she thought gratefully, because she'd hate to have to buy new ones with Creed and a handful of scruffy miners looking on.

She stood nearby while Creed selected a pair of black twill trousers, a dark green wool shirt, and a black hat. To her surprise, he decided to keep the moccasins. He also bought a used Navy Colt and a holster.

He paid for their purchases, tucked their parcels under one arm, and headed for the door.

It was after dark by the time they checked into the hotel.

"You'll have to pretend to be my wife," Creed told her as they crossed the lobby. "We don't have enough money left for two rooms."

Jassy nodded. Contrary to what Creed might think, she was glad they'd be sharing a room.

The hotel clerk's gaze moved over Creed in a long assessing glance that made it clear he didn't cotton to the idea of having a half-breed under his roof.

Creed returned the man's gaze, daring the clerk to ask him to leave. Finally, with a shrug, the man slid the hotel register across the counter.

Glancing over Creed's shoulder, Jassy watched him sign in as Mister and Missus Monroe from Sheridan, Montana.

"We'll need some hot water," Creed said.

"That'll be two bits extra."

"Fine. Send it up right away, will you?"

"Yessir, Mr. Monroe," the clerk replied. He handed Creed two keys, then closed the register with a bang.

Jassy followed Creed up the narrow stairway and down a dark hallway to their room.

Inside, he dropped their packages on the bed, then crossed the floor to the window and stared down at the street below. It was going to be hell, sharing a room with Jassy, he thought as he watched a mud wagon rumble past. The room was small. The bed was small. And she was all too willing . . .

He could hear the rustle of paper as she unwrapped her purchases.

"That hot water should be here soon," Creed remarked, turning away from the window. "I'll go downstairs so you can have some privacy." He buckled on the gunbelt and checked to make sure the Colt was loaded. "Don't leave this room till I get back."

"You will come back, won't you?"

"Yeah." His gaze lingered on her face for a long moment, and then he was gone.

Creed made his way to the town's only saloon and stepped inside. He ordered a glass of whiskey, then stood there, staring into the clear amber liquid. Earlier, he'd gone to the Union Pacific ticket office and bought two second-class tickets to Sacramento. The good news was that the tickets didn't cost quite as much as he had expected; the bad news was that the train wouldn't arrive until Thursday morning. That meant sharing a room with Jassy for the next two nights.

Two nights in the same room. The very idea made him break out in a cold sweat. That day by the river, she had discovered what every woman discovered sooner or later; now that she knew what a powerful weapon her sexuality was, he figured she was going to want someone to practice on. And he was that someone.

Jassy sat at the window, staring down at the street, wondering what was keeping Creed. He'd been gone for over an hour. In that time, she'd bathed and washed and dried her hair. Now, fully dressed, she waited impatiently for his return.

When another thirty minutes went by, she began to wonder if he was ever coming back. She knew he regretted bringing her with him. He thought he was too old for her. He said he had nothing to offer her—no future, no hope. He had escaped from prison, and there was a price on his head. But none of that mattered. Why couldn't he see that? Why wouldn't he admit that they were good together? That he needed her just as much as she needed him?

There had to be something he wasn't telling her, something in his past—but what? He said he had killed people. Was that it? Had he killed someone in cold blood? She knew he was capable of violence, of taking a life, but she couldn't imagine Creed killing for killing's sake.

She glanced over her shoulder when she heard a key turn in the lock. "Creed!"

He nodded at her, trying not to notice how beautiful she looked sitting in front of the window with the lamplight shining on her hair and her eyes glowing with happiness.

As if he had been gone for years instead of hours, she flew across the room and hugged him. "I missed you."

Gently, he disengaged her arms from his

waist. "Why don't you go down to the dining room and get something to eat while I take a bath?"

"I'd rather wait for you."

"I already ate," he lied.

"Oh."

Her disappointment pierced him, sharp as an Apache arrow. But it was better this way. He needed to put some distance between them.

Turning his back to her, he unbuckled his gunbelt and placed it over the back of the chair she'd been sitting in. He started to remove his shirt, then thought better of it.

A few minutes later, a couple of tow-headed boys arrived with hot water. After several trips, the tub was full.

Creed looked at Jassy, one eyebrow raised in question, after the boys left the room the last time.

"I could stay and wash your back," she offered, the flush in her cheeks belying the calm tone of her voice.

"I don't think so. Go on, get something to eat," he said, pressing a greenback into her hand. "You've got to be hungry."

"You can't avoid me forever," Jassy replied tartly.

Jassy was almost to the door when Creed's stomach rumbled twice. Loudly, hungrily.

Very slowly, she turned around to face him, her eyes filled with hurt and silent accusation.

"Jassy . . ."

"Enjoy your bath, Mr. Monroe," she said, and turned away before he could see the tears in her eyes.

Creed swore under his breath as Jassy quietly closed the door behind herself. He didn't like the idea of Jassy going down to the dining room alone, but it couldn't be helped. She was liable to get into a lot more trouble staying here with him than downstairs by herself.

Stripping off his travel-stained buckskins and moccasins, he eased himself into the tub, leaned back, and closed his eyes. What was he going to do about Jassy?

He stayed in the tub until the water grew cool, then washed quickly. Drying off, he pulled on his shirt and pants and moccasins, strapped on his gunbelt, and went downstairs.

At first glance, the hotel dining room appeared to be deserted. Then he saw Jassy sitting at a small table in the far corner. She was smiling, and then he heard her laugh, a sound of pure joy.

As he drew closer, he saw that she wasn't alone.

Jassy clasped her hands in her lap as Creed approached the table. And then she flashed her dinner companion a radiant smile.

"Jassy."

She looked up, as if noticing Creed for the first time. "Oh, Mr. Monroe. Hello." She smiled at the man sitting across from her. "Jim Phillips, this is Creed Monroe. Creed, this is Jim.

He works at the company store."

Jim Phillips stood up, his hand extended. "Pleased to make your acquaintance, Mr. Monroe."

Creed shook the man's hand. Jim Phillips was tall, lean, and pretty-boy handsome, with a shock of blond hair and honest blue eyes. His handshake was firm and friendly. His brown tweed city suit indicated prosperity and good taste.

Creed disliked him on sight.

"Won't you join us, Creed?" Jassy asked, her tone indicating that she didn't really want his company but was merely asking to be polite.

"Thanks," Creed replied. "I think I will."

He drew a chair up to the table and sat down, his face schooled into an impassive mask.

Jassy tried to ignore him, but it was impossible. He didn't say anything, just sat there, glowering at her.

"So, tell me, Jim," she said brightly, "how long have you been here?"

"Just a few months. Will you be staying long?"

"I'm not . . ."

"No," Creed said, fixing Phillips with a hard stare. "She won't be staying long."

Phillips glanced at Jassy. It was obvious, from the expression in his eyes, that he was wondering about her relationship to Creed.

Jassy shifted uncomfortably in her seat, embarrassed by Creed's rudeness.

Creed continued to stare at Phillips, his gaze

openly hostile. Finally, Phillips took the hint, bade Jassy a hasty farewell, and left the dining room.

"So," Creed said, "how'd you meet him?"

"He was alone. I was alone." Jassy shrugged. "He asked if he could join me, and I said yes. Not that it's any of your business."

Creed stared at her, surprised by the jealous rage that swept through him. She was supposed to be in love with him, yet she'd had no trouble at all finding another man. A younger man. A settled man, one with a steady job and no doubt an impeccable reputation. A man who could give her everything she wanted. Everything she deserved.

"Following in your mother's footsteps?" Creed asked nastily, wanting to hurt her.

As soon as the words were out, he wished he could call them back, but it was too late.

Jassy drew back as if he'd slapped her, her eyes growing wide with shock, then narrowing with anger.

"You don't want me," she said quietly. "You've made that very clear, so why should you care?"

"Jassy, I'm sorry."

"Are you?" She stood up, her stance proudly defiant, her eyes glittering with fury. "It was probably a man like you who turned my mother into a whore. Good night, Mr. Monroe."

He stared after her, feeling as though he'd been gutted and left for dead. He stood up.

"Jassy, wait."

But she was gone.

He gave her a few minutes to compose herself, and then he went upstairs. But she wasn't in their room.

"Phillips," he muttered darkly.

He paced the floor, his hands clenched into angry fists. Had she made plans to meet him? Was she with him even now? The image of Jassy in the arms of another man was like a knife cutting into his vitals.

Where was she?

The room seemed to close in on him. Muttering an oath, he grabbed his hat and left the hotel. It was a small town. How hard could it be to find her?

An hour later, he admitted defeat and returned to the hotel. The room seemed strangely empty without her there. He sat in the chair by the window and stared into the darkness, remembering the way she had looked sitting in the same chair earlier that evening, the way her eyes had lit up with welcome when he entered the room.

Swamped by remorse for his unkind words, he rested his head against the back of the chair and closed his eyes. He was a fool, he thought, throwing away happiness with both hands because he didn't think he deserved it, because he had always felt inferior. If his mother hadn't loved him, why would anyone else?

But all the excuses in the world couldn't justify his cruelty. He'd had no right to say what he'd said, no right at all. And now Jassy was alone in a strange town, and it was all his fault.

And if she wasn't alone, that was his fault, too.

Plagued by worry and a guilty conscience, he left the hotel and went to the saloon, hoping a drink would help.

It didn't. Taking the bottle to a table in the back of the room, he sat down and stared out the window, intending to get totally, forgetfully, drunk.

He was draining his second glass when he saw Jassy through the window. She was across the street, walking slowly, her head bowed, her attitude one of total despair. And it was all his fault.

He knew then that he was fighting a losing battle. He loved her. Maybe he had loved her since the first time he saw her in the alley back in Harrison.

Grabbing his hat off the back of his chair, he left the saloon and hurried after her.

"Jassy, wait."

He knew she heard him, but she didn't stop, and she didn't turn around. She just kept walking.

"Jassy!" He caught her arm, forcing her to stop. "Jassy, listen to me, please."

"Leave me alone."

"Jassy, I'm sorry. Please forgive me. I didn't mean it. I swear it!"

"I don't believe you."

He caught her chin between his thumb and forefinger and forced her to look at him.

"I'm sorry, Jassy. I don't have any excuse for what I said except that . . . that I was jealous."

"Jealous? You?"

Creed nodded. "Green with it. I looked at Phillips, and I saw everything you deserve. Everything I'll never be."

Her lips twitched. "You were jealous? Of Jim Phillips?"

"Yeah."

She couldn't help it—she laughed out loud. Imagine, Creed being jealous of Jim Phillips. The idea was ludicrous.

"You wanna tell me what's so funny?" Creed asked.

"You. You're funny. Oh, Creed," she said, laying her hand on his arm. "Don't you see? Your being jealous of Jim Phillips is like a lion being jealous of a kitten."

"Women like kittens," Creed retorted irritably.

"I like lions," Jassy said, running her hand up his arm.

"Forgive me?"

She tilted her head to one side, a mischievous expression in her eyes. "Maybe."

"Maybe?"

"Why were you jealous, Creed?"

"Why do you think?"

"I don't know. You tell me."

"I love you, Jassy. That's why I was jealous.

Because I love you. Is that what you wanted to hear?"

"Oh, yes." She closed her eyes for a moment, thinking he'd never know how she'd longed to hear those words.

"I love you." He drew her into his arms, one arm caressing her back. "I love you." His lips moved over her face, raining kisses over her cheeks, her brow.

She gazed into his eyes, eyes filled with tenderness. "Will you tell me that often, so you don't forget?"

"Every day," he promised.

"All right, then, I forgive you."

Hand in hand, they walked back to the hotel. Creed unlocked the door, lit the lamp, and found himself staring at the bed, which suddenly seemed to fill the room. He was aware of Jassy standing behind him.

Slowly, he turned around to face her. "If you stop looking at me like that, I'll spend the night on the floor," he said, his voice thick.

"And if I don't?"

"I'm gonna make love to you until the sun comes up."

"Really?" She took a step toward him, remembering all the times he'd started to make love to her, then backed away.

"Really."

She closed the distance between them. Rising on her tiptoes, she wrapped her arms around his neck and kissed him.

"Make love to me, Creed," she murmured, her breath warm and sweet against his mouth. "Make love to me until the sun comes up."

"Jassy . . ."

"You haven't changed your mind already?"

"I just don't want you to regret this."

"I won't," she whispered. "I promise I won't."

"I asked you to be my wife a while back, remember?"

Jassy nodded.

"There's bound to be someone in this town who can marry us." He stroked her cheek with his fingertip. "I can wait one more day."

"I can't."

"You're sure?"

She started to say yes, of course she was sure, but then she thought of her mother, and Rose, and all the men they had known—known in the most intimate sense of the word. She had been ashamed of her mother and sister ever since she was old enough to know what they did for a living. If she let Creed make love to her now, she would be no better than the rest of the women in her family.

She looked at Creed, wanting him more than anything she had ever wanted in her life, yet wanting to wait because she knew it was the right thing to do.

"It's okay, Jassy. Like I said, I can wait one more day."

She glanced away, wondering if he was angry, if he thought she was just a tease. "I'm sorry."

"Don't be." He placed a finger under her chin, tipped her face up, and kissed the tip of her nose. And then, resolutely, he put her away from him. "I said I can wait, and I can, but it might be better for both of us if you hopped into bed."

"I love you, Creed."

His hand caressed her cheek. "And I love you." Funny, how easy those words came now, he thought. "And tomorrow I'll show you just how much. But for now, I think you'd better get some sleep."

"All right." She frowned as he picked up his hat. "Where are you going?"

"Downstairs for a few minutes."

Jassy bit down on her lower lip. "You're not going to . . ."

Slowly, Creed shook his head. "No, Jassy," he said with a wry grin. "From now on, you're the only woman for me."

A wave of relief flooded her cheeks with color. "Don't be long."

"I won't. Good night, Jassy."

"'Night, Creed."

He winked at her, then left the room. In the hallway, Creed drew in a deep breath and exhaled it in a long, slow sigh. Then, resolutely, he went downstairs.

An hour later, he had everything he needed.

* * *

A low sigh of pleasure rose in Jassy's throat as a callused hand stroked her cheek.

"Wake up, Jasmine Alexandria McCloud. It's your wedding day."

Wedding day! Her eyelids flew open and she found herself gazing into Creed's laughing black eyes.

"Unless you've changed your mind?" he asked, his lips feathering across her face.

"I haven't."

"Good. Hot water's on the way. Your weddin' dress will be here in a few minutes."

"A dress! You found me a dress?"

Creed shrugged, as if it was of no import. "Hope it fits," he muttered. "Hurry now. I'm going down to get a shave. I'll be back in thirty minutes."

He kissed her, a deep kiss filled with promise, and then he was gone.

Minutes later, there was a knock at the door. Jassy opened it to find a woman of about her size standing in the hallway.

"Yes?"

"Miss McCloud?"

"Yes."

"This is for you." The woman held out a large box. "Congratulations on your forthcoming nuptials," she said. "I hope you'll be very happy."

"Thank you," Jassy said. Closing the door behind her, Jassy placed the box on the bed and lifted the lid. Inside, nestled on a layer of tissue paper, was a wedding dress made of ivory lace.

Reverently, Jassy lifted it out of the box and held it up. It was the most exquisite thing she had ever seen, with a high, stand-up collar, long fitted sleeves, and a full skirt with a small bustle.

"Oh, Creed," she murmured as she stared at herself in the mirror over the commode. "Wherever did you find this?"

Thirty minutes later, Creed knocked at the door. "Ready in there?"

"Yes," she called, and opened the door.

She was a vision in ivory lace. Her brown eyes were glowing, her smile radiant.

"Jassy . . . you're beautiful."

"Am I?"

He nodded, unable to speak past the lump in his throat. He'd never seen anything more beautiful in his life.

"You look beautiful, too," Jassy murmured. And indeed, he did. Freshly shaved, dressed in a black suit, crisp white shirt, black silk cravat, and black boots, she knew she'd never seen a more handsome man in her life.

"Are you ready?" Creed asked.

Jassy nodded, and Creed took her arm and led her downstairs into the dining room.

Jassy gasped when they entered the room. It had been decorated with greenery and wildflowers. A priest stood under an arch made of pine boughs. The hotel clerk and an elderly woman stood beside him. The woman, whom

Jassy recognized as the one who had brought her the dress, held a bouquet of yellow and white daisies, which she handed to Jassy.

"Good luck, dear," she murmured.

Jassy nodded, her eyes brimming with tears. They were in the middle of nowhere, yet Creed had managed to find her a gown and flowers.

The words that united them in marriage were few and simple, yet they were the most beautiful, wonderful words Jassy had ever heard. She hardly minded at all that Creed didn't use his own name; to her, it didn't matter. She was marrying the man, not a name. She spoke the words that made her Creed's wife fervently, and when he kissed her, she knew it was forever.

The hotel clerk and his mother wished them well; the priest smiled benevolently, handed them the marriage license, and took his leave.

Swinging Jassy into his arms, Creed carried her up the stairs to their room. Nudging the door shut with his heel, he kissed Jassy long and hard before setting her on her feet.

Jassy stared up at Creed. He was her husband now, for better or worse, in sickness or health, from this day forward. A riot of emotion welled up within her. Anxiety. Hope. Anticipation. Desire. She could feel the pulse beating rapidly in her throat as his gaze moved over her face.

"Jassy, I'm sorry I couldn't find a ring. I looked, but . . ."

"It doesn't matter."

"I'll try to be a good husband to you, to make

you happy." He took her hand in his. Her hand was so small, so slender, so pale and smooth where his was dark and callused. "I hope you never regret this day."

"I won't."

She saw the doubts in his eyes, and they only made her love him more. Leaning forward, she pressed her mouth to his.

And there was no more room for doubts. He crushed her to him, his lips claiming hers, branding her forevermore. With trembling fingers, he began to unfasten the long row of tiny buttons that fastened her dress. He caressed her out of her undergarments, his hands gentle, eager, until she was gloriously naked, and then he swung her into his arms and carried her to bed.

The heat of his mouth, the exploration of his hands, expelled all trace of modesty or shyness, and it was with bold eagerness that Jassy began removing Creed's clothing. Shivers of delight unfurled within her as her hands encountered warm flesh.

She let her eyes feast on his nakedness, awed by the muscular beauty of him. He was like a statue chiseled from bronze come to life. His back was smooth and dark, marred by the faint white lines of old scars. She found a small puckered scar on his left thigh, another on his right shoulder. With a slight shake of her head, she drew her fingertips over the crooked scar on his left cheek.

"Pretty beat up, huh?" Creed murmured, nuzzling her neck.

"What caused this one?" she asked, touching the scar on his thigh.

"Bullet."

She laid her hand on his shoulder. "And this one?"

"Knife."

"And this one?"

"Tomahawk."

She pressed her lips to each one, wishing she could erase all his old hurts.

"Ah, Jassy," he exclaimed softly, and claimed her lips with his.

And there, in a small narrow bed, amid moans of discovery and quiet cries of delight, Creed made love to Jassy as tenderly as ever a man made love to a woman, hoping she would hear the words trapped in his throat, that she would know he loved her more than life itself, that he needed her more than his next breath.

Later, with her head pillowed on his shoulder, her arm draped over his waist, Jassy let out a long, contented sigh. She felt as if she had waited her whole life for Creed Maddigan, and it had been worth the wait.

Chapter Twenty-two

"Where did you get the dress?" Jassy asked a long time later.

"It belonged to the hotel clerk's mother. I asked him if there was any place to find a wedding dress in this town, and she overheard me and offered to let me borrow hers. She decorated the dining room, too."

"And the suit?"

"Borrowed it from the undertaker," he admitted with a wry grin.

Jassy laughed softly. "Thank you, Creed, for everything."

"You deserve more than a borrowed gown and a bouquet of wildflowers," he replied, his voice laced with bitterness. "Hell, at the very least, you deserve a man who doesn't have to sign a phony name to the marriage license."

"I've got what I want." Jassy traced the line of his jaw with her forefinger. "More than I ever hoped for."

The town held a party at The Big Store for the newlyweds that night. Creed had tried to get out of it. He was a man on the run, after all, and being the center of attention didn't seem like a good idea, but the miners refused to take no for an answer, viewing the occasion as a good excuse to raise hell.

Jassy was embarrassed to be the center of attention, but Creed urged her to join in the spirit of it all, since there didn't seem to be any way to avoid it.

The music was furnished by a fiddle player, who was accompanied by a jug, an accordion, a banjo, and a harmonica. The band, such as it was, played loud and lively, and Jassy found herself dancing with men old enough to be her father and young enough to be her brother.

Creed stood on the sidelines, watching good-naturedly, cutting in every now and then to twirl her around the floor.

Two hours into the celebration, Jassy begged Creed to take her outside. "I need some fresh air," she complained softly, "and my feet hurt."

Smiling proudly, Creed took his wife's arm and led her outside. Wife, he thought. Damn, but that was going to take some getting used to. In all his life, he'd never had to look out for anybody but himself. And now he had Jassy to protect, to provide for. A wife meant responsibility, children. . . . He swore under his breath, hoping she would never be sorry, hoping he would never let her down.

Jassy drew in a deep breath. The night was cool and clear, the sky bright with a million twinkling stars. She slid a glance at Creed. Her husband. He had held her and loved her until she couldn't tell where she ended and he began. She had responded to his caresses with a boldness, a shamelessness, that had embarrassed her even as it had pleased him.

She let her gaze move over his profile, thinking again how handsome he was. She wished he would take her in his arms and hold her close. And then, to her surprise, she reached for him instead.

Creed grinned as Jassy wrapped her arms around his waist. "Something I can do for you, Missus Maddigan?"

"Yes, indeed," she replied.

Jassy pressed herself against him, hoping he would understand what she wanted so she wouldn't have to say the words aloud.

"You wouldn't be wantin' to dance, would you?" Creed drawled, a hint of laughter in his tone.

"No," Jassy replied, letting her hands glide up over his shoulders and down his shirt front.

Creed grunted softly. "A walk, perhaps?"

With a frown, Jassy slipped her hand under

his shirt and caressed his skin. It was warm and solid, and touching it made her whole body quiver with desire. "Creed . . ."

He laughed out loud as he swept her into his arms. "Don't worry, Jassy, I'm pretty sure I know what you want."

A flood of heat burned its way up her neck and into her cheeks. "Do you think I'm terrible?"

"I think you're wonderful." His lips nuzzled her hair. "Don't you think it's what I want, too?

"What about the party?"

His eyes blazed with a fervent heat as his gaze met hers. "We'll have our own party, Missus Maddigan," he replied, his voice thick with desire. "Just you and me."

She buried her face against his shoulder as he carried her down the street to their hotel, her heart hammering with anticipation, her nostrils filling with his scent. She threaded her fingers through the long hair at his nape, loving the way it felt in her hand.

Effortlessly, he carried her up the stairs to their room, and then they were alone, just the two of them. Slowly, deliberately, he lowered her feet to the floor, letting her body slide over his, letting her feel the proof of his need, his desire. His love.

He had promised to tell her he loved her every day of his life, and now, as he undressed her and caressed her, he murmured the words over and over again, fervently, solemnly, so she would never forget.

"And I love you," Jassy replied, her body welcoming his sweet invasion, rising to meet him, to gather him close. "Love you, love you, love you!"

And then she was reaching for the moon and the stars, and he was giving them to her with both hands, until she was wrapped in moonlight and starlight, safely cocooned in her husband's arms.

He had to coax her out of bed in the morning. Weary from a night of lovemaking, shyly eager for his embrace, Jassy tried to pull Creed back into bed with her. Instead, he lifted her into his arms and carried her across the room. Standing her on her feet, he bathed her from head to foot. He might have got through it okay if she hadn't started caressing him, letting her fingertips slide over his chest and down his belly. She poked one finger into his navel, then dropped her hand until it rested on the rising bulge in his trousers.

"Imp," he growled, and made love to her there, on the floor.

The sound of the train whistle reminded him that they didn't have all day. Drawing Jassy to her feet, he tossed the washcloth at her.

"You'd better wash yourself this time," he said, "or we'll miss the train."

* * *

She had never ridden on a train, and she could barely contain her excitement as Creed helped her aboard. She was going to San Francisco!

San Francisco. It conjured up images of miners and mansions and millionaires.

She followed Creed down the narrow aisle until he came to an unoccupied seat. Jassy slid in first so she could sit near the window.

Her heart was pounding so loudly that she thought it would surely drown out the wail of the whistle and the sound of the wheels as the engine lurched forward.

She sat with her nose pressed to the glass, watching the countryside race by. When the conductor came by to punch their tickets, he told her proudly that the train traveled at an amazing speed of twenty-five miles an hour, more than twice as fast as a stagecoach. He also told her that there were thirty thousand miles of track laid from one end of the country to the other.

Spurred on by Jassy's interest, the conductor spent the next ten minutes telling Jassy more about trains than she had ever cared to know. He mentioned that the first locomotive to run on rails had been built in 1825 by Mr. John Stevens of Hoboken, New Jersey. The train ran on a half-mile track located behind Stevens's house.

"Fascinating," Jassy murmured.

"Isn't it?" the conductor agreed, then went on to tell her that the first railroad company in

America had been the Baltimore and Ohio, chartered in 1827.

"Very interesting," Jassy said.

"Enjoy your trip, ma'am," the conductor said, and tipping his hat, he made his way to the next car.

The novelty of riding on a train quickly lost its charm, and Jassy decided that, while traveling by rail might be quicker than traveling by coach, it wasn't a whole lot more comfortable.

As the hours passed, and the train rattled on, she found herself wondering what would happen if the engineer fell asleep. Would the train keep going? Would the cars jump the tracks?

Occasionally, ashes and cinders drifted through a window. She overheard the conductor telling a young boy that trains had once been called brigades of cars, but way back in 1830, the Baltimore and Ohio had used the term "train of cars" in an advertisement, and the word train had stuck.

Later, Jassy heard one of the lady passengers complain that she had once counted thirteen holes burned in her dress due to the engine's constant belching of sparks.

Fortunately, there were stops along the way. At Bryan, there was an hour's delay to change locomotives.

Creed and Jassy left the train to walk through the town. Creed pulled his hat low, his gaze darting right and left as they made their way to a small restaurant.

"What's the matter?" Jassy asked.

"Just being careful. I'm still a wanted man, you know."

"I didn't see a sheriff's office," Jassy said. "Maybe you're worrying for nothing."

"Maybe."

Creed stared out the window, hoping Jassy was right, hoping that he was, indeed, worrying for nothing. They were a long way from Harrison.

They ate quickly, then returned to their seat in the train.

Soon they were on their way again, passing through Evanston on their way to Ogden. The country they passed through was beautiful. The Bear River Mountains rose in the distance and Jassy felt a sudden longing to go exploring, to climb mountains and explore caves, to ride in a canoe, to wander through the vast wilderness.

A new husband, a new world, a new life. She had never been happier, she thought, snuggling against Creed. Gradually, the hum of the wheels and the motion of the train lulled her to sleep.

Carefully, so as not to awaken her, Creed eased Jassy down on the seat, cradling her head in his lap, his hand lightly stroking her hair as he stared out the window. He felt a mild twinge of regret as he realized that his bounty-hunting days were over. Like a bird whose wings had been clipped, he was no longer free to fly from place to place, following the wind or a whim. He had a wife now, responsibilities. Sooner or later, he'd have to find a place to settle down, a job. . . .

He swore under his breath. Who in hell would give him a job? He was wanted by the law. The only things he was any good at were tracking and fast-drawing a Colt.

Damn. He'd thought he had overcome his doubts, but now they rose in full force once again. Who did he think he was, to take on a wife when he had nothing to offer her? He was an escaped convict with a price on his head. A half-breed. People would never forgive him for that, or forgive Jassy for marrying him. And what if she got pregnant? The thought chilled him to the marrow of his bones. What if she was pregnant even now?

He placed a hand over her flat stomach, trying to imagine it swollen with his child. What kind of father would he be? He didn't have any experience at all with kids; he wasn't even sure he wanted any, but most women wanted a passel of kids. Damn, he thought again, why hadn't he kept his hands off Jassy McCloud and left her in Harrison where she belonged? Except she wasn't Jassy McCloud anymore. She was Jassy Maddigan. Missus Creed Maddigan, even though the name on the license said Monroe.

He glanced down at her face and knew why he hadn't left her behind. He needed her, and he loved her, loved everything about her. She was the best thing ever to happen to him, and he was terrified that he would let her down, that he wasn't good enough for her, that in the end he would prove himself to be no better than most people thought.

Damn, but women sure made life complicated.

The Union Pacific line ended in Ogden. Leaving the train, Creed went to the Central Pacific depot and bought two tickets for Sacramento; then they made their way to the hotel.

Creed didn't miss the look of contempt that passed over the hotel clerk's pasty face as he tossed their room key on the counter.

"Room six, top of the stairs, Mr. Jones," the clerk said. His voice was high-pitched and filled with disdain, his gaze speculative as his gaze slid over Jassy.

"She's my wife," Creed said, his voice hard and flat.

"I—what?" the clerk stammered.

"I thought you might be wondering what our relationship was," Creed retorted. "Now you know. So keep your eyes off her."

"Yessir," the clerk replied quickly.

Creed grabbed Jassy by the arm and practically dragged her up the stairs.

"Creed, you're hurting me!" Jassy exclaimed.

He loosened his hold on her arm instantly. "Sorry," he muttered contritely.

"You can't fight the whole world, you know."

He paused on the landing. "Dammit, Jassy, he was leering at you like you were a . . ."

"Whore?" she supplied.

"Yes, dammit, that's just what he thought. Because you were with me."

Anger boiled up inside her—anger at all those thoughtless people who had made Creed feel that he was inferior because he was half-Indian. And anger at Creed himself, because he let those opinions affect the way he saw himself.

"Listen to me, Creed Maddigan," she said, her hands fisted on her hips. "I don't care what anybody else thinks of me, or of you. All that matters is what you think and what I think. And I think you're the most wonderful man in the whole wide world." Her eyes threw a challenge at him. "What do you think?"

"I think you're beautiful when your back is up," he said, grinning broadly as he reached for her hand. "Come on, I want to show you something."

"What?"

"What do you think?"

The expression in his eyes warmed her cheeks and sent shivers of excitement coursing through her as she followed him into the room.

She stood in the middle of the floor while he closed and locked the door, then threw his saddlebags in a corner.

"Come here, Missus Maddigan," he drawled softly.

"Why?"

"Don't you want to see what I have to show you?"

Swallowing the urge to laugh, she tried to

look uninterested. "I think I've already seen it."

Humor glinted in Creed's dark eyes. "Tired of me already, are you?"

"What do you think?"

"I think I'm the luckiest man in the world—or I would be, if you'd get the hell over here."

Hips swaying provocatively, Jassy closed the distance between them. Tilting her head to one side, she gazed up at him, her lips slightly parted, her heart racing at his nearness and the knowledge that he wanted her as much as she wanted him.

"I'm here, Creed."

"Jassy . . ." With a low moan, he swept her into his arms and carried her to bed.

He had thought to make love to her slowly, to seduce her with soft words and gentle hands, but the spark within him roared to life, fanned by her nearness, by the taste of her lips, the touch of her hands delving under his shirt to caress his back.

Pressing her into the mattress, he kissed her deeply, burying his doubts in her sweet acceptance of who and what he was.

And for those few moments, there was nothing in all the world but the woman in his arms.

Chapter Twenty-three

The train left early the next morning. Jassy was still half asleep as she followed Creed out of the hotel toward the train, but not too tired to admire his broad back and the loose-limbed way he walked.

She felt a flush of heat as she recalled how he had made love to her the night before. Making love to Creed was more wonderful than she had ever imagined—and certainly worth the wait!

She smiled up at him as he climbed aboard the train and offered her his hand.

My husband, she thought, and joy bubbled up inside her. She slid across the seat while Creed stowed the carpetbag containing their extra clothing under the seat, then sat down beside her.

With a sigh, she pillowed her head on his shoulder and closed her eyes, utterly content.

Creed wrapped his arm around Jassy's shoulders, all his protective instincts coming to the fore as he held her close. His wife. Damn, but that took some getting used to.

A wry grin twisted his lips. It was no wonder she was tired. He'd made love to her until the early hours of the morning, possessing her again and again as if to prove she was really his, that he could take her as often as he wished. He'd never had a woman like Jassy. She had come alive in his arms, her body like fire and silk beneath his hands. He had buried himself in her warmth, in her smooth softness. And when he'd finally drawn away, forcing himself to leave her alone so she could get some sleep, she had draped herself over him, arousing him anew with her hands and her lips, surprising him with the depths of her passion.

Jassy. He stared out the window, determined to give her everything she wanted, everything she deserved.

His reverie came to an abrupt halt when he saw a tall man clad in a sheepskin jacket and a flat-brimmed black hat walking down the narrow aisle. A warning bell rang in the back of Creed's mind. He'd seen that man before—but where?

The man's eyes, as blue and cold as a frozen lake, flicked over Creed as he passed by.

Damn! Creed felt a sudden itching between his shoulder blades as the man settled into the seat behind them.

Creed froze as the man leaned forward, his voice pitched low.

"Don't make any sudden moves, Maddigan, unless you want your guts splattered all over the lady."

"What do you want?"

"We're getting off the train, real slow. See that *hombre* near the door? The one in the tan duster?"

Creed nodded.

"He's my partner. I want you to pass me your iron, real easy like, using your right hand."

Moving slowly, Creed reached for his gun. Had he been alone, he never would have surrendered his Colt. But he wasn't alone, and he couldn't take a chance on Jassy being hurt.

"I'm waiting," the man hissed.

With a sigh of resignation, Creed slid the .44 out of the holster and passed it, butt first, to the man behind him.

"Good. Now, you get up and make your way toward the door. I'll bring the lady with me."

"Who the hell are you?"

"No time to explain now," Black Hat said. "The train's gettin' ready to pull out."

Creed glanced at Jassy. She was staring at him, her eyes wide with fright.

"You'd best do as he says, Jassy."

"But . . ."

"Just do it."

She nodded, and Creed stood up, then walked slowly down the aisle toward the door. He grunted softly as he recognized the man waiting there for him.

"What's going on, Bishop?" Creed asked.

Carl Bishop shook his head. "Shut up, Maddigan." He jerked his head toward the steps. "Get off the train. I'll be right behind you, so don't try anything."

Creed did as he was told. A few moments later, Jassy stepped off the train and hurried toward him.

Creed's gaze settled on the man wearing the black hat. "Now what?"

"We've got some horses waiting behind the feed store. We're gonna walk over there, nice and slow. And just so's you know how it's gonna be, if you try anything stupid, I'll shoot the woman first. You savvy my meaning?"

"Yeah."

"Good. Let's go."

Minutes later, they reached the rear of the feed store. A young boy stood in the shade, keeping an eye on four horses and a pack mule.

The man in the black hat flipped the kid a coin, and the boy hurried off.

"Hands behind your back, Maddigan," Black Hat ordered brusquely.

"What the hell do you want?"

"Can't you guess?" Black Hat asked.

Pulling a leather thong from the pocket of his jacket, the man tied Creed's hands together, making sure the knots were good and tight.

Creed stared at Bishop, then grimaced. "Never thought you'd take up bounty hunting, Carl."

Black Hat fixed Bishop with a hard stare. "You never told me you knew Maddigan."

"You never asked," Bishop replied succinctly. "Anyway, it was a long time ago."

"So, where do we go from here?" Creed asked.

"We're takin' you back to Harrison," Black Hat said. "Friend of mine doesn't want you runnin' around loose. Said he'd make it worth my while to see you didn't make it to Frisco."

Creed's eyes narrowed thoughtfully. "Coulter?"

Black Hat nodded as he quickly searched Creed for weapons. "Right the first time. Not only will we collect the reward for bringing you in, but a nice bonus from Ray."

Black Hat stepped back. "The reward says dead or alive, so the first time you give me any trouble, you'll be facedown across your saddle. Understand?"

Creed nodded.

Black Hat leered at Jassy. "Maybe we'd better search her, too."

"Leave her alone," Creed said.

"No way," Black Hat said. Holstering his Colt, he ran his hands over Jassy, his thumbs skimming the curves of her breasts.

Rage exploded through Creed as he watched the bounty hunter paw Jassy. He surged forward, then swore as Bishop grabbed him by the arm.

"Dammit, Carl, let me go!"

"Don't be a fool," Bishop said. "There's nothing you can do."

Jassy's cheeks were bright red when the bounty hunter stepped away from her.

"So, Rimmer, did you find any hidden weapons?" Bishop asked dryly.

"No, but I might have to look again later, just in case."

"Keep your filthy hands off her," Creed warned.

"Shut up, Maddigan," Rimmer snapped. "It don't matter to me if I take you in riding that horse, or facedown over its back."

"Let's ride," Bishop said, lifting Jassy onto the back of a zebra dun.

"I'm in charge here, Bishop," Rimmer snapped, "and don't you forget it."

"As if you'd let me."

Bishop steadied Creed as he stepped into the saddle, then, taking up the reins to Maddigan's mount, he swung onto the back of his horse and headed out of town.

Jassy followed Creed, and Rimmer brought up the rear.

They rode until dark, then made camp in a

grove of trees near a shallow stream that was more sand than water.

Rimmer lifted Jassy from the back of her horse, his hands lingering at her waist. "How'd you get hooked up with the 'breed?" he asked.

"We're not 'hooked up'," Jassy retorted, pushing the man's hands away. "We're married."

"Yeah? Well, you'll likely be a widow soon."

"What do you mean?"

Rimmer shrugged. "It's a long ride to Harrison. Anything could happen."

"Is that a threat?" Creed asked, coming up to stand beside Jassy.

"Could be," Rimmer replied with a slow nod. "Just could be." He smiled at Creed, a cold smile laced with venom. "Go sit over yonder," he said, jerking a thumb toward a fallen log. "And you . . ." He gave Jassy a little shove. "Go fix us something to eat."

"Fix it yourself," she retorted.

Rimmer's cold blue eyes bored into Jassy. "If you're smart, lady, you'll do what I tell you, when I tell you. There's matches and grub in my saddlebag."

He stared at her a moment more, then went to look after the horses.

Creed sat with his back against the fallen log, his mind racing. He swore under his breath as he watched Rimmer walk away. John Rimmer. Creed swore again, cursing his bad luck. Rimmer was a bounty hunter to be reckoned with. It was said he had collected bounties on more than twenty men in the last three years, and he had brought them all in facedown.

Damn!

Face impassive, he began to work his hands back and forth. He had to get Jassy out of here, and soon.

"I'll fix the coffee."

Jassy looked over her shoulder to find Bishop squatting on his heels behind her. With a shrug, she thrust the coffeepot at him. She was frightened, more frightened than she had ever been in her life, but she was determined not to let it show. She had to keep her wits about her; she had to be strong. But it wasn't easy, not when Rimmer's threat kept ringing in her ears.

She glanced over her shoulder. Rimmer was a few yards away, unsaddling Creed's mount.

"If you're smart, Miz Maddigan, you won't provoke Rimmer," Bishop said quietly. "He's got a vicious temper, and he likes hurting people, especially women."

"What do you care?"

Bishop grunted. "I'd just hate to see you get hurt, that's all."

"Why are you riding with him?"

"He knows his business. Times are hard, but we've made a bundle of money in the last three years."

"Blood money."

Bishop leveled her with a hard look. "I wouldn't think you'd be in any position to throw stones," he said, filling the coffeepot with water from his canteen. "What with being married to Maddigan and all."

Sharp words sprang to Jassy's lips, but she bit them back. As much as it rankled, she was in no position to judge Bishop, not when Creed himself had once been a bounty hunter.

"What's going on?" Rimmer asked. He glanced from Bishop to Jassy.

"Nothing," Bishop replied, dumping a handful of Arbuckles into the pot. "Just making some coffee. She don't seem too familiar with cooking over a campfire."

"She'll learn. Go keep an eye on the 'breed."

"Why? He ain't goin' anywhere."

"Just do it," Rimmer said curtly.

With a nod, Bishop went to sit on the end of the log, his hand resting on the butt of his gun. "So, Maddigan, how's it going?"

"How do you think?" Creed retorted sarcastically. "Are you gonna let him take me in?"

Bishop's hand caressed the butt of his gun. "I don't know if I can stop him. He's got a draw like greased lightning."

"You owe me one, Bishop."

"Go to hell."

Creed looked over at Jassy. She was kneeling beside the fire, slicing potatoes into a small, cast-iron skillet. Rimmer sat beside her, his cold blue gaze moving over her face and figure like a snake waiting to strike.

"Looks like John's taken a fancy to your lady," Bishop remarked, following Creed's gaze.

"If he touches her, he's dead."

Bishop laughed softly. "How you gonna manage that?" he asked. Then he looked more closely at Maddigan's face, at the hatred glittering in the man's black eyes, and he knew the half-breed wasn't making an idle threat.

"You owe me," Creed said again.

"What do you want me to do?"

"Turn me loose."

"I can't do that!"

"Dammit, Carl, if that bastard lays a hand on her, I'll come after you, too."

Bishop's hand closed over the butt of his gun for reassurance. "I ain't afraid of you," he retorted. But it was a lie, and they both knew it.

Creed's anger grew steadily as the hours passed. Rimmer stayed close to Jassy, forcing her to eat from his plate, his arm frequently brushing against her thigh or her breast. He refused to let her give Creed anything to eat, saying they didn't have enough food for the four of them.

After dinner, Rimmer tied Jassy's hands behind her back, then draped one of his blankets around her shoulders. At Rimmer's orders, Bishop tied Creed's ankles together and checked the rope binding his wrists. Bishop hesitated a minute, then offered Maddigan a drink from his canteen.

"Thanks," Creed muttered.

"Forget it," Bishop said, capping his canteen.

"Unlike some people," Creed said, fixing

Bishop with a hard stare, "I never forget a favor."

"Damn you, Maddigan, what do you want from me?"

"You know what," Creed said.

"I can't!" Bishop hissed. He glanced over his shoulder at Rimmer. "I'm no match for Rimmer, and you know it."

"I'm not asking you to face him in a fair fight."

"What do you expect me to do? Shoot him in the back?"

"If you have to."

"No."

"Then turn me loose."

"I can't do that. Dammit, Maddigan . . ."

"I killed an unarmed kid because of you," Creed said, his voice frigid.

All the color drained out of Bishop's face. And then, shoulders slumped, he nodded and turned away.

Creed watched Bishop walk away, the memory of killing that kid as fresh in his mind as if it had happened only yesterday. They'd been in a saloon in Dodge, playing poker, when Bishop had been caught cheating, something Creed had constantly warned him against, something Carl couldn't seem to resist. Bishop had drawn his gun, warning the other players to keep their hands where he could see them while he scooped up the cash on the table. One of the men had reached for his gun, and Bishop had shot him. Creed had been standing at the bar.

He had drawn his own weapon to discourage anyone else from interfering, and then Carl had yelled, "Creed, on your right!" He had turned and fired instinctively at Bishop's warning, then felt his blood run cold when he realized that the young man he had killed had been reaching for his hat, not a gun.

They rode hard for three days. Rimmer refused to allow Jassy to speak to Creed or to get near him. He was constantly at her side, rubbing up against her, making crude remarks, promising they'd "get to know each other better" once Maddigan was out of the way. He continued to insist that she eat from his plate and drink from his canteen.

Creed endured Rimmer's animosity and Bishop's seeming indifference in tight-lipped silence. Nights, he sat awake long after the others were asleep, trying to free his hands, trying to think of some way to persuade Bishop to cut him loose before it was too late, before he found himself dead or behind bars, before Jassy was totally at the mercy of John Rimmer.

Carl Bishop kept to himself. Once a day, he shared his canteen with Maddigan. At night, he offered Creed another drink from his canteen, then made sure Creed got something to eat, even if it was no more than a chunk of jerky. And each night he read the same tacit words in the half-breed's mind: *I killed an unarmed kid because of you. You owe me.*

And it was true, Bishop thought. He owed Maddigan a debt he could never repay.

Rimmer teased Bishop unmercifully about what he called Bishop's "soft streak."

"You gonna cry for him when he's crow bait?" Rimmer asked one evening.

Bishop refused to answer, but Jassy stayed awake far into the night, Rimmer's unspoken threat repeating itself over and over again in the back of her mind.

They'd been on the trail almost a week when the Indians appeared. There were about twenty of them, armed and painted for war.

"Let me talk to them," Creed said.

"You?" Rimmer shook his head. "I don't think so."

"They're Lakota," Creed said.

"What the hell difference does that make?"

"They're my people."

"Why doesn't that make me feel better?" Rimmer mused. "Forget it. We'll make a run for it."

"Don't be a fool!"

"What kind of fool would I be to trust you?" Rimmer retorted. "Let's ride!"

Grabbing the reins to Jassy's horse, Rimmer raked his spurs across his mount's flanks.

"Bishop, listen to me!" Creed called, but to no avail.

With a muttered curse, Bishop yanked on the reins to Creed's horse and urged his own mount after Rimmer's, which was galloping toward a low rise surrounded by boulders.

As soon as Rimmer took off, the Indians gave chase. Their hellish cries sent shivers of fear skittering along Jassy's spine as she fought to stay in the saddle. Once she risked a glance over her shoulder. She could see Bishop and Creed following close behind, and hard on their heels came the Indians, their faces hideously streaked with paint.

And then the Indians started shooting at them, and Jassy stopped worrying about falling out of the saddle and started worrying about being shot.

Rimmer and Bishop both drew their guns and began firing at the Indians, until her ears rang with the sharp staccato sound of gunfire. They had almost reached the point where Rimmer hoped to make a stand when he toppled from the back of his horse.

She heard one of the Indians shriek in triumph, and then the world spun out of focus as her horse went down.

She screamed as the ground rushed up to meet her.

Chapter Twenty-four

For a moment, time and space ceased to exist. Then, without remembering how it had happened, Jassy found herself lying facedown in the dirt, the breath knocked from her body.

For a moment, she didn't move, and then she realized that the shooting had stopped. Heart pounding with trepidation, she sat up and looked around.

Her horse was thrashing on the ground a few feet away, an arrow through its neck.

Rimmer was dead. Three of the Indians shouted something as they struck his body with feathered sticks.

A few feet behind her, she saw Bishop's body sprawled on the ground. It was obvious that he, too, was dead. She turned away, choking back the urge to vomit, as one of the warriors bent over Rimmer's body, knife in hand.

Where was Creed?

She stood up, concern for Creed overriding fear for her own safety. And then she saw him, lying facedown in the dirt, the back of his shirt soaked with blood. Several Indians were gathered around him, their faces menacing under layers of hideous war paint.

"Leave him alone!" Jassy screamed, and ran toward Creed.

A warrior wearing three eagle feathers in his long black hair grabbed her by the arm before she reached Creed's side.

"Let me go!" Jassy cried. She struck the warrior in the face and kicked him in the shins, but to no avail. "Let me go to him!"

"Inila, winyan." The Indian spoke quietly, but there was no mistaking the authority in his voice or the fact that he was admonishing her to be quiet.

"Please," Jassy said. "Please let me go to him."

The warrior stared at her, his gaze lingering on the beaded choker at her throat before returning to her face.

"Where did you get that?" he asked, his voice sharp.

"He gave it to me," Jassy replied, too worried about Creed to wonder at the Indian's use of English.

The warrior looked at her skeptically, as if he

didn't believe Creed would give a white woman an Indian-made trinket.

Jassy blinked back her tears. "Is he dead?"

"Not yet."

Jassy looked over at Creed. Two Indians knelt beside him. It took a moment for her to realize that they weren't going to hurt him, that they were helping him. While she watched, they bound his wounds, wrapped him in a blanket, and handed him up to a burly warrior mounted on a big piebald gelding.

The warrior holding Jassy released her arm. "Go home, *winyan,*" he said.

"I'm going with you," Jassy said.

"No."

"But he's my husband!"

The warrior made a sound of disbelief low in his throat.

"It's true!" Jassy exclaimed, the thought of being left behind in this wild place almost as frightening as the thought of being parted from Creed.

She gave a little start when one of the Indians fired a bullet into her horse's head, putting the animal out of its misery. Then the warrior was lifting her onto the back of Rimmer's horse.

She felt the bile rise in her throat again as they rode by Bishop's body, and she saw the raw, bloody patch on the back of his head. As they rode past Rimmer's body, she couldn't help seeing that he, too, had been scalped.

She glanced at the warrior riding beside her.

Were they just going to leave the bodies lying in the dirt?

"Aren't you going to bury them?"

The warrior looked at her curiously. "Bury?"

"You know, bury? Put them in the ground?"

The warrior shook his head, his expression telling her more clearly than words what he thought of such a silly idea. The white men were the enemy, undeserving of a proper Lakota burial. Their blood would nourish the earth, their flesh would feed the scavengers.

"How did you learn to speak English?" Jassy asked, her curiosity coming to the fore now that Creed seemed out of danger.

The warrior looked at her as if she weren't too bright. "From a *wasichu*." He paused a moment. "From the whites," he said flatly. "At the reservation."

"Is that where we're going?" Jassy asked hopefully. "To the reservation?"

The warrior looked at her for a long moment. "You ask many questions, white woman."

With a nod, Jassy stared ahead once more, her thoughts turning to Creed. How badly was he hurt? What would happen to them at the hands of these Indians?

They rode all that day, stopping only once to rest and water the horses. Creed was still unconscious, his face deathly pale.

It was dark when they reached the Lakota village. Several men and women gathered around to meet the returning war party. Jassy watched anxiously as Creed was carried into a large tipi near the center of the village. She stood beside her horse for a few moments, and when no one approached her, she ducked into the tipi where they had taken Creed.

No one paid her any attention, so she stood near the doorway, watching quietly. There were three Indians in the lodge. One of them, a stocky man with long gray braids, sat beside a small fire, chanting softly as he sprinkled some kind of ground leaves into the flames. When a pungent aroma filled the air, he reached for an eagle feather, which he passed through the smoke several times.

When that was done, he picked up a knife and knelt beside Creed. She had thought Creed to be unconscious, but now she heard his voice, low and edged with pain as he spoke to the Indians in their own tongue.

Jassy's stomach plummeted to her toes as she got her first glance at the gunshot wound in Creed's chest. To her, it looked enormous. The edges were red and ragged. Blood welled from the wound, trickling down his chest, to be wiped away by one of the other Indians. The stocky Indian, who Jassy had decided was probably the tribal medicine man, began chanting again as he passed the blade of a knife through the smoke, and then he began to probe the wound in Creed's chest.

Creed swore a vile oath as the blade pierced his flesh. At a word from the medicine man, the other two Indians took hold of Creed so he couldn't move.

Jassy turned away, unable to watch, as the medicine man dug the bullet out of Creed's chest.

The low sound of chanting filled the lodge.

Once, she heard Creed cry out in pain.

And then there was a soft grunt of satisfaction, and she guessed the medicine man had dislodged the slug.

She turned around then, her gaze settling on Creed. His face was pale, and he was sweating profusely. His eyes were closed, and she wondered if he had passed out. She fervently hoped so.

She drew back from the doorway as the two warriors left the lodge. The medicine man noticed her then, apparently for the first time. He stared at her for a long moment, and she held her breath, waiting for him to order her from the tipi. Instead, he motioned her to come closer.

"Pehanska," he said, "your woman here."

Creed's eyelids fluttered open. "Jassy?"

"I'm here." Hurrying toward him, she knelt at his side and took his hand in hers. "You'll be all right," she said, but even as she spoke the words, she wondered how he could possibly survive. His hand was hot where it rested in hers; his eyes were fever bright.

Her gaze slid to his chest. The medicine man had packed the wound with a poultice of some kind, then covered it with a strip of cloth. "Can I get you anything?"

"Water."

Jassy looked at the medicine man, who handed her a canteen. Jassy stared at the container, at the letters "U.S." stenciled on the side. Lifting Creed's head a little, she held the canteen to his lips.

The medicine man watched her for a moment, then rose to his feet. "You stay," he said, and left the lodge.

"Jassy, don't be afraid," Creed said. "If anything happens to me . . ."

"Nothing's going to happen," Jassy exclaimed. "You're going to be fine."

"They won't hurt you. If anything happens to me, Tasunke Hinzi—the warrior wearing three eagle feathers—will see you safely back to Rock Springs."

Creed closed his eyes as a wave of pain swept through him. He was badly hurt, and he knew it, just as he knew his chances of survival were slim. But Jassy would be taken care of. She was his wife, and the Lakota would respect that.

"Creed?"

He heard the worry in her voice, and he opened his eyes. "I'll be all right."

She smiled through her tears. "Of course you will."

She sat beside him all that night, wiping his body with a cool cloth in hopes of bringing down the fever, spooning broth into his mouth, covering him with a heavy robe when chills wracked his body.

The hours passed slowly as she endeavored to combat the recurring chills and fever. The medicine man came and went several times through the night, bringing broth and tea for Creed, offering Jassy a bowl of hot venison stew. He changed the poultice every few hours and added sage and sweet grass to the fire. Once, he sat beside Creed for twenty minutes, chanting softly as he drew an eagle feather through the smoke, drawing it over Creed.

Dawn came, and there was no change. Creed was unconscious now, his face ashen, his breathing rapid and shallow. He was going to die, she thought numbly.

Needing to be alone, she left the lodge and walked away from the village, not stopping until she came to a winding river. Kneeling on a patch of dew-damp grass, she folded her hands and stared at the brightening sky, a prayer rising in her heart as the sun climbed in the sky.

"Please," she murmured. "Please let him live. I love him so much. Please, don't take him from me. He's all I have in the world."

She gazed at the brilliant bands of color that spread across the sky, thinking she had never seen anything so beautiful.

"Please," she murmured, knowing that a Being who could create such beauty had the power to heal, to be merciful.

"Please, I'll be so good if You just let him live. . . ."

The sound of a woman weeping drew him from the edge of eternity. With an effort, he opened his eyes. At first, he saw only darkness, and then he saw Jassy sitting beside him, her head bowed, her hands folded in her lap, her cheeks wet with tears. He gazed at her for several minutes, wondering why she was crying. It was an effort to stay awake, to breathe, to think.

Jassy was crying. He longed to take her in his arms and comfort her, but he lacked the strength. The darkness of oblivion whispered in his ear, promising to shield him from the pain that rocked him with every breath. It was tempting, so tempting. For a moment, he considered surrendering to the darkness. All he had to do was close his eyes and let the blackness carry him away.

But then he heard Jassy's voice again. She was praying for him, her words thick with tears. She was crying for him, he thought, crying because he'd been hurt and she thought he was going to die.

Summoning all his strength, he moved away from the velvet cloak of darkness. "Jassy?"

"Creed!" His name was a cry on her lips, a cry of joy, of relief. Of love. "How do you feel?"

"Like hell."

Her smile was bright enough to light a city.

"I've been so afraid," she murmured. "So afraid."

Her hands moved over him, caressing his cheek, adjusting the blanket that covered him, resting on his brow to take his temperature in the way of women the world over.

"I don't understand why the Indians tried to kill you, and then brought you here."

"The Indians didn't shoot me, honey. It was Rimmer."

"Rimmer! Why?"

"I don't know. Are you all right?"

"I'm fine. Are you hungry?" she asked. "Thirsty?"

"Thirsty."

"You need to eat something."

"Later."

He drank the water she brought him, then lay back and closed his eyes. He'd been close to death before, he recalled, but never this close.

"Creed?"

"I'm okay, Jassy. Just tired." He felt her take his hand in hers. "Don't worry, honey. I'll be all right. Why don't you get some sleep?"

He tugged on her hand, pulling her down beside him, his arm slipping around her shoulders to draw her up against him.

Minutes later, he was asleep.

Lying there beside him, her head resting on his shoulder, Jassy offered a silent prayer of thanks to all the gods, both red and white, for sparing the life of the man she loved.

* * *

He did not make a good patient. He was too weak to do more than sit up for a few minutes at a time. He knew it, but he didn't like it. Being idle made him irritable. He didn't like having Jassy wait on him hand and foot. He didn't like being bedridden. He didn't like the fact that he couldn't even get up to relieve himself.

He snapped at Jassy and growled at Mato Wakuwa, the medicine man, until they both threatened to let him lie there and rot.

Tasunke Hinzi came each day to visit, and Jassy learned that Tasunke Hinzi and Creed had been childhood friends. Sometimes she sat near Creed while the two men reminisced about the old days, before the army had attacked their village and taken the survivors to the reservation.

Now was one of those times.

Jassy listened as Tasunke Hinzi spoke of the time on the reservation, unable to believe that the Indians had been driven from their homeland and subjected to such inhumane treatment. She had always been taught that the Indians had been sent to the reservations for their own good, that they were housed and fed and clothed. But Tasunke Hinzi told a different story.

The days at Standing Rock had been hard, he said. There had never been enough food or blankets. The old ones had longed for home, and they had sickened and died at an alarming rate. The children had been hungry all the time.

The women grieved; the men grew angry. After a few months, the warriors began to leave the reservation. One by one, they had slipped away, and after a while, the women and children had followed.

"My people will never go to the reservation again," Tasunke Hinzi said vehemently. "We will live here, or we will die here, but we will never again submit to the *wasichu*."

Tasunke Hinzi glanced at Jassy. She had discarded her *wasicun winyan* clothing for a doeskin dress and moccasins. Her only adornment was the choker at her throat. He remembered it well, remembered Pehanska's pride when his grandmother, Okoka, had made it for him. That had been long ago, he thought sadly. Long ago.

Abruptly, Tasunke Hinzi rose to his feet. *"Ake wancinyankin ktelo, kola,"* he said, nodding at Creed, then Jassy.

"Tanyan yahi yelo," Creed replied. "I'm glad you came."

Jassy watched Tasunke Hinzi duck out of the lodge. He treated her with respect, but she couldn't help wondering if he harbored a secret dislike for her because she was white, because her people had stolen his land and murdered his relatives.

Later that day, Mato Wakuwa came in to check on Creed's wounds. Mato Wakuwa didn't speak much English, but he always had a smile for Jassy, and as the days passed, she grew more and more fond of the old man.

Sometimes, when Creed was asleep, she went outside to sit in the sun. Mato Wakuwa could often be seen sitting outside his lodge surrounded by children and adults alike.

This day was no exception. Sitting with her back against the lodge, Jassy watched the faces of the children, smiling as their expressions changed from awe to humor.

She glanced up as Tasunke Hinzi approached the lodge.

"*Hau,*" he said, dropping down beside her.

"Hello."

"How is Pehanska?"

"Much better, thank you. He's asleep just now."

Tasunke Hinzi nodded. "Rest is good."

"What is Mato Wakuwa telling the children?"

Tasunke Hinzi listened for a moment, then smiled. "He is telling them the story of why people have five fingers."

"Stories, really?"

"*Han.* He is telling them that, in the beginning of the world, there were only animals. One day, no one knows why, the animals held a council and decided to make people. All went well with their design until they came to hands.

"Lizard and Coyote began to argue. Lizard said hands should be like his feet because he could grab things and hold on very tight.

"Coyote said no, hands should be like his, because he could dig and run very fast.

"Lizard said no, his way was best. That made

Coyote angry and he chased Lizard, who ran into some rocks to hide. Then Coyote built a fire to drive Lizard out of his hiding place.

"Lizard climbed on a high rock above the fire and waved to the other animals, crying, 'Here I am. Help me.'

"The other animals saw Lizard waving his hands, and they thought Lizard had won the argument. And that is why people have hands like Lizard, with five fingers."

Jassy clapped her hands, delighted with the winsome tale. She had never imagined Indians telling fairy tales to their children.

"Does he know a lot of stories like that?" she asked.

"*Han*. Among our people, storytellers are valued. Our history and our hero legends are passed from the old to the young. Is it not so among the *wasichu*?"

"Yes, but we also write our histories and our stories in books."

"Books?"

"On paper." Leaning forward, she wrote her name in the dirt. "This is writing. My people can communicate with each other in this way. We write our words in books. . . ." Jassy frowned thoughtfully. "You know how your people keep a winter count on hides? Well, books are like your hides, except they're made out of paper."

Tasunke Hinzi nodded. "Writing seems like a good thing."

"Yes."

He sat there for a moment more, then rose smoothly to his feet. "Tell my *kola* I will be back later."

"I will."

Jassy watched Tasunke Hinzi walk away. Indians were nothing like she had been told. She had been terrified of the Crow, but they had treated her well enough. The Lakota, too, were just people. True, they believed in different gods and their way of life was vastly different from hers, as was their language. But people were people wherever you found them. They loved and laughed; they fought and cried; they worried about their children and cared for their old ones. Some were easy to like, and some were easy to hate. But they were all just people, making the best of what they had.

Knowing that, she didn't feel like such a stranger.

Chapter Twenty-five

Two weeks passed. By the end of the second week, Creed was sitting up for longer and longer periods of time.

By the end of the third week, he was able to go outside to relieve himself.

Another week passed, and he fretted over the weakness that plagued him. The slightest exertion left him exhausted. It galled him to be bedridden. The ache in his chest was bearable but constant. But worst of all was the fact that he was too sore to make love to Jassy.

Ah, Jassy. She tended him day and night, hovering over him like a red-haired angel. She did everything she could to make him comfortable, listening while he complained, ignoring him when he acted like a spoiled child. But he couldn't help it. And he couldn't bring himself to tell her that she was the cause of his most urgent distress, that even though he wasn't physically strong enough to take her in his arms and make love to her, her nearness, her touches, her very scent, kept his body in a constant state of arousal, a fact that he managed to keep hidden beneath a buffalo robe.

Another week passed, and his strength began to return. He spent his mornings walking with Jassy along the river. It was good to be alive, good to be among his people again. Aside from Tasunke Hinzi and Mato Wakuwa, there were only three or four faces he recognized from his childhood. Were all the others dead, he wondered, or enduring the living death of the reservation?

He spent his afternoons resting in the sun, drinking in the sights and sounds of the village. Jassy had become friends with a white woman who had married one of the warriors. Once she was certain Creed was well on his way to recovery, she spent almost every afternoon with Sunlata, learning Lakota ways and helping Sunlata with her four children.

Creed let out a long sigh. Jassy was with Sunlata now, learning to make moccasins, and he was alone in the lodge. Lying there, his eyes closed, he listened to the familiar sounds of his childhood. He could hear women laughing as they erected a new lodge nearby. From somewhere in the distance came the sound of drumming.

He heard Mato Wakuwa telling stories to the children, and he remembered the days when he had sat at the shaman's feet, enraptured by the medicine man's tales. Mato Wakuwa must be a hundred, Creed thought, for he had been an old man when Creed was just a boy.

For a minute, he listened as Mato Wakuwa told the story of why Bobcat's face is flat. It was a Coyote story. Coyote, the trickster, figured in many of the Lakota stories. In this tale, Coyote sang a magic song to put Bobcat to sleep, and then Coyote began to push on Bobcat's face, pushing harder and harder, making Bobcat's face flatter and flatter. When Bobcat woke up, he felt funny, and then he smelled Coyote all around. Certain something was wrong, he ran to a lake and looked at his reflection, and when he saw what Coyote had done, he went looking for Coyote. When he found him asleep, Bobcat sang his own magic song, and then he began pulling on Coyote's nose, until it got longer and longer.

"And that," he heard Mato Wakuwa say, "is why Bobcat has a flat face, and Coyote has a long nose."

The children begged for another story, but Creed's mind drifted away from the account of how Crow came to be black. Instead, he reminisced about his childhood. He had never been ashamed of his Indian blood. It had been a good way to grow up.

Early in life, a Lakota boy learned to take pride in himself and in his people. He was taught to be proud of his accomplishments, to try to be the best in whatever he did. His first kill was honored. When he was fourteen, he went out alone to cry for a vision.

It was one of the things Creed regretted most, that he had never had the opportunity to seek a vision, that he had never received a warrior's name. He wondered now if his life might have turned out differently if he'd had a spirit guide to instruct him.

And then, from out of nowhere, he found himself thinking of his mother, something he hadn't done in years. He recalled his bitterness when she had forced him to leave the People and go back East to Philadelphia. He had despised her then, for forcing him to cut his hair, for burning his buckskins, for insisting that he speak English, for sending him to a private school where he was taunted and teased unmercifully until he blackened one boy's eye and broke another's nose. That had earned the respect of his peers, if not their affection. It had also earned him a severe tongue-lashing from his mother and several swats across his backside from the headmaster.

Most of all, he remembered the time he had been arrested for busting up that saloon. He'd never forgiven her for letting him spend two months sitting in that damn jail.

Creed swore under his breath at the memory. He had never hated anyone the way he had hated his mother for leaving him in that squalid little cell.

Now he wondered if his mother was still alive and if she had ever remarried. With a frown, he realized that he might have some half-brothers or sisters living in the East, maybe some nieces and nephews.

He glanced over his shoulder as Jassy entered the lodge. As always, just the sight of her made his blood race. Dressed in a doeskin dress that was almost white, with her red hair loose about her shoulders, her skin tanned a light golden brown, he thought her the most beautiful creature he had ever seen.

"Hi," she said, smiling.

"Hi."

"Were you sleeping?" she asked.

"No, I was just . . ." He shrugged. "Remembering."

"Oh?" She sat down beside him, automatically taking his hand in hers. "What were you remembering?"

"What it was like growing up here. I hadn't realized how much I missed being with the People."

"I like your people, Creed."

"Do you?"

Jassy nodded. "They aren't anything like I was told."

A wry grin touched his lips. "Did you expect to see them dancing naked around a bonfire while eating their young?"

"Of course not! But, well, I guess I didn't expect your people and mine to have so much in common."

"They like you, too, Jassy."

"I'm glad."

Their eyes met, and Creed felt a rush of heat surge through him as he gazed at Jassy. His woman. His wife. It had been weeks since he had made love to her. Too many weeks.

"Jassy . . ."

"It's too soon," she said, her voice filled with regret. "Your wound . . ."

"It doesn't hurt near as much as another part of my anatomy." He gave her hand a gentle tug. "Come here."

"We shouldn't . . ." she argued, but there was no conviction in her tone. "What if someone comes in?"

"They won't, not as long as the door flap is down."

It was too soon, she thought again, but she wanted him so badly, needed him so desperately, needed to feel his arms around her, to touch him and taste him. She'd come so close to losing him.

He pulled her down beside him and she turned on her side, her arm wrapping around his waist as her lips sought his. He kissed her long and hard, and then his tongue slid over her lower lip, and little flames of desire exploded in the deepest part of her.

They made love slowly, drawing out every kiss, every caress, getting to know each other again. Creed forgot the pain of his wound in the joy of holding Jassy close again. Her scent surrounded him, the silk of her hair teased his chest, and her hands and lips stroked him gently, arousing him as no other woman ever could until, with a low groan, he rose above her, sheathing himself within her.

They fit together like a hand in a glove, he mused, and then all thought was gone, swallowed up by waves of pleasure and sensation as his life poured into her.

Late summer gave way to fall. The trees changed their gowns of green for shimmering leaves of orange and red and yellow. But here, in this place, time had no meaning. Creed ate when he was hungry, slept when he was tired. Here, in the land of his birth, he could put all his doubts and fears behind him. It didn't matter that he was a half-breed, that he was an escaped convict, that he owned nothing but the clothes on his back.

He spent his days with the men, gambling, reminiscing, or simply resting in the shade. Sometimes he sat in the sun, absorbing the sights and sounds of the village. He watched some boys race their ponies along the riverbank, watched a handful of women erect a lodge. And always, his gaze strayed toward Jassy. She was learning to make moccasins, to cook over an open fire, to jerk venison, to tan a hide.

In the five weeks they'd been in the village, she had managed to pick up a smattering of the Lakota language. *Iyuskinyan wancinyankelo* was a phrase she used often. It meant I'm glad to meet you. *Higna* meant husband, *mitawin* meant wife. *Ake u wo* meant Come again; *Le mitawa* meant This is mine; *loyacin he* meant Are you hungry; *tokiya la he* meant Where are you going? She had expressed some surprise when she asked about the Lakota word for good-bye and learned that there wasn't one. Creed had explained that his people felt that the conclusion of a talk was obvious and therefore required no formal word of parting.

Another two weeks passed. Early one morning, he went hunting with Tasunke Hinzi. Although Creed had been too stiff and sore to draw a bowstring, it had been good to sit on a horse again, to ride across the plains in the company of warriors. He had returned feeling better than he had in weeks.

Day by day, his strength increased, as did his appetite. For food and for Jassy. He couldn't seem to get enough of her. Sometimes he made love to her for hours, arousing her slowly, plying her with kisses and soft caresses, bringing her to the brink of ecstasy only to draw back and start again, delighting in her soft moans of pleasure. At other times, he took her swiftly, his hands and lips bringing her to fever pitch in only moments. And sometimes Jassy turned the tables on him, batting his hands away, refusing to let him touch her while she covered his face and body with kisses and sweet caresses until he ached with the pain of wanting her. Only then did she allow him to participate, to taste and touch.

But fast or slow, in command or subject to her will, the flame between them burned ever brighter until he couldn't remember what life had been like without her at his side.

They were sitting in the shade by the river. Another week had passed, and Creed had finally started to feel like his old self.

Lying back on the grassy bank, he stared up at the cloudless blue sky, thinking there was no place else he'd rather be.

"What was your father like?"

He glanced over at Jassy, who was sitting beside him, her feet dangling in the water, one hand splayed across her abdomen.

"He was a medicine man, like Mato Wakuwa. When I was little, I wanted to grow up to be just like him. There was no man in our village who was more respected."

"What was his name?"

"Rides the Wind."

"What does your Indian name mean?"

"White Crane."

Jassy looked thoughtful a moment. "Do the Indians baptize their babies?"

"No." Creed sat up. Plucking a blade of grass, he twirled it between his thumb and forefinger. "Four days after a baby's born, the parents invite everyone to a feast for the naming of the child. The father and the mother's mother give gifts to their friends, to the holy man, and to the poor. When the feast is over, the father announces the name chosen. I was named after my father's father."

Creed gazed into the water. If he'd gone on a vision quest, he likely would have received a new name.

"Is your father still alive?"

"My father was killed in battle when I was thirteen."

"And your mother?"

"I don't know. I ran away from home when I was seventeen, and I never went back."

"How did your parents meet?"

"My mother was wounded in a raid. One of the warriors brought her to the village and left her with my father. He tended her wounds."

"And they fell in love," Jassy exclaimed. "How romantic."

"Not exactly. My father fell in love. My mother hated everything about the Indians, including me."

"I'm sorry, Creed," Jassy said softly.

"Yeah." He tossed the blade of grass into the water and watched the current carry it away.

To this day, he didn't understand why his mother had refused to let him stay with the Lakota. She had made it clear that she didn't approve of him, that she was ashamed of his Indian blood, yet she had insisted on dragging him back East. Why?

"Haven't you ever wondered what happened to her?"

He shook his head. "I can honestly say I'd never given her a thought until we came here."

"Maybe, after we find Rose, we could look for your mother."

"Maybe, although I doubt she'd be too happy to find me on her doorstep."

"It's hard, when your mother doesn't love you," Jassy murmured. "I wish . . ."

"What, honey? What do you wish?"

"I wish I knew where my father is, if he's still alive. It's silly, I guess. I don't even remember what he looked like."

With a sigh, Creed put his arm around Jassy's shoulder and drew her up against him. "I was a pretty good bounty hunter, you know. I could probably track him down if you really want to find him."

Jassy looked up at him, at the tenderness in his eyes. "You'd do that for me?"

"If you want me to."

"I don't know. He probably wouldn't be any happier to see me than your mother would be to see you."

A faint suspicion rose in Creed's mind as his

gaze swept over Jassy. "Why this sudden interest in my mother and your father?" he asked, frowning.

Jassy shrugged and looked away, but she could feel Creed's gaze on her face, feel the heat climbing into her cheeks under his intense scrutiny.

"Jassy . . ." Creed swallowed hard. "You're not pregnant, are you?"

Hesitantly, she turned to meet his gaze. "Would you mind?"

Suddenly speechless, he could only stare at her. Pregnant! He tried to tell himself it was bad news, that he didn't want to be a father, that he had no right to bring a child into the world when his life was such a mess, but none of that seemed to matter now. He felt a smile pull at the corners of his mouth, felt a sudden excitement stir in the pit of his stomach.

Springing to his feet, he grabbed Jassy and held her tight. "I think it's great!" he exclaimed, and lifting her in his arms, he twirled her around and around. The sound of her laughter mingled with his, and then, breathless, he put her down, his hands resting on her shoulders.

"Jassy." He shook his head, overcome with awe to think that she was carrying a child. His child.

She smiled up at him, her eyes shining with love, and he knew she had never been more beautiful than she was at this moment, with her love shining in her eyes and a new life growing beneath her heart.

"I was afraid you'd be mad."

"No." He tilted her chin up, then lowered his head and kissed her. "I'm not mad. I love you, Jassy."

"And I love you!" she whispered fervently, and throwing her arms around Creed's neck, she kissed him with all the love in her heart.

Winter came in a rush of wind and rain. Now that Creed was well again, they moved into a lodge of their own. Creed had traded his horse to Tasunke Hinzi's wife, Wakinyela, for enough hides to make a lodge, and then Sunlata, Wakinyela, and a dozen of the women had got together and sewn the hides for the cover.

Jassy was amazed to find that the Lakota lodge stayed warm and snug, even in the midst of a storm. The inner lining kept out drafts and dampness and prevented rain from dripping off the poles. The warm air rising inside the tipi drew in cold air from the outside, which came in under the cover and went up behind the lining, creating a perfect draft for the fire and taking the smoke out with it.

The liner was sometimes referred to as a "ghost screen" because it prevented the casting of shadows from the fire onto the outer wall, thereby providing not only privacy for the family, but safety as well, giving no enemy who might be lurking in the darkness a target to shoot at.

Jassy glanced at the tipi lining. Unlike the lining in Mato Wakuwa's lodge, which had been covered with drawings that depicted the *shaman's* exploits in battle, the lining of their lodge was bare.

They had virtually no possessions other than the clothes on their backs, two buffalo robes, two willow-rod backrests, which had been gifts from Sunlata, and a few cooking pots which had been given to them by some of the other women.

Sunlata had told Jassy that, to the Lakota, the tipi was considered a temple as well as a home. The floor of the lodge represented the earth, the walls represented the sky, and the poles were the trails from earth to the spirit world. In Sunlata's lodge, directly behind the firepit, was a little space of bare earth which served as the family altar where sweet grass, cedar, or sage was burned.

Sunlata had told her that the Lakota believed that the incense carried the prayers to *Wakan Tanka*, as did the smoke from a pipe. Before each meal, the host said grace and made an offering of a choice piece of meat, either by placing it in the fire or burying it in the earth on the altar.

There were definite rules of etiquette for living in a Lakota lodge. If the door flap was open, friends usually felt free to walk right in. If the flap was closed, they called out or rapped on the hide and awaited an invitation to enter. If two sticks were crossed over the tipi door, it meant that the owners were away or that they wished to be left alone.

As a rule, men sat on the north side of the tipi and women on the south. On entering a tipi, a man moved to the right, a woman to the left. When possible, it was proper to walk behind anyone who was already seated.

So many things to learn and remember, Jassy mused, and yet, in spite of everything, she had never been happier. Creed was alive and well and they were together, and that was all that mattered.

Among the Sioux, winter was a time of storytelling. Men and women moved from lodge to lodge, visiting and listening in rapt attention as the old ones related the ancient legends and tales.

Jassy learned of *Iya*, who was the chief of all evil. He was personified by the cyclone, and his foul breath brought disease. Lesser gods in the demon group were water sprites, goblins, and monsters. *Iktomi* was known as the Trickster. He was a deposed god and reminded Jassy of Lucifer, who had been cast out of heaven for rebellion. There were other evil spirits in Lakota legend: *Waziya*, the Old Man; his wife, *Wakanaka*, the Witch; and their daughter, *Anog-Ite*, the double-faced Woman.

Wakan Tanka was the chief god, but there

were other gods: *Inyan,* the Rock; *Maka,* the Earth; *Skan,* the Sky; and *Wi*, the Sun, were Superior Gods. *Maka* was the mother of all living things. *Skan,* who was a source of power, sat in judgment on all the other gods. *Wi* was the defender of bravery, fortitude, generosity, and fidelity.

Lesser gods included *Hanwi,* the Moon, and *Tate,* the Wind. *Whope* was the daughter of the Sun and the Moon, and *Wakinyan*, the Winged, was the patron of cleanliness.

Jassy was fascinated by the Lakota religion. Four was a sacred number. There were four corners to the earth, four seasons to a year. There were four Superior Gods and four Lesser Gods. There were four classes of animals: crawling, flying, four-legged, and two-legged. There were four parts to all plant life: root, stem, leaves and fruit.

Just as the number four was sacred, so was the circle. The earth, the sun, and the moon were round. The four winds circled the earth; the bodies of animals and the stems of plants were round. Everything in nature, save the rock, was round. So the Lakota lodge was also round.

There were monsters in Lakota lore: *Gnaske,* the Crazy Buffalo, might bring insanity or paralysis. The *Unktehi* captured men and turned them into beasts; the *Nini Watu* were maggots that caused pain and suffering. The *Gica* caused accidents, while *Can Oti* made men lose their direction.

Jassy grinned as she thought of the bogey man her mother had frightened her with. He seemed tame when compared to a monster that could turn you into a beast!

Despite the cold and the snow, Jassy loved spending the winter with the Lakota. There was a freedom to living with the Indians that she had never known before. They ate when they were hungry, slept when they were tired, hunted when it was necessary, and played and sang to buoy their spirits when cold winter winds blew across the plains.

There were no clocks to tell her the time, no highborn ladies to look down on her because her mother had been a whore. There was only Creed, growing stronger each day. They could spend as much time as they wanted alone in the lodge, just the two of them, snuggled together under a warm buffalo robe. A cozy fire crackled in the firepit, but it was Creed's arms that kept her warm, that made her feel loved and cherished.

As the days and weeks passed, Jassy picked up more and more of the language. She found she liked living in a Lakota lodge. She liked the comfort and freedom of wearing a loose-fitting doeskin dress and leggings and fur-lined moccasins. She learned to cook over a fire, to skin rabbits and deer.

And each day, she fell more and more in love with Creed. Here, away from civilization, he smiled more and laughed more. Gradually, the hard shell that had surrounded him fell away. Only then did she realize that she hadn't really known Creed Maddigan at all until now.

Chapter Twenty-six

"What would you think about staying here?"

Jassy looked up from the pot of stew she'd been stirring. "What?"

"I asked how you'd feel about staying here. Indefinitely."

Jassy stared at him for a long moment, her mind racing. Stay here, with the Lakota? Live here? Have the baby here?

Creed was looking at her, waiting for an answer.

"I don't know," she said slowly. "I love your people, and I love it here, I really do, but . . ." She placed her hand over her abdomen.

"You're afraid to have the baby here?"

Jassy nodded.

"The Indians have babies all the time."

"I know."

"But?"

"Well, it's so primitive. I mean, what if something goes wrong, and we need a doctor?"

"Mato Wakuwa is a doctor."

"He's a medicine man."

"It's the same thing."

"But . . ."

"Never mind, Jassy. It was just a thought."

"You don't want to leave, do you?"

"No."

Tears stung Jassy's eyes. Why did she feel so guilty? It wasn't that she didn't love the Indians. She did. But she wanted to be near a real doctor when her time came. She wanted a midwife who spoke English and a doctor if something went wrong. Surely Creed could understand that? This was her first baby, and as much as she wanted it, she couldn't help being a little afraid.

With a sigh, Creed took Jassy in his arms. "Hey, it's all right, honey. We'll go on to Frisco in the spring, like we planned."

"You're disappointed in me, aren't you?"

"No. No." He pressed a kiss to the top of her head. "Don't ever think that, Jassy."

He tipped her chin up and smiled into her eyes. "I love you, Jassy."

"I love you, too."

"Good." He gave her an affectionate swat on the rump. "How about some of that stew?"

* * *

Gradually, the days grew longer, the weather grew warmer, and the snow melted. Creed didn't say anything more about staying with the Indians, but Jassy felt as though she had failed him somehow.

As spring grew nearer, the village seemed possessed of a growing excitement. It was the anticipation of the first spring hunt, Creed explained. Though the winter had been mild, it had been weeks since there was fresh meat in the village. The young men were eager for the hunt. The old ones were anxious for the taste of fresh buffalo hump and tongue.

As soon as the last snow melted, the village packed up and moved.

It was an amazing sight. Warriors mounted on prancing horses. Women talking together as they walked along. Children laughing as they rode the travois ponies. Dogs barking as they raced in and out of the horse herd.

Jassy had never seen anything like it in her whole life. It was like a circus parade. Mounted on a high-stepping bay gelding, she lifted her face to the sun, her heart swelling with love and contentment. Creed rode beside her. Dressed in buckskins, his black hair glinting in the morning sun, he looked like every other warrior. He rode with the same inherent grace and arrogance as the full-blooded Lakota warriors. Tasunke Hinzi had given Creed a bow and a quiver of arrows; Mato Wakuwa had given him a long-legged gray mare.

"Where are we going?" Jassy asked.

"To find the buffalo."

"Oh."

"I'll take you to Frisco, Jassy, I promise. Right after the first hunt."

She nodded, baffled by her churning emotions. One minute she wanted to stay with the Lakota, the next she felt as though Creed cared more for Tasunke Hinzi than he did for her—that it meant more to him to stay and go on some silly buffalo hunt than to get her to San Francisco.

These days, it seemed as though she was always on the verge of tears. Her breasts were tender and swollen. She was always tired. Sunlata had told her it was being with child that made her want to laugh one moment and cry the next, and Jassy supposed it was true. But understanding didn't make her changeable emotions any easier to live with.

She snapped at Creed for no reason at all, turned him away even though she wanted to be held, to be comforted. She felt fat and ugly one minute, beautiful and cherished the next. She was hungry all the time. And sometimes, at night, she craved the most peculiar things, like dill pickles and watermelon, neither one of which was available in a Lakota encampment.

They'd been trailing the buffalo for about two weeks the night she spilled a bowl of soup.

"Jassy, did you burn yourself?" Creed asked. He reached for her hand, but she jerked it away.

"Leave me alone!"

"Jassy . . ."

"You heard me, leave me alone!"

He stared at her for a moment, and then, ignoring her objections, he pulled her into his arms and held her tight.

"Jassy, it's all right. Go on, cry if you want to."

"I don't want to," she said, and burst into tears.

He held her and rocked her until there were no tears left, until she sat spent in his arms, her head cradled on his shoulder.

"I'm sorry, Jassy," he said quietly. "We'll leave for Frisco first thing tomorrow."

As promised, they left the village early the following morning.

Tasunke Hinzi provided them with horses, food, and blankets for their journey.

Jassy felt a twinge of regret as they rode away from the village. Saying good-bye had been harder than she expected. She had come to care for Mato Wakuwa, for Tasunke Hinzi, for Sunlata, and she knew she would probably never see them again.

She couldn't help feeling guilty for taking Creed away from his people. He had been happy with the Lakota, more at peace with himself than she had ever seen him. And yet, for all that, she wanted to go to San Francisco. She wanted to find Rose. Maybe it had something to do with being pregnant, this need to be among her own people. Whatever the reason, she knew she wouldn't rest until they found Rose. She needed to know her sister was all right. And even if Rose didn't want her, she was still the only family Jassy had.

After what had happened on the train, Creed decided they would go cross-country on horseback, avoiding towns and settlements unless they ran out of supplies.

Jassy couldn't help feeling apprehensive as they lost sight of the Lakota camp. It was just the two of them now, alone on the prairie.

The countryside was beautiful. Spring flowers brightened the hills and hollows. The trees were clothed in leaves of bright green. An ocean of new grass spread as far as the eye could see.

There was wildlife everywhere. Birds sang in the treetops. They saw spotted fawns hiding in the shelter of the underbrush and fat bear cubs frolicking near a stream.

Mindful of Jassy's condition, Creed set a slow, careful pace, pausing often to let her rest.

As the days passed, he hovered over her, making sure she had enough to eat and drank plenty of water. In the afternoons, he found a shady place and insisted that she nap for at least an hour. When they made camp, he did everything but the cooking.

In spite of the long hours in the saddle and their primitive campsites, Jassy had never felt so loved or so cosseted in her life.

She was sitting by their campfire a week later,

thinking how lucky she was to have a man like Creed to care for her, when she felt the baby move for the first time. Startled, she gave a little gasp. Immediately, Creed was at her side.

"What is it?" he asked anxiously.

"The baby," Jassy murmured. "It moved." She grabbed Creed's hand and placed it over her belly. "Here, feel."

Creed shook his head. "I don't feel anything."

"Wait."

A moment later, she felt it again—a faint fluttering, like angel wings.

"Did you feel it that time?" Jassy asked.

Creed nodded, his gaze filled with wonder. He'd known Jassy was pregnant, of course, but until now, the child hadn't been real. Now, for the first time, he realized that there was a living being growing beneath Jassy's heart, a child that would need more than just food and shelter. Never had the weight of responsibility felt so heavy. Never had he felt so unprepared, so inadequate.

And then he felt that faint flutter again, and his heart swelled with an emotion he'd never known before. His child, he thought, awed. The living proof of his love for Jassy, and her love for him.

He knew in that moment that he'd never loved her more, that no matter what he did, he'd never be able to repay her for giving him a little piece of immortality.

Moved beyond words, he pulled her into his

arms. "I love you," he murmured. "You know that, don't you?"

"I know."

"I'll try to be a good husband to you, Jassy, a good father to the baby."

"You're already a good husband," she replied. "And you'll be a wonderful father."

"I hope so."

"Stop worrying, Creed. We're in this together, remember?"

"I know, but . . ." He shook his head. He had hunted outlaws and trailed renegades without a qualm, but the thought of being a father scared him right down to his moccasins.

"I've never been a mother before, either, you know," Jassy reminded him. "What we don't know, we'll learn together." She laughed softly. "I remember hearing one of the town ladies say that the good Lord gave first babies hard heads and lots of patience because they had greenhorns for parents."

"I hope she was right," Creed muttered, "because I'm as green as they come."

It was a long ride to San Francisco. Even though Creed kept their hours in the saddle to a minimum, the journey was tiring for Jassy. At the end of a day on the trail, her legs were sore, her back ached, and she wanted only to sleep. Creed did all the chores, both morning and evening; at night he rubbed her back and shoulders and massaged her feet.

He held her when she cried for no reason, assuring her that everything would be all right.

Occasionally, they made love. He was ever so gentle with her then. His kisses were as fervent as ever, but he held her carefully, as though she might shatter in his hands.

She realized that her pregnancy frightened him, that he was afraid of hurting her or the baby. She tried to assure him that it was perfectly normal for them to continue to make love, at least for another month or so, but deep down, she, too, was afraid. She knew next to nothing about babies; she had never even held one.

What she did remember was hearing her mother discussing childbirth with some of the other soiled doves, recounting in vivid detail the pains of giving birth. The other women had talked of their experiences, too, then went on to reminisce about friends who had died in childbirth or spent days in labor only to deliver a stillborn child or die themselves.

She tried not to think of those things. She was young and healthy. She had never been with any man but Creed. She wasn't diseased, or old. She didn't drink hard liquor or smoke cigarettes. She had enough food to eat; she got plenty of rest. Surely she had nothing to fear. Except the pain. Young or old, healthy or infirm, all women agreed that nothing was worse than the pains of childbirth.

"Please, Lord, let us make it safely to San

Francisco," Jassy murmured as they bedded down that night. "Please let my baby be strong and healthy. And thank you, Lord, for Creed."

He was the one constant in her life, the rock she stood on, the hope she clung to. With Creed beside her, she knew she could endure anything.

Chapter Twenty-seven

Jassy felt a wave of relief when she got her first glimpse of San Francisco. One of the girls who had worked in the saloon with Rose had spent a Sunday afternoon regaling Rose and Daisy with stories of San Francisco, recounting how, back in the "old days," eggs had sold for twelve dollars a dozen and houses rented for eight hundred dollars a month. Of course, the thing the city seemed most known for was fires, there being six devastating fires between 1849 and 1851, most of them set to divert attention from plundering and robbery.

But she wasn't interested in the city's history. At the moment, all she wanted was a hot bath and a soft bed.

"We'll be there soon, Jassy girl," Creed remarked.

The trip had been hard on her, he mused, but she never complained. Now, as they rode closer to the town, he wondered if the trip had been worth it. Even if they found Rose, it was unlikely that she still had the money she'd stolen. But even that didn't seem as important as it once had. What mattered now was getting Jassy settled. He'd have to sell their horses to pay for a hotel room, and then he'd have to find a job. He grunted softly. With all the gambling dens in town, finding a job shouldn't be too hard.

A short time later, he drew rein in front of a whitewashed picket fence. The sign on the gate read:

BOARDINGHOUSE.
A. ROSS, Proprietor
VACANCY

He would have liked to be able to settle Jassy into a nice room at one of the better hotels, but weekly rates at a boardinghouse were bound to be a lot less expensive. Not only that, but the price included two meals a day.

Creed helped Jassy from the saddle. She looked tired. There were dark circles under her eyes. Trail dust lingered in her hair and smudged her cheeks. He grimaced as he glanced at their attire, wondering what the landlady would think when she got a look at

Jassy's doeskin dress and his buckskins.

"Why don't you wait here?" he suggested, not wanting to subject her to any rudeness he might encounter.

"All right."

"I'll be back in a minute," he said.

For a moment, he stared at the neatly painted house, the flowerpots that lined the front porch, the blue muslin curtains fluttering in an upstairs window. The place reeked of respectability. Well, there was no help for it. Running a hand through his hair, he opened the gate and walked up to the front door.

A buxom, gray-haired woman in her late fifties answered his knock. She wore a frilly pink-and-white apron over a starched calico dress. She eyed him warily for a moment.

"Can I help you?" she asked, her shrewd brown eyes sizing him up in one quick glance.

"I need a room for myself and my wife."

The woman glanced over Creed's shoulder to where Jassy stood outside the gate.

"You're Indian, aren't you?"

"Yes, ma'am."

The woman stared at Jassy again. "When's your missus expecting that baby?"

"In a couple of months."

"I don't allow no drinking in my house," the woman said sternly. "And no tobacco chewing."

"Yes, ma'am."

"I charge twenty dollars a week for two," she said. "In advance."

Creed nodded. "I don't have any money just now," he said, steeling himself for her rejection. "But I will have as soon as I sell our horses." He took a deep breath, hating to ask this woman for a favor. "I'd appreciate it if you'd let my wife stay until I get back. We've been on the trail a long time, and she needs a place to rest."

"Looks like she could use a bath, too."

"Yes, ma'am."

The woman regarded him for a long moment, taking in his long hair, the trail dust that covered his buckskins, the moccasins on his feet.

"What kind of Indian are you?" she asked.

"Lakota. Sioux."

"You ever scalp anybody?"

"No, ma'am."

A faint smile tugged at the corners of the woman's lips. "You wouldn't lie to me, would you?"

"No, ma'am."

"Well, I'll say one thing for you. You're the most polite Indian I've ever met."

"I'd venture to say I'm probably the only Indian you've ever met. Ma'am."

The woman laughed softly. "Well, now, that's a fact." She studied him a moment more, then sighed. "What's your name?"

Creed hesitated only a moment as he quickly searched his mind for another alias. "Macklin. Creed Macklin, ma'am. My wife's name is Jassy."

"Macklin?" the woman said, frowning. "That

doesn't sound like an Indian name to me."

"I'm a half-breed. My mother was Irish."

He waited while she made up her mind, then felt a rush of relief when she said, "I'm Annie Ross. Go on, get your missus. She shouldn't be standing out there in the sun."

"Thank you," Creed said.

"I imagine she'll be wanting a bath. I'll tell my girl to heat some water."

"Thank you," Creed said again.

Jassy looked at him expectantly as he walked toward her.

"We've got a room," Creed said. He tethered the horses to the fence. "The landlady's heating water so you can have a bath. And then I want you to take a nap while I go see about selling our horses."

A bath, Jassy thought. The mere idea sounded heavenly.

Annie Ross met them in the foyer. Creed introduced the two women. Somewhat shyly, Jassy shook the other woman's hand.

"Dinner's at six," Annie Ross said. "Don't be late. You can have the room upstairs, last door on the right. It has a nice big double bed."

"Thanks," Creed said, and taking Jassy by the arm, he led her upstairs.

The room was neat and clean. A brass bed stood against the far wall. Lace curtains covered the large window that overlooked the side yard. There was a small chest of drawers made of cherry wood, a matching commode, and an armchair covered in a flowered chintz. A small chair stood in front of a curved vanity table.

"It's nice," Jassy said, sinking down in the chair. "Can we afford it?"

"We'll manage. How are you feeling?"

"Fine. A little tired, is all. Stop worrying about me, Creed. Women have babies every day." She smiled at him, wishing she felt as confident as she sounded.

A short time later, a young girl knocked at the door. "Ma says your missus can come down and bathe whenever she's ready."

"Thanks," Creed said. "Come on, I'll walk you downstairs. While you're taking your bath, I'll go see about selling the horses."

"All right." She held out her hand. "Help me up, will you?"

He grinned at her as he pulled her out of the chair and into his arms. "Pretty soon I won't be able to put my arms around you," he teased.

"Very funny," she retorted. "Creed, do you think Rose is still here?"

"I don't know."

"What if she isn't?"

He shrugged. "I don't know, honey. All I know is, we're staying put until that baby's born."

"What if we find her and she doesn't have the money anymore?"

"Hey, stop worrying."

"I can't help it. We don't have any money. We don't even have any clothes . . . I'm sorry, Creed."

"Forget it."

"I don't mean to complain."

"Dammit, you've got every right to complain. You deserve a hell of a lot better than you've gotten so far."

"Creed, don't."

"It's true, and you know it." He took a deep breath. "You might have been killed because of me. And now you're gonna have a baby, and . . ." He swore under his breath. She was pregnant and married to a man with no money and no prospects, an escaped con with a prison record hanging over his head. "Come on," he muttered, "your bath water's getting cold."

There was no point arguing with him, Jassy thought, and even if there was, she was too tired.

He hesitated at the foot of the stairs, kissed her quickly, then went out the door without a backward glance.

With a sigh, Jassy followed Annie Ross down a narrow hallway to a small room that held a large zinc tub. Two large fluffy towels were folded atop a battered bureau.

"Take your time," Annie Ross said, smiling. "None of my other boarders require baths during the middle of the week."

"Thank you, Missus Ross. You've been very kind."

"Pshaw. Mind what I said, dinner's at six. Sharp."

"Yes, ma'am."

"Call me Annie. We don't stand on formality much around here."

"Thank you, Annie."

With a wave of her hand, Annie Ross left the room.

Jassy locked the door behind her, stripped off her dusty dress, and stepped carefully into the tub. She sighed as the water closed over her. She had never realized what a luxury a hot bath was. The Indians had washed every day, but they didn't have bathtubs. Men and women alike had bathed in the river.

She dragged her fingertips through the water, wishing Creed didn't feel that he had failed her. She didn't care about having a house of her own, or fancy clothes, or a lot of money. All she wanted was Creed.

With a sigh, Jassy closed her eyes as the water's warmth seeped into her. Of course, a house and fancy clothes would be nice, too. . . .

An hour later, Creed made his way into the Gold Strike Saloon and ordered a glass of beer. He had sold the horses, bought himself a new pair of trousers. For Jassy, he had bought a couple of dresses and unmentionables, as well as a pair of shoes and stockings and a hairbrush. To save money, he'd kept his moccasins and his buckskin shirt. People would no doubt stare at Jassy if she wandered around town in a doeskin dress, but he doubted that his buckskin shirt and moccasins would draw much attention.

Walking down the street, he had seen men wearing everything from fancy Eastern-cut suits to homespun shirts and Texas chaps.

Frisco seemed to be quite a melting pot. He had passed Mexicans, Chinese, Negroes, even a few Indians. He figured the Chinese were the largest contingent of immigrants. Someone, he couldn't remember who, had told him there were more than two thousand Chinese engaged in the laundry business. In some instances, by switching workers and signs, two firms used the same premises, working around the clock. The Chinese resided in Chinatown, a bustling, noisy section of town that was brightly decorated with calligraphy, fluttering ribbons, and shops crammed with exotic foods and Oriental paraphernalia. Chinatown housed a variety of stores, more than half a dozen pharmacies, a Chinese theater, and several restaurants, which were frequented by many non-Asian citizens.

Most of the black population lived west of Montgomery Street. They were employed as laborers, mechanics, waiters, porters, barbers, and businessmen. The black community had its own cultural organization, as well as its own newspaper, the *Elevator,* which came out weekly.

Then there was infamous Barbary Coast, a hellhole if ever there was one. Pity the poor fool who found himself wandering the streets near the waterfront, where anyone dumb enough to venture into its bawdy houses or gambling dens was considered fair game by the crimps who supplied crews to the ships. Few men who shipped out of the Barbary Coast went voluntarily. Most were plied with doped cigars or doctored gin and shanghaied.

San Francisco was a hell of a town. Women were in the minority, with young men making up the bulk of the population. In spite of their small numbers, the women had managed to make their presence known. Due to their influence, gambling on Sunday had been outlawed in 1855. But there were countless other diversions to be had—parades, dances, banquets, horse races, sing-alongs, concerts, the theater, cockfights, and bullfights were only a few of the ways the men found to entertain themselves.

Creed sipped his beer as he gazed around the room. If Rose was in town, she'd likely be working in one of the cribs, and while he didn't relish the thought of haunting every dive in the city, he knew it was the only way to find her. He just hoped she'd had enough sense to stay clear of the Barbary Coast, because, as much as he could use the money, he valued his hide at considerably more than four thousand dollars.

Chapter Twenty-eight

It was almost suppertime when Creed got back to the boardinghouse. He washed up, using water he found in a pitcher on the commode, while Jassy dressed.

They were the last ones downstairs. He'd never felt comfortable in polite society, and now, as five pairs of eyes swung in his direction, he remembered why. Face impassive, he held Jassy's chair for her, then took the one next to her.

All conversation at the table had stopped at their arrival. Curiosity seemed to roll toward him like the waves that endlessly washed against the beach at Yerba Buena.

Annie Ross stood up and smiled at her boarders. "This is Mister and Missus Macklin," she said, by way of introduction. "Jassy, Creed, may I introduce you to Mabel Downing, Artemis Coleburn, Wyatt and Paul Robinson, and Patricia Spelling."

Conscious only of the speculation in the eyes of the three men and two women seated at the table, Creed hardly heard their names, although he recognized Paul Robinson as the man who had bought their horses.

When Annie Ross finished her introductions, she sat down and passed a platter of fried chicken to Creed. Gradually, conversation at the table returned to normal.

Jassy smiled and made polite chit-chat with the woman beside her. For his part, Creed kept silent. He'd never been good at small talk, and he saw no reason to indulge in it now. Listening to the conversation around him, he learned that the Robinson brothers owned the livery. The Downing woman was the schoolmarm, and unmarried, though he could have guessed that. Patricia Spelling owned a small millinery shop. Artemis Coleburn worked in the bank and was courting Patricia Spelling.

The meal was almost over when Wyatt Robinson asked the question Creed had known was bound to be asked sooner or later.

"Am I wrong, Mister Macklin, or do I detect some Indian blood in your ancestry?"

Creed took a deep breath. Laying his fork aside, he turned to face Wyatt Robinson. "My father was Sioux."

Wyatt grinned at his brother. "Pay up, Paul."

With a grunt, Paul Robinson dug a dollar out of his pocket and slapped it on the table. Then he turned to Creed and explained, "I bet him you were Cheyenne."

"Sorry."

The conversation at the table picked up again, and Creed relaxed. Maybe he had misjudged these people.

After dinner, the two women boarders went into the front parlor, while the men went outside to smoke.

Jassy looked at Creed. "Do you want to join the men?"

"No, I think I'll go upstairs, but you go on and get acquainted with the ladies, if you want."

"Not tonight."

Hand in hand, they walked up the stairs to their room. Creed closed and locked the door, then sat down on the edge of the bed.

For a moment, he watched Jassy as she sat at the vanity table brushing out her hair and then, rising, he crossed the room and took the brush from her hand.

"Let me."

She smiled up at him, then closed her eyes as he began to brush her hair. It was oddly sensual, having him pull the brush through her hair.

"I'll have to look for a job tomorrow," he remarked.

"Where?"

"One of the saloons, most likely."

"Do you think Rose is here?"

"I don't know."

He laid the brush aside, then drew her back against him, his hands lightly kneading her shoulders. "How are you feeling, honey?"

"Fine." More than fine, she thought, basking in the touch of his hands.

She felt his lips brush the top of her head. Then he knelt behind her, his hands cupping her breasts. "Tired?"

"A little."

She heard his sigh of disappointment, felt him begin to draw away. "Not that tired."

"Are you sure?"

"I'm sure."

She turned to face him, lifting her face for his kiss, and as his mouth covered hers, she forgot about Rose and the money, forgot that they were strangers in a strange town. There was only Creed holding her, his hands unfastening the bodice of her gown, slipping under her chemise to caress her skin.

She threaded her fingers through his hair and let her hands slide over his shoulders and down his back, reveling in the muscles that flexed beneath her fingertips. Lifting the edge of his buckskin shirt, she explored the smooth expanse of skin under the soft cloth.

"Jassy . . ."

"Yes." She slid her tongue over his lower lip. "Yes."

With a soft cry, he swung her into his arms and carried her to bed. His hands were trembling with restraint as he removed her shoes and stockings, freed her of her dress and chemise.

"Beautiful," he whispered. Shedding his own clothes, he stretched out beside her. "So beautiful. Motherhood agrees with you."

"Does it?" Overcome with tenderness, she stroked his cheek, the curve of his jaw.

"Hmmm." Propping himself on one elbow, he rained kisses over her breasts and belly. As always, touching her stoked the fires of his own desire, but he kept it in check, afraid to go too fast for fear of hurting her or the child.

But then she began to touch him, to tease him unmercifully. "Jassy," he warned, his voice a low growl. "I don't want to hurt you."

"You won't," she said. "You won't. . . ."

With a low groan, he rose over her, careful not to crush her as their bodies became one.

She drew him closer, wrapping him in her love, until he was a part of her, body and soul.

He held her in his arms long after she'd fallen asleep, one hand splayed over her stomach, marveling at her ability to conceive life, to carry it and nurture it. Marveling at her ability to love him wholly and completely.

With Jassy at his side, he felt that anything was possible.

* * *

By noon the following day, Creed had a job dealing in the Gold Strike Saloon from seven till midnight every night but Sunday. Jassy tried not to let it show, but the thought of spending her nights alone in a strange town filled her with trepidation.

"I'm sorry, honey," Creed said. "It's the best I could do."

"It's all right," she said brightly.

Creed's expression was solemn as he cupped her chin in his hand. "No lies between us, Jassy. I know you don't want me working in a gambling hall. I know you don't like the idea of being alone at night, but . . ." He shrugged. "We need the money."

"I know." She rested her forehead on his chest.

"Jassy . . ."

Her head jerked up, and she glared into his eyes. "Don't you dare tell me I should have married someone else, Creed Maddigan, do you hear me?"

He raised his hands in mock surrender. "Hey, I wasn't gonna say that, honest!"

Head tilted to one side, she continued to stare at him.

"I was just gonna ask if you'd like to go have some lunch. I got an advance on my salary."

"Why, thank you, Mr. Maddigan, I'd like that very much."

* * *

Their days fell into a routine after that. They slept late, then spent the afternoon and early evening together. Creed spent a part of each day prowling from one saloon to another, looking for Rose, but it was Jassy who found her sister.

They had been in San Francisco almost a month. Creed was making good money dealing at the saloon. On this particular day, he was sitting in for one of the dealers who worked days, and Jassy had decided to go shopping.

She was leaving Patricia's Millinery Shoppe when she saw Rose walking across the street. For a moment, Jassy could only stare, unable to believe that the woman she was looking at was her sister. Rose had always been beautiful, vivacious, careful of her appearance. But this woman looked haggard and careworn. Her eyes were dull and her skin pale. Her dress was faded and down at the hem.

Lifting her skirts, Jassy ran across the street. "Rose! Rose, wait!"

With a sigh, the woman turned around. For a moment, she stared at Jassy, her expression blank.

"Rose, it's me. Jassy."

"Jassy?" Rose blinked at her several times. "Jassy?" Slowly, she shook her head. "Jassy, what are you doing here?"

"Looking for you. Rose, what happened?"

"Happened? Nothing."

Jassy glanced up and down the street; then,

taking Rose by the arm, she led her to a small restaurant. The proprietor started to object when he saw Rose, but Jassy stilled his objections with a few coins, then led Rose to a table in the back.

She ordered an enormous lunch for Rose and a glass of tea for herself. Only after Rose had eaten did Jassy question her sister again.

"Tell me, Rose, what happened after you left Harrison?"

Rose stared down into the dregs of her coffee cup. "Everything was fine at first. He bought me a new wardrobe, and we had rooms at the Palace. Ray said we'd get married, but he kept finding reasons to put it off. Then he—he started drinking and gambling. He lost every cent we had. We had to give up our rooms, and he sold all my clothes. . . ."

Rose clenched her hands in her lap. "He said he couldn't find a job. I don't know if it was true or not." Her voice dropped to a whisper. "And then, one night, he brought a man home with him. He said the rent was due, and we were broke, and the only way we could earn any money was for me to—to—"

Rose glanced at Jassy. "He wanted me to whore for him. I've done it most of my life, but I never thought the man I loved, the man who was supposed to love me, would put me up for sale."

She lowered her eyes, too ashamed to face her sister any longer. "I threatened to leave him, and he—he hit me. He told me he'd kill me if I tried to leave him, that I was the best whore in San Francisco, and I was going to make him rich.

"And then I—I got sick."

"Sick?"

"You know," Rose said, not meeting her eyes. "Sick." In truth, she'd had an abortion. "Ray brought me something to help me feel better. I didn't know what it was."

"What was it?"

"Opium."

"Opium! Oh, Rose, how could you?"

"It did make me feel better," Rose said, her voice defiant. "It made me numb."

Jassy gazed at her sister. Somehow, the fact that Rose had stolen four thousand dollars no longer mattered. Rose was the only family she had left, and she needed help.

"You're coming home with me," Jassy said.

"No."

"Yes."

"I can't."

"Why not?"

"Don't you understand? I don't want to leave him."

"Why not?"

"He gives me what I want. What I need. And I . . ."

"And you give him what he wants," Jassy remarked quietly.

"Don't look so shocked, Jassy. I've been doing it most of my life."

"Oh, Rose . . ." Tears of sympathy welled in Jassy's eyes. "What can I do?"

"Nothing." For the first time, Rose met her sister's gaze. "I'm sorry, Jassy," she murmured. "Sorry . . ."

"The money's not important."

"That's not what I meant."

"No? What then?"

Rose sat up straight in her chair and looked at Jassy as if seeing her for the first time. "What are you doing here?"

"I told you. I came here to find you."

"But how did you get here?" Rose frowned. Her gaze ran over Jassy and she blinked, then blinked again. "Jassy, you're—you're pregnant!"

Jassy nodded. "Yes."

"But—but how?"

"The usual way."

"Oh, Jassy."

"It's all right, Rose, I'm married."

"You are? To who?"

"Creed."

Rose stared at her sister, the initial excitement in her eyes changing to disdain. "Creed? Maddigan?"

Jassy nodded.

"You married that dirty, rotten half-breed?"

Jassy lifted her head and squared her shoulders, refusing to be intimidated by Rose's contempt. "I love him, Rose, and he loves me."

"You can't be happy with him!"

"But I am. He's a wonderful man, Rose, so kind, so good to me. . . ."

"He's a hired gun."

"Not anymore."

"Oh, Jassy, I'm sorry, so sorry." Tears welled in Rose's eyes and poured down her cheeks. "So sorry."

Jassy glanced over her shoulder. The other patrons were all staring at them.

"Rose, let's go. We can go to my room."

Rose shook her head. "They won't let me in the hotel."

"We're not staying at the hotel. We have a room at Annie Ross's boardinghouse."

Rose laughed bitterly. "You're crazy if you think old lady Ross would let me set one foot inside her house."

"Let me worry about that. Come on."

Jassy felt every eye in the place follow her as she paid for Rose's lunch, then left the restaurant.

Outside, the sun was warm. Taking Rose by the arm, Jassy led her sister down the sidewalk toward Annie Ross's house. Rose's arm was thin—too thin, Jassy thought, as if she didn't get enough to eat.

Annie Ross stepped onto the porch as they climbed the stairs, her arms folded over her ample breasts.

"Good afternoon, Annie," Jassy said, smiling.

"Good afternoon, Jassy," Annie Ross replied.

She remained in front of the door, her bulk blocking the entrance. "What is *she* doing here?"

"This is my sister, Rose."

"Sister!" Annie Ross exclaimed.

"Yes. She's the reason we came to San Francisco."

"But she's a wh—."

Jassy stared at the older woman, daring her to say the word.

"I mean . . ." Annie Ross shook her head in defeat. "She can visit, but she can't stay the night."

"Thank you, Annie. Do you think you could fix us a pot of tea?"

Annie Ross glared at Rose, then smiled at Jassy. "I'll bring it up when it's ready."

"Thank you, Annie."

"You've developed some gumption since you left Harrison," Rose remarked as she followed Jassy up the stairs.

"A little," Jassy agreed. Opening the door, she pulled off her gloves and removed her hat. "Make yourself comfortable, Rose. The tea should be ready soon."

"Why are you being so nice to me, Jassy? I don't deserve it."

"You're my sister."

"I know, but . . . Never mind." Rose sat down on the chair at the foot of the bed. "How long have you been in Frisco?"

"Not long. It seems like a fascinating city,

what little I've seen of it."

"Yeah, fascinating," Rose muttered.

A few minutes later, Annie Ross knocked on the door. She stared balefully at Rose as she handed the tea tray to Jassy.

"Thank you, Annie," Jassy said.

Annie Ross harrumphed and closed the door.

Jassy put the tray on the dresser, poured two cups, added cream and sugar, and handed one of the delicate china cups to Rose. "Here. This will make you feel better."

"I doubt it," Rose said.

Jassy studied her sister as she sipped her tea. Rose had been a beautiful woman once. Now her hair was dull and lackluster, her skin was sallow, and there were dark circles under her eyes.

Rose stared into her teacup, embarrassed by her sister's scrutiny. How could she make Jassy understand what her life had been like these past months? She had gotten sick after the abortion. If Coulter hadn't given her money for a doctor, she would have died. It was Coulter who had given her a place to stay and opium to ease the pain in her body and dull the guilt that had assailed her when she regained consciousness after the operation to face the stark reality of what she had done.

"You look tired, Rose," Jassy remarked, taking the empty teacup from her sister's hand and setting it aside. "Why don't you get some sleep?"

"Sleep? Yes, I'd like that."

Jassy pulled back the covers on the bed, helped Rose out of her dress and shoes, and tucked her into bed. Moments later, Rose was asleep.

Rose was still sleeping soundly when it was time for Creed to get home from work. Jassy had convinced Annie Ross to let Rosie spend the night, then she had spent the afternoon sitting at the window, watching the traffic in the street below. Not long ago she had hated her sister, hated her for refusing to let her testify at Creed's trial, for hitting her, for stealing her money and papa's watch. But she couldn't hate Rose, not now. Now she felt only pity.

She stood up when she heard Creed's footsteps in the hall. Convincing Annie Ross to let Rose spend the night hadn't been easy, but she knew that convincing Creed would be nigh impossible.

She was smiling when he opened the door. "Hello there," she murmured.

"Hello." He frowned as he tossed his hat on a chair. "Why is it so dark in here? Were you asleep?"

"No."

He pulled her into his arms and kissed her, and for a moment, she forgot everything else.

"So," Creed said, gazing down at her. "Have you already had dinner?"

"No, I waited for you. Annie said she'd keep something warm for us."

"Let's go eat, then," he suggested. "I haven't had anything since noon. I . . ." His words trailed off as he glanced at the bed. "Who's that?"

"Rose."

"Rose? Your sister, Rose?"

Jassy nodded.

"What the hell is she doing here?"

"Shhh. She's sick, Creed." Jassy took his arm and urged him out of the room. "I had to bring her here."

"Dammit, Jassy . . ."

"Creed, listen," Jassy whispered, mindful of the ears of the house. "She's been sick. She couldn't work, and then Coulter gave her opium, and—"

"Opium!" Creed swore under his breath.

"Creed, he's making Rose prostitute herself for him."

"So what? She's been selling herself for years."

"I know, but not like this."

"What difference does it make if she sells herself to one man or a hundred? It's all the same. Dammit, Jassy, if it wasn't for Rose, I wouldn't have spent all that time in jail."

"I know."

"She stole four thousand dollars."

"I don't care about the money."

"Well, I do. I worked damn hard for that money. Dammit, I almost got my head blown off earning it."

Jassy laid a placating hand on her husband's arm. "Creed, I can't turn her away. She's my sister. Except for you, she's all the family I have in the world. I have to help her if I can."

"Help her! I was thinking of having her arrested."

"You're not serious!"

"I was," Creed muttered, "but I guess that's out of the question now. Come on, let's go down and see what Annie left for us to eat."

Chapter Twenty-nine

Rose stretched and yawned, then groaned as she sat up. Where was she? She glanced around the room, then gasped as her gaze came to rest on Creed Maddigan. He was sitting in a chair at the foot of the bed, his expression cold and hard.

Clutching the covers to her chest, Rose pressed herself against the headboard.

"You want to tell me about it?" Creed asked.

"About what?"

"Don't play games with me," Creed said, his voice sharp.

"Where's Jassy?"

"Downstairs, taking a bath. We've got time for a nice long talk."

"I've got nothing to say to you."

"Well, I've got plenty to say to you."

"Does Jassy know you slept with me?"

Creed frowned. "Of course not!"

"What do you think she'd say if she knew?"

"If you're smart, you won't tell her."

"Is that a threat?"

"Damn right!" Creed stood up. "You stole my money, and I don't guess there's any way to get it back, but if you're smart, you won't say anything to hurt Jassy. You understand? She's been hurt enough."

"I understand," Rose replied sullenly. "If you'll leave, I'll get dressed and be on my way."

"My pleasure."

She waited until he left the room, then jumped out of bed and yanked on her dress and shoes. She had to find Coulter. Soon. She would do anything he asked, everything he asked, just as long as he gave her what she craved. What she needed.

"Where's Rose?" Jassy glanced around the room.

"She's gone."

"Gone? Where?"

"I don't know. Come here, I'll brush out your hair."

Frowning, Jassy sat on the edge of the bed. Usually, she loved to have Creed brush her hair, but now all she could think about was Rose.

"She's sick, Creed."

"She's an addict."

"What?"

"She's addicted to opium."

"I don't believe you."

"It's true. I could smell it on her last night."

Jassy shook her head, not wanting to believe it even though she knew it was true. Rosie had admitted as much. *He gives me what I want*, she'd said. *What I need*.

"Listen, Jassy, what do you say we leave here? There's no way we're gonna get the money back, so why don't we make tracks for greener pastures. Montana or Wyoming, maybe?"

"Leave? Without Rose? I can't. She needs me."

"You can't give her what she needs, Jassy. Nobody can."

"What do you mean?"

"I mean," he said, taking her in his arms, "she needs to want to get better. She needs to want to change the kind of life she's living. Until then, nothing you can say or do is gonna change a thing."

"I don't believe that."

"Okay, okay," Creed muttered, brushing her lips with a quick kiss. "Have it your way for now."

Creed dealt the cards automatically. Another hour, and then he could go home. Funny, how quickly he had become accustomed to the idea of having a home to go to, of having Jassy there, waiting for him. It frightened him sometimes, how deeply she was embedded in his heart, in the very fabric of his life. It was hard now to believe there had been a time when she hadn't been there, when he hadn't known the warmth of her smile, the tenderness of her touch. So much love wrapped up in such a neat little package. And soon they'd have a child.

He swore under his breath as he shuffled the cards and dealt a new hand. A baby. As nervous as he was at the thought of being a father, he was beginning to think it might not be so bad.

"Where've you been?"

Rose shrugged, not meeting Coulter's eyes. "Just out."

"You look like hell."

"I'm hurting, Ray."

"I can see that. Where were you all night?"

Rose looked up at him. There was no point in lying. He'd find out the truth one way or another. "My sister's in town. I stayed with her."

"Sister? The one you stole all that money from?"

Rose nodded. "Please, Ray, I'm hurting awful bad."

"Is the 'breed with her?"

Rose stared at Coulter. "Why?"

"The longer it takes you to answer my questions, the longer it'll be till you get what you want."

She nodded slowly, hating herself for her weakness. She'd stolen Jassy's money, and now she'd put Maddigan's life in danger. But it couldn't be helped. She tried to tell herself that Maddigan was no good, that he was a hired gun, an escaped convict, but nothing she said eased her conscience. Jassy had offered to help her, and she was repaying her sister's kindness with treachery. Again.

"Where are they staying?"

"Annie Ross's boardinghouse." Rose placed her hand on Coulter's arm. "Please, Ray, leave them alone. My sister's gonna have a baby."

"So what?"

"She needs her husband."

"I'll take care of her."

"No, Ray."

Rose stared up at him, wondering at her sudden concern for Jassy's welfare. Maybe it was the fact that she was dying that made her long to right the wrong she'd done her sister. Maybe, at long last, she had grown up enough to realize that she'd brought most of her misery on herself. Whatever the reason, it was important that Jassy stay clean, that Jassy's baby have a mother and a father, something neither she nor Jassy had ever had.

Rose licked her lips when Ray unlocked the closet and pulled a small box from the shelf.

He grinned knowingly as he tossed it to Rose. She fell on it like a duck on a June bug, all else forgotten as she sought the relief she craved.

Coulter went to look out the window. So,

Maddigan was here. He cursed viciously. Damn Rimmer! Either he'd been too stupid to trail the 'breed, or he was dead. Either way, Maddigan was in Frisco. He took a deep breath, forcing himself to remain calm, to think. There was a bounty on Maddigan's head. The baby could be sold for a good bit of change. And so could the woman, either into a brothel or to one of the ships that dealt in the white slave trade.

A wry smile tugged at his lips. Yes, he stood to make a tidy sum. The only thing to decide was whether he should kill the 'breed and take the woman now, or wait until the baby was born.

He dragged a hand over his jaw. It would be easier to take the woman first, he decided, and use her for bait.

He turned away from the window. "Rose?" He shook his head in disgust when he saw the slack expression on her face, the blank look in her eyes. "Rose!"

She blinked up at him, and he swore under his breath. He'd have to write the note himself.

Jassy glanced up from the mending in her lap as Annie Ross entered the parlor.

"This just came for you," Annie said, handing Jassy a sealed envelope.

"For me?" Jassy frowned as she opened the envelope and took out a single sheet of paper.

"Everything all right?" Annie asked.

"I don't know." Her gaze moved to the bottom of the note. "It's from my sister."

> Jassy, I need your help. Please come to the Wayfarer Saloon tonight after ten. Take the back stairs. Coulter will be gone from ten to eleven. Please don't tell anyone, especially Creed.

Jassy read the letter a second time. The handwriting wasn't Rose's, but the signature was. Had Rose been too ill to write the note? She felt a flutter of excitement building within her as she wondered if Rose had found the courage to leave Coulter.

She glanced at the clock on the wall. It was almost ten now. Folding the note, she slipped it inside the shirt she had been mending, then stood up.

"I'm going out for a little while," Jassy said. "I won't be gone long."

Annie Ross frowned. "Going out? At this hour?"

"Yes, I . . . Creed wants to meet me for a late dinner."

"You be careful, hear? It's not safe for decent women to be walking the streets this time of night."

"I'll be fine," Jassy said. "Don't worry."

"I'll worry if I want," Annie Ross retorted.

Jassy smiled at the older woman. Annie's voice might be gruff, but she had a heart as big as the Pacific. Annie Ross was one of the few real friends Jassy had ever had, and she treasured her friendship.

Minutes later, Jassy left the house. The Wayfarer Saloon was near the waterfront, a place Jassy had avoided until now. As she made her way down the dark streets, she wondered at the wisdom of going after Rose alone. If Coulter was gone, surely it wouldn't have mattered if she had brought Creed with her, she mused, and then blew out a sigh of resignation. Rose and Creed didn't get along. It was likely they never would.

She heard raucous music and male laughter long before she neared the saloon itself. Taking a deep breath, she made her way to the rear of the saloon. The stairs were clearly visible in the moonlight.

Taking a deep breath, Jassy lifted her skirts and started up the stairway.

Heart pounding with trepidation, she opened the door and stepped into a short, narrow hallway. There was only one door. She hesitated a moment, wondering if she should knock. Deciding against it, she opened the door and stepped inside.

"Rose?"

A low groan sounded from the far side of the room.

"Rose, is that you?" She peered into the darkness. As her eyes grew accustomed to the dark, she saw a bed against the far wall. "Rose?"

The figure on the bed groaned again, and Jassy crossed the room.

She was halfway across the room when she heard the door shut behind her. There was a whiff of sulphur, a flash of light as someone struck a match, and then the flickering glow of a candle.

Jassy spun around, a gasp lodging in her throat when she saw the man standing in front of the door.

She'd forgotten how tall and intimidating Ray Coulter was. He wore a gun on his right thigh and a knife on his left.

A slow smile curved his thin lips as his gaze ran over Jassy. "Evenin', Jassy," he drawled.

Jassy stared at him, unable to speak past the fear congealing in her throat. She glanced over her shoulder. Rose was tossing fitfully on the narrow bed. Her face was pale and sheened with perspiration.

"My . . ." Jassy licked her lips and tried again. "Is my sister all right?"

"Hardly."

"What's wrong with her?"

"Didn't she tell you?"

Jassy shook her head.

"She's dyin'."

"Dying? No! Has she seen a doctor?"

"Yeah."

"Can't they do something?"

"Nope. It's just a matter of time."

"Is there anything I can do?"

Coulter shook his head. "Just stay with her."

"Of course." Jassy took a step toward the door. "I'll need to go back to the boardinghouse and leave a note for my husband, pick up a few things."

"I don't think so."

Jassy met his gaze then. For the first time, she saw the feral gleam in his pale green eyes. "Rose didn't write that note, did she?"

"She wrote what I told her," he said, his voice hard. "She always does what I tell her. If you're smart, you'll do the same."

Jassy took a step backward, her arms wrapping protectively around her stomach. "What do you want?"

"All I can get."

"I don't understand."

"You and that half-breed make up a nice package," Coulter remarked. He leaned back against the door and crossed his arms over his chest. "There's a nice reward for the 'breed." His eyes turned hard and cold. "Though I may just kill him myself for what he did to Harry."

"It was self-defense!"

"Bullshit! Harry was just a kid." He made a vague gesture with his hand. "One way or another, I'll have my revenge." A cruel smile twisted his lips. "I know some folks who'll pay a hefty sum for a white woman and a newborn babe."

Jassy stared at him, more frightened than she'd ever been in her life. Being captured by

Indians had been nothing compared to the horrible fright that clawed its way through her. Her legs suddenly refused to hold her, and she sank down on the floor, feeling dazed and lightheaded. He was talking about selling her baby, about white slavery. She remembered reading an account in one of the papers about women who had been kidnapped and sold into foreign brothels, never to be heard from again.

She stared at Coulter for a long moment, and then she began to laugh hysterically. All her life she had tried to avoid becoming what her mother had been. She had left Harrison, married Creed, and come to San Francisco, certain she had escaped the stigma and threat of becoming a whore. And now this man was going to sell her to a brothel. It was funny, so darn funny that tears streamed down her face.

And then she began to sob. Arms folded over her stomach, she rocked back and forth, hardly aware that her laughter had turned to tears.

She didn't protest when Coulter lifted her from the floor and laid her down on the bed beside Rose. Lost in the horror of what lay ahead, she stared at the ceiling while he tied her hands together. She should have stayed in Harrison, she thought wryly. At least she'd have had a certain amount of freedom. At least she wouldn't have had to go to bed with strangers.

Fresh sobs tore at her throat as she felt her baby stir within her womb. What would become of her child? What would happen to

"When?"

"Oh, about ten, as I recollect. Someone brought her a note. She was right upset when she left."

Creed swore. "Did you see it? The note?"

"No."

"Damn!" He paced the length of the hall, then stopped in front of Annie Ross's door. "If she comes back, you keep her here."

"I will."

"Thanks."

Creed went to their room, stepped inside, and closed the door. Removing his gunbelt, he tossed it over a chair. He had a derringer tucked inside his left boot. Now he slid a knife inside his right boot and hoped it would be enough.

It was midnight straight up when he entered the Wayfarer Saloon. A few men glanced his way as he stepped through the swinging doors. Hard men. Sailors, mostly.

Creed made his way to the bar and ordered a drink, which he held in his right hand but didn't touch.

He didn't have to wait long. Two men walked toward him. The one on the left said, "Follow me," then turned and walked outside. Creed fell into step behind him, aware of the second man close on his heels.

Outside, they turned left and went to the rear of the saloon. Creed stiffened as he felt the nudge of cold steel against his spine. He stood there, rigid, while the first man searched him.

It was a very thorough search. Creed swore under his breath as he felt the man's hands prod between his thighs, in the hollow of his back, down each leg. The man grunted when he found the derringer and the knife.

"The boss said no weapons," the man muttered. "If you're smart, you won't make any more mistakes."

He didn't expect a reply, and Creed didn't offer one. The man at his back gave him a little push, and Creed climbed the narrow staircase.

A short time later, he was standing inside a small room that smelled heavily of unwashed bodies and opium. A movement on the bed drew his gaze, and he swore under his breath when he recognized Jassy. She appeared to be asleep. Her sister lay beside her, obviously heavily drugged.

Creed started toward Jassy, but one of the men behind him warned him not to move.

"Is she all right?" Creed asked.

"She's fine. For now."

Creed turned toward the sound of the voice. Ray Coulter stood inside the doorway, his hand curled around the butt of a well-used Colt revolver.

Coulter nodded to the men standing in the hallway, and one of them closed the door.

"What do you want?" Creed asked.

Coulter tossed him a pair of handcuffs. "For starters, put those on."

Creed stared at the irons, revulsion rising

within him. For a moment, he weighed the odds of jumping Coulter and trying to get his gun, but even as the thought crossed his mind, he knew Coulter was expecting just such a move.

Muttering an oath, Creed clamped the handcuff on his wrists. "Now what?"

"I was gonna turn your body in for the reward," Ray replied, holstering his Colt. "But I decided that would be too quick, too easy. I want you behind bars. I want you to wake up in the morning and go to bed at night thinking about your woman, wondering where she is, if she's still alive."

"Dammit, Coulter, she's got no part in this!"

"That's where you're wrong. She's a pretty woman. After the baby's born, I know a place or two that will pay me a hefty sum for her services."

Nausea churned in Creed's gut as he imagined Jassy locked in a room in some distant brothel, never to be free again, forced to do whatever she was told until she got too sick or too old.

"And the child?"

Coulter shrugged. "Easily sold."

Creed took a step forward, murder in his eye, only to find himself staring into the yawning maw of the other man's Colt. "Don't even think about it."

"Let her go."

"No."

"I've got some money. Not much, but I can get more."

Coulter shook his head. "No. You go back to prison, and she goes to the highest bidder. No loose ends."

"Ray, is that you?"

"Go back to sleep, Rose."

She sat up, rubbing her eyes. And then she saw Creed. "What are you doing?" she asked, glancing at the gun in Coulter's hand, then at Creed and back again.

"Nothing you need to concern yourself about."

Rose stood up, swaying unsteadily. It was then that she saw Jassy. "What's my sister doing here?"

"She came to visit. Don't you remember?"

"No . . . no." Rose looked at Coulter again, her eyes filled with confusion. "The note. You made me sign a note."

"Shut up, Rose."

"Why is my sister tied up?"

"Shut up, dammit!"

Rose disregarded the warning in Coulter's voice. "I want to know what's going on."

"He's sending me back to prison," Creed said, his gaze fixed on Coulter's face. "And then he's gonna sell Jassy to a brothel, after he sells your niece or nephew."

"Ray, you wouldn't!"

Coulter looked at her as if she wasn't too bright. "You fool. Where do you think I get the money to buy that opium you love so much?"

"I don't know. I guess I never thought about it."

Coulter shook his head. "It's a good thing you're pretty," he muttered, " 'cause you sure ain't smart."

Creed glanced at Jassy while Coulter and Rose continued to hurl insults at each other. Jassy was awake now. Creed shook his head slightly, warning her to stay still, to remain quiet.

"I'll do what I damn well please!" Coulter shouted, and Creed's attention was drawn back to the confrontation between Coulter and Rose.

"She's my sister," Rose retorted. "And you're not selling her into slavery."

"She was your sister when we took all that money," Coulter reminded her with a sneer. "That didn't seem to bother you."

"That was your idea and you know it! I let you talk me into it because you promised to marry me."

Coulter snorted. "Who'd marry a whore!"

Rose recoiled as if she'd been slapped, but she refused to back down. "Send Maddigan to prison, if you want. I don't care what you do with him. But you can't hurt Jassy or the baby."

"I'll do whatever I damn well please," Coulter said, drawing out each word. "I own you body and soul, and if you don't want to find yourself in some brothel on the other side of the world, you'll remember that."

Rose stared at Coulter, all the color draining from her face. "You wouldn't!"

"I'll do what I have to do."

"I'm sorry, Jassy, so sorry." With a sob, Rose threw herself on the bed and pulled Jassy into her arms. "Sorry, so sorry," she repeated over and over again.

Coulter swore a vile oath as he watched the two women rock back and forth.

Seeing that he was distracted, Creed took a step forward, but Coulter's gun immediately centered on his chest again.

"I wouldn't," he said, "unless you'd rather be dead. Don't matter to me, you know? The reward says dead or alive."

Creed froze. He'd be no good to Jassy dead, he knew, though he was of damn little use to her now.

And then Rose was standing up, her face buried in her hands, sobbing uncontrollably, staggering toward Coulter, her hand clutching his arm as she begged him not to sell her sister and the baby.

Momentarily thrown off balance, Coulter tried to brush her off, and Creed lunged forward, his cuffed hands reaching for the gun.

Jassy screamed and bounded off the bed, throwing herself in front of Creed as Coulter lined the barrel on Creed's chest.

The sound of gunfire filled the room. Jassy staggered backward, a bright red stain spreading over the bodice of her dress.

With a cry, Rose flung herself on Coulter.

The second gunshot was muffled, and then Rose fell backward, her hands clutching at Coulter, dragging him down with her.

Creed lunged forward, his hand closing around the gun. Jerking it from Coulter's grasp, he brought the butt down on the man's head, then pivoted on his heel, thumbing back the hammer as the door burst open and Coulter's two henchmen filled the doorway.

Creed fired twice, and both men went down.

The ensuing silence was deafening. He waited a minute, listening for the sound of footsteps in the hall, but apparently gunfire was commonplace at the Wayfarer Saloon, and no one came running to find out what was going on.

Shoving the Colt into his waistband, he knelt beside Coulter and fished the key to the handcuffs from the man's pocket.

After removing the irons from his hands, Creed gathered Jassy into his arms, one hand smoothing the hair from her face.

"Jassy? Jassy, can you hear me?"

Her eyelids fluttered open, and she tried to smile. "You're alive. . . ."

"You little fool! You could have been killed."

"Love . . . you . . ." she whispered, and then her head fell back over his arm.

Gently, he eased her down on the floor and unfastened her bodice. Blood poured from a jagged hole high in her right shoulder. Only her shoulder, he thought, weak with relief. Thank God. Tearing a ruffle from her petticoat, he tore it in two. Pressing half of it over the wound to stanch the bleeding, he used the other half to hold the square of cloth in place.

Then, reluctant to leave Jassy, he dragged Coulter across the room and handcuffed the man's hands behind his back When that was done, he shut and locked the door, then went to examine Rose's wound. He knew at a glance that it was fatal.

"Is . . . Jassy . . . ?"

"She'll be all right," Creed said as he placed a wad of cloth over Rose's wound, then bound it in place with another ruffle torn from Jassy's petticoat.

"I need . . . paper."

"Later."

"No . . . now. Must write . . . confession."

"Confession?"

"I saw . . . what happened . . . with Harry."

"You were there?"

Rose nodded. "Saw . . . everything." She closed her eyes. "Paper . . . in desk."

Moving quickly, Creed found a sheet of paper, an inkwell, and a pen.

"You . . . write what I say . . . I'll sign. . . . "

Fifteen minutes later, Rose signed her name to the paper. "Tell Jassy . . . sorry . . . for every . . . thing."

"I will."

"Tell her . . . not to . . . hate me. . . . "

Creed nodded.

"Cold . . ." Rose whispered. "So . . . cold."

With a sigh, Creed gathered Rose into his arms and held her close. Held her and rocked her until the last breath whispered past her lips and she lay still in his arms.

Rising, he placed her on the bed and drew the covers over her.

After folding Rose's confession in half and stuffing it in his pocket, he gathered Jassy into his arms. Holding her close, he carried her to the doctor's office.

Chapter Thirty

Creed paced the floor outside the examining room, his thoughts chaotic. Rose was dead, but she had signed a paper saying she had seen the shooting, that it had been self-defense. Yet none of that mattered now because Jassy was hurt, bleeding.

In labor.

He dragged a hand through his hair as he went to stare out the window. Six hours had passed since he brought her here. Six hours! Damn!

Turning away from the window, he began to pace again, stopping in mid-stride when he heard her cry out, her voice weak and filled with pain as she sought to bring their child into the world.

What if she died? How would he live with himself, knowing it was his fault?

And what if the child died? How would Jassy ever forgive him?

He paused in the middle of the room and raised his arms over his head. Throwing back his head, he closed his eyes. "*Wakan Tanka,*" he murmured, "please don't let her die. It doesn't matter what happens to me, but please don't let her die."

He stood there for a long while, the same prayer repeating itself in his mind over and over again.

He shivered as he heard her scream again, and yet again. "Please . . ."

Another hour passed, and his nerves were raw with waiting. When he couldn't wait another minute, he opened the door and stormed inside.

The doctor looked up, startled by his sudden entrance.

Jassy turned toward the door. Her face was as white as the sheet that covered her. There were dark shadows beneath her eyes, her brow was sheened with perspiration, and her hair was damp.

"Creed . . ." She tried to reach for him, but lacked the strength to lift her arm.

"I'm sorry, Mr. Macklin, but you'll have to leave."

Jassy shook her head weakly. "No."

In two long strides, Creed was at her side, taking her hand in his.

"Mr. Macklin!"

"Shut up, Doc. I'm stayin'."

"This is most irregular. Men are not allowed to be present at the birth."

"You're here."

"I'm a doctor."

"And I'm the father." Creed glared at the man, daring him to deny him his right to be there.

With a sigh, the doctor relented. "Very well, sir, if you insist on staying, you might take that cloth and wipe your wife's face and neck."

"Sure, Doc," Creed said. Lifting the cloth from the table, he dipped it in a bowl of water, wrung it out, and ran it over Jassy's face and neck. "Feel good?"

"Hmmm."

She grabbed his hand, her body arching, every muscle tensing, as a contraction caught her unaware. A low groan rose in her throat.

"Hang on, Jassy, honey."

She nodded, relaxing as the pain receded.

"You've got to ride the pain, honey."

"Ride it?" She stared up at him through eyes glazed with pain and exhaustion.

"Pretend it's a wild mustang. Don't fight it, ride it out."

"I can't." Her eyelids fluttered down. "I'm so tired, Creed. So tired . . ."

"Come on, Jassy, you can do it. Try. For me." He smiled down at her, his hand caressing her cheek. "I'm mighty anxious to see that baby."

His nearness and his words infused her with new strength.

Twenty minutes later, she gave birth to a red-faced, dark-haired baby girl.

Creed sat beside Jassy, holding her hand, while the doctor took care of the baby, disposed of the afterbirth, then laid the baby in Jassy's arms.

"She's beautiful," Creed murmured, daring to run a finger over his daughter's downy hair. "You're beautiful."

"You're not disappointed that it's not a boy?" Jassy asked.

"Hell, no," Creed said, smiling at her. "Boys are no damn good. Everybody knows that."

"Creed, what happened back there? Where's Rose?"

"She's gone, Jassy."

"Gone?"

He swore softly, wishing he didn't have to tell her the truth—not now, not after all she'd been through.

"Creed?"

"She's dead, Jassy. She died to save you and the baby."

"No!"

He squeezed her hand. "I'm sorry, honey."

Two fat tears rolled down Jassy's cheeks.

"I'm sorry," Creed said again, wishing he knew how to comfort her.

Jassy looked up at him. "Would you mind if

we named the baby Rose?"

Creed took a deep breath. He hated like hell to name his daughter after a whore, even though that whore had been Jassy's sister. But one look into Jassy's eyes and he knew he couldn't refuse her.

"Whatever you want, honey," he said, pressing his lips to the back of her hand. "You'd best get some rest now, okay?"

Jassy nodded. "You won't go away?"

"No."

She smiled at him, her eyelids fluttered down, and she was asleep.

"Maddigan."

Creed glanced over his shoulder to see the doctor standing inside the door. The sheriff stood beside the sawbones, gun in hand. Two deputies stood behind the lawman, both armed with rifles.

Slowly, Creed stood up, careful to keep his hands from the gun shoved into his waistband.

"Creed Maddigan?" the sheriff asked.

"Yeah."

"You're under arrest."

"For what?"

"Murder. I want you to pass me that shooter, real easy like."

Creed's gaze flicked over the two deputies. They were both middle-aged, solid, and experienced. Using his left hand, Creed drew the pistol from his waistband and handed it, butt first, to the sheriff.

"Turn around and put your hands behind your back."

Creed did as he was told, his gaze lingering on Jassy and the baby. He hadn't done many things right in his life, he mused, but he'd fathered a beautiful child. He felt his throat close up as he stared at his daughter, sleeping peacefully in her mother's arms.

And then the sheriff was locking a pair of handcuffs in place, hustling him out of the room, down the street, and into the jail.

Creed paced the narrow confines of his cell, frustration and anger churning within him. Damn! He had to get out of here.

He'd shown the lawman the paper Rose had signed, urged the man to send a wire to Judge Parker, but all in vain. The sheriff, whose name was Brick Cameron, didn't give a damn about Rose's statement, declaring it was probably a fraud. Maddigan had killed two men and possibly a woman in his town, and he was determined to see justice done. The fact that the two men were both shady characters with no visible means of support didn't seem to matter. There had been a shooting. Two men and a woman were dead, and Ray Coulter was accusing Maddigan of assault. That was all Cameron seemed to care about. He didn't intend to send Creed back to Harrison to pay for shooting Harry Coulter. He wanted to see Creed brought to justice for what he'd done in San Francisco.

Creed ceased his restless pacing as the door at the end of the cellblock swung open. Moments later, Annie Ross was standing in front of his cell, slowly shaking her head.

"Well, Mr. Macklin, you seem to be in a spot of trouble."

"Yes, ma'am. And the name's Maddigan. Creed Maddigan."

"Maddigan!" Annie exclaimed. "Dear me."

Creed's hands closed around the bars. "Have you seen Jassy? Is she all right?"

"She's fine. Still weak from all the blood she lost, but she's going to be just fine."

"And the baby?"

Annie Ross clasped her hands to her ample breasts. "A lovely child. She's doing right well."

"Does Jassy know I'm in here?"

"Yes, I'm afraid so. Sheriff Cameron spoke to her this morning. He asked her about what happened in Mr. Coulter's room and had her sign a statement."

"Is she still at the doc's?"

"Yes. He wants to keep her there another week or so, until she regains her strength. She's still a mite under the weather from the birthing and from the wound in her shoulder. Don't worry about her, Mr. Maddigan. I'll look in on her to make sure she's being well taken care of. And when Doc Potter says it's all right, she can go home with me."

"What about Coulter?"

"He's in the hospital with a bad concussion.

Wyatt tells me Mr. Coulter spends most of his time telling anyone who'll listen how you broke into his room looking for your wife, and when she said she didn't want to leave, there was a struggle. According to Coulter, Rose tried to help him, and you shot her. And then two of Mr. Coulter's friends came in, and you shot them, too."

"Damn," Creed muttered; then, sensing Annie Ross's censure, he said, "Sorry, ma'am."

"I didn't think that was what happened," Annie Ross said.

"It isn't. Listen, Annie, I need you to do something for me."

"If I can."

"I want you to send a wire to Judge Parker. Tell him I've got a signed statement from someone who saw the shooting in Harrison. Tell him I'm here, and that I need his help."

"I can do that."

"Bless you, Annie," Creed said, gratitude making his voice gruff. "I'm sorry I lied to you, but . . ." Creed shrugged.

"But you didn't think I'd rent a room to a wanted man," Annie Ross remarked candidly. "And you would have been right."

"You're a good woman, Annie."

"Don't try to sweet-talk me, Creed Maddigan. Now, is there anything you want me to tell Jassy?"

"Just tell her I . . ." Creed swallowed. It had been difficult enough to say the words to Jassy;

he didn't think he could ask Annie Ross to carry his love to Jassy.

"I'll tell her," Annie Ross said, her eyes brimming with understanding and compassion. "Can I bring you anything?"

"I'd appreciate a change of clothes. And a razor." Creed grinned at her. "Maybe a cake with a file in it."

Annie Ross chuckled. "I'll see what I can do. And don't you worry, hear? Everything will be all right."

Creed nodded, but deep in his heart, he was afraid nothing would ever be right again.

Nine days passed. He spent most of the time going quietly insane as he paced his cell. His need to hold Jassy, to see for himself that she was all right, gnawed at his vitals like a living thing. And his daughter—she was already nine days old, and he'd never even held her, had seen her for only a short time.

He paused in his restless pacing. Resting his head against the cold iron bars, he closed his eyes and took a deep breath.

Help me, Wakan Tanka, help me to find the center of the earth, to be a part of the great circle of life. Grant me the peace I seek . . .

"Jassy . . ."

He whispered her name, and when he opened his eyes, she was there.

"Creed, I'm so sorry. I would have been here sooner if I could."

"Jassy!" He reached through the bars and wrapped his arms around her, gently pulling her closer. "Oh, girl, you don't know how glad I am to see you!"

She kissed him then, her hands circling his neck, her body yearning toward his, until they were as close as they could be.

"Creed . . ." She murmured his name, and then she kissed him again and again, her hands moving restlessly over his back and shoulders.

"Where's the baby?"

"Annie's watching her."

"How's she doing?"

"She's fine, Creed. She's got your eyes. I'll bring her with me next time."

"No!" He shook his head. "I don't want her in here, Jassy."

"Are you all right?" She drew back a little so she could get a better look at him.

"I'm fine, now that you're here. How are you? How's your shoulder?"

"Better. Stop worrying about me, Creed, I'll be all right. My shoulder's still sore, and I tire easily, but I'm fine, really."

She rested her forehead against his and closed her eyes. It felt so good to be in his arms again, to hear his voice. "What are we going to do about you? I know how much you hate being locked up."

"Did Annie send that wire to Parker?"

Jassy nodded. "He sent a short reply saying he'd look into the matter. That was five days ago, and we haven't heard anything since." She drew back and looked up at him. "What will happen if they send you back to Harrison?"

"I don't know. A new trial, I guess. Even if they find me innocent of murder, I guess I could still find myself doing time for escaping from the Canon City pen."

"But if they find you innocent, that shouldn't matter".

"I hope to hell you're right, but there's no point in worrying about that until we get this mess with Coulter straightened out."

Jassy nodded. She had questioned the sheriff, trying to find out what was going on, but he had refused to tell her anything except that he was also "looking into the matter."

"You'd better go, honey," Creed said. "You look tired."

"I don't want to go, not yet."

"I don't want you to go, but . . ."

She pressed her lips to his and felt his quick response as he pulled her up against him. She didn't care that the bars cut into her breasts, didn't care that her shoulder ached. She needed the reassurance of his touch, needed to feel the solid strength of his arms around her, to know he loved her. She fought down the urge to cry, to pour out her fears. She was so afraid that no one would believe Rose's statement and that Coulter would find a way to convince a jury that Creed had killed her sister and his men.

She blinked back her tears, not wanting him

to know how worried she was, but he knew. She felt it in the way he held her, heard it in the soft words he whispered in her ear.

He drew back, a wry smile on his lips as he cupped her breast. Glancing down, Jassy saw the faint dampness that stained her bodice.

"It's feeding time," she murmured.

"You'd better go then. Give my daughter a kiss for me."

"I will."

He hugged her close and then, reluctantly, let her go.

"I love you," Jassy said.

"I know."

"I'll see you tomorrow."

Creed nodded, unable to speak past the rising lump in his throat. Fists clenched at his sides, he watched Jassy walk down the corridor. She turned at the door, waved, and was gone.

The wire from Parker arrived two days later. Creed read the terse words twice. Parker had reviewed all the evidence in the Coulter case, but was holding his decision pending Creed's trial in San Francisco. Should Creed be found guilty in California, there would be no need to take further action regarding the Coulter incident. Should he be found innocent, he was to be extradited back to Harrison for retrial.

Creed swore a vile oath as he wadded the paper into a ball and hurled it across the cell. Damn!

* * *

The trial was four days later. Creed figured Tuesdays must be a slow day in Frisco, judging by the number of spectators.

He'd met his attorney three days earlier, explained what had happened over and over again while the man—Marcus Feather, his name was—made copious notes.

Creed wanted to believe that he'd get a fair trial, but he couldn't help remembering how things had gone in Harrison. The only thing in his favor now was the fact that Feather seemed to believe him when he said he was innocent. Now all they had to do was convince a judge and twelve of his peers. The thought made him grimace. Twelve of his peers. That was funny.

Jassy came to see him every day, just as she had when he'd been in jail the last time. She put on a brave face for him, always forcing a smile when he knew she wanted to cry. One afternoon she even brought him cookies. Her thoughtfulness, her unending compassion and devotion, almost brought him to his knees. He had blinked back the tears that burned his eyes, knowing that if he surrendered now, they would both be lost.

And then, the day before the trial, she brought the baby to see him.

Creed stared at his daughter. No longer red-faced and wrinkled, she was the most beautiful creature he had ever seen. She stared up at him through unblinking blue eyes, and he felt as if she were probing his soul. In that instant, he regretted every cruel and unlawful thing he had ever done.

He reached out to touch her cheek, and her hand curled around his finger—and around his heart.

"Jassy . . ." He looked at her, unable to put his feelings into words.

"I know," Jassy said, blinking back the tears that welled in her eyes as she looked at her daughter's tiny hand curled around Creed's calloused finger. "I know."

Now, sitting in the courthouse with his hands shackled, Creed held tight to the memory of his daughter's face and his wife's love.

He stood up when the judge entered the room and listened impassively while the magistrate read the charges against him.

The prosecution pleaded eloquently for a guilty verdict, then called Ray Coulter to the stand to testify.

Creed grimaced as he took a good look at the man. In an effort to look like a law-abiding citizen, Coulter wore a boiled shirt, a dark blue suit, obviously brand new, and a black cravat. His hair was slicked back. A stark white bandage was wrapped around his head.

He was sworn in, and then, speaking in a low, humble voice, he told how Mrs. Maddigan had come to see her sister, how Creed had burst into the room and tried to drag his wife away. Fearing for Mrs. Maddigan's well-being, Coulter had tried to defend Mrs. Maddigan. It was then that Creed had drawn a gun. In the ensuing struggle, Maddigan had shot both Rose and Jassy, then killed Bob Sykes and Tom Gillis when they tried to help.

The prosecutor thanked Coulter for his testimony, and then, as he was their only witness, reiterated that Creed Maddigan was a menace to the law-abiding citizens of San Francisco and should be found guilty of murder and hanged forthwith.

Then Creed was called to the stand. After he took an oath to tell the truth and nothing but the truth, Marcus Feather asked him to explain, in his own words, exactly what had happened on the night in question.

When Creed had finished testifying, Feather called Jassy forward.

Rising, Jassy carefully placed her daughter in Annie's arms, then took the stand. Placing a white-gloved hand on the Bible, she spoke clearly and succinctly as she swore to tell the truth.

Marcus Feather guided her carefully through her testimony, offering Rose's note to the judge as Exhibit A, pointing out that the handwriting in the main body of the note matched Ray Coulter's handwriting. Only the signature was Rose McCloud's.

In a deep voice worthy of an old testament prophet, Marcus Feather explained how Ray Coulter had used the note to lure Jassy to his room above the Wayfarer Saloon. He went on to explain that Coulter planned to turn Creed in for the reward, then sell Jassy to a brothel. Lowering his voice, his expression filled with indignation, he informed the jury that Coulter then planned an even more despicable act, that of selling an innocent child to the highest bidder.

When he was certain he had the jury's complete attention, he produced Rose's dying declaration stating that she had seen the shooting in Harrison and that Creed Maddigan was innocent of any and all wrongdoing.

"Would you send an innocent man to the gallows?" Marcus Feather demanded, his voice ringing with fervor. "Would you deprive this beautiful child of its father? Ladies and gentlemen of the jury, I know that you will find it in your hearts to bring forth the only possible verdict in this case and declare Creed Maddigan innocent!"

Creed slid a glance at the jury. It was impossible to tell from their expressions whether they believed Jassy's testimony or whether they had been swayed by Feather's fervent remarks.

His gaze moved to Jassy's face as the judge dismissed the jury. Then the sheriff was taking him by the arm, pulling him down the aisle toward the door.

Creed glanced over his shoulder, searching for Jassy. She smiled at him, and then she was lost from sight as Cameron hustled him out of the courtroom and up the stairs to a small holding cell.

Chapter Thirty-one

Creed paced the floor for several minutes, stopped to stare out the window, then began to pace again as he wondered what was taking the jury so damn long to decide his fate. Was it a good sign, their taking so long, or a bad one?

He paused at the window again, looking down on the people in the street below—people who were free to come and go as they pleased. Would he ever know that kind of freedom again?

He glanced up at the sun. Damn. The jury had been out for more than two hours. His nerves were strung out and raw, and he began to pace again. He hated this small room, which was even smaller than his cell at the jail. Hated being handcuffed. Hated being away from Jassy and his daughter. His daughter. She was almost two weeks old, and he hadn't seen her for more than a few minutes.

"Why don't you sit down, Maddigan? All that pacing ain't gonna make the time go faster."

Creed glared at Cameron. "You ever been locked up, Sheriff?"

" 'Course not," the lawman replied, obviously insulted that Creed would even ask. "Why?"

Creed shook his head. "If you've never been locked up, then you wouldn't understand," he muttered, and began pacing again.

Creed stopped in mid-stride when the bailiff appeared at the iron-barred door. "They've reached a verdict," he said. "The judge wants Maddigan downstairs in five minutes."

"Right," Cameron said. With a sigh, he stood up, his hand resting on the butt of his gun. "Ready?"

Creed nodded, feeling suddenly sick to his stomach now that the waiting was over. In a few minutes, he'd find out if he had any future to look forward to, or if all that awaited him was a trip to the gallows.

Cameron unlocked the door, then stepped back, motioning for Creed to walk out ahead of him.

Taking a deep breath, Creed walked down the stairs that led to the courtroom.

"Maddigan."

Creed glanced over his shoulder, his gaze meeting Cameron's.

"Good luck," the lawman said quietly.

"Thanks."

Squaring his shoulders, Creed entered th courtroom and walked down the aisle towar the table where his lawyer waited for him. H paused when he saw Jassy and the baby. Sh was sitting on the aisle and she reached out t squeeze his hand.

"It'll be all right," she murmured. "I know i will."

Creed nodded, his gaze moving from Jassy' face to his daughter and back again.

"Let's go, Maddigan," Cameron said.

"Yeah." He forced a smile for Jassy, and the he took his place at the defense table.

Moments later, the judge entered the courtroom and took his seat. "Has the jury reache a verdict?" he asked.

The foreman of the jury stood up. "We have Your Honor."

"Very well."

The bailiff took the folded sheet of pape from the foreman and handed it to the judge.

Creed held his breath, his gaze fixed on th judge's face.

"The prisoner will rise while the bailiff read the verdict."

Creed stood up, his hands clenched, as th judge handed the verdict to the bailiff.

The bailiff read it, then cleared his throat "The jury finds Creed Maddigan innocent on al counts."

Relief washed through Creed, warm and sweet.

"The prisoner will be remanded to custody until such time as he can be transported to Harrison, Colorado. Case dismissed."

Creed turned to face his lawyer. "Thank you, Mr. Feather. I appreciate everything you did."

"My pleasure, sir," Marcus said, slapping Creed on the shoulder. "My pleasure. Should you feel the need of my services in Colorado, don't hesitate to let me know."

"I will," Creed said.

And then Jassy was there, throwing her arms around him. "I told you it would be all right," she said, hugging him close.

Lifting his bound hands, Creed put his arms over Jassy and she snuggled against him.

"Where's the baby?" he asked.

"Right here," Annie Ross said. "Sleeping like the angel she is."

Creed glanced over Jassy's shoulder to where Annie Ross stood. Annie drew back the blanket so Creed could see his daughter.

She did look like an angel, he mused. Soft and pink and beautiful.

Behind him, he heard Cameron clear his throat. "Maddigan?"

"Yeah?"

"It's time to go."

Reluctantly, he lifted his arms from Jassy, who took his hand in hers.

"We'll go with you."

"Ma'am, I . . ."

"Surely there can't be any harm in my walking down to the jail with my husband? I can assure you I don't have a weapon hidden in my daughter's diaper."

Creed stifled the urge to smile as Cameron's face turned beet-red.

"No, ma'am, I'm sure you don't but . . ."

"Please, Sheriff?"

"Well, all right." He fixed Creed with a hard stare. "I want your word that you won't try anything, Maddigan."

"You've got it."

"And yours, too, ma'am."

"My word, Sheriff," Jassy said, smiling sweetly.

"You didn't ask, but you've got my word, too," Annie Ross declared.

"Yes, ma'am," Cameron said. "Thank you, ma'am."

They made an odd parade, Creed thought as they left the courthouse. Jassy walked beside him, her head high, her hand on his arm. Annie Ross followed them, the baby cradled in her arms. Cameron brought up the rear.

When they reached the jail, Annie Ross took a seat while Cameron escorted Creed into the cellblock. After locking Creed in one of the cells, he removed the handcuffs and left the cellblock, leaving Creed and Jassy alone.

Creed reached through the bars. Folding his arms around Jassy's waist, he kissed her gently.

"Ah, Jassy," he murmured, "you feel so good."

"You, too. I've missed you so much." She reached up to stroke his cheek, then ran her hand through his hair and let it slide down to curl around his neck, drawing his face closer so she could kiss him again and again.

"How long do you think it will be before they send you back to Harrison?"

"I don't know."

"I hope it will be soon," Jassy said.

Creed nodded, wishing he was as certain as Jassy that everything was going to be all right. Just because he was going to be retried didn't mean Parker would find him innocent. He tried to tell himself that Rose's statement, along with her admission that she had committed perjury at the first trial, would make all the difference. He told himself that a deathbed confession was sure to carry some weight with a jury. But deep down, he didn't believe it. He was a half-breed and, right or wrong, he had killed a white man.

But he couldn't worry about that now, not with Jassy in his arms, her body pressed against the bars in an effort to be closer to him. And then she was kissing him, her hands delving under his shirt, roaming up and down his back. He groaned softly. Her nearness, her touch, aroused him instantly. It had been weeks since they had made love. It would probably be even longer before he made love to her again.

"Jassy . . ."

"I know." A soft moan escaped her lips. "I

know. Touch me. It's been so long. So long."

He kissed her then, his hands caressing her soft curves. It was the sweetest kind of pain, touching her but being unable to possess her. Their kisses became desperate as their bodies yearned toward each other.

"Creed . . ." She gazed up at him, her eyes glazed with desire.

Reluctantly, he drew away and took a deep breath. "You'd better run for the hills if they ever let me out of here," Creed muttered with a wry grin, " 'cause if I catch you, I'm never gonna let you outta my sight again."

"Promise?"

"I promise." He ran his finger over her swollen lips. "I want to see my daughter, Jassy."

"I'll get her."

She left the cellblock, returning a few moments later with the baby cradled in her arms.

"She gets prettier every time I see her," Creed said.

"She is pretty, isn't she?" Jassy remarked.

"Just like her mother."

His praise warmed Jassy's heart. "Say hi to your daddy, sweetie," she crooned. "Yes, that's him," she said, smiling. "He's pretty, too, isn't he?"

Creed snorted. "Pretty, indeed!"

"Beauty is in the eye of the beholder," Jassy reminded him with a saucy grin. "And we think you're beautiful."

"I wish I could hold her."

"You will, Creed."

"Yeah." He ran a hand through his hair and felt the walls closing in on him as he stared at Jassy and the baby, so near, yet out of his reach. "Damn."

"It'll be over soon, Creed. I know it will. And then we'll be together, and I'll be pestering you to take care of her so much you'll be looking for excuses to get away."

Creed nodded, wishing he could play along, praying that what she said was true.

A muscle worked in his jaw as he heard the cellblock door open. "Time's up, Mrs. Maddigan," Cameron called.

"I'm coming," Jassy answered. She looked up at Creed, hating to leave him, knowing how desperately he hated being locked up. "Do you need anything?"

"Just you."

She swayed toward him, lifting her face for his kiss. She wouldn't cry! He didn't need to see her tears, not now.

"I'll see you tomorrow," she said. "Are you sure I can't bring you anything?" She smiled up at him. "Some more cookies, maybe?"

"Yeah, I'd like that."

"I love you," she whispered. "See you tomorrow."

"Tomorrow."

Hands clutching the bars, he watched her walk away. She turned at the door and blew him a kiss, and then she was gone.

* * *

Two days later, they were on an eastbound train. Jassy and Annie Ross had bade each other a tearful farewell at the station, and now Jassy was sitting across from Creed, the baby in her arms. One of Cameron's deputies—a tall, broad-shouldered man named Stuart Flanders—had been detailed to escort Creed back to Harrison. The deputy sat beside Jassy, his long legs crossed, a rifle cradled in his lap.

Creed sat near the window, his right hand cuffed to the seat's iron frame, his face impassive as he watched the countryside roll by. It had been damned humiliating, being marched on board in handcuffs. People had turned to stare as he walked down the aisle. He had heard their remarks as they whispered back and forth, remarking on his Indian blood, wondering what crime he'd been convicted of, assuming that Jassy was the lawman's wife. And that bothered him more than anything else.

Chapter Thirty-two

The trip to Harrison was long but uneventful. They took a stage to Sacramento, then caught a train headed east.

Lacking Jassy's conviction that everything would turn out for the best, Creed grew increasingly morose as the miles slipped past. The thought of going back to prison loomed before him. No matter how many times he told himself that Rose's letter and Jassy's testimony should be enough to clear him of the murder charge, he couldn't shake the feeling that he would soon find himself back in prison. He couldn't bear the thought of being locked up, not now, not when he had so much to live for. He knew he would rather die than spend the next twenty years locked behind iron bars, shut away from Jassy and his daughter.

Daily, his frustration grew—frustration at being handcuffed, at being unable to spend any time alone with Jassy, at the contemptuous looks cast his way whenever the train stopped and Stuart Flanders hustled him off the train so he could stretch his legs.

At one stop, Creed had asked the deputy if he wouldn't turn him loose. "I won't try to escape," he had said, meaning it. "I give you my word."

"Are you serious?" Flanders had asked. "You want me to take them cuffs off?" The lawman had laughed ruefully. "I don't think so."

They had to take a stage into Harrison. Creed was ready to explode by the time they reached town.

Jassy pressed close to Creed, the baby cradled in her arms, while Flanders waited for his valise.

"It'll all work out," she said, giving Creed's arm a squeeze. "You'll see."

Creed nodded. "Go on over to the hotel, Jassy. Get some rest."

Jassy didn't want to leave him, not for a minute. He had a wild, haunted look in his eyes, and she was sorely afraid that he would do something foolish, like try to escape. But as much as she wanted to stay with him, she needed to nurse the baby. And little Rose needed a bath and a nap.

Standing on tiptoe, Jassy pressed a kiss to her

husband's cheek. "We'll be over to see you soon."

Creed loosed a long sigh and nodded. As much as he hated the thought of her visiting him in the jail, the thought of not seeing her at all was unthinkable.

Jassy kissed him again, murmured that she loved him, then hurried down the street toward the Harrison House. The sooner she got settled, the sooner she could see Creed again.

Heads turned as Flanders and Creed walked down the boardwalk toward the jail. Creed looked straight ahead, acutely conscious of the shackles that bound his hands and of the speculative glances that followed him.

Stuart Flanders ushered Creed into the jail, signed the necessary papers to transfer custody of the prisoner from one lawman to another, then left the office to catch the next train west.

Frank Harrington shook his head in wry amusement as he locked Creed in his old cell.

"Just couldn't stay away, huh?" Harrington remarked as he slid the key from the lock. "Well, stick your hands out here, and I'll take those cuffs off."

"Is Parker in town?" Creed asked, rubbing his wrists when the manacles were removed. Damn, he hated being cuffed, hated the feel of cold metal shackling his hands and restricting his movements.

Harrington shook his head. "Naw. He's hearing a case over in Leadville. Sent a wire a couple days ago saying he should be here in a week or so."

A week or so! Creed glanced at the bars that surrounded him and swore under his breath. "I don't guess you'd turn me loose until he shows up."

"What do you think?"

Creed shrugged. "It was worth a try."

Harrington grunted, then left the cellblock, whistling softly as he closed the door behind him.

Wrapping his hands around the bars, Creed pressed his forehead against the cold steel and closed his eyes.

Lord, how he hated being locked up!

Jassy came to see him just after dinner, dressed in a pale yellow dress and matching bonnet. He thought he had never seen anything prettier in his life.

Harrington unlocked the cell and opened the door, then stepped back, his hand resting on the butt of his gun, while Jassy stepped inside.

"Thirty minutes," the sheriff said curtly.

Jassy reached for Creed as soon as the door closed behind them. "Are you all right?"

"I am, now that you're here."

"The sheriff said Judge Parker won't be here for at least a week."

"Yeah, I know."

"I'm sorry, Creed. I know how hard this must be for you."

Creed nodded. His nerves were strung out and raw. "Where's the baby?"

"My friend, Kate Bradshaw, is watching her."

"I didn't know you had any friends in town."

"A couple. Most of the people treated me fine, once they realized I wasn't like my mother." She swallowed hard. "Or Rose."

"I'm glad, Jassy."

Taking her by the hand, he sat down on the edge of the cot and drew her down beside him, his arm sliding around her waist, holding her close. Lord, she felt good. Smelled good.

Jassy leaned against him, her head resting on his shoulder. "They'll like you, too, once they get to know you."

"I doubt that." He'd lived here, off and on, for years, and he could count the people who acknowledged him on one hand.

"Forget about them." She gazed up at him, wishing she could wipe the tension from his face, the pain from his eyes. "I love you."

"Jassy."

She wound her arms around his neck and kissed him, her body straining to be closer to his. Creed groaned low in his throat as her tongue skimmed over his lower lip. Wrapping his arms around her, he drew her down on the cot, his blood racing as her body molded itself to his. Her mouth was warm and sweet, filled with promises and hope for the future, and he clung to her, desperate to believe that they might still have a life together in spite of the doubts that plagued him.

"Creed . . ." Her voice was breathless, filled with longing.

"I know," he replied, his voice husky with desire. "I know." He held her close, breathing in the fragrant scent of her hair and skin. His hands moved lightly over her breasts. They were heavy, swollen with milk. He ached with wanting her, with the knowledge that this might be the full extent of his time with her, that he might never have a chance to make a life for the three of them.

"Jassy, if things go wrong, if they send me back to Canon City—"

"No!" She drew away and pressed her hands over her ears. "I know what you're going to say, and I don't want to hear it."

"Jassy, listen—"

"No!" She shook her head. "You're not sending me away again, Creed Maddigan, do you understand? I'm your wife. No matter what happens, we'll see it through together."

"Dammit, Jassy, be reasonable. What are you gonna do if they send me back to prison? You can't spend the next twenty years of your life waiting for me."

"I can, and I will."

"No." He stood abruptly and began to pace the floor. "I don't want you to spend your whole life alone, waiting. If they send me back, I want you to get a divorce, find yourself a—a good, decent man to . . ." His hands curled around the bars. "I want you to find someone who'll be a father to my daughter."

Jassy looked at Creed. His hands were wrapped around the bars, the knuckles white. She knew just what those words had cost him. He was a proud man, and he loved her deeply, passionately. Jealously. And yet he had only her happiness in mind. Never had she loved him more.

"Promise me, Jassy?"

"I can't."

He turned to face her, his expression bleak. "Seems like we've been through this before," he muttered ruefully.

"But it'll be better this time. I know it will."

He crossed the short space between them and knelt in front of her. Taking her hands in his, he pressed them to his lips. "Jassy, if they send me back to prison, I want your promise that you'll get a divorce and get on with your life. Promise me."

"Please don't ask me."

"I'm not asking you," he said quietly. "I'm begging you. I don't want to spend the next twenty years knowing I've ruined your life, that you're living alone, raising our daughter alone. You're a young woman, too young to spend your life alone." He looked deep into her eyes. "Promise me?"

Her heart was breaking. She knew it. She could feel it shattering, feel the pieces cutting into her soul. She wanted to scream at him, to tell him he was being unfair. How could he expect her to even think of another man now? And yet, how could she lash out at him when she knew he was only thinking of her, wanting the best for her and their daughter? It couldn't be easy for him. And if giving him her promise would ease his mind, she would give it.

"All right, Creed, I promise."

He sighed, as if a great weight had been taken from his shoulders. He buried his face in her lap, and his arms locked around her waist. He sat there for a long while.

Jassy stroked his hair and back, knowing that she'd never be able to keep the promise she had made, knowing she would never love anyone else the way she loved Creed Maddigan. She belonged to him, heart and soul, for now and for always.

Too soon, Harrington came to get her.

"I'll be back tomorrow," Jassy promised as she lifted her face for Creed's kiss. "I'll bring the baby."

Creed nodded.

"I love you."

"I know." He ran his hand over her cheek. "Are you all right? Do you have everything you need?"

"We're fine. Stop worrying." She smiled at him.

Harrington cleared his throat. "You about ready, Missus Maddigan?"

"Yes." She kissed Creed one more time, then walked to the cell door.

"Against the wall, Maddigan," Harrington said brusquely.

Resentment rose up in Creed as he went to stand against the back wall. Standing there, watching the lawman unlock the cell door, he was overcome with a need to lash out, to bury his fist in the lawman's face. He hated being locked up, hated taking orders, hated the fact that his life was no longer his own. He couldn't live like this. If Parker decided to send him back to prison, he'd make a run for it and hope they killed him.

Harrington met Creed's eyes as he opened the door. The two men stared at each other as Jassy left the cell, then Harrington stepped forward and closed and locked the door.

"I know how you feel," the sheriff remarked after Jassy left the cellblock. "I just hope you don't try anything stupid."

Creed shook his head. "I won't," he said tersely. He glanced down the corridor. "I've got too much to lose."

Harrington's features softened a little. "See that you remember that."

It took ten days for Parker to reach Harrison. Creed's nerves were drawn tighter than a Lakota war drum by then. Jassy came to see him twice a day, bringing the baby with her in the morning, coming alone in the evening. As she had before, she brought him cookies. She also brought him the newspaper to read, a change of clothes, and his razor. She made him talk to her when he was feeling sullen and discouraged. She told him that she had renewed her acquaintance not only with Kate Bradshaw, but with Elizabeth Wills, and that both women adored the baby. Mrs. Wellington had offered to give Jassy her old job back, if she wanted it.

It was a cold and cloudy Friday morning when Harrington stepped into Creed's cell. Jace Rutledge stood outside, a shotgun cradled in his arm, while Harrington handcuffed Creed.

"The judge is waiting for you in his office," Harrington said.

Creed frowned. "In his office? Why?"

Harrington shrugged. "I didn't ask."

"I thought I was getting a new trial."

Harrington grunted. "I just do what I'm told. Let's go."

Creed shivered as he stepped out of the jail. A cold wind was blowing down out of the mountains; there was the smell of rain in the air.

Taking a deep breath, he walked down the street toward the judge's office.

Jassy was waiting inside, the baby in her arms.

"Mr. Maddigan," Judge Parker said. He indicated the chair in front of his desk. "Sit down."

Creed did as he was told. Judge Parker was a tall, spare man in his late fifties. His brown hair was peppered with gray, and his brown eyes were shrewd.

"I've read the statement signed by Rose McCloud," Parker said. "And I've listened to your wife's testimony. I'd like you to tell me exactly what happened that night."

"I'd been playing poker in the Lazy Ace. It was about midnight when I left. I was on my way to my room at the hotel when Harry Coulter called me out. He fired first." Creed shrugged. "He missed. I didn't."

"I see." The judge stared at the papers spread on his desk. "You escaped from Canon City some months ago."

Creed nodded.

"Why?"

"Why?" Creed stared at the judge. "You ever been in prison, Your Honor?"

"No."

"Well, if you had, you wouldn't have to ask why I escaped when I got the chance. I did it then, and I'd do it again."

"I see. That's an honest answer, if not a wise one."

Creed took a deep breath. "If it's all the same to you, Judge, I'd just as soon be hanged as sent back to prison."

"No!" Jassy surged to her feet, her hand at her heart. "No."

"Please be seated, Mrs. Maddigan."

Jassy sat down, her face pale as she clutched the baby to her breast.

Parker leaned forward, his gaze steady on Creed's face. "And if I don't hang you and don't send you back to prison, just what do you intend to do with your life?"

"I've got some money I earned working in Frisco," Creed said, his hands clenched. "I own a few acres outside of town. I'd like to build a house there, settle down, and make a home for my wife and my daughter. Maybe raise a few head of cattle."

"Do you think you could do that? Settle down, I mean?"

"Yessir."

Parker glanced at Jassy and the baby, then looked back at Creed. "I'm going to suspend your sentence, Mr. Maddigan. I'm going to give you one year to prove yourself. At the end of that time, I'll reevaluate your case. Any questions?"

"No, sir."

"Very well. Until that time, I'm putting you in the custody of your wife and child."

Creed stared at the judge, unable to believe his ears. He was free. He stood there, jubilant, unable to absorb the full meaning of the judge's words, while Harrington removed the handcuffs. And then Jassy was running toward him, tears streaming down her cheeks as she hugged him close, careful not to crush the baby between them.

Creed's arms closed around his wife and daughter. "Thanks, Judge," he said, blinking back the tears in his eyes. "I . . . thanks."

"Don't make me regret my decision, Mr. Maddigan."

"I won't. I swear it."

Judge Parker smiled. "I believe you, sir." Coming out from behind his desk, he offered Creed his hand. "Good day to you."

Creed shook Parker's hand. "Thanks again."

Jassy smiled at Creed through her tears. "I told you everything would be all right," she said tremulously.

"Yes, ma'am, you did." He gazed down at her, his heart filled to overflowing as she placed his daughter in his arms. "Hi, sweetheart," he murmured.

Jassy smiled at the sight, then frowned. "I didn't know you owned land around here. Where is it?"

"That valley you like so much," Creed said. "It's mine."

"You never told me that!"

"I never thought we'd have a life together, Jassy, especially not here."

"We're going to have a wonderful life," she said. "Just wait and see."

Taking Jassy by the hand, Creed walked out of the judge's office.

Thy sky was still cloudy, but as they walked toward the hotel, the sun came out and a rainbow stretched across the sky. It shimmered overhead like a celestial benediction, Jassy mused, fancifully imagining that it was *Wakan Tanka's* way of promising her a bright future with the man she loved.

Epilogue

Five years later

Jassy stood on the porch, her heart pounding with excitement as she watched Creed work the kinks out of one of the horses. Rose jumped up and down, hands clapping, as the horse began to buck. Standing beside her, her three-year old brother, Clay, hollered encouragement.

She smiled as she watched Creed cling to the horse's back with the tenacity of a cocklebur. Her husband had blossomed in the last five years, she thought, although blossomed hardly seemed an appropriate word for a man. Still, he had lost that hard edge that had been so much a part of him. He smiled more, laughed often. In spite of all his doubts about being a father, she couldn't have asked for a better father for her children or a better husband for herself.

He had built her the house she had once dreamed of, with a big picture window overlooking the lake. They had started off with a small herd of cattle, a herd that had grown steadily each year.

To Creed's surprise, the town had gradually come to accept them both. People no longer remembered that Jassy's mother had been a whore, or that Creed had once earned his living with his gun.

Walking down the stairs, she made her way toward the corral. The battle was over, and Creed had won. Rose and Clay had ducked under the rails, and now they were both chattering a mile a minute, asking what he was going to name the horse, pestering him to let them ride.

"Let's ask your mama what we should call him," Creed suggested as Jassy approached the corral.

"I want to call him Thunder," Clay said.

"And I want to call him Rainbow," Rose said.

"How about if we call him Storm?" Jassy suggested.

"Storm? Why?" Rose asked with a frown.

"Well, when it storms, there's thunder, and then there's a rainbow."

Clay and Rose looked at each other, then nodded. "Storm," they said in unison, and began to giggle.

"Supper's ready," Jassy said. Pulling a hanky

from her apron pocket, she wiped the perspiration from Creed's forehead. "I love you, Mr. Maddigan."

"And I love you, Mrs. Maddigan."

Rose frowned at Clay. "I love you, Clay," she said, imitating Jassy's voice.

Clay grimaced. "I love Storm," he said, ducking when Rose made as if to hit him. "He's prettier than you!"

Creed grinned as he watched his daughter chase her brother toward the house. "See what you started with all that love stuff," he teased.

"Yes, indeed," Jassy said. She looked out over the valley, at their house bathed in the golden glow of the sun, at her two children, now happily tussling in the grass like puppies, at the tall, handsome man at her side. "I wouldn't have had it any other way."

"Me, either," Creed said. Drawing her into his arms, he kissed her, loving the way she leaned into him, the way she always smiled when she saw him. Truly, he had found the treasure at the end of the rainbow the day Jassy McCloud came into his life. And he wouldn't have had it any other way.